New York Times and USA TODAY Bestselling Author

LINDA LAEL MILLER

Ragged Rainbows

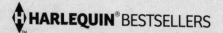

HARLEQUIN® BESTSELLERS

Recycling programs
for this product may
not exist in your area.

ISBN-13: 978-0-373-60589-7

RAGGED RAINBOWS

Copyright © 2011 by Harlequin Books S.A.

The publisher acknowledges the copyright holders
of the individual works as follows:

RAGGED RAINBOWS
Copyright © 1986 by Linda Lael Miller

THE MIRACLE BABY
Copyright © 1997 by Janice Kay Johnson

HARLEQUIN®

™ www.Harlequin.com

Printed in U.S.A.

CONTENTS

For Mary Ann and Stevie,
my cousins and my first friends. I love you.

RAGGED RAINBOWS

New York Times and *USA TODAY* Bestselling Author

Linda Lael Miller

LINDA LAEL MILLER

The daughter of a town marshal, Linda Lael Miller is a *New York Times* and *USA TODAY* bestselling author of more than one hundred historical and contemporary novels, most of which reflect her love of the West. Raised in Northport, Washington, the self-confessed barn goddess now lives in Spokane, Washington. Her most recent *New York Times* bestsellers include her popular McKettricks of Texas series: *Tate, Garrett* and *Austin* and *A Creed Country Christmas*. Dedicated to helping animals in need, Linda is taking this year to offer grants to animal shelters that are desperate for additional funds to help save precious creatures whose whole purpose in life is to love. More information about Linda and her novels is available at www.lindalaelmiller.com. She also loves to hear from readers by mail at P.O. Box 19461, Spokane, WA 99219.

Chapter One

Marvin's toupee was slightly off-center and he was wearing his standard smile, one that promised low mileage to the public in general and headaches to Shay Kendall in particular. She sat up a little straighter in her chair and looked across the wide polished plains of her employer's desk to the view outside the window behind him. Thousands of red, yellow and blue triangular flags were snapping in the wind, a merry contrast to the cloudy coastal sky.

"I'm an office manager, Marvin," Shay said with a sigh, bringing wide hazel eyes back to his friendly face, "not an actress. While I enjoy helping plan commercials, I don't see myself in front of the camera."

"I've been promising Jeannie this trip to Europe for years," Marvin said pointedly.

Richard Barrett, a representative of an advertising agency in nearby Seattle, was leaning back against a burgeoning bookshelf, his arms folded across his chest. He was tall, with nicely cut brown hair, and would have been handsome if not for the old-fashioned horn-rimmed glasses he wore. "You're Rosamond Dallas's daughter," he put in. "Besides, I know a hundred women who would give anything for a chance like this."

Shay pushed back a lock of long, layer-cut brown hair to rub one temple with her fingers, then lifted her head, giving Mr. Barrett an ironic look. "A chance like what, Richard? You make this sound as though it's a remake of *The Ten Commandments* instead of a thirty-second TV spot where I get a dump-truck load of sugar poured over me and say, 'We've got a sweet deal for you at Reese Motors in Skyler Beach!' Furthermore, I fail to see what my being Rosamond's daughter has to do with anything."

Marvin was sitting back in his leather chair and smiling, probably at the image of Shay being buried under a half ton of white sugar. "There would be a sizable bonus involved, of course," he reflected aloud.

He hadn't mentioned a bonus on Friday afternoon, when he'd first presented Shay with a storyboard for a commercial starring herself rather than the infamous "Low-Margin Marvin."

Shay sighed, thinking of all the new clothes her six-year-old son, Hank, would need before school started and of the retirement savings account she wanted to open but couldn't afford. "How much of a bonus?" she asked, disliking Richard Barrett for the smug look that flickered briefly in his blue eyes.

Marvin named a figure that would cover the savings and deposit payment and any amount of jeans, sneakers, jackets and T-shirts for Hank, with money left over.

"Just for one commercial? That's all I'd have to do?" Shay hated herself for wavering, but she was in no position to turn her back on so much money. While she earned a good salary working as Reese Motors's office manager and general all-around troubleshooter, it took all she could scrape together to support herself and her small son and meet the property taxes on her mother's enormous, empty house. Lord in heaven, she thought, if only someone would come along and buy that house....

Marvin and Richard exchanged indulgent looks. "If you hadn't stomped out of here on Friday," Richard said smoothly, "I would have gone on to explain that we're discussing a series of four spots, thirty seconds each. That's a lot of money for two minutes' work, Shay."

Two minutes' work. Shay was annoyed and insulted. Nobody knew better than she did that a thirty-second commercial could take days to perfect; she'd fetched enough antacid tablets for Marvin and made enough conciliatory telephone calls to his wife to know. "I'm an office manager," she repeated, somewhat piteously this time.

"And a damned good one!" Marvin thundered. "I don't know what we'd have done without you all this time!"

Shay looked back over the half dozen years since she'd come to work for Marvin Reese. She had started as a receptionist and the job had been so important to her that she'd made any number of mistakes in her attempts to do it well. Marvin had been kind and his wife, Jeannie, had been a real friend, taking Shay out to lunch on occasion, helping her to find a trustworthy babysitter for Hank, reassuring her.

In many ways, Jeannie Reese had been a mother to Shay during those harried, scary days of new independence. Rosamond—nobody had suspected that her sudden tendency toward forgetfulness and fits of temper was the beginning of Alzheimer's disease—had been living on a *rancho* in Mexico then, with her sixth and final husband, blissfully unconcerned with her daughter's problems.

Now, sitting there in Marvin's spacious, well-appointed office, Shay felt a sting at the memory. She had telephoned her mother right after her ex-husband, Eliott, then principal of a high school in a small town in Oregon, had absconded with the school's sizable athletic fund and left his young and decidedly pregnant wife to deal with the consequences. Rosamond had said that she'd warned Shay not to marry an older man, hadn't she, and that she would love to send money to help out but that that was impossible, since Eduardo had just bought a Thoroughbred racehorse and transporting the beast all the way from Kentucky to the Yucatan peninsula had cost so much.

"Shay?"

Shay wrenched herself back to the present moment and met Marvin's fatherly gaze. She knew then that, even without the bonus check, she would have agreed to be in his commercials. He had believed in her when she had jumbled important files and spilled coffee all over his desk and made all the salesmen on the floor screaming mad by botching up their telephone messages. He had paid for the business courses she'd taken at the junior college and given her regular raises and promotions.

He was her friend.

"It's an offer I can't refuse," she said softly. It was no use asking for approval of the storyboards; Marvin's style, which had made him a virtual legend among car dealers, left no room for temperament. Three years before, at Thanksgiving, he'd dressed up as a turkey and announced to the viewing public that Reese Motors was gobbling up good trade-ins.

Marvin unearthed his telephone from underneath a mountain of paper and dialed a number. "Jeannie? Shay's going to take over the commercials for me. Dust off your passport, honey—we're going on the trip!"

Shay rose from her chair and left Marvin's office for the sanctity of her own smaller one, only to be followed by a quietly delighted Richard.

"I have three of the four storyboards ready, if you'd like to look them over," he offered.

"Why does Marvin want me to do this?" Shay complained belatedly. "Why not one of the salesmen or some actor? Your agency has access to dozens of people...."

Richard grinned. "You know that Marvin believes in the personal touch, Shay. That's what's made him so successful. You should be proud; he must regard you as practically a member of his family."

There was some truth in Richard's words—Jeannie and Marvin had no children of their own, and they had included her and Hank in many of their holiday celebrations and summer camping trips over the past six years. What would she have done without the Reeses?

She eyed the stacks of paperwork teetering in her in-basket and drew a deep breath. "I have a lot to do, Richard. If you'll excuse me—"

The intercom buzzed and Shay picked up her telephone receiver. "Yes, Ivy? What is it?"

Ivy Prescott's voice came over the line. "Shay, that new salesman Mike hired last Tuesday is...well, he's doing something very weird."

Shay closed her eyes tightly, opened them again. With one hand, she opened the top drawer of her desk and rummaged for a bottle of aspirin, and failed to find it. "What, exactly, is he doing?"

"He's standing in the front seat of that '65 Corvette we got in last month, making a speech."

"Standing—"

"It's a convertible," Ivy broke in helpfully.

Shay made note of the fact that Richard was still loitering

inside her office door and her irritation redoubled. "Good Lord. Where is Mike? He's the floor manager and this is his problem!"

"He's out sick today," Ivy answered, and there was a note of panic in her normally bright voice. "Shay, what do I do? I don't think we should bother Mr. Reese with this, his heart, you know. Oh, I wish Todd were here!"

"I'll handle it," Shay said shortly, hanging up the receiver and striding out of the office, with Richard right behind her. As she passed Ivy's desk, she gave the young receptionist a look that, judging by the heightened color in her face, conveyed what Shay thought of the idea of hiding behind Todd Simmons, Ivy's fiancé, just because he was a man.

Shay was wearing slacks and a blue cotton blouse that day, and her heels made a staccato sound on the metal steps leading down into the showrooms. She smiled faintly at the customers browsing among glistening new cars as she crossed the display floor and stepped out onto the lot. Sure enough, there was a crowd gathered around the recently acquired Corvette.

She pushed her way between two of the newer salesmen, drew a deep breath and addressed the wild-eyed young man standing in the driver's seat of the sports car. "Get down from there immediately," she said in a clear voice, having no idea in the world what she would do if he refused.

Remarkably, the orator ceased his discourse and got out of the car to stand facing Shay. He was red with conviction and at least one coffee-break cocktail, and there was a blue stain on the pocket of his short-sleeved white shirt where his pen had leaked. "I was only—" he began.

Shay cut him off swiftly. "My office. Now."

The errant salesman followed along behind Shay as she walked back into the building, through the showroom and up the stairs. Once they were inside her office, he became petulant and not a little rebellious. "No woman orders me around," he muttered. Shay sat down in her chair, folded her hands in her lap so that—she glanced subtly at his name tag—Ray Metcalf wouldn't see that they were trembling just a little. "This woman, Mr. Metcalf, is ordering you out, not around. If you have any commissions coming, they will be mailed to you."

"You're firing me?" Metcalf looked stunned. He was young and uncertain of himself and it was obvious, of course, that he had a problem. Did he have a family to support?

"Yes," Shay answered firmly.

"You can't do that!"

"I can and I have. Good day, Mr. Metcalf, and good luck."

Metcalf flushed and, for a moment, the look in his eyes was ominous. Shay was a little scared, but she refused to be intimidated, meeting the man's contemptuous glare with a level gaze of her own. He turned and left the office, slamming the door behind him, and Shay let out a long breath in relief. When Ivy bounced in, moments later, she was going over sales figures for the month before on her computer.

Despite the difference in their ages—Ivy was only twenty while Shay was nine years older—the two women were good friends. Ivy was going to marry Todd Simmons, an up-and-coming young real-estate broker, at Christmas, and Shay would be her maid of honor.

"Todd's taking me out to lunch," Ivy said, and her chin-length blond hair glistened even in the harsh fluorescent lighting of the office. "You're welcome to come along if you'd like."

"How romantic," Shay replied, with a wry twist of her lips, and went on working. "Just the three of us."

Ivy persisted. "Actually, there wouldn't be three of us. There's someone I want you to meet."

Shay laid down her pen and gave her friend a look. "Are you matchmaking again? Ivy, I've told you time and time again—"

"But this man is different."

Shay pretended to assess Ivy's dress size, which, because she was so tiny, would be petite. "I wonder if Marvin still has that turkey suit at home. With a few alterations, it might fit you. Why didn't I think of this before?" She paused for effect. "I could pull rank on you. How would you like to appear in four television commercials?"

Ivy rolled her blue-green eyes and backed out of the office, closing the door on a number of very interesting possibilities. Shay smiled to herself and went back to work.

The house was a sprawling Tudor mansion perched on a cliff overlooking the Pacific, and it was too damned big for one single, solitary man.

The dining room was formal, lit by two shimmering crystal chandeliers, and there were French doors opening onto a garden filled with pink, white, scarlet and lavender rhododendrons. The walls of the massive library were lined with handcrafted shelves and the fireplaces on the first floor were all large enough for a man to stand upright inside. The master bedroom boasted a checkerboard of tinted and clear skylights, its own hot tub lined with exquisitely painted tiles and a broad terrace. Yes, the place was definitely too big and too fancy.

"I'll take it," Mitch Prescott said, leaning against the redwood railing of the upstairs terrace. The salt breeze rippled gently through his dark blond hair and the sound of the incoming tide, far below, was a soothing song.

Todd Simmons, soon to be Mitch's brother-in-law, looked pleased, as well he might, considering the commission his fledgling real-estate firm would collect on the sale. Mitch noticed that Todd's hand trembled a little as he extended it to seal the agreement.

Inwardly, Mitch was wondering what had possessed him to meet the outrageous asking price on this monster of a house within fifteen minutes of walking through the front door. He decided that he'd done it for Ivy, his half sister. Since she was going to marry Simmons, the sale would benefit her, too.

"When can I move in?" Mitch asked, resting against the railing again and gazing far out to sea. His hotel room was comfortable, but he had spent too much of his life in places like it; he wanted to live in a real house.

"Now, if you'd like," Simmons answered promptly. He seemed to vibrate with suppressed excitement, as though he'd like to jump up in the air and kick his heels together. "In this case, the closing will be little more than a formality. I don't mind telling you that Rosamond Dallas's daughter is anxious to unload the place."

The famous name dropped on Mitch's weary mind with all the grace of a boxcar tumbling into a ravine. "I thought Miss Dallas was dead," he ventured.

A sad expression moved in Todd's eyes as he shook his head and drew a package of gum from the pocket of his blue sports jacket. He was good-looking, with dark hair and a solid build; he and Ivy would have beautiful children.

"Rosamond has Alzheimer's disease," he said, and he gave a long sigh before going on. "It's a shame, isn't it? She made all those great movies, married all those men, bought this house and half a dozen others just as impressive all over the United States, and she winds up staring at the walls over at Seaview Convalescent, with the whole world thinking she's dead. The hell of it is, she's only forty-seven."

"My God," Mitch whispered. He was thirty-seven himself; it was sobering to imagine having just ten good years left. Rosamond, at his age, had been at the height of her powers.

Todd ran a hand through his dark hair and worked up a grin. "Things change," he said philosophically. "Time moves on. Rosamond doesn't have any use for a house like this now, and the taxes have been a nightmare for her daughter."

Mitch was already thinking like a journalist, even though he'd sworn that he wouldn't write again for at least a year. He was in the beginning stages of burnout, he had told his agent just that morning. He'd asked Ivan to get him an extension on his current contract, in fact. Now, six hours later, here he was thinking in terms of outlines and research material. "Rosamond Dallas must have earned millions, Todd. She was a star in every sense of the word. Why would the taxes on this place put a strain on anybody in her family?"

Todd unwrapped the stick of gum, folded it, accordion-fashion, into his mouth and tucked the papers into his pocket. "Rosamond had six husbands," he answered after a moment or two of sad reflection. "Except for Riley Thompson—he's a country and western singer and pays for her care over at Seaview—they were all jerks with a talent for picking the worst investments and the slowest horses."

"But the profit from selling this house—"

"That will go to clear up the last of Rosamond's personal debts. Shay won't see a dime of it."

"Shay. The daughter?"

Todd nodded. "You'll meet her tonight. She's Ivy's best friend, works for Marvin Reese."

Mitch couldn't help smiling at the mention of Reese, even though he was depressed that someone could make a mark on the world the way Rosamond Dallas had and have nothing more to pass on to her daughter than a pile of debts. Ivy had written him often about her employer, who was something of a local celebrity and the owner of one of the largest new-and-used car operations in the state of Washington. Television commercials were Reese's claim to fame; he had a real gift for the ridiculous.

Mitch's smile faded away. "Did Shay grow up in this house, by any chance?" he asked. He couldn't think why the answer should interest him, but it did.

"Like a lot of show people, Rosamond was something of a vagabond. Shay lived here when she was a little girl, on and off. Later, she spent a lot of time in Swiss boarding schools. Went to college for a couple of years, somewhere in Oregon, and that's when she met—" Todd paused and looked sheepish. "Damn, I've said too much and probably bored you to death in the process. I should be talking about the house. I can have the papers ready by tonight, and I'll leave my keys with you."

He removed several labeled keys from a ring choked with similar ones and they clinked as they fell into Mitch's palm. "Ivy mentioned dinner, didn't she? You'll be our guest, of course."

Mitch nodded. Todd thanked him, shook his hand again and left.

When he was alone, Mitch went outside to explore the grounds, wondering at himself. He hadn't intended to settle down. Certainly he hadn't intended to buy a house. He had come to town to see Ivy and meet her future husband, to relax and maybe fish and sail a little, and he'd agreed to look at this house only because he'd been intrigued by his sister's descriptions of it.

Out back he discovered an old-fashioned gazebo, almost hidden in tangles of climbing rosebushes. Pungently fragrant pink and yellow blossoms nodded in the dull, late morning sunshine, serenaded by bees. The realization that he would have to hire a gardener as well as a housekeeper made Mitch shake his head.

He rounded the gazebo and found another surprise, a little girl's playhouse, painted white. The miniature structure was perfectly proportioned, with real cedar shingles on the roof and green shutters at the windows. Mitch Prescott, hunter of war criminals, infiltrator of half a dozen chapters of the Ku Klux Klan, trusted confidant of Colombian cocaine dealers, was enchanted.

He stepped nearer the playhouse. The paint was peeling and the shingles were loose and there were, he could see through the lilliputian front window, repairs to be made on the inside as well. Still, he smiled to imagine how Kelly, his seven-year-old daughter, would love to play here, in this strangely magical place, spinning the dreams and fantasies that came so easily to children.

Shay stormed out of Marvin's office muttering, barely noticing Ivy, who sat at her computer terminal in the center of the reception room. "Bees…a half ton of sugar…that could kill me.…"

"Todd sold the house!" Ivy blurted as Shay fumbled for the knob on her office door.

She stopped cold, the storyboards for the outrageous commercials under one arm, and stared at Ivy, at once alarmed and hopeful. "Which house?" she asked in a voice just above a whisper.

Ivy's aquamarine eyes were shining and her elegant

cheekbones were tinted pink. "Yours—I mean, your mother's. Oh, Shay, isn't it wonderful? You'll be able to clear up all those bills and Todd will make the biggest commission ever!"

Shay forgot her intention to lock herself up in her office and wallow in remorse for the rest of the afternoon. She set the storyboards aside and groped with a tremulous hand for a chair to draw up to Ivy's desk. Of course she had been anxious to see that wonderful, magnificent burden of a house sold, but the reality filled her with a curious sense of sadness and loss. "Who bought it? Who could have come up with that kind of money?" she asked, speaking more to the cosmos than to Ivy.

Her friend sat up very straight in her chair and beamed proudly. "My brother, Mitch."

Shay had a headache. She pulled in a steadying breath and tried to remember all that Ivy had told her, over the years, about her brother. He and Ivy did not share the same mother; in fact, Mitch and his stepmother avoided each other as much as possible. Shay had had the impression that Mitch Prescott was very successful, in some nebulous and unconventional way, and she remembered that he had once been married and had a child, a little girl if she remembered correctly. Probably because of the rift between himself and Ivy's mother, he had rarely been to Skyler Beach.

Ivy looked as though she would burst. "I knew Mitch would want that house, if I could just get him to look at it," she confided happily. But then she peered at Shay, her eyes wide and a bit worried. "Shay, are you all right? You look awful!"

Shay stood up and moved like a sleepwalker toward the privacy of her office.

"Shay?" Ivy called after her. "I thought you'd be pleased. I thought—"

Shay turned in the doorway, clutching the storyboards to her pale blue blouse. She smiled shakily and ran the fingers of her left hand through her hair, hoping the lie didn't show in her eyes.

"I am happy," she said. And then she went into the office, closed the door and hurled the storyboards across the room.

"Dinner?"

Ivy was clearly going to stand fast. "Don't you dare say no, Shay Kendall. You wanted to be free of that house and Todd sold it for you and the least you can do is let us treat you to dinner to celebrate."

Shay gathered up the last of the invoices she had been checking and put them into the basket on her desk. It had been a difficult day, what with the planning of the commercials and that salesman making his speech on the front lot. Of course, it was a blessing that the house had been sold and she was relieved to be free of the financial burden it had represented, but parting with the place was something of an emotional shock all the same. She would have preferred to spend the evening at home, lounging about with a good book and maybe feeling a little sorry for herself. "Your brother will be there, I suppose."

"Of course," Ivy replied with a shrug. "After all, he's the buyer."

Shay felt a nip of envy. What would it be like to be able to buy a house like that? For a very long time, she had nursed a secret dream of starting her own catering business and being such a smashing success that she could afford to keep the place for herself and Hank. "I have to stop by Seaview to see Rosamond on my way home," she said, hoping to avoid having dinner out. "And then, of course, there's Hank...."

"Shay."

She sighed and pushed back her desk chair to stand up. "All right, all right. I'll spend a few minutes at Seaview and get a sitter for the evening."

Ivy's lovely face was alight again. "Great!" she chimed, turning to leave Shay's office.

"Wait," Shay said firmly, stopping her friend in the doorway.

Ivy looked back over one shoulder, her pretty hair following the turn of her head in a rhythmic flow of fine gold. "What?"

"Don't get any ideas about fixing me up with your brother, Ivy, because I'm not interested. Is that clear?"

Ivy rolled her eyes. "Oh, for pity's sake!" she cried dramatically.

"I mean it, Ivy."

"Meet us at the Wharf at eight," Ivy said, and then she waltzed out, closing Shay's door behind her.

Shay locked her desk, picked up her purse and cast one last disdainful look at the storyboards propped along the back of her bookshelf before leaving. She tried to be happy about the assignment and the money it would bring in, tried to be glad that the elegant house high above the beach was no longer her responsibility, tried to look forward to a marvelous dinner at Skyler Beach's finest restaurant. But, as she drove toward Seaview Convalescent Home, it was all Shay could do to keep from pulling over to the side of road, dropping her forehead to the steering wheel and crying.

Chapter Two

Shay Kendall looked nothing like her illustrious mother, Mitch thought as he watched her enter the restaurant. No, she was far more beautiful: tall with lush brown hair that fell past her shoulders in gentle tumbles of curl, and her eyes were a blend of green and brown, flecked with gold.

She wore a simple white cotton sundress and high-heeled sandals and when Ivy introduced her and she extended her hand to Mitch, something in her touch crackled up his arm and elbowed his heart. It was a sudden, painful jolt, a Sunday punch, and Mitch was off balance. To cover this, he made a subtle production of drawing back her chair and took his time rounding the table to sit down across from her.

Ivy and Todd, having greeted Shay, were now standing in front of the lobster tank, which ran the length of one wall, eagerly choosing their dinner. Their easy laughter drifted over the muted chatter of the other guests to the table beside the window.

Shay was looking out through the glass; beyond it, spatters of fading daylight danced on an ocean tinted with the pinks and golds and deep lavenders of sunset. Her eyes followed the gulls as they swooped and dived over the water, giving their raucous cries, and a slight smile curved her lips. An overwhelming feeling of tenderness filled Mitch as he watched her.

He had to say something, start a conversation. He sliced one irate glance in Ivy's direction, feeling deserted, and then plunged in with, "Ivy tells me that the house I bought belonged to your mother."

The moderation with which Mitch spoke surprised him, considering that he could see the merest hint of rosy nipples through the whispery fabric of Shay's dress. He took a steadying gulp of the white wine Todd had ordered earlier.

The hazel eyes came reluctantly to his, flickered with pain and then inward laughter at some memory. Mitch imagined Shay as a little girl, playing in that miniature house behind the gazebo, and the picture slowed down his respiration rate.

"Yes." Her voice was soft and she tossed a wistful glance toward Ivy and Todd, who were still studying their unsuspecting prey at the lobster tanks. In that instant Shay was a woman again, however vulnerable, and Mitch was rocked by the quicksilver change in her.

He tried to transform her back into the child. "That little house in back, was that yours?"

Shay smiled and nodded. "I used to spend hours there. At the time, it was completely furnished, right down to china dishes—" She fell silent and her beautiful eyes strayed again to the water beyond the window. "I only lived there for a few years," she finished quietly.

Mitch began to wish that he had never seen Rosamond Dallas's house, let alone bought it. He felt as though he had stolen something precious from this woman and he supposed that, in a way, he had. He was relieved when Ivy and Todd came back to the table, laughing between themselves and holding hands.

He was so handsome.

Nothing Ivy had ever said about Mitch Prescott had prepared Shay for the first jarring sight of him. He was a few inches taller than she was, with broad shoulders and hair of a toasted caramel shade, but it was his eyes that unsettled her the most. They were a deep brown, quick and brazen and tender, all at once. His hands looked strong, and they were dusted with butternut-gold hair, as was the generous expanse of chest revealed by his open-throated white shirt. He had just the suggestion of a beard and the effect was one of quiet, inexorable masculinity.

Here was a man, Shay decided uneasily, who had no self-doubts at all. He was probably arrogant.

She sat up a little straighter and tried to ignore him. His vitality stirred her in a most disturbing way. What would it be like to be caressed by those deft, confident hands?

Shay's arm trembled a little as she reached out for her wineglass. Fantasies sprang, scary and delicious, into her mind, and she battled them fiercely. God knew, she reminded herself, Eliott Kendall had taught her all she needed or wanted to know about men.

Ivy was chattering as she sat down, her eyes bright with the love she bore Todd Simmons and the excitement of having her adored brother nearby. "Aren't you going to pick out which lobster you want?" she demanded, looking from Shay to Mitch with good-natured impatience.

"I make it a point," Mitch said flatly, "never to eat anything I've seen groveling on the bottom of a fish tank. I'll have steak."

Ivy's lower lip jutted out prettily and she turned to Shay. "What about you? You're having lobster, aren't you?"

Shay grabbed for her menu and hid behind it. Why hadn't she followed her instincts and stayed home? She should have known she wouldn't be able to handle this evening, not after the day she'd had. Not after losing— *selling* the house.

"Shay?" Ivy prodded.

"I'll have lobster," Shay conceded, mostly because she couldn't make sense of the menu. She felt silly. Good Lord, she was twenty-nine years old, self-supporting, the mother of a six-year-old son, and here she was, cowering behind a hunk of plastic-covered paper.

"Well, go choose one then!"

Shay shook her head. "I'll let the waiter do that," she said lamely. I'm in no mood to sign a death warrant, she thought. Or the papers that will release that very special house to a stranger.

She lowered the menu and her eyes locked with Mitch Prescott's thoughtful gaze. She felt as though he'd bared her breasts or something, even though there was nothing objectionable in his regard. Beneath her dress her nipples tightened in response, and she felt a hot flush pool on her cheekbones.

Mitch smiled then, almost imperceptibly, and his eyes— God, she had to be imagining it, she thought—transmitted a quietly confident acknowledgment, not to mention a promise.

A wave of heat passed over Shay, so dizzying that she

had to drop her eyes and grip the arms of her chair for a moment. Stop it, she said to herself. You don't even know this man.

A waiter appeared and, vaguely, Shay heard Todd ordering dinner.

Ivy startled her back to full alertness by announcing, "Shay's going to be a star. I'll bet she'll be so good that Marvin will want her to do all the commercials."

"Ivy!" Shay protested, embarrassed beyond bearing. Out of the corner of one eye she saw Mitch Prescott's mouth twitch slightly.

"What's the big secret?" Ivy complained. "Everybody in western Washington is going to see you anyway. You'll be famous."

"Or infamous," Todd teased, but his eyes were gentle. "How is your mother, Shay?"

Shay didn't like to discuss Rosamond, but the subject was infinitely preferable to having Ivy leap into a full and mortifying description of the commercials Shay would begin filming the following week, after Marvin and Jeannie departed for faraway places. "She's about the same," she said miserably.

The salads arrived and Shay pretended to be ravenous, since no one would expect her to talk with her mouth full of lettuce and house dressing. Mercifully, the conversation shifted to Todd's dream of building a series of condominiums on a stretch of property south of Skyler Beach.

Throughout dinner, Ivy chattered about her Christmas wedding, and when the plates had been removed, Todd brought out the papers that would transfer ownership of Rosamond's last grand house to Mitch. Shay signed them with a burning lump in her throat and, when Ivy and Todd went off to the lounge to dance, she moved to make her escape.

"Wait," Mitch said with gruff tenderness, and though he didn't touch Shay in any physical way, he restrained her with that one word.

She sank back into her chair, near tears. "I know I haven't been very good company. I'm sorry...."

His hand came across the table and his fingers were warm and gentle on Shay's wrist. A tingling tremor moved through her and she wanted to die because she knew Mitch had felt it and possibly guessed its meaning. "Let me take you home," he said.

For a moment Shay was tempted to accept, even though she was terrified at the thought of being alone with this particular man. "I have my car," she managed to say, and inwardly she despaired because she knew she must seem colorless and tongue-tied to Mitch and a part of her wanted very much to impress him.

He rose and pulled back her chair for her, escorted her as far as her elderly brown Toyota on the far side of the parking lot. There were deep grooves in his cheeks when he smiled at Shay's nervous efforts to open the car door. When she was finally settled behind the steering wheel, Mitch lingered, bending slightly to look through the open window, and there was an expression of bafflement in his eyes. He probably wondered why there were three arthritic French fries, a fast-food carton and one worn-out sneaker resting on the opposite seat.

"I'm sorry, Shay," he said.

"Sorry?"

"About the house. About the hard time Ivy gave you."

Shay was surprised to find herself smiling. She started the car and shifted into Reverse; there was hope, after all, of making a dignified exit. "No problem," she said brightly. "I'm used to Ivy. Enjoy the house."

Mitch nodded and Shay backed up with a flourish,

feeling oddly relieved and even a bit dashing. Oh, for an Isadora Duncan–style scarf to flow dramatically behind her as she swept away! She was her mother's daughter after all.

She waved at Mitch Prescott and started into the light evening traffic just as the muffler fell off her car, clattering on the asphalt.

Mitch was there instantly, doing his best not to grin. Shay went from wanting to impress him to wanting to slap him across the face. The roar of the engine was deafening; she backed into the parking lot and turned off the ignition.

Without a word, Mitch opened the door and when Shay got out, he took her arm and escorted her toward a shiny foreign status symbol with a sliding sunroof and spoked wheels. The muffler wouldn't dare fall off this car.

"Where do you live?" Mitch asked reasonably.

Shay muttered directions, unable to look at him. Damn. First he'd seen her old car virtually fall apart before his eyes and now he was going to see her rented house with its sagging stoop and peeling paint. The grass out front needed cutting and the mailbox leaned to one side and the picture windows, out of keeping with the pre–World War II design, gave the place a look of wide-eyed surprise.

By the time Mitch's sleek car came to a stop in front of Shay's house, it was dark enough to cover major flaws. The screen door flew open and Hank burst into the glow of the porchlight, his teenage babysitter, Sally, behind him.

"Mom!" he whooped, bounding down the front walk on bare feet. "Wow! That's some awesome car!"

Shay was smiling again; her son had a way of putting things into perspective. Sagging stoop be damned. She was rich because she had Hank.

She turned to Mitch, opening her own door as she did

so, and put down a foolish urge to invite him inside. "Good night, Mr. Prescott, and thank you."

He inclined his head slightly in answer and Shay felt an incomprehensible yearning to be kissed. She got out of the car and cut Hank off at the gate.

"Who was that?" the little boy wanted to know.

Shay ruffled his red-brown hair with one hand and ushered him back down the walk. "The man who bought Rosamond's house."

"Uncle Garrett called," Hank announced when they were inside.

Shay paid the babysitter, kicked off her high-heeled sandals and sank onto her scratchy garage-sale couch. Garrett Thompson had been her stepbrother, during Rosamond's Nashville phase, and though Shay rarely saw him, their relationship was a close one.

Hank was dancing from one foot to the other, obviously ready to burst. "Uncle Garrett called!" he repeated.

"Did he want me to call him back?" Shay asked, resting her feet on the coffee table with a sigh of relief.

Hank shook his head. "He's coming here. He bought a house you can drive and he's going fishing and he wants me to go, too!"

Shay frowned. "A house—oh. You mean a motor home."

"Yeah. Can I go with him, Mom? Please?"

"That depends, tiger. Maggie and the kids will be going, too, I suppose?"

Hank nodded and Shay felt a pang at his eagerness, even though she understood. He was a little boy, after all, and he needed masculine companionship. He adored Garrett and the feeling appeared to be mutual. "We'd be gone a whole month."

Shay closed her eyes. "We'll talk about this tomorrow,

Hank," she said. "I've had a long day and I'm too tired to make any decisions."

Anxious to stay in his mother's good graces, Hank got ready for bed without being told. Shay went into his room and gave his freckled forehead a kiss. When he protested, she tickled him into a spate of sleepy giggles.

"I love you," she said moments later, from his doorway.

"Ah, Mom," he complained.

Smiling, Shay closed the door and went into her own room for baby-doll pajamas and a robe. After taking a quick bath and brushing her teeth, she was ready for bed.

She was not, however, ready for the heated fantasies that awaited her there, in that empty expanse of smooth sheets. She fell asleep imagining the weight of Mitch Prescott's body resting upon her own.

The next day was calm compared to the one before it. Shay's car had been brought to Reese Motors and repaired and she left work early in order to spend an hour with her mother before going home.

Rosamond sat near a broad window overlooking much of Skyler Beach, her thin, graceful hands folded in her lap, her long hair a stream of glistening, gray-marbled ebony tumbling down her back. On her lap she held the large rag doll Shay had bought for her six months before, when Rosamond had taken to wandering the halls of the convalescent home, day and night, sobbing that she'd lost her baby—couldn't someone please help her find her baby?

She had seemed content with the doll and even now she would clutch it close if anyone so much as glanced at it with interest, but Rosamond no longer cried or questioned or walked the halls. She was trapped inside herself forever, and there was no knowing whether or not she understood anything that happened around her.

On the off chance that some part of Rosamond was still aware, Shay visited often and talked to her mother as though nothing had changed between them. She told funny stories about Marvin and his crazy commercials and about the salesmen and about Hank.

Today there were no stories Shay wanted to tell, and she couldn't bring herself to mention that the beautiful house beside the sea, with its playhouse and its gazebo and its gardens of pastel rhododendrons, had been sold.

She stepped over the threshold of her mother's pleasant room and let the door whisk shut behind her, blessing Garrett's father, Riley Thompson, for being willing to pay Seaview's hefty rates. It was generous of him, considering that he and Rosamond had been divorced for some fifteen years.

"Hello, Mother," she said quietly.

Rosamond looked up with a familiar expression of bafflement in her wide eyes and held the doll close. She began to rock in her small cushioned chair.

Shay crossed the room and sank into another chair, facing Rosamond's. There was no resemblance between the two women; Rosamond's hair was raven-black, though streaked with gray now, and her eyes were violet, while Shay's were hazel and her hair was merely brown. As a child Shay had longed to be transformed into a mirror image of her mother.

"Mother?" she prompted, hating the silence.

Rosamond hugged the doll and rocked faster.

Shay worked up a shaky smile and her voice had a falsely bright note when she spoke again. "It's almost dinnertime. Are you getting hungry?"

There was no answer, of course. There never was. Shay talked until she could bear the sound of her own voice no longer and then kissed her mother's papery forehead and left.

The box, sitting in the middle of the sidewalk in front of Shay Kendall's house, was enormous. The name of a local appliance store was imprinted on one side and, as Mitch approached, he saw the crooked coin slot and the intriguing words, Lemmonad, Ten Sens, finger-painted above a square opening. He grinned and produced two nickels from the pocket of his jeans, dropping them through the slot.

They clinked on the sidewalk. The box jiggled a bit, curious sounds came from inside, and then a small freckled hand jutted out through the larger opening, clutching a grubby paper cup filled with lemonade.

Mitch chuckled, crouching as he accepted the cup. "How's business?"

"Vending machines don't talk, mister," replied the box.

Some poor mosquito had met his fate in the lemonade and Mitch tried to be subtle about pouring the stuff into the gutter behind him. "Is your mother home?" he asked.

"No," came the cardboard-muffled answer. "But my babysitter is here. She's putting gunk on her toenails."

"I see."

A face appeared where the cup of lemonade had been dispensed. "Are you the guy who brought my mom home last night?"

"Yep." Mitch extended a hand, which was immediately clasped by a smaller, stickier one. "My name is Mitch Prescott. What's yours?"

"Hank Kendall. Really, my name is Henry. Who'd want people callin' 'em Henry?"

"Who indeed?" Mitch countered, biting back another grin. "Think your mom will be home soon?"

The face filling the gap in the cardboard moved in a nod. "She visits Rosamond after work sometimes. Rosamond is weird."

"Oh? How so?"

"You're not a kidnapper or anything, are you? Mom says I'm not supposed to talk to strangers. Not ever."

"And she's right. In this case, it's safe, because I'm not a kidnapper, but, as a general rule—"

The box jiggled again and then toppled to one side, revealing a skinny little boy dressed in blue shorts and a T-shirt, along with a pitcher of lemonade and a stack of paper cups. "Rosamond doesn't talk or anything, and sometimes she sits on my mom's lap, just like I used to do when I was a little kid."

Mitch was touched. He sighed as he stood upright again. Before he could think of anything to say in reply, the screen door snapped open and the babysitter was mincing down the walk, trying not to spoil her mulberry toenails. At almost the same moment, Shay's Toyota wheezed to a stop behind Mitch's car.

He wished he had an excuse for being there. What the hell was he going to say to explain it? That he'd been awake all night and miserable all day because he wanted Shay Kendall in a way he had never before wanted any woman?

Mitch was wearing jeans and a dark blue sports shirt and the sight of him almost made Shay drop the bucket of take-out chicken she carried in the curve of one arm. Go away, go away, she thought. "Would you like to stay to dinner?" she asked aloud.

He looked inordinately relieved. "Sounds good," he said.

Sally wobbled, toes upturned, over to stand beside Shay. "Who's the hunk?" she asked in a stage whisper that sent color pulsing into her employer's face.

Shay stumbled through an introduction and was glad when Sally left for the day. Mitch watched her move down the sidewalk to her own gate with a grin. "I hope her toenails dry before the bones in her feet are permanently affected," he said.

"Dumb girl," Hank added, who secretly adored Sally.

The telephone was ringing as Shay led the way up the walk; Hank surged around her and bounded into the house to grab the receiver and shout, "Hello!"

"Why are you here?" Shay asked softly as Mitch opened the screen door for her.

"I don't know," he answered.

Hank was literally jumping up and down, holding the receiver out to Shay. "It's Uncle Garrett! It's Uncle Garrett!"

Shay smiled at the exuberance in her son's face, though it stung just a little, and handed the bucket of chicken to Mitch so that she could accept the call.

"Hi, Amazon," Garrett greeted her. "What's the latest?"

Shay was reassured by the familiar voice, even if it was coming from hundreds of miles away. The teasing nickname, conferred upon Shay during the adolescent years when she had been taller than Garrett, was welcome, too. "You don't want to know," she answered, thinking of the upcoming commercials and the attraction she felt toward the man standing behind her with a bucket of chicken in his arms.

Garrett laughed. "Yes, I do, but I'll get it out of you later. Right now, I want to find out if Maggie and I can borrow Hank for a month."

Shay swallowed hard. "A month?"

"Come on, mother hen. He needs to spend time with me, and you know it."

"But…a month."

"We've got big stuff planned, Shay. Camping. Fishing." There was a brief pause. "And two weeks at Dad's ranch."

Shay was fond of Riley Thompson; of all her six stepfathers, he had been the only one who hadn't seemed to regard her as an intruder. "How is Riley?"

"Great," Garrett answered. "You've heard his new hit, I assume. He's got a string of concerts booked and there's talk that he'll be nominated for another Grammy this year. You wouldn't mind, would you, Shay, our taking Hank to his place, I mean? Dad wants to get to know him."

"Why?"

"Because he's your kid, Amazon."

Shay felt sad, remembering how empty that big beautiful house overlooking the sea had been after Riley and Garrett had moved out. Everyone knew that the divorce had nearly destroyed Riley; he'd loved Rosamond and chances were that he loved her still. "I want you to tell him, for me, how much I appreciate all he's done for my mother. God knows what kind of place she'd have to stay in if he weren't paying the bills."

"Shay, if you need money—"

Shay could hear Hank and Mitch in the kitchen. It sounded as though they were setting the table, and Hank was chattering about his beloved Uncle Garrett, who had a house that could be "drived" just like a car.

"I don't need money," she whispered into the phone. "Don't you dare offer!"

Garrett sighed. "All right, all right. Maggie wants to talk to you."

Garrett's wife came on the line then; she was an Australian and Shay loved the sound of her voice. By the time the conversation was over, she had agreed to let Hank spend the next four weeks with the Thompsons and their two children.

She hung up, dashed away tears she could not have explained, and wandered into the kitchen, expecting to find Mitch and Hank waiting for her. The small table was clear.

"Out here, Mom!" Hank called.

Shay followed the voice onto the small patio in back. The chicken and potato salad and coleslaw had been set out on the sturdy little picnic table left behind by the last tenant, along with plates and silverware and glasses of milk.

"Do I get to go?" Hank's voice was small and breathless with hope.

Shay took her seat on the bench beside Mitch, because that was the way the table had been set, and smiled at her son. "Yes, you get to go," she answered, and the words came out hoarsely.

Hank gave a whoop of delight and then was too excited to eat. He begged to be excused so that he could go and tell his best friend, Louie, all about the forthcoming adventure.

The moment he was gone, Shay dissolved in tears. She was amazed at herself—she had not expected to cry—and still more amazed that Mitch Prescott drew her so easily into his arms and held her. There she was, blubbering all over his fancy blue sports shirt like a fool, and all he did was tangle one gentle hand in her hair and rock her back and forth.

It had been a very long time since Shay had had a shoulder to cry on, and humiliating as it was, silly as it was, it was a sweet indulgence.

Chapter Three

"Tell me about Shay Kendall," Mitch said evenly, and his hand trembled a little as he poured coffee from the restaurant carafe into Ivy's cup.

Ivy grinned and lifted the steaming brew to her lips. "Are you this subtle with stool pigeons and talkative members of the Klan?"

"Dammit," Mitch retorted with terse impatience, "don't say things like that."

"Sorry," Ivy whispered, her eyes sparkling.

Mitch sat back in the vinyl booth. The small downtown restaurant was full of office workers and housewives with loud little kids demanding ice cream; after a second night in that cavernous house of his, he found the hubbub refreshing. "I asked about Ms. Kendall."

Ivy shrugged. "Very nice person. Terrific mother. Good office manager. Didn't you find out anything last night? You said you had dinner with Shay."

Mitch's jaw tightened, relaxed again. "She was married," he prompted.

Ivy looked very uncomfortable. "That was a long time ago. I've never met the guy."

Mitch sipped his coffee in a leisurely way and took his time before saying, "But you know all about him, don't you? You're Shay's friend."

"Her best friend," Ivy confirmed with an element of pride that said a great deal about Shay all by itself. A second later her blue eyes shifted from Mitch's face to the sidewalk just on the other side of the window and her shoulders slumped a little. "I don't like talking about Shay's private life. It seems…it seems disloyal."

He sighed. "I suppose it is," he agreed.

Ivy's eyes widened as a waitress arrived with club sandwiches, set the plates down and left. "Mitch, you wouldn't—you're not planning to write a book about Rosamond Dallas, are you?"

Mitch recalled his telephone conversation with his agent that morning and sorely regretted mentioning that the house he'd just bought had once belonged to the movie star. Ivan had jumped right on that bit of information, reminding Mitch that he was under contract for one more book and pointing out that a biography of Ms. Dallas, authorized or not, would sell faster than the presses could turn out new copies.

He braced both arms against the edge of the table and leaned toward his sister, glaring. "Why would I, a mild-mannered venture capitalist, want to write a book?"

Ivy was subdued by the reprimand, but her eyes were suspicious. "Okay, okay, I shouldn't have put it quite that way." She lowered her voice to a whisper. "Are you writing about Shay's mother or not?"

Mitch rolled his eyes. "Dammit, I don't know," he

lied. The truth was that he had already agreed to do the book. Rosamond Dallas's whereabouts, long a mystery to the world in general, were now known, thanks to the thoughtless remark he'd made to Ivan. Mitch knew without being told that if he didn't undertake the project, his agent would send another writer to do it, and unless he missed his guess, that writer would be Lucetta White, a barracuda in Gucci.

Lucetta was no lover of truth, and she made it a practice to ruin at least three careers and a marriage every day before breakfast, just to stay in top form. If she got hold of Rosamond's story, the result would be a vicious disaster of a book that would ride the major best-seller lists for months.

"Shay's husband was a coach or a teacher or something," Ivy said, jolting Mitch back to reality. "He was a lot older than she was, too. Anyway, he embezzled a small fortune from a high school in Cedar Landing, that's a little place just over the state line, in Oregon."

"And?"

"And Shay was pregnant at the time. She found out at her baby shower, if you can believe it. Somebody just walked in and said, 'guess what?'"

"My God."

"There was another woman involved, naturally."

Mitch was making mental notes; he would wait until later to ask his sister what had prompted her to divulge all this information. For the moment, he didn't want to chance breaking the flow. "Does anybody know where they are, Shay's ex-husband and this woman, I mean?"

Ivy shrugged. "Nobody cares except the police. Shay received divorce papers from somewhere in Mexico a few weeks after he left, but that was over six years ago. The creep could be anyplace by now."

"Who was the other woman?"

"Are you ready for this? It was the local librarian. Everybody thought she was so prim and proper and she turned out to be a mud wrestler at heart."

If it hadn't been for an aching sense of the humiliation Shay must have suffered over the incident, Mitch would have laughed at Ivy's description of the librarian. "Appearances are deceiving," he said.

"Are they, Mitch?" Ivy countered immediately. "I hope not, because when I look at you, I see a person I can trust."

"Why did you tell me about Shay's past, Ivy? You were dead set against it a minute ago."

Ivy lifted her chin and began methodically removing frilled toothpicks from the sections of her sandwich. "I just thought you should know why she's...why she's shy."

Mitch wondered if "shy" was the proper word to describe Shay Kendall. Even though she'd wept in his arms the night before, on the bench of a rickety backyard picnic table, he sensed that she had a steel core. She was clearly a survivor. Hadn't she picked herself up after what must have been a devastating blow, found herself a good job, supported herself and her son? "Didn't Rosamond do anything to help Shay after Kendall took off with his mud wrestler?"

Ivy stopped chewing and swallowed, her eyes snapping. "She didn't lift a finger. Shay makes excuses for her, but I think the illustrious Ms. Dallas must have been an egotistical, self-centered bitch."

Mitch considered that a distinct possibility, but he decided to reserve judgment until he had the facts.

After they had eaten their club sandwiches, Mitch drove his sister back to Reese Motors and her job. One hand on the inside handle of the car door, she gazed at her brother with wide, frightened eyes. "All those things in your books, Mitch—did you really know all those terrible people?"

He had hedged enough for one day, he decided. "Yes. And unless you want all those 'terrible people' to find out who and where I am, you'd better learn to be a little more discreet."

Tears sparkled in Ivy's eyes and shimmered on her lower lashes. "If anything happened to you—"

"Nothing is going to happen to me." How many times had he said that to Reba, his ex-wife? In the end, words hadn't been enough; she hadn't been able to live with the fears that haunted her. The divorce had at least been amicable; Reba was married again now, to a chiropractor with a flourishing practice and a suitably predictable lifestyle. He made a mental note to call and ask her to let Kelly come to visit for a few weeks.

Ivy didn't look reassured, but she did reach over and plant a hasty kiss on Mitch's cheek. A moment later she was scampering toward the entrance to the main showroom.

Mitch went shopping. He bought extra telephones in one store, pencils and spiral notebooks in another, steak and the makings of a salad in still another. He reflected, on his way home, that it might be time to get married again. He didn't mind cooking, but he sure as hell hated eating alone.

Shay carried a bag of groceries and several sacks containing new clothes for Hank's trip with Garrett and Maggie. She resisted an urge to kiss the top of her son's head after setting her purchases down on the kitchen table.

"How was work?" he asked, crawling onto a stool beside the breakfast bar that had, like the picture windows in the living room, been something of an architectural afterthought.

Shay groaned and rolled her eyes. "I spent most of it being fitted for costumes."

Hank was swinging his bare feet back and forth and there was an angry-looking mosquito bite on his right knee. "Costumes? What do you need costumes for? Halloween?"

Shay brought a dozen eggs, a pound of bacon and other miscellaneous items from the grocery bag. "Something similar, I'm afraid," she said ruefully. "I'm going to be doing four commercials."

Hank's feet stopped swinging and his brown eyes grew very wide. "You mean the kind of commercials Mr. Reese does? On TV?"

"Of course, on TV," Shay answered somewhat shortly. "Mr. and Mrs. Reese are going to be away, so I'll have to take Mr. Reese's place."

"Wow," Hank crowed, drawing the word out, his eyes shining with admiration. "Everybody will see you and know you're my mom! I betcha I could get a quarter for your autograph!"

A feeling of sadness washed over Shay; she recalled how people had waited for hours to ask Rosamond for her autograph. She had signed with a loopy flourish, Rosamond had, so friendly, so full of life, so certain of her place in a bright constellation of stars. Did that same vibrant woman exist somewhere inside the Rosamond of today?

"You're thinking about your mom, aren't you?" Hank wanted to know.

"Yes."

"Sally's mother says you should write a book about Rosamond. If you did, we'd be rich."

Shay took a casserole prepared on one of her marathon cooking days from the small chest freezer in one corner of the kitchen and slid it into the oven. She'd been approached with the idea of a book before, and she hated it. Telling Rosamond's most intimate secrets to the world would be a betrayal of sorts, a form of exploitation, and besides, she was no writer. "Scratch that plan, tiger," she said tightly. "There isn't going to be a book and we're not going to be rich."

"Uncle Garrett is rich."

"Uncle Garrett is the son of a world-famous country and western singer and a successful businessman in his own right," Shay pointed out.

"Rosamond was famous. How come you're not rich?"

"Because I'm not. Set the table, please."

"Sally's mother says she had a whole lot of husbands. Which one was your dad, Mom? You never talk about your dad."

Shay made a production of washing her hands at the sink, keeping her back to Hank. How could she explain that her father had never been Rosamond's husband at all, that he'd been the proverbial boy back home, left behind when stardom beckoned? "I didn't know my father," she said over the sound of running water. In point of fact, she didn't even know his name.

Hank was busily setting out plates and silverware and plastic tumblers. "I guess we're alike that way, huh, Mom?"

Shay's eyes burned with sudden tears and she cursed Eliott Kendall for never caring enough to call or write and ask about his own son. "I guess so."

"I like that guy with the blue car."

Mitch. Shay found herself smiling. She sniffled and turned to face Hank. "I like him, too."

"Are you going to go out with him, on dates and stuff?"

"I don't know," Shay said, unsettled again. "Hey, it'll be

a while until dinner is ready. How about trying on some of this stuff I bought for your camping trip? Maggie and Garrett will be here Saturday, so if I have to make any exchanges, I'd like to take care of it tonight."

The telephone rang as Shay was slicing cucumbers for a salad, and there was a peculiar jiggling in the pit of her stomach as she reached out one hand for the receiver. She hoped that the caller would be Mitch Prescott and then, at the nervous catching of her breath in her throat, hoped not.

"Shay?" The feminine voice rang like crystal chimes over the wires. "This is Jeannie Reese."

Mingled relief and disappointment made Shay's knees weak; she reached out with one foot for a stool and drew it near enough to sit upon. With the telephone receiver wedged between her ear and her shoulder, she went on slicing. "All ready for the big trip?" she asked, and her voice was as tremulous as her hands. If she didn't watch it, she'd cut herself.

"Ready as I'll ever be, I guess. We couldn't get away if it weren't for you. Shay, I'm so grateful."

"It was the least I could do," Shay replied, thinking of how frightened and alone she'd been when she had come back to Skyler Beach hoping to take refuge in her childhood home and found herself completely on her own. The Reeses had made all the difference. "What's up?"

"I know it's gauche, but I'm throwing my own going-away party. It'll be at our beach house, this Saturday night. Can I count on you to be there?"

By Saturday night, Hank would be gone. The house would be entirely too quiet and the first television commercial would be looming directly ahead. A distraction, especially one of the Reeses' elegant parties, would be welcome. "Is it formal?"

"Dress to the teeth, my dear."

Shay tossed the last of the cucumber slices into the salad bowl and started in on the scallions. Her wardrobe consisted mostly of work or casual clothing; she was either going to have to buy a new outfit or drag the sewing machine out of the back of her closet and make one. "What time?"

"Eight," Jeannie sang. "Ciao, darling. I've got fifty-six more people to call."

Shay grinned. "Ciao," she said, hanging up.

Almost instantly, the telephone rang again. This time the caller was Ivy. "You've heard about the party, I suppose?"

"Only seconds ago. How did you find out so fast?"

"Mrs. Reese appointed me to make some of the calls. Shay, what are you going to wear?"

"I don't know." The answer was sighed rather than spoken.

"We could hit the mall tomorrow, after work."

"No chance. I've got too much to do. It's tonight or nothing."

Ivy loved to shop and her voice was a disappointed wail. "Oh, damn! I can't turn a wheel tonight! I've got to sit right here in my apartment, calling all the Reeses' friends. Promise me you'll splurge, buy something really spectacular!"

Shay scraped a pile of chopped scallions into one hand with the blade of her knife and frowned suspiciously. "Ivy, what are you up to?"

"Up to?" Ivy echoed, all innocence.

"You know what I mean."

"No, I don't."

"You're awfully concerned, it seems to me, about how I plan to dress for the Reese party."

"I just want you to look good."

"For your brother, perhaps?"

"Shay Kendall!"

"Come on, Ivy. Come clean. He's going to be there, isn't he?"

"Well, I did suggest…"

Shay laughed, even though the pit of her stomach was jumping again and her heart was beating too fast. "That's what I thought. Has it occurred to you, dear, that if Mitch wanted to see me again he would call me himself?"

"He did drop in for chicken last night," Ivy reminded her friend.

Shay blushed to remember the way she had sobbed in Mitch's arms like a shattered child. She'd probably scared him off for good. "That didn't go too well. Don't get your hopes up, Ivy."

"Buy something fabulous," insisted the irrepressible Ivy. And then she rang off.

By the time Hank had paraded through the kitchen in each of his new outfits—by some miracle, only one pair of jeans would have to be returned—the casserole was finished. Mother and son sat down to eat and then, after clearing the table and leaving the dishes to soak, they went off to the mall.

Exchanging the jeans took only minutes, but Shay spent a full hour in the fabric store, checking out patterns and material. Finally, after much deliberation, she selected a material that would make a nice floaty black skirt. In a boutique across the way, she bought a daring silver and black top, holding her breath the whole while. The shirt, while gorgeous, was heavy and impractical and far too expensive. Would she even have the nerve to wear it?

Twice, on the way back to her car, Shay stopped in her tracks. What was she doing, spending this kind of money for one party? She had to return the shirt.

It was Hank who stopped her from doing just that. "You'll look real pretty in that shiny shirt, Mom," he said.

Shay drew a deep breath and marched onward to the car. Every woman needed to wear something wickedly glamorous, at least once in her life. Rosamond had owned closetfuls of such things.

The telephone was ringing when Shay entered the house, and Hank leaped for the living room extension. He was a born positive-thinker, expecting every call to bring momentous news.

"Yeah, she's here. Mom!"

Shay dropped her purchases on the couch and crossed the room to take the call. She was completely unprepared for the voice on the other end of the line, much as she'd hoped and dreaded to hear it earlier.

"You've heard about the party, I presume?" Mitch Prescott asked with that quiet gruffness that put everything feminine within Shay on instant red alert.

"Yes," she managed to answer.

"I don't think I can face it alone. How about lending me moral support?"

Shay couldn't imagine Mitch shrinking from anything, or needing moral support, but she felt a certain terrified gladness at the prospect of being asked to go to the party with him. "Being a sworn humanitarian," she teased, "I couldn't possibly refuse such a request."

His sigh of relief was an exaggerated one. "Thank you."

Shay laughed. "Were you really that afraid of a simple party?"

"No. I was afraid you'd say no. That, of course, would have been devastating to my masculine ego."

"We can't have that," Shay responded airily, glad that

he couldn't see her and know that she was blushing like a high-schooler looking forward to her first prom. "The Reeses' beach house is quite a distance from town. We'd better leave at least a half an hour early."

"Seven?"

"Seven," Shay confirmed. The party, something of an obligation before, was suddenly the focal point of her existence; she was dizzy with excitement and a certain amount of chagrin that such an event could be so important to her. Shouldn't she be dreading her son's imminent departure instead of looking past it to a drive along miles and miles of moon-washed shore?

While Hank was taking his bath, under protest, Shay washed the dishes she'd left to soak and then got out her sewing machine. She was up long after midnight, adjusting the pattern and cutting out her silky skirt. Finally she stumbled off to bed.

The next day was what Hank would have called "hairy." Three salesmen quit, Ivy went home sick and the people at Seaview called to say that Rosamond seemed to be in some kind of state.

"What kind of 'state'?" a harried Shay barked into the receiver of the telephone in her office.

"She's curled up in her bed," answered the young and obviously inexperienced nurse. "She's crying and calling for the baby."

"Have you called her doctor?"

"He's playing golf today."

"Oh, at his rates, that's just terrific!" Shay snapped. "You get him over there if you have to drag him off the course. Does Mother have her doll?"

"What doll?"

"The rag doll. The one she won't be without."

"I didn't see it."

"Find it!"

"I'll call you back in a few minutes, Mrs. Kendall."

"See that you do," Shay replied in clipped tones just as Richard Barrett waltzed, unannounced, into her office.

"Bad day?"

Shay ran one hand through her already tousled hair and sank into the chair behind her desk. "Don't you know how to knock?"

Richard held up both hands in a concessionary gesture. "I'm sorry."

Shay sighed. "No, I'm sorry. I didn't mean to snap at you that way. How can I help you?"

"I just wanted to remind you that we're going to shoot the first commercial Monday morning. You've memorized the script, I assume?"

The script. If Shay hadn't had a pounding headache, she would have laughed. "I say my line and then read off this week's special used-car deals. That isn't too tough, Richard."

"I thought we might have a rehearsal tonight."

Shay shook her head. "No chance. My mother is in bad shape and I have to go straight to the convalescent home as soon as I leave here."

"After that—"

"My son is leaving on a camping trip with his uncle, Richard, and he'll be gone a month. I want to spend the evening with him."

"Shay—"

Now Shay held up her hands. "No more, Richard. You and Marvin insisted that I take this assignment and I agreed. But it will be done on my terms or not at all."

A look of annoyance flickered behind Richard's glasses. "Temperament rears its ugly head. I was mistaken about you, Shay. You're more like your mother than I thought."

The telephone began to jangle, and Ivy wasn't out front to screen the calls. Shay dismissed Richard with a hurried wave of one hand and snapped "Hello?"

A customer began listing, in irate and very voluble terms, all the things that were wrong with the used car he'd bought the week before. While Shay tried to address the complaint, the other lines on her telephone lit up, all blinking at once.

It was nearly seven o'clock when Shay finally got home, and she had such a headache that she gave Hank an emergency TV dinner for supper, swallowed two aspirin and collapsed into bed.

Bright and early on Saturday morning, Garrett and his family arrived in a motor home more luxuriously appointed than many houses. While Maggie stayed behind with her own children and Hank, Shay and Garrett drove to Seaview to visit Rosamond.

Because the doll had been recovered, Rosamond was no longer curled up in her bed weeping piteously for her "baby." Still, Garrett's shock at seeing a woman he undoubtedly remembered as glamorous and flippant staring vacantly off into space showed in his darkly handsome face and the widening of his steel-gray eyes.

"My God," he whispered.

Rosamond lifted her chin—she was sitting, as always, in the chair beside the window, the rag doll in her lap—at the sound of his voice. Her once-magical violet eyes widened and she surprised both her visitors by muttering, "Riley?"

Shay sank back against the wall beside the door. "No, Mother. This is—"

Garrett silenced her with a gesture of one hand, approached Rosamond and crouched before her chair. Shay realized then how much he actually resembled his father, the Riley Thompson Rosamond would remember and recognize. He stretched to kiss a faded alabaster forehead and smiled. "Hello, Roz," he said.

The bewildered joy in Rosamond's face made Shay ache inside. "Riley," she said again.

Garrett nodded and caught both his former stepmother's hands in his own strong, sun-browned ones. "How are you?" he asked softly.

Tears were stinging Shay's eyes, half blinding her. Through them, she saw Rosamond hold out the doll for Garrett to see and touch. "Baby," she said proudly.

As Garrett acknowledged the doll with a nod and a smile, Shay whirled away, unable to bear the scene any longer. She fled the room for the small bathroom adjoining it and stood there, trembling and pale, battling the false hopes that Rosamond's rare moments of lucidity always stirred in her.

When she was composed enough to come out, Rosamond had retreated back into herself; she was rocking in her chair, her lips curved into a secretive smile, the doll in her arms. Garrett wrapped a supportive arm around Shay's waist and led her out of the room into the hallway, where he gave her a brotherly kiss on the forehead.

"Poor baby," he said, and then he held Shay close and rocked her back and forth in his arms. She didn't notice the man standing at the reception desk, watching with a frown on his face.

Chapter Four

When Hank disappeared into Garrett and Maggie's sleek motor home, a lump the size of a walnut took shape in Shay's throat. He was only six; too young to be away from home for a whole month!

Garrett grinned and kissed Shay's forehead. "Relax," he urged. "Maggie and I will take good care of the boy. I promise."

Shay nodded, determined not to be a clinging, neurotic mother. Six or sixty, she reminded herself, Hank was a person in his own right and he needed experiences like this one to grow.

Briefly, Garrett caressed Shay's cheek. "Go in there and get yourself ready for that party, Amazon," he said. "Paint your toenails and slather your face with gunk. Soak in a bubble bath."

Shay couldn't help grinning. "You're just full of suggestions, aren't you?"

Garrett was serious. "Devote some time to yourself, Shay. Forget about Roz for a while and let Maggie and me worry about Hank."

It was good advice and Shay meant to heed it. After the motor home had pulled away, a happy chorus of farewell echoing behind, she went back into the house, turned on the stereo, pinned up her hair and got out the skirt she'd made for the party. After hemming it, she hurried through the routine housework and then spent the rest of the morning pampering herself.

She showered and shampooed, she pedicured and manicured, she gave herself a facial. After a light luncheon consumed in blissful silence, she crawled into bed and took a long nap.

Upon rising, Shay made a chicken salad sandwich and took her time eating it. Following that, she put on her makeup, her new skirt and the lovely shimmering top. She brushed her hair and worked it into a loose style and put on long silver earrings. Looking into her bedroom mirror, she was stunned. Was this lush and glittering creature really Shay Kendall, mother of Hank, purveyor of "previously owned" autos, wearer of jeans and clear fingernail polish?

It was. Shay whirled once, delighted. It was!

Promptly at seven, Mitch arrived. He wore a pearl-gray, three-piece suit, expertly fitted, and the effect was at once rugged and Madison Avenue elegant. He was clean shaven and the scent of his cologne was crisply masculine. His brown eyes warmed as they swept over Shay, and the familiar grooves dented his cheeks when he smiled.

"Wow," he said.

Shay was glad that it was time to leave for the Reeses' beach house; she had rarely dated in the six years since her divorce and she was out of practice when it came to amenities like playing soft music and serving chilled wine and making small talk. "Wow, yourself," she said, because that was what she would have said to Hank and it came out automatically. She could have bitten her tongue.

Mitch laughed and handed her a small florist's box. There was a pink orchid inside, delicate and fragile and so exotically beautiful that Shay's eyes widened at the sight of it. It was attached to a slender band of silver elastic and she slid it onto her wrist.

"Thank you," she said.

Mitch put a gentlemanly hand to the small of her back and steered her toward the door. "Thank you," he countered huskily, and though Shay wondered what he was thanking her for, she didn't dare ask.

As his fancy car slipped away from the curb, Mitch pressed a button to silence the blaring music.

The drive south along the coastal highway was a pleasant one. The sunset played gloriously over the rippling curl of the evening tide and the conversation was comfortable. Mitch talked about his seven-year-old daughter, Kelly, who was into everything pink and ballet lessons, and Shay talked about Hank.

She wanted to ask about Mitch's ex-wife, but then he might ask about Eliott and she wasn't prepared to discuss that part of her life. It was possible, of course, Shay knew, that Ivy had told him already.

"Have you started furnishing the house yet?" Shay asked when they'd exhausted the subject of children.

Mitch shook his head and the warm humor in his eyes cooled a little, it seemed to Shay, as he glanced at her and then turned his attention back to the highway. "Not yet."

Shay was stung by his sudden reticence, and she was confused, too. "Did I say something wrong?"

"No," came the immediate response, and Mitch flung

one sheepish grin in Shay's direction. "I was just having an attack of male ego, I guess."

Intrigued, Shay turned in her seat and asked, "What?"

"It isn't important."

"I think maybe it is," Shay persisted.

"I don't have the right to wonder, let alone ask."

"Ask anyway." Suddenly, Shay was nervous.

"Who is that guy who was holding you in the hallway at Seaview this morning?" The question was blurted, however reluctantly, and Shay's anxieties fled—except for one.

"That was Garrett Thompson. His father was married to my mother at one time." Shay folded her hands in her lap and drew a deep breath. "What were you doing at Seaview?"

The Reeses' beach house was in sight and Mitch looked longingly toward it, but he pulled off the highway and turned to face Shay directly. "I was asking about your mother," he said.

Shay had been braced for a lie and now, in the face of a blunt truth, she didn't know how to react. "Why?" she asked after several moments of silence.

"I don't think this is a good time to talk, Shay," Mitch replied. "Anyway, it isn't anything you need to worry about."

"But—"

His hand closed, warm and reassuring, over hers. "Trust me, okay? I promise that we'll talk after the party."

Mitch had been forthright; he could have lied about his reason for visiting Seaview, but he hadn't. Shay had no cause to distrust him. And yet the words "trust me" troubled her; it didn't matter that Mitch had spoken them: she heard them in Eliott's voice. "After the party," she said tightly.

Moments later she and Mitch entered the Reeses'

spacious two-story beach house. It was a beautiful place with polished oak floors and beamed ceilings and a massive stone fireplace, and it was crowded with people.

Marvin took one look at Shay's shiny shirt and bounded away, only to return moments later wearing a pair of grossly oversized sunglasses that he'd used in a past commercial. Shay laughed and shook her head.

"I hope his tie doesn't squirt grape juice," Mitch commented in a discreet whisper.

Shay watched fondly as Marvin turned away to rejoin the party. "Don't let him fool you," she replied. "He reads Proust and Milton and speaks two languages other than English."

Mitch was still pondering this enlightening information—Marvin's commercials and loud sports jackets were indeed deceptive—when Ivy wended her way through the crowd, looking smart in pale blue silk. Her aquamarine eyes took in Shay's outfit with approval. "Jeannie sent me to bid you welcome. She's in the kitchen, trying to pry an ice sculpture out of the freezer. Would you believe it's a perfect replica of *Venus de Milo?*"

"Now we know why the poor girl has no arms," Todd quipped, standing just behind Ivy.

Both Ivy and Shay groaned at the joke, and Ivy added a well-aimed elbow that splashed a few drops of champagne out of Todd's glass and onto his impeccable black jacket.

"Six months till the wedding and I'm already henpecked," he complained.

"I've been thinking about those condos," Mitch reflected distractedly. "From an ecological standpoint…"

"Business!" Ivy hissed, dragging Shay away by one arm. They came to a stop in front of a table spread with plates of wilted crab puffs, smoked oysters, crackers and cheeses.

Shay cast one look in Mitch's direction and saw that he

was engrossed in his conversation with Todd. It hurt a little that he apparently hadn't even noticed that she was gone. She took a crab puff to console herself.

Ivy frowned pensively at the morsel. "Isn't that pathetic? You'd think a place as big as Skyler Beach would have one decent caterer, wouldn't you? Mrs. Reese had to have everything brought in from Seattle."

The crab puffs definitely showed the rigors of the journey, and it was a miracle that *Venus de Milo* had made it so far without melting into a puddle. Shay's dream of starting her own catering business surfaced and she pushed it resolutely back onto a mental shelf. She had a child to support and there was no way she could afford to take the financial risks such a venture would involve.

"You look fantastic!" Ivy whispered. "Is that shirt heavy?"

"It weighs a ton," Shay confided. Her eyes were following Mitch; she was memorizing every expression that crossed his face.

"Let's separate those two before they start drawing up plans or something," Ivy said lightly.

Shay wondered how long it would be before Todd balked at Ivy's gentle commandeering but made no comment. A buffet supper was served soon afterward, and she and Mitch sat alone in a corner of the beach house's enormous deck, listening to the chatter of the tide as they ate. Stars were popping out all over a black velvet sky and the summer breeze was warm.

When silences had fallen between herself and Eliott, Shay had always been uncomfortable, needing to riddle the space with words. With Mitch, there were no gaps to fill. It was all right to be quiet, to reflect and to dream.

Presently, a caterer's assistant came and collected their empty plates and glasses, but Mitch and Shay remained in that shadowy corner of the deck. When the Reeses' speakers began to pipe soft music into the night, they moved together without a word. They danced, and the proximity of Mitch's blatantly masculine body to Shay's softer one was an exquisite misery.

Shay saw his mouth descending to claim her own and instead of turning to avoid his kiss, she welcomed it. Unconsciously she braced herself for the crushing ardor Eliott had taught her to expect, but Mitch's kiss was gentle, tentative, almost questioning. She felt the tip of his tongue encircle her lips and a delicious tingling sensation spread into every part of her. His nearly inaudible groan rippled over her tongue and tickled the inner walls of her cheeks as she opened her mouth to him.

Gently, ever so gently, he explored her, his body pinning hers to the deck railing in a tender dominance that she welcomed, for rather than demanding submission, the gesture incited a passion so intense that Shay was terrified by it. Had it been feelings like these that had caused Rosamond to flit from one husband to another, dragging one very small and frightened daughter after her?

Shay turned her head, remembering the bewilderment and the despair. No one knew better than she did that the price of a grand passion could be a child's sense of security, and she wasn't going to let that happen to Hank.

"I'd like to go home," she managed to say.

Mitch only nodded, and when Shay dared risk a glance at his profile, turned now toward the dark sea, she saw no anger in the line of his jaw or the muscles in his neck.

They left minutes later, pausing only to make plausible excuses to Marvin and Jeannie Reese, and they had traveled nearly half an hour before Mitch broke the silence with a quiet, "I'm sorry, Shay."

Shay was miserable; she was still pulsing with the raw

desire Mitch had aroused in her. Her breasts were weighted, as though bursting with some nectar only he could relieve them of, the nipples pulled into aching little buds, and a heavy throbbing in her abdomen signaled her body's preparation for a gratification that would be denied it. "I just—I guess I'm just not ready." Like hell you're not ready, she taunted herself.

"I wasn't going to make love to you with half of Skyler Beach just a wall away," Mitch pointed out reasonably. "Nor did I intend to fling you down in the sand, though now that I think about it, it doesn't sound like such a bad idea."

Shay had forgotten all about the party while Mitch was kissing her anyway and the reminder of that stung her to fury. "What exactly was your plan?" she snapped.

"I was in no condition to plan anything, lady. We're talking primitive responses here."

Shay lowered her head. She'd been trying to lay all the blame for what had nearly happened on Mitch and that was neither fair nor realistic. The only sensible thing to do now was change the subject. "You said we would talk after the party. About why you were at Seaview this morning."

"And we will. My place or yours?"

Did he think she was insane? Either place would be too private and yet a restaurant might be too public. "Mitch, I want to know why you're interested in my mother's illness, and I want to know right now."

"I never explore potentially emotional subjects in a moving vehicle."

"Then stop this car!"

"Along a moonlit beach? Come on, Shay. Surely you know what's going to happen if I do that."

Shay did know and she still wanted him to stop, which made her so mad that she turned in her seat and ignored him until they reached Skyler Beach. He drove toward her house, chivalrously giving her a choice between asking him in or spending a whole night in an agony of curiosity about his visit to Seaview. There would be agony aplenty without that.

"I'll make some coffee," Shay said stiffly.

He simply inclined his head, that brazen tenderness dancing in his eyes. Moments later he was seated at the table in Shay's small spotless kitchen, his gray jacket draped over the chair back. "What did Ivy tell you about me?"

Shay, filling the coffeepot with cold water, stiffened. "Not much. Come to think of it, I don't even know what you do for a living." It was humiliating, not knowing even that much about a man who had nearly made love to her on a sundeck.

"I'm a journalist."

Shay set the coffeepot aside, water and all, not even bothering to fill the basket with grounds. She fell into a chair of her own. "I don't understand."

"I think you do understand, Shay," he countered gently.

Shay felt tears gather in her eyes, stinging and hot. To hide them, she averted her face. "You plan to write about my mother, I suppose."

"Yes."

Swift, simmering anger made Shay meet his gaze. Damn, but it hurt to know that he hadn't taken her to the party just because he found her attractive and wanted her company! "I think you'd better leave."

Mitch sat easily in his chair, giving no indication whatsoever that he meant to do as Shay had asked. "I could have lied to you, you know. Won your confidence and then presented you with a fait accompli."

"I imagine you're very practiced at that, Mr. Prescott. Winning people's confidence, I mean, and then betraying them." She remembered the coffeepot and went back to measure in the grounds, which sprinkled the counter because she was shaking, put the lid on and plug the thing in. "Surely you don't write for one of those cheap supermarket scandal sheets—that would never pay you enough money to buy a house like yours."

"I write books," he said, unruffled. "Under a pen name."

Shay leaned back against the counter's edge, the coffeepot chortling behind her, and folded her arms across her glitzy chest. "So my mother rates a real book, does she? Well, I'm sorry, Mr. Prescott, but there will be no book!"

"I'm afraid there will."

Shay went back to the table and sat down again. "I won't permit it! I'll sue!"

"You don't have to permit anything—unauthorized biographies are perfectly legal. Moreover, nothing would make my publisher happier than a lawsuit filed by Rosamond Dallas's daughter. The publicity would be well worth any settlement they, or I, might have to pay."

Shay felt the color drain from her face. What Mitch said made a dreadful sort of sense.

"I would have turned the project down cold, Shay," he went on, "except for one thing."

Shay sat up a little straighter. "What 'one thing' was that? Money?"

"I have plenty of money. Have you ever heard of Lucetta White?"

Lucetta White. Shay searched her memory and remembered the woman as the one person Rosamond had truly feared. Ms. White's books could be lethal to a career, every word as sharply honed as a razor's edge. "She ruined half a dozen of my mother's friends."

Mitch nodded. "Lucetta and I have the same agent. If I don't write this book, Shay, she will."

Shay felt sick at the prospect. "What assurance do I have that you'll be any kinder?"

"This. I'd like you to coauthor the book. The byline is yours, if you want it."

Thinking of other books written by the children of movie stars, Shay shook her head. "I couldn't."

"You couldn't help, or you couldn't claim the byline?"

"I won't exploit my own mother," Shay said firmly. "Besides, I'm no writer."

"I'll handle that part of it. All I want is your input: memories, old scrapbooks, family pictures. In return, I'll pay you half of the advance and half of the royalties."

Shay swallowed hard. "You're talking about a considerable amount of money."

Again he nodded.

A kaleidoscope of possibilities fanned out and then merged in Shay's mind. She could provide for Hank's education, start her catering business....

"Would I have full control?"

Mitch was turning a teaspoon from end to end on the tabletop. "'Full control' is a very broad term. You can read all the material as we go along. I'll be as kind as I can, but I won't sugarcoat anything, and if I find a skeleton, I'll drag it out of the closet."

Shay's color flared, arching on her cheekbones and flowing in a hot rush down her neck. "That sounds like Lucetta White's method."

"Read a few of her books," Mitch answered briskly. "Lucetta invents her own skeletons, bone by grizzly bone."

The coffee was done, but Shay couldn't offer any,

couldn't move from her chair. She rested her forehead in her palms. "I'll have to think about this."

She heard Mitch's chair scrape the linoleum floor as he stood up to go. "Fair enough. I'll call you in a few days."

Shay did not move until she had heard the front door open and close again. Then she went and locked it and watched through one of the picture windows as Mitch Prescott's fancy car pulled away.

Mitch waited for three days.

During those seventy-two endless hours, he hired a cook and a housekeeper and a gardener. He sent for the contents of his apartment in San Francisco, and he read everything he could find concerning Rosamond Dallas until the muscles in the small of his back threatened spasmodic rebellion.

On Tuesday morning, he drove to Reese Motors.

"Damn," Shay grumbled as she came out of the plush RV on the back lot.

Ivy tried very hard not to smile as she took in the yellow-and-black-striped suit Shay was wearing. "I think you make a terrific bee," she said.

"Flattery," Shay answered bitterly, "will get you nowhere. Don't you dare laugh!"

Ivy put one hand over her mouth and the diamonds in her showy engagement ring sparkled in the sunshine. "Put the hat on. Here, let me help you."

Shay submitted to the hat, which was really more of a hood. It was black, with nodding antennae on top.

Richard Barrett approached with long strides. "The wings!" he thundered. "Where are the wings?"

"He thinks he's Steven Spielberg," Ivy whispered.

Shay, standing there in the hot sun, sweltering in her

padded velveteen bee suit, wanted to slap him. "Wings?" she hissed.

"Of course," Richard replied with the kind of patience usually reserved for deaf dogs. "Bees do have wings, you know."

The wings were hunted down by Richard's curvaceous young assistant, who was taking this taste of show biz very seriously. She wore her sunglasses on top of her head and constantly consulted her clipboard.

"I don't need this job, you know," Shay muttered to no one in particular as she was shuffled onto an *X* chalked on the asphalt in front of a new-model sedan with all the bells and whistles.

"Do you remember your lines?" Richard's cretin assistant sang, blowing so that her fluffy auburn bangs danced in midair.

"Sure," Shay snapped. "To bee or not to bee, that is the question."

"Sheesh," the assistant marveled, not getting the joke.

"All right, Shay," Richard said, indicating one of two cameras with a nod of his head. "We'll be filming from two angles, but I want you to look into this camera while you're delivering your line."

"Since when is 'bzzzz' a line?"

"Just do as I tell you, Shay." A muscle under Richard's right eye was jumping. Shay had never noticed that he had a twitch before.

"I'm ready," she conceded.

The cameras made an almost imperceptible whirring sound and a clapboard was snapped in her face.

"Take One!" Richard cried importantly.

"Bzzzzzz," said Shay, dancing around the hood of the sedan as though to pollinate it. "Come to Reese Motors, in Skyler Beach, 6832 Discount Way! You can't afford to miss a honey of a deal like this!" She moved on to a red pickup. So far, so good. "Take this model right here, only nineteen-ninety—nineteen-ninety—"

Shay's voice froze in her throat and her concentration fled. Mitch Prescott was standing beside Ivy, looking stunned.

"Cut!" Richard bellowed.

Shay swallowed, felt relieved as she watched Mitch turn and walk resolutely away. Were his shoulders shaking just a little beneath that pristine white shirt of his?

"I'm sorry," she said to Richard, who looked apoplectic. It seemed to Shay that he took commercials a mite too seriously.

"Take Two," Richard groaned. "God, why do I work with amateurs? Somebody tell me why!"

He wouldn't have dared to talk to Marvin that way, Shay thought. And why had she apologized, anyway? Nobody got a commercial right on the first take, did they?

Shay started over, offering the folks in Skyler Beach a bunny of a deal.

"That's Easter!" Richard screamed, frustrated beyond all good sense.

"Don't get your stinger in a wringer!" the bee screamed back and every salesperson on the lot roared with laughter.

On the third take the spot was flawless. Shay scowled at Richard and stomped into the RV with Ivy right behind her. The younger woman kept biting back giggles as she helped with the cumbersome costume.

When Shay was back in her slacks and golden, imitation-silk blouse, her hair brushed and her makeup back to normal, she left the RV with her chin held high. The salesmen formed a double line, a sort of good-natured gauntlet, and applauded and cheered as she passed.

Shay executed a couple of regal bows, but her cheeks were throbbing with embarrassment by the time she closed her office door behind her and sank against it. It was bad enough that half of Washington state would see that stupid commercial. Why had Mitch had to see it, too?

Chapter Five

The very fact of Marvin's absence seemed to generate problems and Shay was grateful for the distraction. Dealing with the complaints and questions of customers kept her from thinking about the three commercials yet to be filmed and the very enticing dangers of working closely with Mitch Prescott.

At five minutes to five, Ivy waltzed into Shay's office with a mischievous light in her eyes and a florist's bouquet in her hands. "For you," she said simply, setting the arrangement of pink daisies interspersed with baby's breath and white carnations square on top of Shay's paperwork.

At the sight and scent of the flowers, Shay felt a peculiar shakiness in the pit of her stomach. Reason said the lovely blossoms had been sent by the salespeople downstairs or perhaps the Reeses. Instinct said something very different.

Her hands trembling just slightly—she couldn't remember the last time anyone had sent her flowers—Shay reached out for the envelope containing the card. Instinct prevailed. "If you're free tonight, let's discuss the book over dinner at my place. Strictly business, I promise. R.S.V.P. Mitch."

Strictly business, he said. Shay remembered Mitch's kiss and the sweet, hard pressure of his body against her own on the Reeses' darkened deck the night of the party and wondered who the hell he thought he was kidding. She felt a certain annoyance, a tender dreading, but mingled with these emotions was a sensation of heady relief. With a sigh, Shay admitted to herself that she would have been very disappointed if the flowers had come from anyone else on the face of the earth.

"Mitch?" Ivy asked, the impish light still dancing in her eyes.

Shay grinned. "How very redundant of you to ask. You knew."

"I did not!" Ivy swore with conviction and just a hint of righteous indignation. "I just guessed, that's all."

Shay's weariness dropped away and she moved the vase of flowers to clear the paperwork from her desk. She sensed all the eager questions Ivy wanted to ask and enjoyed withholding the answers. "Well," she said with an exaggerated sigh, picking up her purse and the flowers and starting toward the door, "I'll see you tomorrow. Have a good evening."

Ivy was right on her heels. "Oh, no you don't, Shay Kendall! Did my brother ask you out or what? Why did he send you flowers? What did the card *say,* exactly?"

Smiling to herself, Shay walked rapidly toward the stairs. To spare her friend a night of agonizing curiosity, she tossed back an offhanded "He wants to start work on the book about Rosamond. Good night, Ivy."

"What book?" Ivy cried desperately, hurrying to keep up

with Shay as she went down the stairs and across the polished floor of the main display room. "You don't mean—you're not actually—you said you'd never—"

Fortunately, Todd was waiting for Ivy outside, or she might have followed Shay all the way to her car, battering her with questions and fractured sentences.

Ivy looked so pained as her fiancé ushered her into the passenger seat of his car that Shay called out a merciful, "I promise I'll explain tomorrow," as she got behind the wheel of her own car.

Shay did not drive toward home; Hank wouldn't be there and she needed some time to prepare herself for the strange quiet that would greet her when she unlocked her front door. She decided to pay her mother a visit.

More than once during the short drive to Seaview Convalescent Home, Shay glanced toward the flowers so carefully placed on the passenger seat and wondered if it wouldn't be safer, from an emotional standpoint anyway, to forget Mitch Prescott and this collaboration business altogether and take her chances with Lucetta White. Granted, the woman was a literary viper, but Ms. White couldn't hurt Rosamond, could she? No one could hurt Rosamond.

Shay bit her lower lip as she turned into the spacious asphalt parking lot behind the convalescent home. Rosamond was safe, but what about Hank? What about Riley and Garrett? What about herself?

Stopping the car and turning off the ignition, Shay rested her forehead on the steering wheel and drew a deep breath. Each life, she reflected, feeling bruised and cornered, touches other lives. If Miss White chose to, she could drag up all sorts of hurtful things, such as Eliott's theft all those years before, and his desertion. Shay had long since come to terms with Eliott's actions, but how could Hank, a six-year-old, be expected to understand and cope?

Shay drew another deep breath and sat up very straight. Except for his personal word, she had no assurances that Mitch Prescott would be any fairer or any kinder in his handling of the Rosamond Dallas story, but he did seem the lesser of two evils, even considering the unnerving effect he had on Shay's emotions. The book would be written, one way or the other, and there was no going back.

She got out of the car, crossed the parking lot and entered the convalescent home resolutely. Shay was not looking forward to another one-sided visit with her mother and the guilt inspired by that fact made her spirits sag. What was she supposed to say to the woman? "Hello, Mother, today I dressed up as a bee?" Or maybe she could announce, "Guess what? I've met a man and he wants to tell all your most intimate secrets to the world and I'm going to help him and for all that, Mother, I do believe he could seduce me without half trying!"

As Shay hurried through the rear entrance to the building and down the immaculate hallway toward her mother's room, the inner dialogue gained momentum. *I'm afraid, Mother. I'm afraid. I'm starting to care about Mitch Prescott and that's going to make everything that much more difficult, don't you see? We'll make love and that will change me for always but it will just be another affair to him. I don't think I could bear that, Mother.*

Overcome, Shay stopped and rested one shoulder against the wall beside Rosamond's door, her head lowered. The fantasy was futile: Rosamond couldn't advise her, probably wouldn't bother even if she were well. That was reality.

A cold, quiet anger sustained Shay, made her square her shoulders and lift her chin. She walked into her mother's room, crossed to her chair, bent to bestow the customary forehead kiss. Then, because her own reality was that she loved her mother, whether that love had ever been returned or not, Shay sat down facing Rosamond and told her about being a bee in a car-lot commercial, about a bouquet of pink daisies, about a man with brash brown eyes and a smile that made grooves in his cheeks.

After half an hour, when Rosamond's dinner was brought in, Shay slipped out. She hesitated only a moment before rummaging through her purse for her cell phone. Mitch answered on the second ring.

"Thank you for the flowers," Shay said lamely. She'd planned a crisper approach, but at the sound of his voice, the words had evaporated from her mind in a shimmering fog.

His responding chuckle was a low, tender sound, rich with the innate masculinity he exuded so effortlessly. "You're welcome. Now, what about dinner and the book?"

Shay, whose job and personal responsibilities had always forced her to be strong, suddenly ached with shyness. "Strictly business?" she croaked out.

Mitch's silence was somehow endearing, as though he had reached out to caress her cheek or smooth her hair back from her face, but it was also brief. "Until we both decide otherwise, princess," he said softly. "You're not walking into any heavy scenes, so relax. You're safe with me."

Tears filled Shay's eyes, coming-home tears, in-out-of-the-rain tears. She would be safe with Mitch, and that was a new experience for Shay, one she had never had with Rosamond or Eliott. "Thanks," she managed to say.

"No problem," came the velvety yet gruff reply. "Remember, though, I'm not promising that I won't tease you about this morning."

Shay found herself laughing, a moist sound making its way through receding tears. "If you think the bee debacle was bad, wait until you hear about my next epic."

"The suspense is killing me," Mitch replied with good-natured briskness, but then his voice was soft again, at once vulnerable and profoundly reassuring. "It looks as though it might rain. Drive carefully, Shay."

"What time do you want me?"

Mitch laughed. "You name a time, baby, and I want you."

"Let me rephrase that," retorted Shay, smiling. "What time is dinner?"

"Now. Whenever." He paused, sighed in exasperation. "Shay, just get over here, before I go crazy."

"Can you stay sane for half an hour? I want to change clothes."

She could almost see his eyebrows arch. "Wear the bee suit," he answered. "It really turns me on."

Shaking her head, Shay said goodbye and hung up. Her step was light as she hurried down into the hallway and outside to her car. The sky had clouded over, just as Mitch had said, and there was a muggy, prestorm heaviness in the summer air. Shay blamed her sense of sweet foreboding on the weather.

At home, she quickly showered, put on trim gray slacks and a lightweight sweater to match, reapplied her makeup and gave her damp hair a vigorous brushing. It was a glistening mane of softness, tumbling sensuously to her shoulders and she decided that the look was entirely too come-hither. With a few brisk motions, she wound it into a chignon and then stood back from the bathroom mirror a little way to assess herself. Yes, indeed, she looked like the no-nonsense type all right. "Strictly business," she reminded her image aloud, before turning away.

Since his new housekeeper, Mrs. Carraway, had left for the day, Mitch answered the door himself. He knew the visitor would be Shay, and yet he felt surprised at the sight of her, not only surprised, but jarred.

She was wearing gray slacks and a V-necked sweater to match. Her makeup was carefully understated and her hair was done up, instead of falling gracefully around her shoulders as it usually did, and Mitch suppressed a smile. Obviously she had made every effort to look prim, but the effect was exactly the opposite: she had achieved a sexy vulnerability that made him want her all the more.

For several moments, Mitch just stood there, staring at her like a fool. The cymballike clap of thunder roused him, however, and he remembered his manners and moved back from the doorway. "Come in."

Shay stepped into the house with a timid sort of bravado that touched Mitch deeply. Were her memories of the place sad ones, or were they happy? He wanted to know that and so much more, but getting close to this woman was a process that required a delicate touch; she was like some wild, beautiful, rarely seen creature of the forests, ready to flee at the slightest threat.

"Your things haven't arrived," she said, her eyes sweeping the massive empty foyer swiftly, as though in an effort not to see too much.

Gently, Mitch took her elbow in his hand, still fearing that she would bolt like a unicorn sensing a trap. "Actually," he answered in a tone he hoped sounded casual, "some of them have. All the most impractical things, anyway: pots and pans but no plates, sheets and pillows but no bed..."

He instantly regretted mentioning the bed.

Shay only smiled. She was relaxing, if only slightly.

They ate in the library, picnic-style, before a snapping, summer-storm fire, their paper plates balanced on their laps, their wine contained in supermarket glasses. For all that, there was an ambiance of elegance to the scenario, and Mitch knew that it emanated from the woman who sat facing him. What a mystery she was, what a tangle of vulnerability and strength, softness and fire, humor and tragedy.

Mitch felt his own veneer of sophistication, something he had long considered immutable, dissolving away. His reactions to that were ambivalent, of course; he was a man who controlled situations—at times his life had depended on that control—but now, in the presence of this woman, he was strangely powerless. The surprising thing was that he was comfortable with that.

When the meal was over he disposed of the plates and the plastic wineglasses and returned to the library to find Shay standing in the center of the room, studying every bookcase, every stone in the fireplace.

"Were you happy here?" he asked, without intending to speak at all.

She started and then turned slowly to face him. "Yes," she said.

The ache in Shay's wide hazel eyes came to settle somewhere in the middle of Mitch's chest. "Feel free to explore," he said after a rather long silence.

A quiet joy displaced the pain in Shay's face and Mitch was relieved. "But we were going to work," she offered halfheartedly. "I brought the photo albums you wanted. They're in the car and—"

Mitch spoke with the abruptness typical of nervous people. "I'll get them while you look around. Maybe you can give me a few decorating ideas. Right now, this place has all the cozy warmth of an abandoned coal mine."

She looked grateful and just a little suspicious. "Well…"

Mitch pretended that the matter had been settled and left the house. Her car was parked in the driveway, only a few strides from the front door, and the box containing Rosamond Dallas's memorabilia was sitting in plain sight on the seat. He took his time carrying the stuff inside, setting it on the library floor, sorting through it. Instinctively he knew that Shay needed time to wander from room to room, settling memories.

The room that had been Shay's was empty, of course. The built-in bookshelves were bare and dusty, the French provincial furniture and frilly bedclothes had been removed, along with the host of stuffed animals and the antique carousel horse, a gift from Riley Thompson, that had once stood just to the left of the cushioned windowseat. The nostalgia Shay had braced herself for did not come, however; this had been the room of a child and she felt no desire to go backward in time.

She wandered across the wide hallway and into the suite that had been Rosamond's, in a strange, quiet mood. The terrace doors were open to the rising rain-and-sea-misted wind and Shay crossed the barren room to close them. She smiled as she stepped over the tangled sleeping bag that had been spread out on the floor, and a certain scrumptious tension gripped her as she imagined Mitch lying there.

He was downstairs, waiting for her, but Shay could not bring herself to hurry. She reached down and took a pillow from the floor and held it to her face. Its scent was Mitch's scent, a mingling of sun-dried clothing and something else that was indefinably his own.

Shay knelt on the sleeping bag, still holding the pillow close and, unreasonably, inexplicably, tears filled her eyes. She couldn't think why, because she didn't feel sad and she didn't feel happy, either. She felt only a need to be held.

It was as though she had called out—in the future Shay would wonder many times whether or not she had—because

Mitch suddenly appeared in the double doorway of the suite. "Are you all right?" he asked, and Shay knew that he was keeping his distance, honoring his promise that she would be safe with him.

And she didn't want to be safe. "No," she answered. "Actually, no."

Mitch crossed the room then, knelt before her, removed the pillow from her grip and cupped her face in his strong hands, his thumbs moving to dry away her tears.

Shay was reminded of that other time when he'd held her, before the party, when she had dissolved over a bucket of take-out chicken at the backyard picnic table. "I'm not usually such a c-crybaby," she stammered out. "You must think—"

"I think you're beautiful," he said. It was what any healthy man on the verge of a seduction would say, Shay supposed, but coming from Mitch Prescott it sounded sincere. A tremulous, electric need was surging through her, starting where his hands touched her face so gently, settling into sweet chaos in her breasts and deep within her middle. She couldn't think.

"Hold me," she said.

Mitch held her and she knew that the line had been irrevocably crossed. He kissed her, just a tentative, nibbling kiss, and the turmoil within her grew fierce. This facet of Shay's womanhood, denied for six years and largely unfulfilled before that, was now beyond the realm of good judgment: it was a thing of instinct.

But Mitch drew back, his hands on Shay's shoulders now, his expression somber in the shadowy half light of that enormous, empty room. "Remember what I said earlier, Shay? About both of us being ready?"

Shay couldn't speak; her throat was twisted into a raw knot. She managed to nod.

The low timbre of Mitch's voice resounded with misgivings. "I don't want this to be something you regret later, Shay, something that drives a wedge between us. Being close to you is too important to me."

Shay swallowed hard and was able to get out a soft, broken "I need you."

"I know," came the unhurried answer, "and I feel the same way. But for you this house is full of ghosts, Shay. What you need from me may be something entirely different than what I need from you." As if to test his theory, he held her, his hands strong on her back, comforting her but making no demands.

She rested her forehead against his shoulder, breathing deeply, trying to get control of herself. "You're wrong," she said after a long, careful silence. "I'm not Rosamond Dallas's little girl, haunting this house. I'm—I'm a woman, Mitch."

He chuckled, his breath moving warm in her hair, his hands still kneading the tautness of her back. "You are definitely a woman," he agreed. "No problems there."

Shay moved her hands, sliding them boldly beneath his sweater so that she could caress his chest, and her touch brought an involuntary groan from him, along with a muttered swearword.

Shay laughed and fell to the down-filled softness of the sleeping bag, and Mitch descended with her, one of his hands coming to rest on her thigh with a reluctant buoyancy that made it bounce away and then return again, albeit unwillingly.

"We're both going to regret this," he grumbled, but his hand was beneath her sweater now, caressing the inward curve of her waist.

That remark made sense to Shay, but she was beyond caring. There was only the needing now. "It was inevitable...."

Mitch was kissing the pulsing length of her neck, the outline of her jaw. "That it was," he agreed, and then his mouth reached hers, claiming it gently.

Shay shuddered with delicious sensations as his hand roamed up her rib cage to claim one lace-covered breast. With a practiced motion that would have been disturbing if it hadn't felt so wonderful; he displaced her bra and took her full into his hand, stroking the nipple with the side of his thumb.

She felt a shudder to answer her own move through his body as he stretched out beside her, the kiss unbroken. A primitive, silent whimpering pounded through Shay and she was glad that Mitch couldn't hear it. She wriggled to lie beneath him, needing the weight and pressure of him as much as she needed the ultimate possession they were moving toward.

He groaned at this and ended the kiss, but only to slide Shay's sweater upward, baring her inch by inch. She felt the garment pass away, soon followed by the skimpy bra beneath. She wondered why she'd worn that bra, when she'd dressed to fend off just what was happening now. Or had she dressed to invite it?

"Oh," she said, gasping the word, as Mitch's mouth closed boldly around her nipple and drove all coherent thought from her mind. His hand found the junction of her thighs, still covered by her slacks and panties, and the skilled motions of his fingers caused her hips to leap in frenzied greeting. Just when she would have begged for closer contact, he gave it, deftly undoing the button and zipper of her slacks, sliding them away into the nothingness that had taken her sweater and all her inhibitions. Her panties and sandals were soon gone, too.

"God in heaven," Mitch muttered as he drew back to look at her. He stripped off his own clothes and returned to her unwillingly, as though flung to her by forces he could not resist.

Mitch's hands caressed and stroked every part of her, until she was writhing in a tender delirium, searching him out with her fingers and her mouth, with every part of her. Finally he sat back on his muscled haunches and lifted Shay to sit astraddle of him, and she cried out as they became one in a single, leisurely stroke.

Even at the beginning, the pleasure was so great as to be nearly unbearable to Shay; she flung her head back and forth in response to the glorious ache that became greater with every motion of their joined bodies, and her hair fell from its pins and flew about her face and shoulders in a wild flurry of femininity.

All that was womanly in Shay called out to all that was masculine in Mitch and they moved as one to lie prone on the tangled sleeping bag, their bodies quickening in the most primal, most instinctive of quests. And then there was no man and there was no woman, for in the blinding explosion of satisfaction that gripped them and wrung a single shout of triumph from them both, they were one entity.

Afterward, as Shay lay trembling and dazed upon that sleeping bag, she tried to brace herself for the inevitable remorse. Incredibly she felt only brazen contentment. It was fortunate, in her view, that she didn't have the strength to talk.

Apparently, Mitch didn't either. He was lying with one leg thrust across hers, his chest moving in breaths so deep that they must have been carrying air all the way to his toes, his face buried in the warm curve where Shay's neck met her shoulder.

Long minutes had passed before he withdrew from her and crossed the room to take a robe from the closet and pull it on. The wrenching motions of his arms were angry, and the glorious inertia that had possessed Shay until that moment fled instantly.

Mitch left the room without speaking and Shay was too proud to call him back. She sat upright on the sleeping bag and covered herself with his shirt, chilled now that the contact had been broken not only physically, but emotionally. She waited in a small hell of confusion and shame, willing herself to put on her clothes and leave but unable to do so.

Finally, Mitch returned. He flipped on the lights, revealing the starkness of the room, the scattering of Shay's clothes and his own, the reality of the situation. Shay closed her eyes and let her forehead fall to her upraised knees.

He nudged her shoulder with something cold and she looked up to see that he was offering a glass of chilled wine. Blushing, Shay took it in both hands, but she could not meet his eyes.

"You're angry," she said miserably.

"Shocked would be a more appropriate word," he answered, sitting down nearby and clinking his own glass against hers.

Now, Shay's eyes darted to his face. She was stung to an anger that made her forget the one she had sensed in Mitch. "Shocked? You? The adventurer, the sophisticate?"

His expression had softened; in his eyes Shay saw some lingering annoyance, but this was overshadowed by a certain perplexity. "I wasn't casting aspersions on your moral character, Shay, so settle down."

"Then what were you doing?"

He only smiled at the snap in her voice, setting his wineglass aside with a slow, lazy motion of one hand. "From the moment I met you, you've been trying to keep me at a distance. You might as well have worn a sign saying Look, but Don't Touch. Yet tonight, you—"

She couldn't bear for him to say that she'd seduced him, though it was true, in a manner of speaking. "I'm a modern woman," she broke in, shrugging nonchalantly and lifting her wineglass in an insolent salute, though in truth she felt like sliding down inside the sleeping bag and hiding there.

"No," Mitch replied wryly. "You aren't."

"I resent that!"

He took her wineglass and set it aside. "Strange. That's one of the most interesting things about you, you know. Despite what we just did, you're an innocent."

"Is that bad or good?"

He took the shirt she'd been clutching and flung it away, giving her bare breasts a wicked assessment with those quick, bold eyes of his. "I haven't decided yet," he said, and then they made love again, this time in the light.

Chapter Six

The box containing what remained of the Rosamond Dallas legend was a silent reprimand to Mitch. He rolled his head and worked the taut muscles in his neck with one hand. *You'll be safe with me,* he'd told Shay. No heavy scenes, he'd said.

He heard that ridiculous old car of hers grind to a start in the driveway and swore. She'd come there to have dinner and to work and instead she was making a getaway in the gray light of a drizzling dawn, afraid of encountering his housekeeper.

Mitch shook his aching head and swore again, but then a slow, weary smile broke over his face. He regretted buying the house and he regretted ever mentioning Rosamond Dallas to his agent, but he couldn't regret Shay. For better or for worse, she was the answer to all his questions.

He walked to the middle of the library floor, knelt on the carpet and began going through the photographs, diaries and clippings that made up Rosamond Dallas's life.

* * *

At home Shay took a hot, hasty shower and dressed
for work. She kept waiting for the guilt, the remorse, the
regret, but there were no signs of any such emotion. Her
body still vibrated, like a fine instrument expertly played,
and her mind, for the first time in years, was quiet.

While she brushed her hair and applied her makeup
with more care than usual, Shay remembered the nights
with Eliott and wondered what she'd seen in him.

She paused, lip pencil in midair, and gazed directly
into the mirror. "Hold it, lady," she warned her reflection
out loud. "One night on a man's sleeping bag does not
constitute a pledge of eternal devotion, you know. Don't
forget that you threw yourself at him like a—like a brazen
hussy!" Shay frowned hard, for emphasis, but even those
sage words, borrowed in part from one of her mother's early
movies, could not dampen her soaring spirits. She was in
love with Mitch Prescott, really in love, for the first time
in her life, and for the moment, that was enough.

Of course, it made no sense to be so happy—there was
every chance that she'd just made a mistake of epic propor-
tions—but Shay didn't let that bother her, either. Mitch's
feelings, whatever they might be, were his own problem.

She drove to Reese Motors and soared into her office,
only to find Ivy waiting in ambush. Even though the phones
were ringing and Richard's camera crew was crowded into
the reception room, Ms. Prescott sat quietly on Shay's
couch, her legs crossed, her hands folded in her lap.

Shay smiled and shook her head. Love was marvelous.
Richard's crew was proof positive that she was going to
have to film another commercial that very day and here
was Ivy, waiting to grill her about the evening with Mitch,
and she still felt wonderful. "I hate to pull rank, Ivy," she

said brightly, "but get out there and take care of business. Now."

Ivy looked hurt but nonetheless determined as she stood up and smoothed the skirt of her blue cotton dress. "At least promise to have lunch with me," she said with dignity. "You did say that you'd tell me all about everything, you know."

Shay thought about "everything" and blushed. There was no way she was going to tell everything. "We may not have time for lunch today, Ivy. There's another commercial scheduled, isn't there? And by the way that phone is jumping around on the desk, I'd say it's going to be a crazy day."

Ivy was sulking and just reaching for the doorknob when the door itself suddenly sprang open, the chasm filled by an earnest and somewhat testy Richard. "I know we planned to wait a week before we filmed the second spot, but something has come up and—"

Shay smiled placidly, knowing that the advertising executive had been prepared for a battle. "Come in, Richard," she said in a sweet voice. "Don't bother to knock."

Richard looked sheepish and somewhat baffled. He ran one hand through his already mussed hair and stared at Shay in speechless bewilderment.

She laughed. "Which one are we doing today?" she prompted lightly as Ivy dashed out and began answering the calls that were lighting up all the buttons on the telephone.

"The one you hated."

Shay was still unruffled. "That figures. When are they airing yesterday's artistic triumph?"

"Next week," Richard answered distractedly, glancing at his watch and frowning as though it had somehow displeased him. "Do you want the makeup done here, or down on the lot, in the RV?"

"I don't want it done at all, but I know wishful thinking when I see it. I'll be on down there in five or ten minutes."

Shay's intercom buzzed and she picked up the telephone receiver. "Yes, Ivy?"

"Hank's on line two," the secretary said pleasantly, her ire at being put off having faded away.

Delighted, Shay punched the second button on her telephone. "Hi, tiger!" she cried. "How are you?"

The sound of Hank's voice was the reward, Shay supposed, for some long-forgotten good deed. "I'm great, Mom! We're at this lake in Oregon and we caught two fish already!"

"That's fantastic!" Shay ignored Richard Barrett's alternating glares of impatience and consultations with his watch and turned to the windows. The sky was gray and drops of rain were bouncing off the cars in the rear lot. It was strange, she reflected fancifully, that she hadn't noticed the weather on her way to work. "Is it raining there?"

The conversation with her son was sweetly mundane and when it ended, five minutes later, Shay stoically followed Richard through the outer office and down the stairs. Due to the rain, the RV had been parked close to one of the rear entrances and the showroom itself would be the set.

Inside the roomy motor home, Shay was helped into a neck-to-toe bodysuit with metallic bolts of thunder stitched to it, and glittery cartoon superheroine makeup was applied to her face. As gooey styling mousse was poured into her hair, she tried to be philosophical. This was the silliest commercial of the lot, but it was also the easiest. She had only to say one line, and the remainder of the spot would show used cars with prices painted on their windshields.

"I bet you hate having your friends see you like this," commiserated Richard's assistant, she of the fluffy bangs and ever-present clipboard, as she pulled Shay's mousse-saturated tresses into points that stuck straight out, all over her head.

Shay only rolled her eyes, telling herself that the girl was young.

"I'd die," insisted the little helper.

"If you keep working for Richard," Shay replied, "your life will probably be short."

"Huh?"

"Here but for the grace of God go you."

"I still don't get it."

"Never mind," Shay said with a sigh. The mousse was drying and her scalp itched. The bodysuit was riding up in all the wrong places. She told herself that that was why she suddenly felt so uncharitable.

The door of the RV squeaked open and made the hollow sound typical of all motor homes when it closed behind Richard. He looked at Shay as though he'd just beaten her at some game and his mouth twitched. "I," he said with quiet pomposity, "am a genius."

"Don't press your luck, Richard," Shay snarled. Her body was no longer vibrating, and there was a headache unfolding behind her right temple.

"I said I'd die if I had to dress like that and she said my life might be short if I went on working for you," broke in the assistant in a breathless babble. "What'd she mean by that, Richard? She won't tell me what she meant!"

"Wait outside, Chrissie," Richard said, all but patting the girl on the head.

Reluctantly, Chrissie obeyed.

"Does your wife know about her?" Shay asked, just to be mean.

Richard cleared his throat and pressed at his hopelessly old-fashioned glasses with one index finger. Despite this display of nervousness, he was not an easy opponent. "You have an audience outside," he said. "It seems your fame is spreading."

Shay stood up with a sigh, and when they entered the showroom moments later, she was even more annoyed to find that she did indeed have an audience. All of the salesmen were there, along with their wives and even a few children. It was the presence of the children that kept Shay from showing them that she was Rosamond Dallas's daughter by making a scene.

"Stand right there on your *X*, darlin'," Richard drawled. "This'll be over before you can say—"

"Oh, shut up!" Shay grumbled, taking her mark.

The lights were blaring in her face. She drew a deep breath and tried to be professional, which wasn't easy in a thunderbolt bodysuit and outrageous makeup. Mentally she went over her line. Oh, to do this in one take and have it behind her!

The clapboard snapped in her face and Shay smiled broadly, trying not to think of how her hair was standing out from her head in mousse-crusted points. She knew she looked as though she had just stuck her finger into a light socket, and that, of course, was the whole idea. "Come out and see for yourselves, folks," she crowed winningly. "Our prices here at Reese Motors, 6832 Discount Way, are so low that they'll shock you!"

It was a wrap! Shay wanted to jump up into the air and click her heels together.

"Do it again," Richard said with exaggerated patience.

Shay couldn't have been more surprised if he'd doused her in cold water. "What?" she demanded. "Richard, that take was perfect!"

"It wasn't anything of the sort. I want more emphasis on the word 'shock.'"

He was repaying her for all the barbs they'd exchanged and that knowledge infuriated Shay. "I think this gunk in my hair makes that point on its own, don't you?"

"No," Richard responded flatly.

He made her go through the scene half a dozen times before he would admit to any sort of satisfaction with it, and that, when he gave it, was grudging.

Shay muttered as she stomped back into the RV and slammed the door behind her. Refusing help from the vacuous Chrissie, she slathered cleansing cream onto her face and carefully wiped away the glittery makeup. After that, she squeezed into the vehicle's miniature bathroom and took a tepid shower, muttering through shampoo after shampoo. A bathrobe that probably belonged to Marvin was hanging on the hook inside the door, and Shay helped herself to it.

When she left the bathroom she was startled to find Mitch Prescott sitting at the RV's tiny table, his hair moussed into an elongated crew cut rising a good four inches above his head. "May I say," he told her blandly, "that I was shocked by your behavior this morning?"

The utter ridiculousness of the moment dissolved Shay's foul mood, and she began to laugh. "You're crazy!"

Mitch caught her hand and pulled her onto his lap. "About you," he said, on cue.

Shay knew that she shouldn't be sitting on this man's lap in an oversized bathrobe with all of Reese Motors's employees gathered outside, but she was powerless to move away. She looked at Mitch's hair and into his laughing brown eyes and she thought, *I love you. God help me, I love you.*

Mischievously he opened the front of her robe, revealing

her breasts, and she could not lift a hand to stop him. "It's a good thing you washed that stuff out of your hair," he mumbled distractedly, and she could feel his breath on her right breast, feel the nipple tensing for the touch of his tongue. It came soon enough, and Shay gasped, the sensation was so wickedly delicious.

"Why?" she groaned.

"Because we might have mated and produced a punk rocker," he answered sleepily, still busy with her breast.

Using laughter and the last bit of her willpower, Shay thrust herself off Mitch's lap and out of his reach. Watching her, he helped himself to a hairbrush left behind by Chrissie and returned his hair to some semblance of normalcy. Shay wanted to use that time to dress and escape, but she couldn't seem to work up the momentum.

When the maestro held out his hands, she moved into them, moaning softly as she stood before Mitch, shivering as she felt the robe open. The intermezzo was a sweet one, brief and soaring, underscored by Shay's own soft cries of pleasure as she was taught a new tune, note by glorious note.

Minutes later, fully dressed, she left the RV with her head held high and her body humming. The vibrations carried her through the rest of the day.

If the night before had been given over to dalliance, that one was all business. The rest of Mitch's furniture had arrived and he and Shay sat on a sinfully soft sofa in his library, facing each other instead of the crackling fire, half-buried in scrapbooks and old photographs.

As she explained what she knew of her mother's life, Shay found herself thrust from one emotional extreme to another, from laughter to tears, from love to anger. Mitch only listened, making no move to touch her.

"Sometimes," Shay confided pensively as the long evening drew toward a close, "I think she was the most selfish person on earth. Riley loved her so much, and yet…"

She looked at the small recorder between them.

"Yes?" prompted Mitch.

"I think that was the very reason that Rosamond began to lose interest in him. Finally she seemed to feel nothing but contempt. But Riley was such a good man, so decent and solid—it just doesn't make sense!"

"Since when are legendary movie stars expected to make sense?"

Shay shrugged and then yawned. "Rosamond certainly didn't."

"She must have made you angry," Mitch remarked, snapping off the recorder with a motion of his hand.

The words jarred Shay out of her sleepy stupor. Suddenly she didn't want to talk about Rosamond anymore, and she didn't want to talk about herself. "I'd better be going," she said, moving to rise off the sofa.

Mitch stopped her by taking her arm in a gentle grasp. "She did make you angry, didn't she?" he persisted quietly.

"No."

"You're lying."

Shay bounded off the couch and this time there was no stopping her. "Who do you think you are?" she snapped. "Sigmund Freud?"

Mitch sat back in that cushy sofa, damn him, and cupped his hands behind his head, not saying so much as a word. Shay was reminded of the scandalous way he'd loved her in the RV earlier and she sat down in a nearby chair, her knees weak.

"Everybody has hang-ups about their mother," she sputtered when the silence grew too long and too damning. She glared at Mitch, remembering all that Ivy had told her over the past few years. "Or their stepmother."

Mitch sighed and stared up at the ceiling, still maintaining his attitude of relaxed certainty. "The difference is, my dear, that I can talk about my stepmother. She and I don't get along because she was my father's mistress before he and my mother were divorced. In effect, you could say that she took him away from us."

"My God," Shay whispered, feeling sympathy even though there was nothing in Mitch's voice or manner that asked for it.

"It was traumatic at the time," Mitch said evenly. "But Dad was a good father to me and, eventually, my mother remarried. She's disgustingly happy."

"But Ivy's mother—"

"Elizabeth does the best she can. She loved my father."

Shay was silent.

"Your turn," Mitch prompted.

She stared into the snapping fire for a while, drifting back to another night. "Rosamond was her own greatest fan," she said. "And yet she could humiliate herself so easily. I remember one of her lovers—a tennis bum—he was good-looking but if you tapped on his forehead, nobody would answer the door."

Mitch chuckled. "Go on."

"He was part of the reason that Mother got bored with Riley, I guess. After Riley and Garrett were gone, he decided that it was time to get back on the old circuit. He was going to walk out and I'll never forget—I'll never forget the way Mother acted. He was trying to get into his car and she was on her knees in the driveway, with her arms wrapped around his legs, begging him to stay." Shay turned shadowed, hurting eyes to Mitch's face. "It was awful."

"You saw that?" Mitch must have tried, but he failed to keep the annoyance out of his voice.

"I've seen a lot worse," she answered.

"Stay with me," he said, clearing away aging memorabilia to make a space beside him on the sofa.

Shay couldn't leave, but she suddenly felt too broken and vulnerable to stay. "I don't want—"

"I know," he said, standing up and extending one hand to her. After a moment or so, she rose and took the offered hand and Mitch led her gently up the stairs and into his bedroom.

Furnished now with a massive bed, chairs and bureaus and a freestanding chess table set up for play, the room didn't seem so vast.

Deftly, as though he did such things as a part of his daily routine, Mitch undressed Shay and then buttoned her into one of his pajama tops, a royal blue silk affair with piping and a monogram on the pocket.

"You do not strike me as a man who wears pajamas," she said, aware of the inanity of her remark but too shaky to say anything heavier.

"A Christmas present from Ivy," he explained, disappearing into the adjoining bathroom. A moment later Shay heard the shower running.

"Why am I staying here?" she asked the cosmos, holding her arms out from her sides.

When the cosmos didn't answer, she followed Mitch into the steamy chamber and helped herself to one of the new toothbrushes she found in the cabinet drawer. As she brushed, she fumed. Six toothbrushes, still in their boxes. The man expected to entertain a harem!

Behind the beautifully etched door of the double shower, Mitch sang at the top of his lungs. Shay glared at her reflection in the steamy mirror. "If you had any sense at all," she muttered, "you'd go home! This is a man who keeps extra toothbrushes, for God's sake!"

Having said all this, Shay went back to the bedroom and crawled into bed. The sheets were as smooth as satin and the song of the tide coming in through the terrace doors reduced her to a sleepy, languid state.

She felt the bed give as Mitch got into it, heard the click of the lamp switch, stirred under the sweet weight of the darkness. "Are you going to make love to me?" she asked.

He chuckled and drew her close, holding her. "No," he said.

Shay yawned. "Don't let go, okay?"

"Okay," came the hoarse reply.

They both slept soundly, huddled close in that gigantic bed, neither asking anything of the other except their nearness.

Mitch awakened to an exquisite caress and opened his eyes to see a tumble-haired vamp kneeling on the bed beside him, her whole face lit by a wicked grin. "Ummm," he said, stretching, luxuriating in the pleasure she was creating. "The truce is over, I take it?"

"Every man for himself," she agreed.

"In that case…" He stretched again, with deceptive leisure, and then flipped over suddenly, carrying Shay with him, imprisoning her soft body beneath his own.

Her eyes widened in mock surprise and he laughed, using his nose to spar with hers.

She caught her hands together at the back of his neck and drew him into her kiss; it was a soft, nurturing thing, and yet it sent aching waves of desperate need crashing through him. He sensed that she was exerting some tender vengeance for the way he'd pleasured her in the RV the day before and he was all for it.

When the opportunity afforded itself some moments later, Mitch pulled back far enough to rid Shay of the pajama top and then fell to her again, settling against her but reluctant to take her.

Suddenly she parted her legs and the warmth of her was too compelling to be resisted. He entered her almost involuntarily, thrust into the agonizing comfort she offered by the strength of her hands and the upward thrust of her hips.

She guided him, she taunted him, she rendered him mindless with need. For all Shay's beautiful treachery, however, her moment came first and Mitch marveled at the splendor in her face as she cried out, tossing her head back and forth on the pillow and grasping at his shoulders with her hands.

"I love you," he said.

It was clear enough that Ivy's feelings were hurt. Entering the office, after a hasty shower and change of clothes at home, Shay remembered her promise to have lunch with her friend the day before and was chagrined, even though there had been no time to go out to eat.

"Hi," she said, standing before Ivy's desk.

Ivy kept her eyes on her computer screen. "Hi," she said remotely.

"Free for lunch?"

Ivy looked up quickly, and the clouds separated, revealing the sunlight that was integral to her nature. "We might have to stay in. I got kind of behind yesterday."

Shay was relieved that no permanent damage had been done to this most cherished friendship. Ivy might be nosy, but it was only because she cared so much. "We could always call Screaming Hernando's and have them send over a guacamole pizza."

Ivy made a face and then giggled.

The morning went smoothly, and when noon came, Ivy and Shay were able to slip away. They had chicken sandwiches at the coffee shop across the street.

"I thought you were mad at me," Ivy confided between delicate bites from her sandwich. "I guess I shouldn't have called Mitch and told him you were filming another commercial."

Shay leaned forward, forgetting her sandwich. "So that was how he knew. I should have guessed. Ivy Prescott, what possessed you?"

"Actually," Ivy replied, "it wasn't anything quite as dramatic as possession. It was plain old bribery. Mitch promised to try to get along with my mother if I would call him whenever you were doing a spot."

"Traitor!"

"What can I tell you? I love my mother and I love Mitch and I want to see them bury the hatchet, especially with the wedding coming up."

Shay remembered what Mitch had told her the night before, when they were talking about hang-ups. "Is it working?"

"They've been civil to each other," Ivy said, shrugging. "I guess that's a start. So, are you and Mitch an item, or what?"

"An 'item'? Have you been reading old movie magazines or something?"

Ivy executed a mock glare. "Stop hedging, Shay. You don't need to tell me, you know. You can just sit by and see me consumed by my own curiosity."

Shay sighed. "If you're talking about the love-and-marriage kind of item, we're not."

Ivy's eyes were wide with delight. "That's what they all

say," she replied. "So the gossip is true! You and Mitch are doing more than working together!"

"Now that is definitely none of your business, Ivy Prescott," Shay said firmly. "And exactly what gossip is this?"

"Well, you two were inside the RV together for quite a while yesterday...."

Shay willed herself not to blush at the memory and failed. She hoped Ivy would ascribe the high color in her face to righteous indignation. "What were you doing, standing out there with a stopwatch?"

"Of course not!" Ivy's feathers were ruffled. She squirmed in her chair and looked incensed and then said defensively, "I don't even own a stopwatch!"

Chapter Seven

"This is some pile of bricks," Ivan announced, gazing appreciatively up at the walls of the house while Mitch was still recovering from the surprise of finding his agent standing on his doorstep. "Pretty big for one person, isn't it?"

Mitch stepped back to admit the small, well-dressed man with the balding pate. Ignoring Ivan's question, he offered one of his own. "What's so important that it couldn't have been handled by telephone, Ivan?"

Ivan patted his breast pocket and grinned. "An advance check of this size warrants personal delivery," he answered.

Mitch turned and walked back toward the library where he'd been working over his notes for the Rosamond Dallas book, leaving Ivan to follow. Mrs. Carraway, who had been upstairs cleaning most of the morning, magically appeared with coffee and warm croissants.

Once the pleasant-faced woman had gone, Ivan helped

himself to a cup of coffee and a croissant. "Nice to see you living the good life at last, Prescott. I was beginning to think you were going to spend the rest of your days crawling through jungles on your belly and hobnobbing with the Klan."

Despite his sometimes abrasive manner, Mitch liked and respected Ivan Wright. The man was always direct, and he played hardball in all his dealings. "I guess I'm ready to settle down," he said, and his mind immediately touched on Shay.

"That could be good, and it could be bad," Ivan replied. "What are your plans for after?"

"After what?"

"After you finish the Rosamond Dallas book." Ivan added jam and cream to his croissant.

"I haven't made any plans for another project, if that's what you're getting at. I may retire. After all, I'm a rich man."

"You're also a young man," Ivan pointed out. "What are you, thirty-seven, thirty-eight?" Without waiting for an answer, the agent went on. "Your publishers want another book, Mitch, and they're willing to pay top dollar to get your name on the dotted line."

The thought made Mitch feel weary. He was having a hard enough time working up enough enthusiasm to write about Rosamond, but he supposed that was because of Shay. No matter how delicately the project was handled, she would, to some degree, be hurt by it. "We're talking about a specific subject here, I assume."

Ivan nodded, licking a dab of cream from one pudgy finger. "You've heard of Alan Roget, haven't you? That serial murderer the FBI picked up in Oklahoma a few months back?"

Mitch remembered. The man had been arraigned on

some thirty-two counts of homicide. "Sweet guy," he reflected.

"Roget may be a pyscho, but he's a fan of yours. If anybody writes his story, he wants it to be you."

"They don't need his permission to do a book," Mitch pointed out, and he remembered saying a similar thing to Shay.

"No," Ivan agreed readily, calmly. "The difference is that he's willing to talk to you, tell you the whole disgusting saga from his point of view. Another writer could do the job, of course, but they'd be operating on guesswork."

"What about my anonymity? How could we trust this maniac to respect that?"

"He wouldn't have to know your real name. That can be handled, Mitch, in the same way we've handled it in the past. What do you say?" A master of timing, Ivan waited a moment and then laid the sizable check Mitch and Shay would share on the coffee table between them.

"I need time to think, Ivan. For one thing, I'm not sure I even want to hear all the rot this space-case probably plans to spill."

"Going soft, Prescott?"

"Maybe."

Ivan gave a delicate sigh and stood up. "Well, I've got a cab waiting. Got to get back to the airport, you know."

Mitch only shook his head. He was half Ivan's age, but even in his jungle-crawling, Klan-breaking days, he hadn't lived at the pace that Ivan did.

"You'll call?" Ivan asked, tugging at the jacket of his Brooks Brothers' suit to straighten it.

"I'll call." Mitch sighed the words.

Shay raised one eyebrow when Ivy informed her that the bank was calling. She couldn't be overdrawn, could she?

She'd just deposited the bonus check Marvin had signed before he left, making payment for the four commercials.

"Ms. Kendall?"

Shay drew a deep breath and set aside the stack of paperwork, also left behind by Marvin, that she'd been wading through. "Yes?"

"My name is Robert Parker and I'm calling in reference to your account."

Shay tensed and then willed herself to relax. She had balanced her checkbook only a few days before, and her figures had tallied with the bank's. "Yes?"

"It seems that a sizable amount of money has been deposited and, well, we were just wondering if a mistake had been made. This sum is well beyond what the Federal Reserve will insure in any single account, you know."

"I don't understand," Shay said, resting her forehead in the palm of one hand. "Surely a couple thousand dollars—"

"A couple thousand?" The bank officer laughed nervously. "My, my, this deposit is many times that amount. I was certain that there had to be some error."

Shay was a little stung that the banker could be so incredulous, even though she was incredulous herself. Maybe she'd never had more than eight hundred dollars in her account at any one time, but she wasn't a deadbeat and if she'd been overdrawn a time or two, why, that had been accidental. "Wait just a moment, Mr. Parker, wasn't it? Where did this deposit come from?"

"The check itself was drawn on the account of a Mr. Mitch Prescott."

It was a moment before Shay remembered the book she and Mitch were supposed to be writing together; her mind hadn't exactly been on the professional aspects of their relationship. "Then the money is mine," she said, as much to herself as to Mr. Parker. "Would you mind telling me the exact amount?"

The sum Mr. Parker replied with made the pit of Shay's stomach leap and sent her head into a dizzying spin. Mitch had told her that her share would be a "lot" of money, but never in Shay's wildest dreams had she expected so much.

"We'll have to verify this, of course," Parker said stiffly, seeming to find Shay's good fortune suspect in some way.

"Of course," Shay answered. And then she hung up the receiver, folded her arms on the desktop and lowered her head to them.

She was rich.

The more Mitch thought about the Alan Roget project, the more it appealed to him. It would be a study in human ugliness, that book, but for once in his life he had something to counterbalance that. He had Shay.

Eager now to get the Rosamond Dallas book behind him, he began composing a comprehensive outline of the material he had on hand, working from his notes and the tapes containing Shay's observations about her mother.

He was interrupted, at intervals, by the telephone. Mrs. Carraway tried to field his calls, but there were several that could not be avoided, one from a pedantic bank clerk questioning the deposit he'd made to Shay's account after Ivan had left, one from his daughter, Kelly, who wanted to tell him that she could visit over Christmas vacation, and one from Lucetta White. Lucetta had heard, through the grapevine, that he'd landed a "plum" of an assignment and asked for details. Mitch had talked for fifteen minutes and told Ms. White exactly nothing.

He was sitting back in his desk chair, his hands cupped

behind his head, when the telephone rang again. To spare Mrs. Carraway the problem, he answered it himself with a crisp "Hello?"

"Hello," Shay replied, and the single word resounded with bewilderment. "About that money…"

Mitch waited for her to go on, but she didn't, so he replied, "Your share, as agreed. Is anything wrong?"

"Wrong? Well, no, of course not. A-are we working tonight?"

"I'm working. From now on, your part will be an occasional consultation. Of course, I'll need you to read over the material, too, as I write it."

"Oh," she said, and she sounded disappointed. Perhaps even a little hurt.

"Shay, what's the matter?"

She sighed. "I feel a little—a little superfluous, I guess. And overpaid for it in the bargain."

Mitch laughed. "You could never be superfluous, my love. Listen, if you want a more active part in writing the book, you can have it."

He could almost see her shaking her beautiful, leonine head. "No, no. I have things of my own to do, now that I'm a woman of means."

Mitch arched an eyebrow, not sure he liked the sound of that. "Like what?"

"Oh, getting solid financial advice, talking to the tax people, starting my catering service. Things of that nature."

Mitch hadn't known that Shay had aspirations to go into business for herself and he was a little peeved that she'd failed to confide something so important. He scowled down at his watch and saw that it was nearly five o'clock. "I won't keep you, then," he said stiffly, and even as he spoke the words he wondered what it was that made him want to put space between himself and this woman when he needed her so much.

There was a brief silence, and then Shay answered, "No. Well, thank you." She hung up and Mitch sat glaring at the receiver in his hand.

No. Well, thank you, he mimicked in his mind. She had what she wanted now, the money; apparently their lovemaking and the special rapport they'd formed weren't important anymore. Mitch hung up with a bang that was no less satisfying for Shay's not hearing it.

As Shay wandered up and down the aisles of the public library that evening, choosing books on the operation of small businesses, she was awash in a numbing sort of despair. All of her dreams were suddenly coming true, or, at least, most of them, and she should have been happy. She hugged the stack of self-help books close to her chest. Why wasn't she happy?

She knew the answer, of course, and was only torturing herself with the question. She had thought she meant something to Mitch Prescott and found out differently. She had provided the research material he needed for his book and he'd paid her and, as far as he was concerned, the transaction was complete. There would be a few "consultations," and he wanted her input as the book progressed, but he'd made it clear enough that she wasn't to expect anything more.

Shay drove home slowly, heated a can of soup for her supper and immersed herself in the books she had checked out at the library, making notes in a spiral notebook as she read. It wasn't as though she needed Mitch Prescott to be happy, she told herself during frequent breaks in her concentration. She had Hank, she had her job, and she had the money and the determination to make her life what she'd always dreamed it could be.

Well, almost what she'd dreamed it could be.

For the rest of that week, Shay concentrated on her job at Reese Motors, grateful that she would have a little time before she had to do another commercial. She talked to Hank frequently by telephone and visited Rosamond every afternoon. From the convalescent home she invariably went to the public library, exchanging the books she'd scanned the night before for new ones. She told herself that she was preparing for her own entry into the world of private enterprise and she was learning a great deal, but the main reason for her marathon study fests was Mitch Prescott. Being absorbed in business theories kept her from thinking about him.

By Saturday morning, she was haggard. Ivy, showing up on her doorstep bright and early, was quick to point that out.

Shay yawned, feeling rumpled and dissolute in her old bathrobe. "How do you expect me to look at nine o'clock on a Saturday morning? Don't you ever sleep in?"

The weather was nice and Ivy looked disgustingly vibrant in her old blue jeans and summery cotton top. "Sleep in?" she chimed. "And let the world pass me by?"

"The world wouldn't dare pass you by," Shay responded dryly, staggering toward the kitchen, homing in on the coffeepot which, blessedly, operated on a small timer set the night before. "Where's Todd?"

Ivy settled herself in a chair at Shay's table, shoving aside the current stack of business books with a slight frown. "He's working. Ambition is his curse, you know." She stopped for a breath. "I'm going to this great auction today. Want to come along?"

Shay poured coffee for herself and Ivy and stumbled

over to the table to collapse into a chair. "Why would I want to go to an auction?"

"To buy something, silly. This is an estate sale, and they're holding it in a barn."

"I'm not in the market for harnesses and milk stools," Shay muttered, beginning to come alive as caffeine surged through her veins.

"The newspaper ad says they have a lot of great stuff, Shay. Antiques."

"Milk stools."

"You're impossible. I bought my brass bed at a sale like this, and for a song, too."

"They probably just wanted you to stop singing."

"Very funny. Come on, Shay, come with me. For the drive. For the fresh air. Good Lord, you look terrible."

Shay knew she couldn't face another day of studying. Maybe it would be fun to poke through a lot of junk in some old barn and then treat Ivy to lunch. "You haven't asked me why I look terrible, Ivy. For you, that's a drastic oversight."

Ivy sat up very straight and smiled. "I haven't asked because I already know. You and Mitch are on the outs."

"You're pleased about that?"

"I know it's temporary. Now, are you going to the sale with me or not?"

"I'm going. Just let me finish my coffee."

"No." Ivy shook her head. "They sell coffee at the sale. They sell it in little stands along the road. They sell it everywhere. Take your shower and let's go!"

Muttering, Shay abandoned her coffee and made her way to the bathroom.

The carousel horse stood, its once-bright paint chipped and faded, in the middle of the barn where the auction would be held, as though waiting for Shay.

She drew in her breath and moved toward it, her eyes wide. It couldn't be Clydesdale!

Shay crouched to look at the horse's right rear hoof. Sure enough, splotches of Rosamond's favorite fire engine–red fingernail polish still clung to the wood. The marks had been made one glum and rainy afternoon in the long-ago, by Shay herself.

Another woman came to look at the horse. "Wouldn't that make a marvelous planter, Harold?" she was saying. "We could strip off the paint and then varnish it...."

Shay put down an urge to slap the woman away and glanced back over one shoulder at Ivy, who was inspecting a sterling-silver butter dish, one of hundreds of items set out on portable display tables.

The carousel horse, like the playhouse, had been a gift from Riley, before his divorce from Rosamond, and Shay had cherished it. The piece was valuable, and, after shipping Shay off to a summer camp, Rosamond had sold it on a whim.

The anger came back to Shay—or maybe it had never left. In any case, it was all she could do not to fling one arm over the neck of that battered, beloved old horse and cling to it, fending off all prospective buyers with her purse.

"That's nice," Ivy said suddenly from beside Shay, her eyes moving over the hand-carved and painted relic. "Are you going to bid on it?"

The woman and Harold were still standing nearby, pondering their plans to make a planter of Shay's horse. "I might," she said through tight lips, shrugging to give her words an air of indifference and nonchalance.

By the time the bidding finally began, Shay was in a state of anxiety, though she managed to appear calm. When Clydesdale—Garrett and Shay had considered a multitude of names for the horse before coming up with that one—came on the docket, she waited until the auctioneer had gotten a number of bids before entering one of her own.

Harold and the missus drove the price well beyond what Riley had paid for the piece originally, and it had been expensive then, but Shay didn't care. When the competition fell away and hers was the highest bid, she had to choke back a shout of triumph.

"What are you going to do with that, Shay?" Ivy whispered, sounding honestly puzzled.

It was a reasonable question. While Hank would consider the horse an interesting addition to their hodge-podge decorating scheme, he would not see it as a spinner of magic. "I'll explain later," Shay whispered back.

Ivy shrugged and jumped into the bidding for the silver butter dish. Later, after Shay had written a check and arranged for the horse to be delivered, she posed her original question.

Settled into the passenger seat of Ivy's car, Shay shrugged self-consciously. "He was mine, once. One of my mother's husbands gave him to me when I was a little girl. I'd just had my tonsils out, and Riley wanted to spoil me."

"Oh," said Ivy, in a fondly sentimental tone. "That's sweet."

They stopped for a late lunch and Shay was ravenous, but she was also anxious to get home. The horse would be delivered around six o'clock that evening, and she wanted to have sandpaper and fresh paints ready.

In fact, she did. She had newspapers spread out on her living room floor, too, and the deliverymen made jokes about that as they set the beloved old toy on the paper and unwrapped the blankets that had protected it.

Shay smiled wanly at their attempt at humor and had to

restrain herself from shooing them out so that she could begin the restoration project. Once they'd been given their tip, they left.

Gently, Shay applied a special paint-stripping compound to the horse, removing as much of the scratched and faded finish as she could. Then she sanded. And sanded. And sanded.

It was therapy, she said to herself. She would restore Clydesdale to his former glory and when she opened her catering service, he would stand in the office, where customers could admire him. Maybe he would even become her personal insignia, his image emblazoned on her letterhead....

Letterhead. Shay smiled and shook her head. Before there could be letterhead, there had to be a business, didn't there?

As she knelt beside the carousel horse, sanding away what remained of the silver paint on one hoof, Shay felt real trepidation. It wouldn't be easy to hand in her resignation; while she could go no further in her job at Reese Motors, it was a secure position and it paid decently. The work might be trying sometimes, but it was never dull, and Marvin and Jeannie had been so kind to her.

On the other hand, Shay had money now, and a chance to follow her dreams. How many people got an opportunity like this? she asked herself. How many?

Shay sanded more vigorously, so intent on her task and her quandary that, when the doorbell rang, she was startled. Rubbing her hands down the front of an old cotton work shirt that Eliott had left behind, she got to her feet and hurried to answer the persistent ringing.

Mitch Prescott was standing on the worn doormat, looking both exasperated and contrite. He was wearing a white T-shirt and jeans, his hands wedged into his hip pockets.

Shay's heart slid over one beat and then steadied. She was painfully conscious of her rumpled hair and solvent-scented clothes. "Yes?" she said with remarkable calm.

"Dammit, Shay," he grumbled. "Let me in."

Shay stepped back and Mitch opened the screen door and came inside the now-cluttered living room. His dark eyes touched on the carousel horse, now stripped nearly to bare wood, but he made no comment.

Remembering his coolness on the telephone, Shay was determined to keep a hold on her composure, such as it was. She wasn't about to let Mitch know how his disinterest had hurt her. "May I help you?" she asked stiffly.

He looked patently annoyed. "I came here to apologize," he snapped. "Though I'm not exactly sure what it was that I did wrong."

Coolness be damned. Shay simmered, and her voice came out in a furious hiss. "You made love to me, Mitch Prescott. You laughed with me and you held me and you listened to my deepest secrets! Then, when you'd found out all you wanted to know about my mother, when you'd paid me for my trouble—"

Mitch's strong, beard-stubbled jawline tensed, and his coffee-colored eyes snapped. "That's not fair, Shay," he broke in. "The deal we made has nothing to do with what's going on between us."

"Doesn't it? Strange, but I noticed a definite decrease in your interest level once I'd told you about my mother and shared your bed a couple of times!"

"You think that's why I slept with you? To get the inside skinny on your mother?" He paused, made an angry sound low in his throat, and then ran one hand through his hair in frustration. "Good God, Shay, don't you see how neurotic that is?"

"Neurotic? You're calling me *neurotic?*"

His expression, in fact his whole demeanor, softened. "No. No, sweetheart. I'm not. You're probably the sanest person I know. But when it comes to intimate relationships, you've got some problems." Mitch sighed and spread his hands. "Little wonder, considering your mother's exploits and that bastard you married."

Shay wavered, not sure whether to be angry or comforted. There was something inside her that needed to believe Mitch, no matter what he said, and down that path lay risks that she couldn't take. She'd believed Eliott, after all, and she'd believed Rosamond's promises that each marriage would be the one that would last. "Don't you dare slander my mother," she whispered.

"Rosamond hurt you, Shay. You're angry. Why can't you admit that?"

"She's a poor, sick woman!" Shay cried. "How could I be angry at her? How?"

"You couldn't—not at the Rosamond of today, anyway. But that other Rosamond, the young, vital one who didn't have time for her own daughter—"

Shay whirled away, furious and afraid. "Why are you doing this to me? Why are you pushing me, pestering me? Why?"

He caught her upper arms in his hands and gently turned her to face him. "Shay, get mad. Admit that the woman hurt you, disappointed you. You're not going to be able to let go of that part of your life unless you face what you really feel."

Shay's chin quivered, but her eyes flashed as she looked up into Mitch's face. "How do you know what I feel?" she choked out. "How could anybody know what it's like to mean less than the latest tennis pro in your mother's life? Less than a racehorse, for God's sake?"

"Tell me what it's like, Shay. I'll listen."

Shay trembled. "Making mental notes for your book all the while, I'm sure! Get out of here, Mitch, leave me alone. I've told you all I can."

He gave her a slight shake. "Will you forget that damned book? I'm not talking about Rosamond, I'm talking about you, about us!"

"What about us, Mitch?" The question was a challenge, a mockery, an attempt to drive this man away before he could become important enough to Shay to hurt her. He already had become just that, of course, but there was such a thing as cutting one's losses and making a run for it. God knew, she thought frantically, Rosamond had taught her that if nothing else.

Mitch's hands fell slowly from Shay's shoulders and, once again, he looked toward the carousel horse. She sensed that he knew all about Clydesdale.

After a long time, Mitch sighed and started toward the door. In the opening, he paused, his eyes searching Shay's face for a moment and then shifting away. "You know, I really thought we'd be able to communicate, you and I. I really thought we had a chance."

Shay's throat tightened and tears burned in her eyes. She turned away from Mitch and took up her sandpaper.

"You can't bring back your childhood, Shay," he said, and then the door closed quietly behind him.

Shay wiped her eyes on the sleeve of her work shirt and sanded harder.

Chapter Eight

Shay stood back from the carousel horse, her hands on her hips, her head tilted to one side. She had been working on the project every night for a week and now it was done: Clydesdale was restored to his former pink, silver and pale blue glory. He looked fabulous.

She sighed, wiping her hands on her shirt. Now what was she going to do to keep herself from going mad? Hank wouldn't be home for another ten days and Shay couldn't stand the thought of reading another book or scanning another article on the internet on the management of a small business. She'd reached her saturation point when it came to studying. Besides, she had learned the rudiments of free enterprise by working for Marvin Reese; it was time to take real action.

Shay glanced at the clock on the wall above the TV and grimaced. It was nearly two in the morning, and the third commercial was scheduled for nine-fifteen. If she didn't get some sleep, she would never get through it.

Though Shay kept herself as busy as she possibly could, teetering always on the brink of utter exhaustion, she dreaded lying down in bed and closing her eyes. When she did, she always saw Mitch on the inner screen of her mind, heard him saying that she couldn't bring back her childhood.

She turned her gaze to the beautiful wooden horse and wondered why anyone would want to bring back a childhood like hers. There had been so many disappointments, so many tears; she'd lived in luxurious neglect, having about as much access to Rosamond as any other adoring fan.

Shay bit her lower lip and shook her head in an effort to curtail that train of thought. No, Mitch Prescott had been wrong: she had no desire to relive those little-girl days. Clydesdale was merely a pleasant reminder that there had been happy, whimsical times, as well as painful ones.

With one hand, Shay tried to rub away the crick in her neck and started off toward the bathroom, looking forward to a hot, soothing shower. But she paused and looked back and it occurred to her that Clydesdale might not be just a memento—he might be a sort of emotional Trojan horse.

"May I say that you look absolutely dreadful?" Richard Barrett asked as Shay riffled through the mail on her office desk and picked out a postcard from Jeannie and Marvin. There was a picture of the Eiffel Tower on the front of the card, and Shay felt a pang at the thought of telling the Reeses about her decision to resign and start her own business.

"You have bags under your eyes, for God's sake!" Richard persisted.

Shay smiled ruefully and reread the almost illegible script on the back of the postcard. The Reeses would be home in another week and a half; she would break the news to them once they'd had time to get over their jet lag and settle in. "That gives me an idea," she teased, enjoying Richard's annoyance over the smudges that betrayed her lack of sleep. "For a commercial, I mean. You could show me, close up, and I could say, 'Come down to Reese Motors and bag yourself a good deal!' Get it, Richard? *Bag* yourself a good deal?"

"You're not only exhausted, you're insane. Shay, what's the matter with you?"

"Nothing a half ton of sugar wouldn't cure. This is Sugar Day, isn't it, Richard?"

Richard had the good grace to look just a little shamefaced. "Yes. Shay, it's safe, really. I wouldn't ask you to do anything dangerous."

"By all means, let's confine ourselves to the merely ridiculous."

Mr. Barrett sighed dramatically and flung up his hands. "You knew what doing these commercials entailed, Shay, and you agreed to it all!"

"At the time, I needed the money."

"Are you trying to back out of the deal?" Richard's voice was a growl.

Shay shook her head. "No. When I make a promise, I keep it. Even when it means making a fool of myself." Her association with Mitch Prescott and his stupid book, she added, to herself, was a case in point.

"Well, let's get this over with before it rains or something. I've got a dump-truck load of sugar down there waiting." Richard looked truly beleaguered. "I'll be just as glad when that last commercial is in the can as you will, you know!" he barked.

"Nobody could possibly be that glad, Richard," Shay

replied tartly. "Now get out of my office, will you please? I need some time to prepare for my big scene."

Richard muttered a single word as he left. It might have been "witch," but Shay wasn't betting on it.

The moment she was alone, she punched the button on her intercom. "Ivy? Would you get Todd on the phone, please?"

Instead of giving her answer over the wire, Ivy dashed into the office to demand in person, "Why? Shay, what are you planning to do?"

Shay sank into her desk chair with a sigh. Because she didn't have the strength to spar with Ivy, she answered readily. "I've decided that it's time to step out on my own, Ivy. I'm going to open my catering business and I'll need a place to work from."

Ivy's expression revealed two distinct and very different emotions: admiration and disappointment. "Wow," she said.

"Make the call, Ivy," Shay replied briskly, shuffling papers around on her desk in a pretense of being too busy to talk.

Five minutes later Todd was on the line. He listened to Shay's comments on the sort of building she needed and, bless him, asked no personal questions whatsoever. He had two good prospects, in fact: a Victorian house on Hill Street and a small restaurant overlooking the ocean. Both were available for lease with options to buy, and both had been abandoned for a considerable length of time.

Shay smiled into the telephone receiver. "You're telling me that they're fixer-uppers, aren't you, Todd?"

Todd laughed. "Yes, but the prices are right. Do you want to look at them?"

"Oh, yes, and as soon as possible."

"How about tonight, after you get off work?"

Despite her weariness, Shay felt a thrill of excitement. After all, she was doing something she had only dreamed about before: she was starting her own business. "That will be great. Why don't we make an evening of it? I'll order a pizza and throw together a salad and you and Ivy can have dinner with me."

"Sounds terrific," Todd agreed warmly. "See you at five."

"Five-thirty would be better. I've got a commercial to do this morning, and that always makes me fall behind on everything else."

"Five-thirty, then," Todd confirmed.

To save Ivy the trouble of an inquisition, Shay went out to her desk and relayed the plan. Ivy, who loved any sort of get-together no matter how casual or how highbrow, was delighted.

Chuckling, Shay started toward the stairs, ready for the third commercial. On the top step, she paused and turned to look back at her friend. "Don't you dare call your brother, either!"

Ivy beamed, sitting up very straight behind her computer terminal. "Too late!" she sang back.

Shay's hopeful mood faded instantly. She glared at her friend and stomped down the metal stairs to meet her singular and ignoble fate.

The dump truck was parked in the rear lot, as Richard had said, and the camera people were checking angles. Surreptitiously, Shay looked around as she walked toward the RV allotted for her use. If Mitch was there, she didn't see him.

This time her makeup was simple; merely a heavier version of what she normally wore. She shooed Richard's chattering assistant out of the RV and got ready, leaving the coveralls she would wear for last.

Outside—thank heaven, there was still no sign of Mitch—she read off the list of special car deals Marvin had authorized before his departure for Europe and then braced herself as the clapboard snapped and the cameras focused on her and on the dump truck parked nearby.

Smiling brightly, she announced, "Come on down to Reese Motors, folks! We guarantee you a sweet deal!"

On cue, the back of the dump truck ground upward and an avalanche of white sugar cascaded down onto Shay, burying her completely. She fought her way to the surface, sputtering and coughing, silently vowing that she would kill Richard Barrett if he wasn't satisfied with the first take.

"It's a wrap!" Richard shouted joyously and a laughing cheer went up from the salesmen, who had, as usual, gathered to watch.

Shay's hair and eyelashes were full of sugar. It filled her shoes, like sand, and even made its way under her clothes to chafe against her skin. She vowed she'd never put the stuff in her coffee again as she hurried back toward the RV, desperate to shower and change her clothes.

She began ripping them off the moment she'd closed the door behind her, flinging them in every direction. When the RV's engine suddenly whirred to life and the vehicle lurched into motion, she was stark naked.

Her first thought was that the salesmen were playing some kind of prank. Half amused and half furious, she wrenched a blanket from the bed above the RV's cab and wrapped it around herself.

"Stop!" she yelled.

The RV stopped, but only for a second. It was soon swinging into midmorning traffic. Just when Shay would have screamed, a familiar masculine voice called from the front, "Don't worry, it's all arranged! You have the day off!"

Too furious to think about the fact that she was crusted with white sugar and wrapped in a blanket, Shay flung aside the little curtain that separated the cab of the RV from the living quarters and raged, "Mitch Prescott, you stop this thing right now! I'm getting out!"

He looked back at her, his mouth serious, his eyes laughing. "In this traffic? Woman, are you mad? You'd make the six o'clock news, and if you think the commercials were embarrassing..."

"You'll be the one who makes the news!" Shay screamed, outraged. "This is not only kidnapping, it's grand theft auto!"

"I'll have you know that I rented this rig," he answered calmly.

"Well, you didn't rent me! Turn this thing around, now!"

"I'd need a football field to do that, sweets," came the happily resigned reply. "We're in this for twenty-four hours, plus mileage, I'm afraid."

"You idiot! You—you *caveman*—" Shay paused, breathless, and looked around for something to throw.

"I like the idea of dragging you off to a cave, I must admit," Mitch reflected good-naturedly. "It's the whacking you over the head with a club and hauling you off by the hair that I can't quite deal with."

"You'd never prove that by me!"

Mitch laughed and someone honked as he switched lanes to fly up a freeway ramp. Shay gave a choked little cry and slumped down on the floor in a bundle of sugared synthetic wool. There, she considered her options.

Jumping out of a vehicle traveling at fifty-five miles per hour was definitely out. So was putting her clothes back on without showering first, and she couldn't face the thought of taking a shower with this maniac at the wheel.

A sweet, throbbing warmth moved beneath Shay's skin as she reviewed her situation. There were worse things than being alone with Mitch Prescott, whatever their differences. "Was Ivy in on this?"

"I'm pleading the Fifth on that one, sugar plum."

Just the mention of sugar made Shay itch all over. She squirmed in her blanket and wailed, "When I get my hands on her—"

There was, for the first time since that crazy ride had begun, a serious note in Mitch's voice. "We have to talk, Shay."

"You didn't have to kidnap me for that!"

"Didn't I? The last time I tried, you were something less than receptive."

Shay yawned. It was crazy, but all her sleepless nights seemed to be catching up to her, demanding their due. Now, of all times! She curled up in her blanket and closed her eyes. The swaying, jostling motion of the RV lulled her into a languorous state of half slumber. "Why…are you… doing this?" she asked again.

She could have sworn he said it was because he loved her.…

Nah. She'd only dreamed that.

Mitch paced the length of the secluded beach, his hands pushed into the hip pockets of his jeans. What had he done? Was he losing his reason? For all his exploits, he'd never stooped to anything like this. Never.

He looked back at the RV he'd taken such pains to rent and sighed a raspy sigh that grated in his throat. Shay was still asleep, he supposed. When she woke up, she was going to fly into his face like a mother eagle defending her nest. He bent and grasped a piece of driftwood in one hand, and flung it into the surf.

Maybe it was that week of twenty-hour workdays. Maybe that had shorted out his brain or something.

The door of the RV creaked open and Mitch braced himself. Shay was going to give him hell, and the knowledge that he deserved whatever she might say didn't make the scenario any easier to prepare for.

She was still wearing the blanket, and little grains of sugar glimmered like bits of crystal in her hair, in her eyebrows, on her skin. Barefoot, she made her way toward him through the clean brown sand.

"I'm sorry, Shay," he said gruffly when she finally stood facing him, her wide hazel eyes unreadable. "I don't believe I did this—"

She raised the fingers of one hand to his lips, silencing him. Hidden birds chirped in the towering pine trees that edged the beach; gulls squawked in the distance; the tide made whispery music against the shore. It was a poetic interlude where only the earth and the waters spoke.

A primitive, grinding need possessed Mitch; he wanted Shay, craved her. But he didn't dare touch her, or even speak. How was he going to explain this?

Her fingers moved from his lips to caress his jawline and then trace the length of his neck. He shuddered with the aching need of her.

"They forgot to fill the water tank," she announced.

Mitch had been expecting a glorious, violent rage, expecting anything but this inane remark. He gaped at her, and his breath sawed at his lungs as it moved in and out. "What?"

"There isn't any water for the shower," Shay answered, holding the blanket in place with one hand and stroking Mitch's neck with the other. "In the RV, I mean."

She was a constant surprise to Mitch; just when he expected her to be furious, she was quiet. Or was this just the calm before the storm? "A shower?" he echoed stupidly.

Shay's lush lips curved into a smile. "If you'd just had a half ton of sugar dumped on you, you'd want a shower, too."

His frustration doubled and redoubled. Was she tormenting him deliberately? Was she making him want her, just so she could exact revenge by denying him when his need was greatest? "Dammit, Shay, I just shanghaied you and you're standing there talking about showers! Get back in the RV and I'll take you home."

The sweet lips made a pout. "I told you," she said. "I'm covered with sugar. I can't go home like this."

It was revenge; Mitch was sure of it. He made a growling sound in his bafflement and started to turn away. She caught his arm in her small, strong hand and urged him back around to face her.

The blanket seemed to waft to the sand in slow motion and Mitch couldn't breathe, couldn't move, couldn't think.

Shay stood on tiptoe, and when her lips touched Mitch's, he was lost. He groaned and gathered her to him with both hands, her soft flesh warm and gritty beneath his palms. He lowered her to the blanket, taking no time to smooth it, his mouth desperate for hers, his hands stroking her, shaping her for the taking. But he denied himself that possession, denied her, choosing instead to break the kiss and taste Shay's sugared breasts, her stomach, her thighs.

She writhed in pleasure, tossing her head back and forth, her fingers fierce in his hair. If she was setting him up for a last-second denial, she was doing a damned good job of it; Mitch wasn't sure he'd be able to stop if she asked that of him. He felt as though he'd stumbled into some jungle river, as though he were being flung along by currents too strong to swim against.

He didn't remember taking off his clothes, but suddenly he was naked, his flesh pressed against the strange roughness of hers. In silence she commanded his entry, in obedience and passion he complied.

They moved together in a ferocious rhythm, every straining thrust of their bodies increasing the pace until they both cried out, each consumed by the other, their flesh meeting in a final quivering arch. They fell slowly from the heights, gasping, sinking deep into the warm sand.

It took some time for Shay to coerce her lax, passionsated muscles to lift her from that tangled blanket on the sand. When she managed to stand up, she stumbled toward the surf, into it.

The water was cold, even though it was August, and the chill of it nipped at Shay's knees and thighs and hips as she waded farther out. Mitch was beside her in a moment and she smiled to think that he might be afraid for her.

Shivering, his lips blue with cold, he caught her upper arms in his hands. "Shay."

She didn't want to hear an apology. Nothing could be allowed to spoil the sweet ferocity of the minutes just past. She cupped both hands in the sea and flung salty water into Mitch's face, laughing as he cursed, lost his balance and came up sputtering with cold and fury.

Shay held her breath and submerged herself, letting the ocean wash away the last of the sugar from her body and came up to be pulled immediately into a breathless kiss.

When that ended, Mitch lifted her into his arms, carried her back onto the shore. He lowered her to the sand, the blanket forgotten, and made slow, sweet love to her. Her cries of pleasure carried high into the blue summer sky, tangling with the coarse calls of the seabirds.

"I really have to go back," Shay said quietly. She was dressed again, the dream was over. "Todd has a couple of buildings to show me."

"Buildings?" Mitch, too, was fully dressed, and he sat across the RV's tiny table from Shay, looking strangely defeated.

"I've decided to take the plunge and start my catering business."

Mitch's jaw tightened. "Oh."

"Why does that bother you so much?" Shay asked. "Despite your caveman tactics this afternoon, you don't give the impression of being a chauvinist."

"I'm not a chauvinist, dammit!" Mitch snapped, looking for all the world like a wounded and outraged little boy. "We made love, Shay. We worked together. Maybe we haven't known each other very long, but we've shared a lot. It hurt that you didn't mention something that important."

Shay shrugged, confused. "Until you gave me that money for helping with the book, it was just a dream, Mitch. I have a child to support and I couldn't have taken the risks. What would be the point in talking about something I didn't expect to be able to do?"

There was a short silence while Mitch absorbed the things Shay had said. "I guess I did overreact a little," he finally admitted. His eyes met hers. "I'm sorry about this morning, too. I had no right to do that."

"It was pretty crazy," Shay agreed, but she couldn't bring herself to be angry. Instead her whole being seemed to resonate with a feeling of contentment. "What made you do it?"

Mitch's broad shoulders moved in a shrug and he rubbed

his beard-stubbled chin with one hand as he thought. "It was a hell of a way to show it, but I love you, Shay."

Shay swallowed hard. She had really heard the words; this time she wasn't dreaming or so caught up in the throes of passion that she couldn't be sure she'd understood them correctly. She tried to speak and failed.

"You don't believe me?"

Shay swallowed again. "We haven't known each other very long, Mitch. Oth-other things are so good between us that—well, we could be confusing that with love, couldn't we?"

"Marry me," he said.

"No," she replied. "I can't."

"Why not?"

"Because."

"Oh, that's a great answer. God, I hate it when I ask someone a simple question and they say 'because'!"

Shay couldn't resist a smile, though it was a sad one. "I guess the day is over, huh?"

Mitch was glaring at her. "I guess it is. But we aren't over. Is that clear, Shay? You and I are not over."

"For a bestselling writer, you have terrible grammar. Speaking of that, how's the book going?"

"I'm halfway through the first draft," Mitch answered in clipped and somewhat grudging tones. "Why won't you marry me, Shay? Don't you love me?"

"As crazy as it seems, I think I do love you. If I didn't, I would have been on the main highway, trying to flag down a state patrolman."

"But?"

"But I've seen my mother fail at marriage over and over. I've failed at it myself. I can't go through that again, Mitch."

"If you need to prove that you can make it on your own, well, it seems to me that you've already done that."

"Have I, Mitch? Until you came along and offered me a fat fee for my help in writing that book about my mother, I was barely making it from one payday to the next. I haven't proved anything; I've just been lucky."

Mitch shook his head. "So now it's the catering business. If you make that fly, you're a valid person. Is that it, Shay?"

"I guess it is."

"Then I feel sorry for you."

The words came as a slap in the face to Shay; she sat back on the narrow bench, her eyes wide, her breath caught in her throat. "What?"

"You're in a trap, Shay. You're an intelligent woman, so you must know that the value of a person has nothing to do with what they prove or don't prove."

Shay felt distinctly uncomfortable. Next he'd be saying that she was just using her need to succeed at something to avoid taking a chance on marriage. "I suppose if we were married, you'd want me to give up the whole idea of starting a catering service."

"On the contrary, Shay, I'd help you in any way I could." He looked grimly smug. "Wriggle your way out of that one."

Shay was stumped. "Okay, so I'm afraid. It's human to be afraid when you've been hurt."

"This conversation is getting us nowhere." Mitch stood up, took the keys to the RV from the pocket of his jeans. "Can we at least agree that we'll give this relationship or whatever the hell it is a sporting chance?"

Shay could only nod.

"That's progress, at least. Let's go."

They were both settled in the front seat and the RV was

jolting up the narrow road to the highway before either of them spoke again.

"I want to read what you've written so far, Mitch. About Rosamond, I mean."

Mitch did not take his eyes from the road. "Buckle your seat belt. You're free to read the manuscript whenever you want."

Shay snapped the belt into place and sighed. "Ivy and Todd are coming over for pizza after I look at those properties. Why don't you join us?"

"Now that was an enthusiastic invitation if I've ever heard one. Are you afraid I'd end up staying the night?"

"I *know* you would end up staying the night."

Mitch cast a sidelong look at her and shook his head. "Woman, you defy logic. Caution is your middle name, and yet you seem to enjoy walking on thin ice."

"I'm as confused as you are, if that helps," Shay admitted ruefully. "Are you coming over for pizza or not?"

"I'm coming over for one hell of a lot more than pizza, lady, and you know it. Am I still invited?"

Shay thought for a long time. "Yes," she finally answered. "The invitation stands."

Chapter Nine

If Ivy and Todd were surprised when Shay arrived at Reese Motors promptly at five-thirty, they had the good grace not to show it. Freshly showered and made up, Shay went into her office long enough to check her telephone messages and align her work for the next day.

When she came out, her friends were waiting, Ivy wide-eyed and just a bit pale, Todd blithely unaware that anything was amiss.

Shay gave Ivy a scorching look that warned of an imminent confrontation and said, "Well, let's look at those buildings. We'll pick up the pizza on the way to my place, afterward."

Ivy swallowed visibly and croaked, "Okay."

Their first stop was the large Victorian house Todd had mentioned. It had been empty for a long time, but Shay could see vast potential in it; if she renovated the place, she would have room not only for her business, but for half a dozen small shops. She wouldn't run these herself, of course, but rent them to other people.

Todd assured her that the house was basically sound, though it needed a great deal of work. The plaster in most of the rooms was either stained or falling off the walls in hunks, and the ceilings sagged.

Shay liked the house; it had personality. The kitchen, while much in need of repair, was large enough to accommodate the needs of a catering service, and the spacious dining room could be converted to a reception area of sorts. The pantry, almost as big as Shay's kitchen in her rented house, would make a suitable private office.

"I have some rough estimates on the renovation, if you'd like to see them," Todd offered.

Shay was pleased by his thoroughness. Here was a man who would go far in the business world. She reviewed the estimates submitted by various construction companies as they drove to the other potential site. The amounts of money involved were staggering.

The second site was a small restaurant overlooking the water. The ceiling had fallen down, coming to rest across a counter still equipped with a cash register. Debris of every sort was scattered on the floor, seeming to pool around the bases of the tattered stools that lined the counter. The smell of mice was potent.

"It does look out over the water," Ivy ventured. She'd been very quiet all along.

"That's about all it has going for it," Shay replied. "If I were going to open a bistro or something, I might be interested, but I don't think a view is going to be any particular plus for a catering service."

Todd nodded his agreement.

Suddenly, Shay was very tired. After all, it had been a crazy day. "I'll need some time to think this over, Todd, but I'm interested in the other place. Do you think I could get back to you in a few days?"

Again, Todd nodded. "You might want to get some other estimates. The ones I gave you were meant to give an idea of what would be required."

Shay looked down at the sheaf of papers in her hand. "Do you recommend these people, Todd?"

He held the door open and Ivy sort of skulked through, just ahead of Shay. "I've dealt with all of them at one time or another and they do fine work. But you should still get other estimates, it's always good business."

They stopped at a pizza-to-go place and, as Shay waited at the counter for her order, she happened to glance through the front window. Ivy and Todd appeared to be having some kind of serious consultation in the car. Ivy's head was bent and Shay found her irritation with her friend fading away.

Ivy was a meddler extraordinaire, but she meant well. She was happy with Todd and she wanted everyone else she knew to be happy, too. Still, Shay thought the young woman deserved the lecture she was probably getting at that moment.

The pizza was ready and Shay was distracted from the scene in the car for a few moments. When she reached it, carrying the pizza, Ivy and Todd were sitting as far from each other as they possibly could. Shay let herself into the backseat, wrestling the huge pizza box as she did so and, of course, made no comment on the chill inside the car.

At Shay's house, a very subdued Ivy took over the making of the salad. When Mitch arrived she started and looked even more guilty and disconsolate than before.

Mitch gave Shay a quick kiss on the lips and turned to his sister, who tossed him a defiant look and made a face.

Mitch laughed and then reached out to rumple Ivy's gossamer hair, but he spoke to Shay. "Ivy didn't know why I wanted to rent that RV until it was too late."

Ivy startled everyone by bursting into tears and fleeing through the back door. Todd started to follow, but Shay stopped him with a gesture of one hand and a quiet "No. I'll talk to her."

She found Ivy sitting at the picnic table, her head resting on her folded arms, her small shoulders shaking.

Shay laid a hand on her friend's quivering back and said, "Hey. It's all right, Ivy. I'm not mad at you."

"I could kill that brother of mine!" Ivy wailed, sniffling intermittently. "Oh, Shay, I never thought he'd do anything like that!"

Shay couldn't help smiling a little. "No harm was done. Let's forget it."

Ivy turned and flung herself into Shay's arms for a quick hug. After that, she recovered quickly.

During dinner, served on that same picnic table, the conversation centered mostly on the house Shay was thinking of taking for her catering business and her ideas about renting out the other rooms as small shops.

Mitch said very little, but the light in his brown eyes revealed a certain amused respect that told Shay he liked the idea. Ivy, of course, was bursting with suggestions: she knew a woman who made beautiful candles and would be overjoyed to be a part of such a project, was acquainted with another who had been wanting to import Christmas ornaments to sell to the tourists as souvenirs but had had no luck in finding a shop she could afford.

When the pizza and salad were gone and the paper plates had been thrown away, Ivy and Todd made an abrupt, if cheerful, exit.

"Was it something I said?" Shay said with a frown.

Mitch grinned. "Don't be naive," he replied.

While Mitch brewed a pot of coffee, seeming as at home in Shay's kitchen as if it had been his own, she settled onto the couch with the pages of his manuscript. She had never known a writer before, but she had expected a first draft to be a mass of scribbles and cross-outs and have scrawled notes in the margins. Mitch's pages were remarkably neat and there was something in his style that grabbed Shay's attention, made her read as someone who had never met Rosamond Dallas might.

Presently, Mitch set a steaming cup on the coffee table in front of her, but she didn't pause to reach for it. She was fascinated, seeing a side of Rosamond that she hadn't consciously noticed before.

By the time she'd raced through a hundred and fifty pages of concise, perceptive copy, her coffee was cold in the cup and her view of Rosamond—and Mitch himself—had been broadened by the length of a horizon.

"Wow," she said.

Mitch took away her coffee cup, refilled it and returned to the living room. "You approve, I take it?"

"I'm not sure if I approve or not, but I'm impressed. The writing is good, Mitch, really good. How could you have learned so much about Rosamond from a few pictures and scrapbooks and a couple of conversations with me?"

Mitch was settled into the overstuffed chair nearest the couch. "I did a lot of research, Shay. For instance, I talked to all six of her ex-husbands by phone. And your grandmother—"

"My grandmother?" Shay felt a quickening inside, one of mingled surprise and alarm. "I don't have a grandmother."

Mitch lowered his eyes to his coffee, taking a sip before he answered, "Yes, you do."

Shay set the pages of the manuscript aside, fearing that she would drop them if she didn't. "Speaking of things people don't bother to mention…"

Mitch set aside his cup and raised both hands in a gesture of peace. "I didn't find out about her until this afternoon, Shay, after I'd dropped you off here. One of my research people had tracked her down and he gave me her name and phone number."

Shay swallowed. "You called her?"

"Yes. Her name is Alice Bretton and she lives in Springfield, Missouri. Your father—"

"Is her son," Shay's voice was shaky.

"Was her son, I'm afraid. He was a navy pilot, Shay, and he was shot down in combat." Mitch was sitting beside Shay on the couch now, holding her gently and not too tightly.

"They're sure? So many pilots—"

"He's dead, Shay. He was positively identified."

An overwhelming feeling of betrayal and hurt washed over Shay. "I didn't even know him. Rosamond wouldn't tell me his name."

"His name was Robert Bretton."

"Tell me about him!"

Mitch sighed. "I don't know the whole story. He and Rosamond were 'going steady,' as they called it back then. When things went wrong, your mother bought a bus ticket to Hollywood and from what Mrs. Bretton told me, Robert finished college and then joined the navy."

Shay was dizzied by the sudden influx of information that had been denied her throughout her life, first by Rosamond's reluctance to talk, then by her illness. "There are so many things I want to know.…"

"Why don't you get in touch with your grandmother tomorrow? She'll be able to tell you a lot more than I can."

"She might not want anything to do with me!"

Mitch shook his head. "She asked me a thousand questions about you, Shay." He pulled a wry face meant to lighten the mood. "Of course, I didn't tell her how you taste when you've just had a half ton of sugar dumped over your head."

Shay was making a sound, but she wasn't sure whether she was laughing or crying or both. She gave Mitch a shove and then allowed her forehead to nestle into his broad shoulder.

"Make love to me, Mitch," she said after a very long time.

"Here?" he teased in a hoarse voice, but he picked Shay up in his arms and carried her into the room she pointed out to him. The night was a long one, full of tender abandon.

The pit of Shay's stomach quivered with nervousness as she dialed the number Mitch had given her. What, exactly, was she going to say to this grandmother she had never known, never heard a word about?

Mitch puttered around the kitchen, getting breakfast, while the call went through.

"Mrs. Bretton?" Shay's voice shook. "My name is Shay Kendall and—"

"Shay!" The name was a soft cry of joy, full of tears and laughter. "Is it really you?"

"It's really me," Shay answered, and she made a face at Mitch as he shoved a dishtowel into her hands. Then she dried her eyes with it. "T-tell me about my father. Please."

"There is so much to tell, darling, and so much to show. Could you possibly come to Springfield for a visit?"

Shay wanted to hop on the next plane, but she had responsibilities to Marvin and Jeannie and she couldn't go away without letting Hank know. Suppose he got sick and Garrett brought him home and there was no one there to take care of him? "This is a bad time—my job—my son—"

"Then I'll come there!" Alice Bretton interrupted warmly. "Would that be all right, Shay? I could bring the photo albums and we could talk in person."

"I'd love to have you, Mrs. Bretton."

"In that case, I'll make arrangements and call you right back."

"That would be wonderful."

They said goodbye and Shay set the phone receiver back in its cradle as Mitch poured scrambled eggs into a pan of hash browns and chopped onions and bits of crisp bacon.

"I take it she's flying out for a visit?" Mitch asked moderately, looking back at Shay over one bare shoulder.

Shay nodded. "I can't make sense of what I feel, Mitch. I'm happy that I'm finally going to meet my grandmother and I'm sad because my father died and I'm furious with Rosamond! Here she is, this poor, sick, wretch of a woman, and I could cheerfully wring her neck!"

"That's normal, Shay. The important thing is that you wouldn't really do it."

"I want to thank you for this, Mitch. F-for my grandmother."

He turned from the stove, grinning, almost unbearably handsome in just his jeans. His hair was rumpled and his feet were bare and, as always, he needed to shave. "Don't be too hasty with your gratitude, kid," he warned. "For all you know, she's a bag lady with bad breath, bunions and bowling shoes."

"That was alliterative, in a tacky sort of way," Shay responded. She slid off the stool near the wall phone and put her arms around Mitch's lean waist.

He kissed the tip of her nose and gave her bottom a squeeze that brought back memories of the night before. Shay blushed to recall what a greedy wanton she'd been.

"I'm not sure whether you bring out the best in me, or the worst," she commented.

Mitch's eyebrows went into brief but rapid motion. "If that was your worst," he said in a Groucho Marx voice, "I'm all for it."

Shay tipped her head back and laughed. It was a throaty, gleeful sound, and it felt oh, so good. If she could be sure that life with Mitch Prescott would always be this way, she would have married him in a second. But in her deepest mind, marriage was linked with betrayal, with pain. She sobered, thinking of Eliott's desertion and the fickle vanity of her mother.

Mitch lifted his index fingers to the corners of Shay's mouth and stretched her lips into a semblance of a smile. "No sad faces allowed," he said.

He went to dish up the scrambled egg concoction he'd made for their breakfast, and Shay sat down in a chair at the table. It was strange, having a man not only cook for her, but serve her as well. "I could get used to this," she said as he set a steaming, fragrant plate in front of her.

"Good. We'll get married and make it a ritual. I'll fix your breakfast every morning and then take you back to bed and make wild love to you."

Shay blushed again, but some vixen hiding deep inside her made her say, "Keep making threats like that, fella, and I'll accept your proposal."

Mitch's eyes were suddenly serious. "Eat," he ordered in a gruff tone, looking away.

Before Shay could say anything at all, the telephone rang. Alice Bretton had made her flight arrangements and she would be arriving in Seattle the following afternoon at two. Shay wrote down the name of the airline and the flight number and when she turned away from the phone, Mitch was disconsolately scraping their plates.

Standing behind him, Shay wrapped her arms around his middle and rubbed his stomach with tantalizing motions of both hands. "I seem to remember something about a threat," she said softly, her lips moving against the taut flesh of his back as she spoke.

Shay was late for work that morning.

Just talking to Alan Roget over the telephone gave Mitch a creepy feeling, as though a massive spiderweb had settled over him or something. He frowned as he listened to the first accounts of the murderer's childhood, entering notes on the screen of his computer throughout the conversation.

The night with Shay had been magical, and so had the morning. Life was so damned ironic: one minute, a man could be eating scrambled eggs or making love to a woman, the next, talking to someone who personified evil. Like most psychotics, Roget exhibited no remorse at all, from what Mitch could tell. He seemed to feel that civil and moral laws applied only to other people and not to him.

By the time Mitch hung up the telephone, he was a little sick. He immediately dialed Reba's number in California, and when she answered, he asked to talk to Kelly.

"You're in luck, big fella," Reba responded warmly. "The munchkin happens to be home from school today."

Mitch sat up a little straighter in his desk chair. "Is she sick?"

"Nothing serious," his ex-wife assured him promptly. "Just the sniffles. So, how have you been, Mitch?"

Mitch couldn't help smiling. Reba definitely wasn't your standard ex-wife. She was happy with her new husband

and that happiness warmed her entire personality. "I'm in love," he confided, without really expecting to.

"Oh, Mitch, that's great!" Worry displaced a little of the buoyancy in her voice. "It *is* great, isn't it? Maybe great enough to keep you out of jungles and hotbeds of political unrest?"

"No more jungles, Reba," he said solemnly. He'd made changes in his life recently that he had refused to consider while he and Reba were married, and he wondered if she would resent that.

Not Reba. He should have known. "We'll all breathe a sigh of relief," she chimed. "On the count of three, now. One, two—"

Mitch laughed. He remembered the good times with Reba and, for a fleeting moment, mourned them.

When Kelly's piping voice came on the line, he forget about Roget and all the other ugliness in the world. But the house seemed even bigger than it was after he'd talked to his daughter, and even emptier.

He threw himself into his work, concentrating on Rosamond Dallas and what had made her tick.

The need to throttle Rosamond was gone by the time Shay visited her that afternoon; in its place was a certain sad acceptance of the fact that mothers are women, human and fallible.

She approached her mother's chair, kissed her forehead. "How can I hate you?" she whispered.

Rosamond rocked and clutched the ever-present doll. It seemed to Shay that she was retreating deeper and deeper into herself and growing smaller with every passing day.

Tired because of a most delicious lack of sleep the night before, a day of work and telephone conversations with half a dozen contractors, Shay sighed and sank into the chair facing her mother's. "I'm going to meet my grandmother tomorrow," she said, hardly able to believe such a thing could be possible and expecting no reaction at all from Rosamond.

But the woman sat stiffly in her chair, her famous eyes widening.

Shay was incredulous. "Mother?"

The fleeting moment of lucidity was over. Rosamond stared blankly again, crooning a wordless song to her doll.

Shay looked at the doll and, for the first time ever, wondered if that raggedy lump of cloth and yarn could, in Rosamond's mind, represent herself as a baby. It was a jarring thought, but oddly comforting, too. Maybe, Shay thought, she loved me as well as she was able to love anyone. Maybe she did the best she could.

On her way home from the convalescent home, Shay stopped at a bookstore, looking for the four titles Ivy had written down for her. Mitch's work was published under the odd code name of Zebulon, with no surname of any kind given and, of course, with no photograph on the back or inside flap of the book jackets.

Shay felt a little shiver of fear as she looked at the covers and thought of all the dangerous people who must hate Mitch Prescott enough to kill him. She was trembling a little as she laid the books on the counter and paid for them.

At home, she did housework, ate a light supper and took a bath, then curled up on the couch with one of Mitch's books. The one she'd selected to read first was an account of the capture of a famous Nazi war criminal, set mostly in Brazil. It was harrowing, reading that book, and yet Shay was riveted to it, turning page after page. In the morning, she awakened to find herself still on the couch, the open book under her cheek. Groaning, she raised herself to a sitting position and ran her fingers through her hair.

This was the day that she would meet Alice Bretton, her grandmother, for the first time. She was determined to think of that and not the horrors Mitch had to have faced in order to write that book.

After showering and dressing, she wolfed down a cup of coffee and half an English muffin and drove to work to find the usual chaos awaiting her. At least Richard Barrett wasn't around, wanting to film the last commercial. That was a comfort.

Shay delved into her work and the hours passed quickly. Soon it was time to drive to the airport and meet Mrs. Bretton's plane.

She wondered how she would recognize her grandmother and what she would say to her first. There were so many things to tell and so many questions to ask.

As it happened, it was Alice Bretton who recognized Shay. A tiny, Helen Hayes–type, with snow-white hair done up in a bun and quick, sparkling eyes, Mrs. Bretton came right up to her granddaughter and said, "Why, dear, you look just like Robert!"

Shay was inordinately glad that she resembled someone; Lord knew, she looked nothing like Rosamond and never had. It was that gladness that broke the ice and allowed her to hug the small woman standing before her. "I'm so happy to see you," she said, and then she had to laugh because, looking down through a mist of tears, she could see that Alice was wearing bowling shoes with her trim, tasteful suit.

"They're so comfortable, don't you know!" Alice cried in good-natured self-defense.

Shay looked forward to telling Mitch that Mrs. Bretton

did indeed wear bowling shoes, though she obviously wasn't a bag lady and it was doubtful that she had bunions.

Talking with her grandmother proved remarkably easy, considering all the years and all the heartaches that might have separated them. The two women chattered nonstop all the way back to Skyler Beach, Shay asking questions, Alice answering them.

Shay's eyes were hazel because hazel eyes ran in the Bretton family, she was told, and yes, Robert had wanted to marry Rosamond, but she'd refused. He had tried to see Shay many times, but she had always been away in some school, out of his reach. Rosamond had never allowed any of his letters or phone calls to Shay to get through.

Alice patted her sensible, high-quality purse. "But I have most of those letters right here. When they came back, Robert saved them."

Shay worked at keeping her mind on her driving, and it was hard. She wanted to pull over to the side of the freeway and read all of her father's letters, one after another. "Why didn't Rosamond want him to see me or even talk to me?"

Alice sighed, and if she bore Rosamond Dallas any ill will, it wasn't visible in the sweet lines of her face. "Lord only knows. She wasn't very happy as a child, you know, and I guess she didn't want anything to do with anyone from Springfield. Not even her own baby's father."

Rosamond had said very little about her life in Springfield, only that her mother drank too much and her father, a railroad worker, had died in an accident when she was four years old. "Did you know Rosamond as a girl?"

Alice shook her head. "I only met her after she'd started to date Robert. She was beautiful, but I—well, I had my misgivings about her. She was rather wild, you know."

Shay could imagine her mother as a young girl, looking

for approbation and love even in those prefame days. It was strange that the search had never stopped, that Rosamond had gone from man to man all her life. "I wish I'd known about you and about my father."

Alice reached across the car seat to pat Shay's knee. "You'll know me, and I've brought along things to help you know your father, too." Suddenly the elderly woman looked alarmed. "I do hope I'm not keeping you from your work, dear!"

Shay thought of the commercials and the irate customers and the stacks of contracts and factory invoices she had left behind at Reese Motors. "My work will definitely keep until tomorrow. You can stay for a while, can't you?"

"Oh, yes. Nobody waiting at home but my parakeet, my cat and my bridge club. Now tell me all about this boy of yours. Hank, isn't it? You know, it's a funny thing, but your great-grandfather's name was Henry and they called him Hank, don't you know...."

Chapter Ten

Shay bit her lower lip as the ringing began on the other end of the line. It was just plain unconscionable to awaken someone at that hour of the night, but after reading her father's gentle, innocuous letters, she felt a deep need to touch base.

On the third ring, Mitch answered with an unintelligible grumble.

"She wears bowling shoes," Shay said.

"You woke me up to tell me that?" He didn't sound angry, just baffled.

"I thought you'd want to know." She paused, drew a deep breath. "Oh, Mitch, Alice is a wonderful woman."

"She's your grandmother. What else could she be besides wonderful?"

"Flatterer."

"You love it."

I love you, Shay thought. "Good night, Mitch," she said.

He laughed, a wonderful rumbling, sleepy sound. "Good night, princess."

Shay was glad that no one could see her, there in the darkness of her kitchen. She kissed the telephone receiver before she put it back in place.

Alice was still sleeping the next morning when Shay left for work. Rather than disturb her grandmother, she scribbled a note that included her office telephone number and crept out. Alice had made it very clear, the night before, that she didn't want to disrupt Shay's life in any way.

On the way to Reese Motors, Shay marveled that life could follow the same dull and rocky road for so many years, and then suddenly take a series of crazy turns. She'd met Mitch, she'd found her grandmother, she was about to start the business she had only dreamed of—and all this had taken place in a period of a few weeks.

When Shay arrived at work, she found Richard waiting in her office with the fourth and final storyboard. She was relieved; after this, she would never have to make a fool of herself on camera again.

"It's a giant, hairy hand," Richard said with amazing enthusiasm.

"I can see that, Richard," Shay replied dryly, frowning at the storyboard. "When are we filming this one?"

"Tomorrow, I hope. We had to special order that hand, you know."

Shay sighed inwardly. "It won't collapse or anything, will it?"

"Absolutely not. Would I risk your life that way?"

Shay shrugged philosophically. "I don't know, Richard. You almost smothered me in sugar the other day, so I thought I'd ask."

"Marvin's going to be pleased with these commercials, Shay," Richard said on an unexpectedly charitable note.

"You've done a great job. The first spot aired late last night. You looked great, even in a bee suit."

Shay grinned, unable to resist saying, "I'll bet people are buzzing about it."

Richard laughed and left the office, taking the story-board with him.

At noon, Alice arrived at Reese Motors by taxi, all dressed up for the lunch date she and Shay had made the night before. Shay proudly introduced her to Ivy, all the salesmen and even the mechanics in the repair section.

"I saw you on television today, dear," the elderly woman announced moderately over a chef's salad. "You were dressed as a bee, of all things." Alice looked puzzled, as though she thought Shay might say she was mistaken.

Briefly, Shay explained about Marvin's penchant for creative advertising.

"We have a car dealer like that in Springfield," Alice said seriously, and there was an endearing look of baffle-ment in her eyes. "He let a mouthful of water run down his chin and said he was liquidating last year's models."

"Oh, Lord," Shay groaned. "Do me a favor and don't mention that around Reese Motors. Marvin would prob-ably get wind of it and come up with some version of his own."

"Is there a young man in your life, dear?"

The abrupt change in subject matter caught Shay off guard. "I—well—yes, sort of—"

Alice smiled. "Good. They're not all wasters like that Eliott person, you know."

Shay wondered what Alice would think of Mitch if she knew how he had hijacked her granddaughter to a private beach and made love to her in the sand. The memory of her own responses brought throbbing color to Shay's cheeks.

"What is his name, dear? What does he do?"

"His name is Mitch Prescott. He's the man who found you for me," Shay said, somewhat hesitantly.

Alice did not pursue the matter. "My, but you do look like your father," she said in a faraway voice.

That evening, after work, Shay drove to the Victorian house she hoped to restore and parked at the curb. The place was derelict, and yet, in her mind's eye, she could see so many possibilities for it. Suddenly she wanted that disreputable old white elephant with a consuming ache.

She drove home to find Alice happily cooking dinner and Mitch helping. The way the two of them were chattering, they might have known each other for ten years instead of ten minutes. It was crazy, but Shay was just a little jealous of both of them.

"Sit down, dear, sit down," Alice ordered, gesturing toward a chair at the kitchen table. "You look all worn out."

Over Alice's neatly coiffed and blue-rinsed head, Mitch gave Shay an evil wink.

Shay sighed and sat down, grateful for the coffee that was immediately set before her. "You two are going to spoil me if you keep this up. What will I do without you?"

The question, so innocently presented, caused a stiff silence. Mitch gazed off through the window over the sink, but Alice recovered quickly. "I was just telling your young man that I might sell my house and move out here for good. I could get a little apartment, don't you know."

Shay's eyes widened. "You would do that? You would actually move here, just to be near Hank and me?"

"You're my family," Alice said softly. "All I have in the world. Of course I'd move to be near you. That's if you'd want—if I wouldn't be in the way—"

"Never." Shay rose from her chair and embraced this

woman who had come to mean so much to her in such a short time. "You could never be in the way."

"Our Mr. Prescott might have a thing or two to say about that," Alice pointed out with a misty wryness as she and Shay drew apart. "He has plans for you, you know."

Mitch was no longer looking out the window, and a grin tilted one side of his mouth and lit his eyes. His entire demeanor said that he did indeed have plans for Shay, and none of them could be mentioned in front of her grandmother.

Shay waited until Alice wasn't looking and gave Mitch a slow, saucy wink.

Color surged up from the neck of his dark blue T-shirt and he tossed Shay a mock scowl in return. "Actually," he said, "I think Shay needs a grandmother around to keep her in line. I've tried, but the job is too big for me."

Alice chuckled and gave him a slight shove. "Step aside, handsome," she said. "I've got to get these biscuits in the oven or they won't be ready in time for supper."

Mitch caught Shay by the hand as he passed her, pulling her out of her chair and into the living room, where he promptly drew her close and kissed her. It was a thorough kiss that left Shay unsteady on her feet and just a bit flushed in the face.

Holding her close, Mitch whispered against the bridge of her nose, "If your grandmother wasn't in the next room, lady…"

Shay trembled with the delicious feeling of wanting him. In a low, teasing voice, she retorted, "You shameless rascal, how can you say such a thing when you've been flirting with another woman under my very nose?"

Mitch grinned. "What can I say? I took one look at Alice and I was smitten."

"Smitten?"

He pulled her toward the couch, sat down, positioned her on his lap. His hand moved beneath her skirt to stroke her thigh. "Smitten," he confirmed.

Shay's breath had quickened and her blood felt warm enough to melt her veins. She slapped away his hand and it returned, unerringly, to create sweet havoc on the flesh of her upper leg.

"So," he said, as though he weren't driving her wild with the brazen motion of his fingers. "Have you decided whether or not to take the house Todd showed you?"

Shay could barely breathe. "I'm...waiting for...estimates."

"I see."

Again, Shay removed his hand; again it returned. "Rat," she muttered.

Alice was humming in the kitchen, happy in her work, probably pleased with herself for giving the young lovers some time alone. Mitch continued to caress Shay, slowly, rhythmically, skillfully.

She buried her mouth in the warmth of his neck to muffle the soft moan his attentions forced her to utter.

"You look a bit flushed, dear," Alice commented, minutes later, over a dinner of chicken, green beans and biscuits, her gentle eyes revealing worry. "I hope you aren't coming down with something."

"She's perfectly healthy," Mitch replied with an air of authority.

Beneath the surface of the table, Shay's foot moved and her heel made solid contact with Mitch's shin. He didn't even flinch.

After dinner, he and Shay did the dishes together while Alice rested on Hank's bed. She'd closed the door behind her, but Shay still felt compelled to keep her voice down.

"If you ever do a thing like that again, Mitch Prescott..."

He wrapped the dishtowel around Shay's waist, turned

slightly and pulled her against him. "You can be sure that I'll do it again," he muttered. "And you'll react just the same way."

Shay knew that he was right and flushed, furious that he had such power over her and yet glad of it, too. Her body was still reverberating with the force of her response to those stolen moments of pleasure. "You are vain and arrogant!" she whispered.

He put one hand inside her blouse to cup her breast, his thumb moving her bra out of place and then caressing her nipple. "I'm going to forget that copy of my manuscript when I leave here tonight," he said, his lips barely touching Shay's. "You, of course, will throw up your hands in dismay and tell your grandmother that you've got to return it to me immediately."

Shay shuddered with desire, still held close to solid proof of his masculinity by the dishtowel. His fingers were plucking gently at her nipple and she couldn't reason, let alone argue. "B-bastard," she said, and that was the extent of her rebellion.

Mitch slid the top of her blouse aside and bent his head to taste her now-throbbing nipple with an utterly brazen lack of haste. In fact, he satisfied himself at leisure before tugging her bra back into place and straightening her blouse. And then he left.

Shay finished the dishes and then, hating herself, tapped at the door of Hank's room. "Alice?"

The answer was a sleepy, "Yes, dear?"

"Mitch forgot something here, and I've got to take it to him. I'll be back soon."

Two hours later Shay returned, hair and clothes slightly rumpled, lips swollen with Mitch's kisses. Alice was knitting, the television tuned to a mystery program, and even in the dim light of the living room, Shay could see the sparkle in her grandmother's eyes. The lady was clearly nobody's fool.

"Did you have a nice time, dear?"

Every part of Shay was pulsing with the "nice time" she'd had in Mitch Prescott's arms. "Yes," she said, in classic understatement, and then she excused herself to take a bath and get ready for bed.

Because the last commercial was being taped the next morning and Alice wanted to watch, Shay arrived at work with her grandmother in tow.

The enormous hairy hand towered in the middle of the main showroom, and Shay shook her head as she looked at it. She was given a flowing white dress to put on in the restroom, and Richard's assistant applied her makeup.

At least the showroom had been closed for whatever length of time it would take to get the spot on videotape, Shay noted with relief. Using a stepladder, she climbed into the palm of that hand and stretched out on her side, trying to keep the dress from riding up. Richard followed her up and carefully closed the huge fingers of the hand around her.

Before going back down the stepladder he winked at Shay and told her again that Marvin was going to be proud of her.

"This is really the way Fay Wray got her start, huh?" Shay muttered, trying to be a good sport about the whole thing. After all, this was the last commercial she would ever appear in.

Looking down, Shay saw her grandmother talking with Ivy, but there was no sign of Mitch. Her feelings about that were mixed. On the one hand, she hated to have him see her in such a ridiculous position. On the other, it was always comforting to know that he was there somewhere.

This time the cameras were above her, on the mezzanine, along with an enormous fan. A microphone had been hidden in the neckline of Shay's chiffon dress.

"Ready?" Richard called from his place between the two cameramen.

Shay nodded; she was as ready as she was ever going to get.

The fan started up and Shay's dress and hair moved in the flow of air. She practiced her smile and mentally rehearsed her line as the cameras panned over the selection of cars available in the showroom. When she saw them swing in her direction, she beamed, even though the fan was buffeting the air from her lungs, and gasped, "You'll go ape when you see the deals we're making at Reese Motors! Come on down and talk to us at 6832 Discount Way, right here in Skyler Beach!"

"Perfect!" Richard exulted, and Shay's relief was such that for a moment she sank into the hollow of that giant ape hand and closed her eyes. One of the salesmen came to help her out from under the hairy fingers and down the ladder.

"You were magnificent!" Alice said when Shay came to stand before her, but there was an expression of profound relief in her eyes.

"I'm just glad it's over," Shay answered, wondering if Alice would tell her friends back home that her granddaughter earned her living by dressing up as a bee or lying in a huge and hairy hand.

"Well," Alice announced brightly, "I'm off to look at apartments with Ivy's young man. I may be late, so I took the liberty of setting out one of the casseroles you had in your freezer." The older woman's eyes shifted from Shay to Ivy, and they sparkled with pride. "My granddaughter is a very organized young woman, don't you know. She'll make a fine caterer."

The vote of confidence uplifted Shay; she said goodbye to Alice and went into the restroom to put on her normal clothes and redo her makeup. Within twenty minutes, she was so involved in her work that she'd forgotten all about her brief stint as the captive of a mythical ape.

After work, Shay met briefly with one of the contractors providing an estimate on the renovation of the old house. His bid was higher than the one Todd had gotten, but she reviewed it carefully anyway.

Over the next three days, the rest of the estimates came in, straggle fashion. Shay looked them all over and decided to go with Todd's original choices all the way down the line. She called her friend and, after taking one deep breath, told him that she would lease the house he'd shown her if the option to buy later still stood.

"You're certainly efficient, Todd," she said after the details had been discussed. "Alice loves that apartment you found for her. She's looking forward to becoming a 'beach bunny,' as she put it."

Todd laughed. "She's something else, isn't she? I'm glad you and Alice found each other, Shay."

Shay was glad, too, of course, for her own sake and for Hank's. What a surprise Alice would be to him when he came home from his trip! Even before her illness, Rosamond had never been very interested in the child, but now he would have someone besides Shay to claim as family.

For all these good things that were happening, there was one dark spot on Shay's horizon. "H-have you talked to Mitch in the last few days?"

There was intuitive understanding in Todd's voice as he replied, "He's working like a madman, Shay. I think he's got another project lined up for when he's done with Rosamond's book, and he's anxious to get to it."

Another project. Shay thought of Mitch's earlier books—she'd skimmed through all four of them during the past few days—and she was alarmed. Good God, did he mean to tangle with the Mafia again? With drug dealers and Nazis and militant members of the Klan? He'd be killed!

She said goodbye in the most moderate voice she could manage, then hung up the telephone with a bang and rushed out of her office, past Ivy's empty desk, through the deserted showroom downstairs and across the parking lot to her car.

Ten minutes later she was knocking on Mitch Prescott's front door.

His housekeeper, Mrs. Carraway, answered. "Hello, Mrs. Kendall," she said warmly. She probably knew a great deal about Shay's relationship with her employer, but Shay couldn't take the time to consider all the embarrassing ramifications of that now.

"Is Mr. Prescott at home? I really must see him as soon as possible."

Mrs. Carraway looked surprised. "Why, no, Mrs. Kendall. He's away on a research project or some such. I don't expect him back for nearly a week."

A week! Mitch was going to be gone for a whole week and he hadn't even bothered to say goodbye. Shay was devastated and she was angry and she was afraid. So afraid. Had he gone back to the jungles of Colombia, or perhaps to Beirut or Belfast or some other dangerous place? She swallowed her pride.

"Do you know if Mr. Prescott has left the United States?"

The housekeeper's face revealed something Shay found

even harder to bear than surprise, and that was sympathy. "I really don't know, Mrs. Kendall. I'm sorry."

Shay muttered something polite and quite insensible and turned away. She should have known better than to get involved with a man who lived his life in the fast lane, she thought fiercely. She should have known better.

When Shay arrived home she found her grandmother packed to leave for Springfield on an early morning plane. Alice was eager to tie up the loose ends of her life in Missouri and get back to Skyler Beach.

Shay didn't want her to go, even for such a short time. Everyone she loved, it seemed, was either away or about to leave. "If you'd stay just a few more days, you could meet Hank—"

Alice left her packing to kiss Shay's cheek. "I'll be back soon, don't you worry. Besides, the boy will need his room."

"It isn't going to be the same without you," Shay said as Alice went back to the two suitcases propped on the living room sofa to arrange and rearrange their contents.

Alice went on working, but there was gentle understanding in the look she passed to Shay. "You think I'm going to get back there and change my mind, don't you?"

Shay sank into the easy chair nearest the couch. "Your friends are there. Your house, your memories."

The old woman gestured toward the stack of photo albums she'd brought with her. They constituted a loving chronicle of Robert Bretton's life, virtually from birth. "My memories are in my mind and my heart and in those albums over there. And my future is right here, in Skyler Beach. In fact, I'm thinking seriously of renting one of the shops in your building and opening a little yarn shop. I've always wanted to do something like that."

Shay reached out and took one of the albums from the

coffee table, opening it on her lap. Lord knew, she'd studied them all so many times that every last picture was permanently imprinted in her mind, but seeing her father's face, so like her own, was a comfort. "A yarn shop?" she echoed, not really absorbing what Alice had said.

"Robert's father provided very well for me," Alice reflected, "and I've got no worries where money is concerned." She closed the suitcases and their fastenings clicked into place one by one. "In my time, very few women had their own businesses, but I always dreamed of it."

Shay looked up and closed the album. "You could teach knitting classes, as well as sell yarn," she speculated, getting into the spirit of things.

Alice nodded. "I've arranged for Ivy to come and pick me up, Shay. She's driving me to a hotel near the airport."

Shay set the album aside, stung. "I would have been glad to—"

"I know, dear. I know. You would have been glad to drive me to the airport tomorrow at the crack of dawn and interrupt your entire day, but I won't let you do it."

"But—"

"No buts. My mind is made up. You've been running yourself ragged, what with our talks about your father and your job and those silly commercials, not to mention the catering service. I want you to eat a good supper, take a nice bath and go to bed early."

Shay couldn't help smiling, though she felt sad. Mitch was gone, Hank was gone, and now Alice was going, too. "Spoken like a true grandmother. Won't you at least let me drive you to your hotel?"

"Absolutely not. Ivy and her young man are taking me and that's final." Alice lowered her voice and bent toward Shay, her eyes sparkling. "I do believe they're planning a rather romantic evening; though, of course, I'll never know."

Shay laughed and shook her head, but inside she wished that she were looking forward to just such an evening with Mitch.

The call came within minutes of Alice's departure with Todd and Ivy. There would be no quiet dinner, no comforting bath, no going to bed early. Rosamond had taken an abrupt turn for the worse, the doctor told Shay, and the diagnosis was pneumonia. Rosamond was being taken by ambulance to the nearest hospital.

Shay raced to Skyler Beach's only hospital, driving so recklessly that it was a miracle she didn't have an accident and end up in the intensive care unit with her mother.

Rosamond had arrived several minutes before her daughter, but it was some time before Shay was permitted to see her. Lying there, she looked small and incredibly emaciated, and there were so many tubes and monitoring devices that it was difficult to get close to her.

Shay had expected this to happen, but now, standing beside her mother's hospital bed, she found that expecting something and being prepared for it are two very different things. She wept silently as she kept her vigil and, toward morning, when Rosamond passed away, there were no more tears to cry.

Shay walked out of the hospital room, down the hallway, into the elevator. She drove home in a stupor—there was a storm gathering in the sky—and somehow gathered the impetus to dial the telephone number Garrett had left for her. The first person to learn of Rosamond's death, besides Shay herself, had to be Riley.

After talking to a housekeeper and then a secretary, Shay was finally put through to Garrett, who told her that Hank and Riley were on another part of the ranch, participating in a roundup.

As the storm outside broke, flinging the rain and the wind at the walls of her tiny house, Shay sank onto her sofa, the telephone balanced on her knees. "Garrett, it's Rosamond. She—she—"

Garrett waited, probably guessing what was coming, for Shay to go on.

"She died early this morning. Pneumonia. Will you tell Riley for me?"

"Of course," Garrett answered gently. "I'm sorry, Amazon. I'm really sorry. Have any arrangements been made?"

"Not yet. I just—" Shay paused, pushing rain-dampened hair back from her forehead. She didn't remember getting wet. "I just got home."

"Are you all right?"

"I think so."

"Call someone. You shouldn't be alone."

No, I shouldn't, Shay thought without any particular emotion, but I am. "I think I'll be all right. You'll—you'll bring Hank home right away?"

"Right away, sweetheart. Hang tough; we're as good as on the road right now."

Shay mumbled a goodbye and hung up the telephone. Then she got up and made her way into her room. Clydesdale, her carousel horse, stood in one corner, his head high, his painted mane flowing.

Shay rested her forehead against his neck and this time she wept for all the happiness that might have been.

Chapter Eleven

Of all Rosamond's husbands, only Riley came to the funeral. A tall man with rough-hewn features and a deep melodic voice that echoed in the hearts of his hearers, he seemed, after all those years of fame, perpetually baffled by the attention paid him. Looking uncomfortable in his dark suit, he delivered a simple and touching eulogy to the remarkably small gathering. It seemed apt that the sky was dark and heavy with an impending storm.

Ivy and Todd were there to offer moral support, though neither of them had really known Rosamond at all. Marvin and Jeannie Reese, recently returned from their trip and still showing signs of jet lag, were present, too, also for Shay's sake. That left Riley, Garrett and Shay herself as true mourners. Garrett's wife, Maggie, was looking after the children.

It wasn't much of a turnout, Shay thought, looking around her. Rosamond had made such a mark on the world, but it appeared that she had touched few individual lives in any lasting way. There was a lesson in that, but Shay was too distracted to make sense of it at the moment.

She wished for Mitch with a poignancy that came from the depths of her and when she turned away from the graveside, he was there. He took both her hands in his.

"I just heard," he said hoarsely. "Shay, I'm sorry."

Shay nodded, her throat thick with tears that made speech impossible.

It began to rain and the mourners dispersed, carrying black umbrellas, their heads down. Shay stood in the open, facing Mitch, wanting nothing so much as to be held by him. He took her arm and led her toward his sleek blue car, parked behind the somber trio of limousines.

After settling her in the passenger seat and closing the door against the drizzling rain, he approached Riley and Garrett. Shay watched through the droplets of water beading on the windshield as he offered his hand, probably in introduction, and said something. The two other men nodded in reply and then Mitch came back to the car.

Shay didn't ask what he'd told them; in essence, she didn't care. "You're here," she remarked. That, for the moment, was enough.

Mitch patted her arm and started up the powerful car. "I'll always be here," he said, and then they were leaving the cemetery behind.

They were almost to Mitch's house when Shay came to her senses. "I should go home. Hank is there, and—"

"Hank is all right."

Shay knew that was true. Hank was safe with Maggie. He'd barely known Rosamond anyway; her death had little meaning to him except as something that had upset his mother. "I didn't expect to grieve, you know," she said in a small voice. "Rosamond and I weren't close."

Mitch was concentrating on the sharp turn onto his property. "She was your mother," he answered, as though that made sense of everything. And in a way, Shay supposed, it did.

The rain was beating down by the time Mitch stopped the car in the driveway, and Mrs. Carraway stood holding the front door open as they dashed toward the house.

"I've made dinner," the housekeeper said in the entryway as Mitch began peeling Shay's sodden suit jacket from her shoulders. "I'll go home now, if that's all right."

"Be careful," Mitch said, without looking at the woman. "It's nasty out there."

Mrs. Carraway hesitated. "Mrs. Kendall?" she said, her eyes steady on Shay's face though it was clear that she would rather have looked away. "I'm truly sorry about your mother."

"Thank you," Shay answered. Her teeth began to chatter and she hugged herself, trying to get warm.

Mrs. Carraway went out and Mitch lifted Shay into his arms and carried her up the stairs and into his bedroom. The hot tub had been filled and the water steamed invitingly.

Mitch set Shay on her feet and, after flipping a switch that made the water in the tub churn and bubble, he gently removed the rest of her clothes. Then he lowered her into the wondrously warm, welcoming water.

Shay shuddered violently as her cold-numbed body adjusted itself to the change of temperature. "F-feels go-good," she said.

Mitch sat on his heels beside the tub and reached out to touch her hair. "You look like a lady in need of a glass of brandy and a good meal. Are you hungry?"

Shay felt guilty surprise. "Yes," she marveled. "That's awful, isn't it?"

"Awful? I don't follow your logic, princess." His hand lingered in her hair, and it felt as good to her as the surging warmth of the hot tub.

"I just left my mother's funeral. I shouldn't be here."

Mitch shook his head in exasperation, but his eyes were gentle and so was his voice. "Next you'll be asking for a hair shirt. You belong here, with me. Especially now."

"But Hank—"

"If you want Hank, I'll go and get him."

Shay bit her lower lip. "You'd do that?"

"Of course I would."

"I—I'd like to call him later, to make sure he's okay."

"Fine." Mitch bent, kissed her forehead and then left the room. He returned several minutes later carrying a tray of food, two crystal snifters and a bottle of brandy.

Shay ate without leaving the hot tub and then slid the tray away. Mitch was sitting on the tiled edge, wearing a blue terry-cloth bathrobe and dangling his hairy legs in the water.

Having finished her dinner and a hefty dose of brandy, the warm water soothing her further, Shay began to yawn. With a tender light in his dark eyes, Mitch helped her from the tub, dried her gently with a soft towel and bundled her into a bathrobe much like the one he was wearing. That done, he guided Shay to the bed and tucked her in.

He kissed her forehead and then turned away. Shay watched, half-awake, as he shed his blue bathrobe and flung it back toward the bed, just missing the target, and then lowered himself into the hot tub, his tanned and muscled body hidden from view.

Shay was disappointed. "Did you know that you're beautiful?" she yawned.

Mitch chuckled and braced himself against the edge of

the tub, his arms folded on the tiles, his brandy glass in one hand. "Am I?"

"Ummm-hmmm."

"Sleep, princess."

Shay stretched, warm in Mitch's bathrobe and his bed, her mind floating. "I wished for you…and you were there… just like a prince in a fairy tale. You won't…you won't leave me, will you?"

"I won't leave you." The words were gruff, and they seemed to come from a great distance. "Go to sleep, my love."

"Come here. Hold me."

She heard a splashing sound as Mitch got out of the hot tub, and watched as he dried himself with a huge green towel. And then he was there, beside her, strong and warm, his flesh a hard wall that kept the rest of the world at bay.

They slept for a long time, and then awakened simultaneously to make love. The world was dark and the only sound Shay could hear, besides her own breathing and Mitch's, was the bubbling of the hot tub.

She crooned and stretched in luxurious abandon as he kissed and tongued her breasts and her stomach, stroked her with his hands. Shay was seized by a keening tension as Mitch loved her and she clasped his shoulders in her hands. "Now, now," she breathed.

He parted her legs with a motion of one knee and took her in one swift, masterful stroke, filling her with himself, driving out all thoughts of death and sadness and loss.

With a cry, Shay arched against him, her body acting on its own, clutching at life, affirming life, demanding life. "Oh, God," she gasped, breathless. "Mitch, Mitch—"

He fit his hands beneath her quivering bottom and lifted her up, to possess her more fully, to be possessed by her.

"It's all right," he said to that part of Shay that was ashamed to feel such primitive need. There were no words, however, as their bodies waged their tender and furious battle, rising and falling in a feverish search for fulfillment that ended in a hoarse shout for Mitch and a sob for Shay.

He held her, his chest heaving and damp beneath her cheek, as she cried.

"How could I—how could I do that? My mother—"

Mitch's hand smoothed her hair back from her face and then his arm tightened around her. "Shhh. You're alive, Shay. Your body was reminding you of that. It's an instinctive thing, so stop tormenting yourself."

"You're just trying to make me feel better!"

"Of course I am, I love you. But what I said was true, nevertheless. Any brush with death, direct or indirect, will produce that response in a healthy person."

He spoke with such authority. Shay thought of Mitch's encounters with death, all chronicled so forthrightly in his books, and wondered whom he'd been with afterward. Some Colombian señorita? "That lady pilot, in Chapter Six of *The Connection*—"

Mitch gave an exaggerated snore.

Shay jabbed him in the ribs and then, conversely, cuddled even closer. She fell asleep and dreamed that she and Mitch were making love on the lush floor of a Colombian jungle, vines and tropical plants and enormous, colorful flowers making a canopy for their bed.

Life went on, Shay discovered, and it carried her with it. She said goodbye to Riley and Garrett and Maggie, got Hank into school and gave two weeks' notice at her job.

"We'll be sorry to see you go," Marvin said quietly, sitting behind his broad, paper-littered desk. "But Jeannie and I both wish you the best of luck wth your business."

Shay let out a sigh of relief. Marvin was a reasonable man, but she had been worried that he'd think her ungrateful. "Thank you."

Behind his fashionable wire glasses, Marvin's eyes twinkled. "Those commercials you made were first-rate, Shay. I couldn't have done a better job myself."

Shay grinned. "It'll be years before I live those spots down," she answered. "Yesterday, in the supermarket, a little girl recognized me as the bee and called her mother over to meet me. It was half an hour before I could get back to my shopping. To make matters worse, Hank is selling my autograph."

Marvin sat back in his chair, chuckling. His checkered jacket appeared capable of leaping into the conversation on its own, and Shay blinked as he replied, "You've definitely hit the big time."

Shay sighed philosophically. "Not really. He charges more for Riley's signature. The poor man must have written his name a hundred times while he was with Hank, just to keep the kid in spending money."

"Enterprising boy, that Hank," Marvin said with quiet pride. "Takes after his mother."

"That's a compliment, I hope."

"Absolutely. If you need help of any kind, Shay, you come to Jeannie and me."

Shay nodded and looked away, to hide the sudden tears that sprang to her eyes. "I'd better get back to work," she said softly, turning to go and then pausing at the door. "About my replacement—"

"I think Ivy can handle the job, don't you?"

Shay was delighted. She'd planned to suggest Ivy, but Marvin had saved her the trouble. "Yes."

"Get a new receptionist, then," Marvin said brusquely, tackling his paperwork with a flourish meant to hide emotions of his own. "Do it right away. Ivy will need to concentrate on learning your job and I want the transition to be made as smoothly as possible."

Shay saluted briskly, her lips twitching, and hurried out. Ivy was standing up at her computer terminal, at hopeful attention.

"The job is yours," Shay whispered.

"Ya-hoo!" Ivy shrieked.

Shay had obviously painted part of the old house herself, in a very light shade of blue and a pristine white. Both colors were well represented not only on the front of her coveralls but on her chin and her nose, too. Watching her, Mitch ached with the love of her, the need of her.

He'd been hard at work on Rosamond's book for several weeks and now it was done, ready for Shay's final approval. He cleared his throat and she lifted her eyes to his face, her conversation with a similarly clad Alice falling off in midsentence.

"Mitch," she said.

Alice rubbed her hands down the legs of her tiny coveralls and did a disappearing act.

"The book?" Shay whispered.

Mitch extended a fat manila envelope. "Here it is, princess."

She approached him, took the envelope, but her wide eyes never left his face. "I'll read it tonight," she said.

"I've missed you," he replied.

"We've both been busy." Her eyes were averted now. "Y-you're starting a new book, aren't you?"

Mitch sighed. The Alan Roget project was something they hadn't discussed. "I've gathered some material, yes."

She paled. "I—I guess I'd better get back to work," she said.

Something in her manner panicked Mitch. He wanted to shout at her, grasp her arm, anything. Instead he simply said her name.

Shay turned away from him, holding the manuscript in both arms. "It's over now, I guess," she said distractedly. "You have your life and I have mine."

"Over?" Mitch was stunned. He reached out then and caught her arm in one hand and wrenched her around to face him. "What the hell are you talking about?"

"W-we'll both be so busy now—"

"Busy?"

There were tears gathering along her eyelashes and her lower lip was quivering. "Shall I call you if there are any changes to be made? In—in the book, I mean?"

Mitch looked around him then, at the beautifully restored walls and ceilings, and suddenly he thought he understood what was happening. He'd served his purpose and now there was no place in Shay's life for him. "Yeah," he bit out, letting go of her arm. "You do that." He turned and walked out, not daring to look back.

Shay sat down on the newspaper-covered floor and opened the packet containing Mitch's manuscript. She had to rub her eyes several times before the words would come into focus.

"Where's Mitch?" Alice asked innocently, holding out a cup of coffee to Shay and sipping at one of her own.

Shay felt hollow and broken. "He's gone."

Alice manuevered herself into a cross-legged position on the floor, facing her granddaughter. "Gone? I don't like the sound of that, Shay. It has a permanent ring."

"It is permanent," Shay confirmed sadly.

"Are you mad?" Alice asked in a low incredulous tone. "That man loves you, Shay, and you love him!"

"You don't understand. H-he's writing another book."

By now, Alice was a member of the necessarily small group of people who knew that Mitch Prescott and the mysterious "Zebulon" were one and the same person. She had read his books avidly, one after another, Shay knew, so she should have gotten the point. It was obvious from what she said next she hadn't. "Isn't that what writers do? Finish one book and start another?"

Shay was suddenly annoyed, and the sharpness of her tone reflected that, as did the hot color in her cheeks. "It isn't the writing that bothers me! It's the research! Alice, he could be killed, captured, tortured!"

"That's why you're throwing him over? Shay, I thought you were made of better stuff."

Alice's words, though moderately spoken, stung Shay. "I'd be sweating blood every time he left the house, Alice! I love him too much to—"

"On the contrary, dear," Alice broke in quietly. "It seems to me that you don't love him enough."

Shay leaped to her feet, insulted, and stomped out of the room, out of the house. Alice could get back to her apartment on her own, she knew; she had bought a small car from Marvin Reese and was already an expert at navigating every part of Skyler Beach. Shay got into her own car and drove away, going far too fast.

She got a speeding ticket before she had traveled four blocks, and the fact that she deserved it did nothing to temper her mood. By the time she got back to her house, she was a wreck.

When Hank came home from school, he took one look at his mother and asked if he could go over to his friend Louie's house to play until dinner. Feeling guilty, Shay smiled and ruffled his hair. "Have you got any homework?"

"They don't give much homework in the first grade, Mom. I can do it when I get home," he said indulgently.

"Oh."

Hank was perched on the arm of her chair, his eyes taking in the paint smudges on her face, her tangled hair, the coveralls. "Do you like your new job, Mom?"

"I haven't started it yet, but I'm sure I'll like it a lot."

"Will you have to dress like that?"

Shay laughed. "No. I painted my office today, that's all."

"I thought the contractors were supposed to do all that stuff."

"I wanted to do my office myself. And don't ask me why, tiger, because I don't know."

"Are we going to live over there, where your office is, I mean?"

Shay shook her head. "There won't be room, once all the other shops open. I rented the last one today."

"You didn't rent Grammie's knit shop out, did you?" Hank demanded. Rosamond had always been Rosamond to him, but Alice, who had won his affections instantly, was "Grammie."

"Of course I didn't," Shay said with a frown. "What made you ask a thing like that?"

Hank's thin shoulders moved in a shrug. "I was just wondering."

Shay didn't believe him. Somehow, in the uncanny way of a child, he'd sensed that she and Alice had had words. She felt ashamed of her outburst now and made a mental note to call Alice and apologize the moment Hank went outside to play. "Grammie's looking forward to having you help her at the shop."

Hank looked manfully apologetic. "I won't be able to go every day. I've got Little League practice and stuff like that."

"I'm sure Grammie will understand."

"And the guys might tease me if they see me messing around with yarn and junk."

Shay kept a straight face. "They might."

Hank brightened. "I'd better go and find Louie now. See ya."

"You be back here in half an hour, buddy," Shay warned. "Supper will be ready then."

"Okay, Mom," he called, the sound mingling with the slamming of the front door.

Shay got out of her chair, took a quick shower and put on her bathrobe and slippers. This was a night to be dissolute, she decided as she put hot dogs on to boil and opened a can of pork and beans to serve with them. After tearing the top off a bag of potato chips, she dialed Alice's number.

"I'm sorry," she said without preamble.

"Call Mitch Prescott and tell him the same thing," Alice immediately responded.

Shay stiffened. "I will not."

"You're a fool, then," Alice answered. "A man like that doesn't come around every few months, like quarterly taxes and the newest reality show, you know."

"You're impossible!"

"Yes," Alice agreed. "But you love me."

Shay laughed in spite of herself. "That's true. I'll see you tomorrow, then?"

"Absolutely. My cash register and some of my yarn are supposed to be delivered."

Shay was hanging up the telephone just as Hank dashed in, flushed from some backyard game and ready for his supper. He ate and took his bath without complaint, then settled down to watch the one hour of television allowed him on a school night.

Shay settled into the easy chair in the living room and began reading Mitch's manuscript again. It was a great improvement over the first draft, which had been wonderful in its own right, and she again had the feeling that she was meeting Rosamond Dallas for the first time. She stopped long enough to see that Hank brushed his teeth and said his prayers, but the story of her mother's life drew her back.

She turned the last page at three-fourteen that morning, wide awake and awed by the quiet power of Mitch's writing. She had expected the book to need minor changes. But it was perfect as it was. Unfortunately. Revisions would have given her an excuse to work closely with Mitch again.

Stiff and sore, Shay set the manuscript carefully aside and rose from her chair. Working with Mitch would have been a foolish indulgence, considering her decision to end the relationship. No, it was better this way, she told herself—she would simply call him in the morning and tell him that she could see no problems with the book being published just as it was. Their association would then be officially ended, and Shay could go on with her life.

What kind of life was it going to be, without Mitch? The question chewed at Shay long after she'd fallen into bed. Sure, she had Hank and Alice and her business, but what was she going to do without those fevered bouts of lovemaking that always left her exhausted but strangely revitalized, too? What was she going to do without the laughter and the fights and the adventures?

Adventures. Shay sighed. That was the key word. She simply wasn't cut out to sit at home, chewing her fingernails, while the man she loved risked his life in order to research some new journalistic feat.

Alice's accusation came back to haunt her then, echoing

in her mind. She did *too* love Mitch enough. She loved him, as she had maintained to Alice, too much. If she married Mitch and then he was killed, she would be devastated.

She sat up in bed with a jolt. Only in that moment did it occur to her that she would be just as devastated if he died without ever marrying her, ever touching her again. Why had she thought that separating herself from Mitch would save him?

The next morning was splashed in the singular glory of early October and Shay drove slowly up the hill to Mitch's house. The distant sound of a hammer made her walk around back instead of ringing the doorbell.

Mitch was kneeling on the roof of the playhouse, half a dozen nails jutting from his mouth, his tanned chest and shoulders bared to the crisp bite of the weather. Shay stood watching him for a moment, her heart caught in her throat.

He stopped swinging the hammer to look at her, and there was no welcome, no tenderness, in his eyes. "Well," he said.

Shay was careful not to reveal how much his coolness hurt her. "If you have a minute, I'd like to talk."

He began to drive another nail into another tiny shingle. "I'm busy."

Shay was shaken to her core, but she stood her ground. "I came to return the manuscript, Mitch," she lied. In truth, the book had been an afterthought, an excuse.

He went on working. "Leave it with Mrs. Carraway," he said brusquely.

"You aren't going to let me apologize, are you?" Shay reddened, embarrassed and hurt and yet unable to turn and walk away.

"Apologize all you want. I'm through playing the game, Shay."

"The game? What game?"

Now, Mitch set the hammer aside, but he remained on the roof of the playhouse and his manner was no friendlier. "You know what I'm talking about, Shay. You come to me when you need comfort or a roll in the hay, and then you run away again."

"A roll in the—my God, that's crude!"

The broad, sun-browned shoulders moved in a shrug cold enough to chill Shay. "Maybe so, but it's the truth. You want the fun, but you're too cowardly to make a real commitment, aren't you? Well, get yourself another flunky."

"You said you loved me!"

A small shingle splintered under the force of a blow from Mitch's hammer. "I do," he said, without looking at Shay. "But I don't want to play house anymore. I need the real thing."

Baffled and as broken as that shingle Mitch had just destroyed, Shay turned and hurried away.

Chapter Twelve

If there was one thing Shay learned in the coming weeks, it was how little she knew about the catering business. She made all the standard mistakes and a few new ones to boot. By the end of October her confidence was sorely shaken.

Alice lifted the furry Halloween costume she was making for Hank to her mouth and bit off a thread with her teeth. While her grandmother sewed at the kitchen table, Shay was frantically mixing the ingredients for enough lasagne to feed fifty people.

"You expected starting your own company to be easy, Shay?"

Shay sighed as she wrapped another panful of lasagne and put it into the freezer. "Of course I didn't. But I have to admit that I expected a lack of business to be the problem, not a surplus. I have four wedding receptions and people are already calling about Thanksgiving. Who ever heard of having Thanksgiving dinner catered, for heaven's sake?"

Alice chuckled. "The solution seems obvious. Hire some help."

Shay leaned back against the counter in a rare moment of indolence. "I hate to do that, Alice. If things slow down, I'd have to let people go."

"You'll just have to make it clear from the beginning that the work could be temporary."

"All right, fine. But how am I going to make the time to interview these people, let alone train them to cook?"

Alice let the costume rest in her lap. "Dear, dear, you are frazzled. You simply call the junior college. They have a culinary program, you know. Ask them to send over a few prospects. I'll do the interviewing for you, if you'd like, right in my shop. If any seem promising, I'll send them on to you."

"You're brilliant," Shay said, bending to plant a kiss on her grandmother's forehead. "How in the world did I ever get along without you?"

Alice chuckled and went back to her sewing. "What are you wearing to the Reeses' Halloween party?" she asked over the whir of Shay's portable machine.

Shay was mixing tomato sauce to pour over a layer of ricotta cheese. "I'm not going."

The sewing machine stopped. "Not going? But it's going to be marvelous, with everyone in costume.…"

"I plan to drop off the food and then leave, Alice, and that's that."

"You're no fun at all. Where's your spirit of adventure?"

Shay remembered a few of the "adventures" she'd had with Mitch Prescott and felt sad. "I've never been the adventurous type. Besides, I don't have a costume."

"You've got that bee suit. Wear that."

"Wear it? When I've been all this time trying to live

it down? No way. I'll stay home and greet the trick-or-treaters, thank you very much."

"Party pooper."

Shay laughed. "What are you going to wear, by the way?"

The sewing machine was going again. "I'm dressing up as a punk rocker," Alice answered placidly.

Shay shook her head. It seemed odd that her grandmother was so full of life and she herself could think of nothing but work. She should wear the bee suit for Halloween after all, she thought. It was a costume that suited a drone.

Mitch was tired from the flight and sick to his stomach. Meetings with unrepentant serial killers tended to have that effect on him.

Mrs. Carraway was busy carving an enormous pumpkin at the kitchen table. "Hello, Mr. Prescott," she said, beaming. "Welcome back." She started to get up and Mitch gestured for her to stay put.

The last thing he wanted was food. He rummaged through a cupboard until he found a bottle of Scotch and poured himself a generous helping. "What are you doing?" he asked, frowning at the pile of pumpkin pulp and seeds on the table.

Mrs. Carraway arched an eyebrow, either at his drink or his question; Mitch didn't know which and didn't care. "Why, I'm making a jack-o'-lantern. It's Halloween."

Mitch lifted his glass in a silent salute to the holiday. He needed a shower and a shave and about eighteen hours of sleep and he'd just spent two days talking to a man who was a whole hell of a lot scarier than your run-of-the-mill hobgoblin. "How fitting," he said.

The housekeeper gave him a curious look, probably

thinking that she'd signed on with a reprobate. "Are you all right, Mr. Prescott?"

He thought of Shay and how badly he needed her to hold him in her arms and remind him of all the things that made life good and wholesome and right. "No," he answered, refilling his glass and starting toward the doorway. He paused. "The world can be a very ugly place, Mrs. Carraway. You see, for some people, every day is Halloween." He lifted the glass and took a burning gulp of Scotch. "The trouble is, they're bona fide ghouls and they don't wear costumes so that you can recognize them."

Mrs. Carraway looked really worried. "Won't you have something to eat, Mr. Prescott? It's almost suppertime."

"I may never eat again," Mitch answered, thinking of the things Alan Roget had confessed to him. He shook his head as he climbed the stairs, drink in hand. The tough journalist. He had walked out of that interview feeling as though he'd been exposed to some plague of the spirit and he'd been back in his hotel room all of five seconds before being violently ill.

Mitch entered his massive bedroom and it was empty, though specters of Shay were everywhere: lounging in the hot tub, kneeling on the bed, counting the extra tooth-brushes he kept in the bathroom cabinet.

He drained the glass of Scotch and rubbed his eyes, tired to the very core of his being. "Shay," he said. "Shay."

Shay felt an intuitive pull toward Mitch's house; the sensation was so strong that it distracted her from the food she'd prepared for the Reeses' Halloween party. She hurried to finish packing the cheeseballs and puff pastries and then went into her office to dial the familiar number.

This is silly, she told herself as Mitch's phone began to ring.

"Prescott residence," Mrs. Carraway answered briskly.

Shay bit her lower lip. She should hang up. Calling Mitch was asking for rejection; he'd made his feelings perfectly clear that day when Shay had gone to him to apologize. "Th-this is Shay Kendall, Mrs. Carraway."

"Thank heaven," the housekeeper whispered, with a note of alarm in her voice that made Shay's backbone go rigid. "Oh, Mrs. Kendall, I have no right interfering like this—I'll probably be fired—but Mr. Prescott is in a terrible way."

"What do you mean? What's wrong?"

"He's been away on business for several days, and he just got home an hour or so ago. He said some very strange things, Mrs. Kendall, about every day being Halloween for some people."

Shay closed her eyes, thinking of the monsters that had populated Mitch's books. "Is he there now?"

Mrs. Carraway suddenly burst into tears. "Please come, Mrs. Kendall. Please. I don't know what to do!"

Shay looked down at her watch and bit her lower lip. She had to deliver the food to Jeannie and Marvin's town house, but after that the evening would be free. "I'll be there as soon as I can," she promised. "Don't worry. Everything will be all right."

Lofty words, Shay thought as she hung up the telephone in her office. Suppose everything wasn't all right? Suppose Mitch wouldn't even see her?

After loading the Reeses' hors d'oeuvres into her new van, Shay went back inside her building to find Alice just closing up her yarn shop. "Something is wrong with Mitch," she told her grandmother bluntly. "I've got to go to him as soon as I deliver the Reeses' order. Hank is going trick-or-treating with his friend Louie at six, but if I'm late…"

Alice looked concerned. "Of course I'll look after him, my dear. You take all the time you need."

Shay kissed her grandmother's lovely crinkled cheek and hurried out to her car. She made the drive to Marvin and Jeannie's house in record time, and virtually shoved the boxes of carefully prepared cheeseballs and crab puffs and paté-spread crackers into the hands of a maid hired to serve that evening.

Everything within Shay was geared toward reaching Mitch at the soonest possible moment, but some niggling little instinct within argued that she needed a way to get past whatever defenses he might have erected against her. She stopped at her house for a few minutes and then went on to Mitch's.

Mrs. Carraway answered the doorbell almost before Shay had lowered her finger from the button. If Mitch's housekeeper was surprised to find a velveteen bee standing on the doorstep, she didn't show it.

"Upstairs," she whispered. "In his room."

Shay made her cumbersome way up the stairs. This was no time to try to hide the fact that she knew the way to Mitch Prescott's bedroom.

She tapped at the closed door.

"Go away!" Mitch bellowed from within. His voice was thick. Was he drunk?

Shay drew a deep breath and knocked again, harder this time.

There was muffled swearing and then the door swung open. "Dammit, I said—" Mitch's voice fell away and his haunted eyes took in Shay's bee suit with disbelief.

"Trick or treat?" she chimed.

"Good God," Mitch replied, but he stepped back so that Shay could enter the room.

She immediately pulled off the hood with its bobbing

antennae and tossed it aside. After that, she struggled out of the rest of the suit, too. Mitch looked a little disappointed when he saw that she was wearing jeans and a T-shirt underneath, but then he turned away from her, his broad shoulders tensed.

"What's wrong, Mitch?" she asked softly, afraid to touch him and yet drawn toward him at the same time. She stood close behind Mitch and wrapped her arms around his middle. "Tell me what's the matter."

He turned in her arms, and she saw hurt in his eyes, terrible, jarring hurt, and disillusionment, too. "You don't want to know," he said hoarsely.

"Yes, I do, so start talking."

Remembering all the times when Mitch had been there for her, Shay took the glass from his hand—he'd clearly had too much to drink—and set it aside. She filled the empty hot tub with warm water and flicked the switch that activated the jets beneath the surface. She took Mitch's T-shirt off over his head and then removed his shoes and his jeans, too. He was still gaping at her when she began maneuvering him toward the bubbling hot tub.

"Get in, Prescott," she said in a tough, side-of-the-mouth voice, "or it won't be pretty!"

A grin broke through the despair in Mitch's face, though just briefly, and he slid into the tub. Shay kicked off her shoes, and then stripped completely, enjoying the amazement in his eyes.

She stepped into the tub, standing behind Mitch, working the awesome tension from his shoulders with her fingers. "Talk to me, Mitch."

Haltingly, he began to tell her about his interviews with Alan Roget. Shay had read about Roget, knew that he was a vicious killer with a penchant for calling attention to himself. She listened staunchly as Mitch poured out the ugly, inhumane things he'd be expected to write about.

When Mitch turned to her, there were tears on his beard-stubbled cheeks. Shay held him, her hands moving gently up and down his heaving back, her tears flowing as freely as his.

"How can I write about this bastard?" he demanded once, in raspy horror. "It makes me sick just to think about him!"

Shay caught Mitch's strong face in her hands and held it firmly. "You have to write about him, Mitch, because there are a lot of other psychos out there and if one woman recognizes the type and stays alive because of it—just *one woman,* Mitch—it will be worth all the pain!"

"I can't do it!" Mitch roared, and then a grating sob tore itself from the depths of him. He shuddered in Shay's arms. "Dammit, I can't do it anymore!"

"Yes you can, Mitch. I'll help you."

He drew back from her, studying her face with those tormented, fatigue-shadowed eyes. "You'll what?"

"I know you don't want a relationship with me," Shay said, wondering where she'd found the strength to admit to something that had been impossible to face only an hour before. "So there won't be any strings attached."

"Strings?"

"I love you, Mitch, regardless of how you feel about me. Tonight, I'm going to drag you back from everything that's ugly and base if I have to drive you out of your mind to do it."

She held her breath and plunged under the water to pull the plug, and the water began to drain away, but neither she nor Mitch made any move to climb out of the tub. "Your therapy begins right now," Shay said.

* * *

Because of Shay, and only because of Shay, Mitch was able to fly back to Joliet for one final interview with Roget and then to return home and write about the man. It was hell, and he swore he'd never tackle a project like it again, but by Thanksgiving he'd roughed out the skeleton of a first draft.

Shay sat on her sofa with her feet tucked underneath her, reading the last chapter. The scent of the turkey Alice had cooked still hung in the air, mingling with the spicy aroma of the pumpkin pie that would be served later. Mitch tried not to watch Shay's every expression as she read, but his eyes strayed in her direction at regular intervals.

Hank, worn out by a day of celebrating, was asleep on the couch, his head resting on Shay's lap. Mitch grinned, remembering the game of Dungeons and Dragons he and the boy had played earlier.

To keep from looking at Shay again, he watched Alice, who was sitting in a rocking chair, knitting a bright red sweater. These two women and the boy made up a family Mitch wanted very much to be a part of, but he couldn't risk proposing to Shay again; their relationship was too delicate for that.

Sitting on the floor, Mitch cupped his hands behind his head and leaned back against the chair he didn't feel like sitting in, grinning when Alice caught him staring at her and winking mischievously in response.

Shay finally finished reading and set the manuscript aside. Her eyes were averted and there was a slight flush in her cheeks and Mitch sat bolt upright.

"You don't like it," he said, hating his own vulnerability to this woman's opinion.

Shay met his gaze with a level stare of her own. "You

detest this guy, Mitch. The other chapters were okay, but this one is a—a vendetta."

"Of course I detest Roget! He's a murderer!"

"Your emotions have no place in the book, Mitch. You're a journalist and you've got to be objective."

Hank stirred and muttered something and Mitch thrust himself to his feet, bending to gather the little boy up in his arms. "I'll put him to bed," he said through his teeth.

Shay smiled. "My, but you take criticism well, Mr. Prescott."

Mitch carried Hank into his room, helped him out of his clothes and into bed. "I wish you were around all the time," the child said with a yawn as Mitch tucked the blankets in around him. "It's almost like having a dad."

Mitch smiled and rumpled Hank's hair with one hand. "I'm doing my best, fella," he said quietly. "I'm doing my best."

"Are you going to marry my mom?"

Mitch thought for a moment, trying to find the right words. "I hope so," he finally said.

Hank snuggled down into the covers and yawned again, his eyes closed now. "I hope so, too," he answered.

When Mitch returned to the living room he was shocked to find Shay standing on the couch, holding out a chair, lion-tamer style, and pretending to brandish a whip with one hand. "Back, back!" she cried. To Alice, she said, "There's nothing more dangerous than a writer who's just been told that his last chapter stinks!"

Mitch was having a hard time keeping a straight face. "Oh, so now it stinks, does it?"

Shay clamped her nose with two fingers and Mitch was lost. He laughed, wrested the chair from her and pulled her down off the couch and into his arms.

"I think the pie's done," Alice chimed, beating a hasty retreat into the kitchen.

Mitch kissed the bridge of Shay's nose. "You wanna know what makes me maddest of all, lady? You're right about that last chapter. Still, you could have spared my feelings."

Impishly, she pinched him with the fingers of both hands. "I ask you, did you spare my feelings when my cheeseballs bombed at the mayor's party? No. You said you wouldn't feed them to a dog!"

"Actually, I may have spoken prematurely. I met a Doberman once, in Rio, who richly deserved one."

She laughed and the sound made a sweet, lonely ache inside Mitch. He'd never wanted anything as much as he wanted to marry this woman and share his life and his bed with her. As it was, they were together only when their schedules permitted, which wasn't often. "I love you," he said.

There was a puzzled look in her wide eyes for a moment, then she stood on tiptoe to kiss his chin. "Stay with me."

"I can't and you know it," Mitch snapped, irritated. "What would we tell Hank in the morning? That we're carrying on a cheap affair?"

Her lower lip jutted out. "Is that what you think this is, Mitch?"

He held Shay closer, desperate for the feel and scent and warmth of her. "You know damned well that that isn't what I think!"

She pinched him again, her eyes dancing with mischief. "Not even after what we did in my office yesterday?" she whispered.

Heat flowed up over Mitch's chest in a flood, surging along his neck and into his face. He swatted Shay's delectable rear end, hard, with both hands. "You little vamp, are you trying to drive me crazy or what?"

She wriggled against him. "Ooo-la-la!" she teased.

"Shay!"

She was running her hands up and down his hips and his sides. He remembered the episode she had mentioned a moment before, and Halloween night, when she'd saved him from demons that had nothing to do with the thirty-first of October. "Stay with me," she said again. "We'll set the alarm and you can leave before Hank gets up."

He set her away from him. "No, dammit. No."

Shay's eyes widened with confusion and hurt as he snatched up his jacket and the copy of the new book and started toward the door. "Mitch—?"

He paused, his hand on the knob. "I'll call you tomorrow," he said, and then he opened the door and went out.

She followed him down the walk, to the front gate and as he tried to outdistance her, she broke into a run. "What's wrong?" she asked, taking hold of his sleeve and stopping him. "Tell me what's wrong!"

"We're wrong, Shay. You and I."

"You don't mean that."

"Not the way you're taking it, no." Mitch sighed and scanned the cold November sky before forcing his eyes back to her face. "We should be able to share a bed without having to orchestrate it, Shay."

She receded. "You mean, we should be married."

"You said it, I didn't. Remember that." He opened the gate, went through it and got into his car.

Alice was in the kitchen dishing up pumpkin pie. Shay had baked so much of it for her Thanksgiving customers that she couldn't face the stuff, so she poured herself a cup of coffee and sat down at the table.

"Since nobody's volunteering anything, I'll butt my nose in and ask. What's the matter now?" Alice might have looked like a mild-mannered little old lady, but she was really a storm trooper, Shay had decided, undaunted by any assignment.

"Mitch wants to get married," Shay said despondently.

"Gee, that's terrible," came the sardonic response. "The man ought to be horsewhipped."

"It could be terrible," Shay insisted sadly. "I might be just like my mother and she was—you know how she was."

"Your great-uncle Edgar was a chicken thief, but I've yet to catch you in somebody else's coop."

Shay had to chuckle. Maybe she'd have a piece of pie after all. "Your point is well taken, but the fact remains that marriage scares me to death."

Alice refused to smile; she was clearly annoyed. "Mitch Prescott is a very fine man and you're going to fool around and lose him," she fretted.

"Have some pie," Shay said.

"I've lost my appetite," Alice snapped. "Good night and I'll see myself out."

Shay stood up. "Please, don't go."

"You should have said that to your man, Shay," Alice replied, and she walked stiffly out into the living room.

Shay followed, clenching and unclenching her hands, feeling like a miserable child. "I did. He wouldn't stay with me. He didn't want Hank to wake up and find him here."

"At least one of you has some sense," Alice murmured, her exasperation fading into tenderness. "If Mitch were your husband, there wouldn't be so many logistical problems, Shay."

"I can't marry him just so we won't have to explain going to bed!"

"You can't marry him because you're afraid, yet you love him, I know you do. And he loves you." Alice sighed, poised to leave. "Take a chance, Shay. Take a chance."

"I did that once before! And the man I loved ran off with a librarian!"

"It's a damned good thing that he did, kiddo, or you might never have found yourself. Look at you. You're in business for yourself. You're strong and you're smart and you're beautiful. What in Sam Hill do you want, a written guarantee from God?"

Shay just stared at her grandmother, stuck for an answer.

"That's what I thought. Well, you'd better not hold your breath, Shay, because we don't get any guarantees in this life." With that, Alice Bretton opened the door and walked out.

Shay went to the window and watched until her grandmother was safely in her car, then returned to the kitchen and sat staring at her half-eaten piece of pumpkin pie with its dollop of whipped cream. She stuck a finger into the topping and dolefully licked at it.

Some Thanksgiving this was. Hank was asleep and Alice had gone home in a huff and Mitch… She didn't even want to think about Mitch.

The next day she woke up with a chest cold and had to stay home, trusting Barbara and Louise, the two women she'd hired through the culinary program at the college, to run the business.

Half-buried in tissue boxes and decongestants of all sorts, Shay lay on her sofa, grimly watching game shows and soap operas and trying to be civil in the face of Hank's determined attempts to nurse her back to health.

By the time he finally gave up and went out to play with his friends, Shay was in a dreadful mood. The telephone began to ring and she made her way across the room, grumbling all the way.

"Hello," she said through her nose.

The response was a rich masculine chuckle. "Good Lord," Mitch marveled. "What's the matter with you?"

"I'm thick," Shay answered with dignity.

He laughed. "I would describe you as thin."

"Thick ath in not well," Shay labored to say.

"I'll be over in ten minutes."

Before Shay could protest that plan, Mitch had hung up. Her head pounding, she stumbled back to the couch and huddled under the afghan she'd crocheted during her earth-mother phase. She coughed and pulled the cover up over her head.

It would save the paramedics the trouble.

Chapter Thirteen

The two small shops on the first floor of Shay's building were all decorated for Christmas. She marveled at the industry of their proprietors; Jenna and Betty must have worked all of Thanksgiving weekend to assemble such grandeur, she thought.

Though her own office and kitchen were, of course, on the first floor, too, Shay climbed the stairs to see if Alice and the woman who owned the candle shop had followed suit. They had.

Shay crammed her hands into the pockets of her coat and went downstairs by the back way, feeling a little guilty because she hadn't put out so much as a sprig of holly.

Both Barbara and Louise were busy in the huge kitchen, with its big tables and commercial refrigerators. Shay watched them for a few moments, unnoticed, trying to imagine what their lives had been like.

Barbara, a plump woman with beautifully coiffed hair,

was rolling out dough for an order of quiche. She had signed up for the culinary program at the college after her husband of twenty-eight years had divorced her for another woman. Louise, a small and perpetually smiling blonde, had lost her husband in a car accident a year before. She, like Barbara, had never held a paying job in her life, and yet she'd been faced with the prospect of earning a living.

Inwardly, Shay sighed. These two women had given their best to their marriages, and where had it gotten them? They had been betrayed, abandoned.

At that moment Barbara spotted her and smiled. "Good morning, Ms. Kendall. Feeling better?"

The inside of Shay's chest still felt raw and hollow, while her sinuses were stuffed, but the worst was past. Mitch had coddled her shamefully. "Yes," she said. "Yes, I feel better."

"You look like you dragged yourself down here," Louise observed in her forthright way. "Why don't you go home and rest? We can manage things on this end."

Shay looked upon the two women with admiration. Okay, so life hadn't gone as they'd planned, but they were survivors. They had tallied what skills they had—neither was a stranger to cooking for a crowd—and they'd gone out and found a market for what they knew. "I've got some book work to do in the office," she said in reply to Louise's well-meant suggestion. "But it probably would be better if you two handled the cooking today."

"I could make the deliveries, too," Barbara ventured.

I must look like I'm on my last legs, Shay thought. She nodded and went into her small office, closing the door behind her.

Her desk was piled with telephone messages, bills from food suppliers, catalogs offering fancy ice molds and serving dishes. She sighed as she sat down in her chair. She had her own business now, and she was keeping her head above water financially, which was something in the first year, so where was all the delight, all the fulfillment, all the pride of accomplishment?

Barbara and Louise were laughing in the kitchen, their voices ringing. They sounded happy.

Shay opened a ledger and tried to concentrate on debits and credits, but her mind kept straying back to those two women in the kitchen. She found herself envying them. Why was that?

She tapped the eraser end of her pencil against her chin. She guessed she was like them, in a way—life had certainly thrown her a few curve balls, like Eliott leaving her—and she'd landed on her feet, but she didn't remember laughing the way Barbara and Louise were laughing now. She remembered fear and uncertainty and a constant struggle, and she remembered leaving Hank with a babysitter on cold winter mornings when she would have given anything to stay home and take care of him herself.

Shay sighed again, laying down her pencil. That was it, that was what she envied. For all the heartache they'd suffered in recent months, Louise and Barbara had had their time with their children. They'd been there for the first giggle, the first step, the first word.

Resolutely, Shay took up her pencil again and forced her eyes to the neat columns written in the ledger. There was no point in bemoaning such things now; she was a career woman, whether she liked it or not. And on that cold, windy November day, she didn't like it very much.

At noon Alice breezed in with chicken sandwiches from the deli down the street, her cheeks pink from the cold weather. The two women chatted about inconsequential things as they ate, and then Alice went back to her yarn shop upstairs.

Shay marveled at the woman's energy, at the same time wondering what had happened to her own. She finished balancing the books and then went into the kitchen to help Louise and Barbara box fragrant crab quiche for delivery. Once the boxes had been loaded into the back of her van, Shay confessed that she didn't think she could make it through the rest of the day and her helpers promised to take up the slack.

She delivered the quiche to the home of a prominent surgeon and his wife and then drove around aimlessly, not wanting to work, not wanting to go back to her empty house. Finally, in desperation, she went to Reese Motors to say hello to Ivy.

The office was in an uproar. Marvin was about to make another commercial and Ivy was simultaneously going over an invoice with a salesman and sparring with Richard Barrett. It gave Shay a pang to see that she'd been so easily replaced.

She would have sneaked out without speaking to Ivy at all if her friend hadn't spotted her and called out, "Shay, wait. I need to talk to you about the wedding."

Ivy got rid of the salesman and Richard in record time and all but dragged Shay into her office. It was disturbingly neat, that office.

"How have you been, Shay? Good heavens, I haven't seen you in ages!"

"I've been…fine."

Ivy's gaze was level. "You don't look fine. Is everything okay?"

"Please don't start, Ivy. I get enough analysis from Mitch and Alice."

Ivy grinned and lifted both hands, palms out. "Say no more." She sat down in the chair behind the desk and Shay took a seat on the sofa and it all seemed strange. It was amazing that a person could jog along in the same rut for six years and then suddenly find herself living a whole different life. "When can you work in a fitting for your dress?"

Shay stared blankly for a moment and then realized that Ivy was talking about the gown she would wear as a bridesmaid in her friend's wedding. "Flexibility is my middle name," she said awkwardly. "Name a date."

"How about tomorrow night, at my apartment? Bring Hank and Alice and we'll have supper after the sewing fairies close their little tufted boxes and steal away into the night."

Shay smiled, hoping that she didn't look forlorn. "I think I can collar Hank for the occasion, but Alice has a big date with a knitting-needle salesman."

That brought a grin from Ivy, though her eyes were serious. It was obvious that she wanted to ask how things were going with Mitch. Shay was grateful that she didn't. "How's the catering business?"

"Hectic," Shay replied without thinking. She felt foolish, sitting there in Ivy's office when she should have been in her own, working. "Do you like your new job?"

Ivy smiled pensively. "Most of the time, I thrive on it."

"And the rest of the time?"

Ivy glanced toward the office door, as if to make certain that it was tightly closed, leaned forward and whispered, "Shay, I think—I think—"

"What, Ivy?"

"I think I'm pregnant," Ivy answered in a low rush of words, and it was impossible to tell whether she was happy or not.

Shay knew what *she* felt, and that was plain, old-fashioned envy. "Have you discussed this with Todd?"

Ivy nodded. "He's thrilled."

"Are you thrilled, Ivy?"

"Yes, but I'm not looking forward to telling my mother. She'll have a fit, because of the white dress and everything."

I should have such a problem, Shay thought. "Don't worry about your mother, Ivy. Just enjoy the wedding and take things as they come."

Ivy started to say something but the telephone on her desk began to buzz. Shay mouthed a goodbye and left, feeling even more bereft than she had before she'd arrived. Her life was in limbo and she didn't know which way to turn or how to go on. She wanted to go to Mitch, but that would have been a weak thing to do, so she drove around until it was time for Hank to get out of school.

She brightened as she drew the van to a stop in front of her son's school. He'd be surprised to see her, and they'd go out for hamburgers and maybe an early movie, just the two of them. Shay had it all planned out.

Only Hank scowled at her and got into the car grudgingly, his eyes averted.

"I'm glad to see you, too," Shay said. "What's the problem, tiger?"

"Nothin'."

Shay shut off the car's engine and turned to her son. She moved to ruffle Hank's hair, but he pulled away. "You're mad at me, aren't you?"

He flung her a defiant look. "Yes. You found out about your dad, but you won't tell me anything about mine!"

Shay shrank back a bit, stunned by the force of the little boy's rage. "I didn't think you were ready," she said lamely.

"I wonder about him all the time and there's nobody to tell me! It isn't fair, Mom!"

Shay closed her eyes for a moment, trying to gather strength. Hank was right. Keeping him in the dark about Eliott had not been fair. Hadn't she been angry with Rosamond for not telling her about Robert Bretton? "I'll tell you everything you want to know."

Over take-out food and the few photographs Shay had kept of Eliott, she told Hank the whole story. She told him, as kindly as she could, about the stealing and about the librarian and she ached at the hurt she saw in her son's eyes.

Hank listened in stony silence and when Shay had finished talking, he snatched up one of the snapshots of his father and went out into the backyard to sit disconsolately at the picnic table. It was cold out there, and windy, and Shay had all she could do not to go out and drag her son back inside.

Presently, he came in on his own, his small shoulders slumped, his eyes averted. Shay, conscious of his dignity, did not speak or move to touch him.

"I'll take my bath now, I guess," he said.

"Okay," Shay replied, looking out the window so that she could hide the expression on her face. The picture of Eliott was blowing across the surface of the picnic table in pieces.

At breakfast the next morning, Hank was in better spirits and Shay blessed the resiliency of children. In fact, she tried to emulate it.

She was humming when she got to the office and, just to give the day a little pizzazz, she went into the Christmas-ornament shop on the first floor and bought a fancy cornhusk wreath for the reception room. Clydesdale was positioned in the curve of the bay windows, and Shay hung the wreath on his head. "Hail, Caesar," she said, before going off to find a hammer and a nail.

The entire day went well and Shay was feeling better than she had in days when she got home. Hank was there, idly pounding one fist into his baseball glove and watching Sally, his babysitter, paint her toenails.

"Spruce up, fella," Shay said brightly. "We're due at Ivy's place for supper in an hour."

Hank's freckled face twisted into a grimace, then brightened. "Is Mitch going to be there?"

"I don't know. Why don't you call Ivy and ask her?"

The babysitter picked up a blow dryer, switched it on and aimed it at her toes. The roar drove Hank to make his call from the kitchen.

By the time Sally had dried her toenails and gone home, Shay was through with her shower and wrapped in her bathrobe, carefully applying fresh mascara. Sensing Hank's presence behind her, she asked, "Well? Is Mitch going to be there?"

Hank was silent for so long that Shay finally turned to look at him, mascara wand poised in midair. His lower lip was quivering and everything inside Shay leaped with alarm.

"He's bringing a stupid girl!" Hank wailed.

Shay swallowed. "A girl?"

Hank nodded. "I called him up and told him off! I told him *you* were supposed to be his girl!"

"Oh, Lord," Shay breathed, closing her eyes for a moment. "Hank, you shouldn't have done that. You had no right."

"I don't care!" Hank shouted. "He's just like my dad! He's a creep!"

"Hank!"

Hank stormed into his bedroom and slammed the door and Shay knew it was useless to talk to him before he'd had a chance to calm down. She went into the living room and tried to make sense of what was happening.

Mitch and a girl? There had to be some misunderstanding. There had to be.

There was. Fifteen minutes after Hank's outburst, there came a knock at the door. Shay opened it to find Mitch standing on the porch, a small, brown-eyed girl huddling shyly against his side. "This," he said, "is the other woman."

Shay smiled and stepped back. She hoped her relief didn't show. "You must be Kelly," she said to the child, helping her out of her coat.

Kelly nodded solemnly. "I'm seven," she said.

"Where, may I ask," Mitch drawled, "is the staunch defender of your honor as a woman?"

"In his room," Shay answered, and as Mitch strode off to knock at Hank's door, she offered Kelly her hand. "Would you like a cup of cocoa?"

"Yes, please." Kelly's dark eyes made a stunning contrast to her pale hair and they moved from side to side as Shay led her toward the kitchen. "Daddy said you had a real carousel horse," she said. "I don't see him around, though."

Shay hid a smile. "I keep him at my office. We could stop there later, if you want."

"I'd like that, thank you." Kelly settled herself at the table and Shay felt a pang as she put milk on to heat for the cocoa. Her mother must be beautiful, she thought.

In a few minutes Mitch appeared in the doorway with a sheepish and somewhat sullen Hank at his side. "Another domestic crisis averted," muttered the man.

"I don't wanna go anywhere with any stupid girl," added the boy.

"I spoke too soon," Mitch said.

"Hank Kendall," Shay warned, "you go to your room, this instant!"

Kelly smoothed the skirts of her little dress. "I'm not a stupid girl," she threw out, just loud enough for a retreating Hank to hear.

"Is she always this good?" Shay whispered once Kelly had finished her cocoa and gone off to the living room to sit quietly on the couch and thumb through a copy of a magazine.

Mitch shook his head. "I'm still a novelty," he answered, trapping Shay neatly against the kitchen counter and bending to steal one mischievous kiss. "She's only staying a few days, Reba and her husband are attending some conference in Seattle." Liking the taste of the first kiss, he gave her another. "Hank's pretty upset, isn't he?"

Shay nodded. "I told him about Eliott."

Mitch's hand was in Shay's hair, his thumb tracing the rim of her ear. "You did the right thing, princess. He's going to need some time to come to terms with what happened, that's all."

"You were remarkably patient with him."

Mitch kissed her again. "I'm a remarkably patient man." His voice dropped to a whisper. "But I'd sure like to take you to bed right now, lady."

Shay trembled, needing Mitch and knowing that her need would have to be denied. "I'd sure like to go," she replied honestly.

Mitch laughed and nuzzled her neck once. "I'll try to arrange something," he said, and then they coaxed Hank out of his room and went to Ivy's apartment for the evening.

Mitch called Shay at the office first thing the next morning. "Keep the weekend open," he said. "I'm going to take you somewhere private and love you until you're crazy."

A hot, anticipatory shiver went through Shay. "What about the kids? Where would we—"

"Reba is picking Kelly up tomorrow night. Maybe Hank could stay with Alice."

"Well…"

"Ask her, Shay. You're talking to a desperate man, a man consumed with lust."

Shay laughed. "I'll check with Alice and call you back."

Alice asked no questions. She simply agreed to keep Hank for the weekend and returned to the group of knitters gathered at the back of the shop.

The rest of that week crept by, even though Shay was busy day and night. She didn't see Mitch at all, but he managed to keep her blood at an embarrassing simmer by calling her at intervals and making scandalous promises.

Finally, Friday afternoon arrived. Shay left the office early, picked Hank up at school and brought him back to Alice's shop.

Alice immediately set him to work unpacking a new shipment of yarn. "You just go along, dear," she whispered, half pushing Shay out through the shop's open door and into the hallway. "Hank and I will be fine."

Shay pulled a crumpled piece of paper from her coat pocket and handed it to Alice. "This is a telephone number, where you can reach us, er, me."

Alice glanced at the number, which constituted the sum total of what Shay knew about where she would be that weekend, nodded her head and tucked the paper into the pocket of her apron. "Have a lovely time, dear," she said, dismissing Shay with a wave of one hand.

Because Shay had to leave the van with Barbara and Louise so that they could make deliveries, Mitch picked her up in front of the building. She felt like a fool, standing there on the front steps with her suitcase at her feet.

"I didn't even know what clothes to pack!" she snapped once she'd gotten into Mitch's car and fastened her seatbelt.

"You probably won't need any," he replied.

Their destination turned out to be a log cabin in the foothills of the Olympics. There was smoke curling from the stone chimney and lights glowed at the windows. Pine trees towered behind the small house, scenting the crisp evening air, and among them were maples and elms, a few bright orange leaves still clinging to their branches.

Mitch took the box of supplies that he'd picked up at the store down the road, and carried it to the porch step, setting it down to unlock the door. Shay took as long as she could to get her suitcase and follow.

The inside of the cabin was simplicity at its finest. The wooden floors were bare, except for a few brightly colored scatter rugs, and polished to a high shine. A fire snapped and chattered on the hearth of the rustic rock fireplace, tossing darting crimson shadows onto the plush sofa that faced it. There was a tiny bathroom and an even tinier kitchen, where Mitch immediately busied himself putting away the food.

"Whose place is this, anyway?" Shay asked, oddly nervous considering all the times she'd been intimate with Mitch.

Mitch closed the door of the smallest refrigerator Shay had ever seen and turned to unzip her jacket and slide it off her shoulders. "It belongs to a friend of Todd's," he answered, but his mind clearly wasn't on such details. His eyes were on the third button of Shay's flannel shirt and it was a wonder that the little bit of plastic didn't melt under the heat.

"There isn't any phone. I gave Alice a number—"

"My cell doesn't work out here, so that's the number for the store down the road. If anything happens, Alice will have no problem getting through to us."

Shay's arms were still in her jacket sleeves, the garment only half removed, when Mitch slipped out of his own coat and began unbuttoning her shirt. She quivered, unable to utter so much as a word of protest, as he undid the front fastening on her bra and bared her breasts.

When he touched her, with one tentative hand, she gasped with pleasure and let her head fall back, her eyes drifting shut. Mitch stroked her gently, shaping each of her breasts for his pleasure and her own, teasing her nipples until they tightened into pulsing little pebbles.

Finally he removed her jacket entirely, then her shirt and her already-dangling bra, her jeans and her shoes, her socks and, last of all, her panties. A low crooning sound came from Shay's throat as Mitch caressed every part of her with his hands, slowly, as if memorizing her shape, the texture of her flesh. One by one, he found and attended the spots where her pleasure was most easily roused.

After what seemed a dazzling eternity to Shay, he took off his clothes and they knelt, facing each other, before the fire. Now, while Mitch's hands brazenly cupped Shay's breasts, she used her own to explore him, learning each muscle in his powerful thighs with her fingers, each hollow and plane in his broad back and on his chest. At last she tangled her fingers in his hair and moved astraddle of him, catching his groan of surrender in her mouth as she kissed him and at the same time sheathing him in her warmth.

They moved slowly at first, their mouths still locked in that same kiss, their tongues mimicking the parries and thrusts of their hips.

But finally the need became too great and Shay leaned

back in triumphant submission, bracing herself with her hands, her breasts swollen and heaving under the attentions of Mitch's fingers. She groaned with each slow thrust of his hips, pleaded senselessly at each lingering withdrawal.

He stopped plying her nipples with his fingers to suckle and tongue them instead and Shay was driven to madness. She threw her legs around Mitch and he shouted in a madness of his own, plunging deep.

Shay would not allow him to escape the velvety vengeance that cosseted him, rippled over him, sapped his strength. Her triumph was an elemental thing, and she shouted with the joy of it even as Mitch growled in a release of his own.

Once they'd recovered enough to rise from that rug in front of the fire, where they'd fallen in a tangle of perspiration and breathless laughter, they ate sandwiches and drank wine and then made the sofa out into a bed and made love again.

In the darkest depths of the night Shay awakened and lay listening, in perfect contentment, to the calls of the owls and the cry of some lonely, faraway beast. She felt her spirit, crumpled by the rigors of day-to-day life, unfolding like a soft cloth. She snuggled closer to Mitch and wished that they could stay there in that cabin far longer than just a weekend.

The morning was cold and the sky was a brassy blue, laced with gray clouds. Mitch and Shay consumed a hastily cooked breakfast of scrambled eggs and toast and then went outside.

They found a silver ribbon of a creek, hidden away among the trees and watched a deer dashing up a hillside, white tail bobbing. It was all so beautiful that Shay ached with the effort of trying to draw it all inside herself, to keep.

Early in the afternoon snow began to fall, drifting down in big, lazy flakes that seesawed their way to the ground. Mitch built up the fire and then came to stand behind Shay at the window, kneading her shoulders with his strong hands, his chin propped on the top of her head.

"What are you thinking, princess?"

Shay knew there would be tears in her voice and made no effort to hide them. "That two days isn't going to be enough."

"Two centuries wouldn't be enough," he agreed quietly, and his arms slid around her and tightened.

They watched the snow for hours, it seemed, and then they went back to the bed. There was no lovemaking; they were too tired for that.

When Shay was prodded awake by hunger, she sat up in bed and yawned. It was dark outside and the fire was almost out. She squinted at her watch and was shocked at the time; it was after midnight!

She prodded Mitch with one hand. "Wake up!"

He stirred briefly and then rolled over, hauling most of the covers with him and burying his face in his pillow.

Shay swatted his backside. "I said, wake up!"

He muttered something and burrowed deeper.

Disgusted, Shay scrambled out of bed and hop-danced to the window because the floor was so cold under her bare feet. The snow was deep now and it glowed in the moonlight, so white and glittery that Shay's throat went tight as she looked at it.

Her stomach rumbled and she remembered that she was hungry. She found her robe and slippers and put them on, then began ransacking the kitchen, making as much noise as she possibly could.

Mitch woke up reluctantly, grumbling and groping for his jeans. "What the—"

Shay shoved a bacon, lettuce and tomato sandwich into his hands and began wolfing down one of her own. "I challenge you to a duel, my good man," she said, eating and putting on her clothes at the same time.

"Name your weapon," Mitch muttered with a disgraceful lack of enthusiasm.

Shay stepped outside the door for a moment, wincing at the cold, and then let him have it. "Snowballs!" she shouted as the first volley struck Mitch's bare chest.

Chapter Fourteen

On Sunday morning the snow began to melt away, leaving only ragged patches of white here and there on the ground. In a like manner, Shay's dreams seemed to waste away, too. She had hoped that Mitch might propose to her again—she felt ready to accept now—but as the time for them to leave the cabin drew closer, his mood went from pensive to distant to downright sullen.

Shay watched him out of the corner of one eye as they drove past the small country store on the highway—the proprietor had been the one to build the fire and turn on the lights in the cabin before they arrived—but she didn't ask Mitch what was wrong because she thought she knew. He probably dreaded the inevitable return to the realities of the relationship as much as she did.

When Mitch reached out for the radio dial on the dashboard, Shay gently forestalled the motion.

"You've almost finished the Roget book," she threw out, to make conversation. "What's next?"

Mitch tossed one unreadable look in Shay's direction and his jawline tightened as he turned his attention back to the road. "I suppose Ivan will sift through the dregs of humanity until he finds some other scum for me to write about."

Shay stiffened. "Is that what my mother was, Mitch? The dregs of humanity?"

He cursed under his breath. "I was talking about Roget and you damned well know it. Don't bait me, Shay, because I'm not in the mood to play your games."

It was an uncomfortable reminder of the last time Mitch had accused her of playing games and Shay felt defensive. Still, she tried hard to keep her voice level. "Do you really think I want to argue with you, especially now? Especially after—"

"After what, Shay? Two days of reckless passion?" His tone was blade-sharp. Lethal. "That's our only real way of communicating, isn't it?" He paused, drew a deep, raspy breath. "I'll say one thing for us, love—we relate real well on a sexual level."

Shay was wounded and her voice sounded small and shaky when she spoke. "If you feel that way, why did you ask me to marry you?"

The brown eyes swung to her, scoured her with their anger. "I guess I lost my head," he said bluntly. Brutally. "Rest easy, sugar plum. I won't risk it again."

"Risk—"

"If you want to marry me—and I don't think you have the guts to make that kind of commitment to any man— you'll have to do the proposing. Rejection hurts, Shay, and I'm not into pain."

Shay turned her head, and the tall pine trees along the roadside seemed to whiz past the car window in a blurry rush. The terrible hurt, the three-hundred-and-sixty-degree turn in Mitch's attitude, all of it was proof that she'd been wrong to expect consistent, unwavering love from a man. Why hadn't she learned? She'd watched Rosamond enter into one disastrous relationship after another. She'd nearly been destroyed by a failed marriage herself. Why in God's name hadn't she learned?

"Shay?" Mitch's voice was softer now, even gentle. But it was too late for gentleness.

She let her forehead rest against the cool, moist glass of the window, trying to calm herself. "Leave me alone."

The sleek car swung suddenly to the side of the road and came to a stomach-wrenching stop. "Shay."

She shook his hand from her shoulder, keeping her face averted. "Don't touch me, Mitch. Don't touch me."

There was a blunt sound, probably his fist striking the steering wheel or the dashboard, followed by a grating sigh. "I'm sorry. It's just that I get so frustrated. Everything was so good between us and now it's all going to hell again and I can't handle that, Shay."

"That's obvious."

She heard him sigh again, felt a jarring motion as he shifted furiously in the car seat. "Don't give any ground here, dammit. Whatever you do, don't meet me halfway!"

Shay could look at Mitch now; in fact, her pain forced her to do that. She sat up very straight in her seat, heedless of her tousled hair and the tears on her cheeks. "I've met you more than halfway, Mitch. I came up on this damned mountain with you. I shared your bed. And you turned on me."

"I didn't turn on you, Shay. I got angry. There's a difference."

"Is there?"

"Yes, dammit, there is!"

"If you truly love somebody, you don't yell at them!"

Mitch's nose was within an inch of Shay's. "You're wrong, lady, because I love you and I'm yelling at you right now! And I'll keep yelling until you hear me! I LOVE YOU! Is that coming through?"

"No!" Shay closed her eyes tightly. Memories of her mother filled her mind—Rosamond screaming, Rosamond throwing things, Rosamond driving away everyone who tried to love her. "No!"

Mitch's hands were clasping her shoulders then. "Open your eyes, Shay. Look at me!"

Shay did open her eyes, but only as a reflex.

"I'm still here, aren't I? You can get mad at me, Shay, and I can get mad at you, and it's still all right. Don't you see that? It's all right."

She fell against him, burying her face in his shoulder, clinging to him with her hands. She had always been afraid of anger, in other people, in herself. And she trembled in fear of it then, even as she began to realize that Mitch was right. Getting mad was okay, it was human. It didn't have to mean the end of something good.

Presently, Mitch cupped one hand under her chin and lifted, brushing her lips with his own.

"All weekend," he said, "you've been telling me what your body wants, what it needs. Your mind and your spirit, Shay, what do they want?"

She sniffled. That one was easy. With her whole heart and soul she wanted Mitch Prescott. She wanted to laugh with him and bear his children and, yes, fight with him, but she couldn't bring herself to say those things aloud. Not yet. She was still coming to terms with too many other emotions and her right to feel them.

Mitch overlooked her complete inability to answer and kissed the tip of her nose. "We'll get this right, Shay.

Somehow, I'm going to get past all that pain and fear and make you trust me."

Shay swallowed hard. "I—I trust you."

He started the car again. "I'll believe that, my love, when you ask for my hand in marriage."

"It's supposed to be the other way around, isn't it?" Shay caught her breath as the car sped onto the highway again.

"Not in this case," Mitch answered, and the subject was closed.

The boxed manuscript landed in the middle of Ivan's desk with a solid, resounding thump—Mitch had printed it out just so he could make the impact.

Ivan looked at the box and then up at Mitch's unyielding face. "Good Lord," the older man muttered. "You're not serious!"

"I'm serious as hell, Ivan. I'm through writing this kind of book."

Ivan gestured toward one of several chairs facing his desk. "Sit down, sit down. Let's at least talk this over. You didn't fly three thousand miles just to throw a ream of paper in my face, did you?"

Mitch ignored the invitation to sit—he'd had enough of that flying from Seattle to New York—and paced the length of Ivan's sumptuous office, pausing at the window to look down on Fifth Avenue. He thought of Shay, back home in Skyler Beach and probably up to her eyes in cheeseballs, and smiled. "I flew three thousand miles, Ivan, to tell you face-to-face that you're going to have to get yourself another Indiana Jones."

"You're older now, more settled. I can see why you wouldn't want to do the kind of research your earlier books required, but your career has taken a different course anyway, between the Rosamond Dallas biography and the Roget case. What's the real problem, Mitch?"

"A woman."

Ivan sighed. "I should have known. Don't tell me the rest of the story, let me guess. She's laid down the law. No husband of hers is going to fly all over the country chasing down leads and interviewing murderers. Am I right?"

Mitch was standing at the window, still absorbed in Fifth Avenue's pre-Christmas splendor. "You couldn't be further off base, Ivan. If it hadn't been for Shay, I wouldn't have had the stomach to write about Alan Roget."

"So she's supportive. Three cheers for her. I still don't understand why a writer would turn his back on his craft, his readers, his publishers, his—"

"I never do anything halfway, Ivan," Mitch broke in patiently. "And right now holding that relationship together takes everything I've got."

"If it's that shaky, maybe it isn't worth the trouble."

"It's worth it, Ivan."

Ivan sat back in his swivel chair, his eyes on the manuscript box in front of him. "I almost dread reading this," he observed after several moments of reflective silence. "I suppose it's just as good as your other stuff?"

"Better," Mitch said with resignation rather than pride.

Ivan was, for all his professional tenacity, a good sport. And a good friend. "This lady of yours must be something. Once the dust settles and you want to write again, you give me a call."

Mitch grinned, already at the door of Ivan's office, ready to leave. "I expect her to propose any time now," he said, enjoying the look of surprise on his agent's face. "Goodbye, Ivan, and merry Christmas."

"Bah humbug," Ivan replied as Mitch closed the door behind him.

* * *

"Doesn't anybody cook their own Christmas turkey anymore?" Shay grumbled as she read over the work schedule Barbara had just brought into her office.

Barbara was wearing a bright red apron trimmed in white lace and there was a sprig of holly in her hair. Everybody seemed to have the Christmas spirit this year. Everybody, that is, except for Shay. "If you don't mind my saying so, Ms. Kendall, most people would be glad to have so much business."

Shay sighed. "I suppose you're right."

"You don't care much for all this, do you?"

The directness of Barbara's question set Shay back on her emotional heels. "I've dreamed of owning this catering business for years!"

Barbara was undaunted. "Sometimes, we dream of something and we work and sweat and pray to get it and, when we do, we find out that it wasn't what we really wanted after all. What is it that you really want, Ms. Kendall?"

Shay blushed. Damn the woman and her uncanny perception! "I'm almost embarrassed to admit to it, in this day and age, but I'd like to be married and have babies. I'd like to have the luxury of being weak sometimes, instead of always having to be strong. I'd like to be there when my son comes home from school and I'd like to watch soap operas and vacuum rugs." Shay caught herself. Barbara would be horrified. Any modern woman would be horrified. "Aren't you sorry you asked?"

Barbara chuckled. "I was married for a long, long time, Ms. Kendall, and those were some of the things I liked best about it."

"You're not shocked?"

"Of course I'm not. You're a young woman and it's natural for you to want a man and a home and babies."

Shay was gazing toward the window. There wasn't any snow and she wanted snow. She wanted to be alone in the mountains with Mitch again. "I'm not at all like my mother," she mused in a faraway voice threaded through with a strand of pure joy. "I'm myself and I can make my own choices."

Barbara must have slipped out. When Shay looked back, she was gone.

Shay propped her chin in her hands, running over her dreams, checking each one for soundness, finding them strong. All she had to do was find the courage to act on them.

Mitch wanted a marriage proposal, did he? Well, she'd give him one he'd never forget. She reached for the telephone book and leafed through the yellow pages until she found the listings she wanted. There was no way she could put her plan into action until after Christmas, what with the business and Ivy's wedding and the general uproar of the holiday itself, but it wouldn't hurt to make a few calls.

Kelly cast one questioning look up at her mother. Reba nodded, her eyes suspiciously bright, and the child scampered through the crowd of Christmas travelers and into Mitch's arms.

He lifted her, held her close. There was no time to tell Reba that he was grateful; he and Kelly had to catch a northbound plane within minutes. He nodded and Reba nodded back. A second later, she had disappeared into the crowd.

"Look, Daddy," Kelly chimed over the standard airport hubbub, pointing to a pin on her coat. "Mommy bought me this. Santa and his nose lights up when you pull the string!"

Mitch chuckled hoarsely. "Your mommy is a pretty special lady. Shall we go catch our plane?"

Kelly nodded. "Mommy already checked my suitcase and I've got my ticket right here."

Minutes later they were settled in their seats on the crowded airplane and Mitch ventured, "I know this is the first Christmas you've ever been away from your mother...."

Kelly smiled and patted his hand as though Mitch were the child and she the adult. "Don't worry, Daddy. I won't cry or anything like that. It'll be fun to be with you and be in Aunt Ivy's wedding and, besides, I get a whole other Christmas when I get back here."

The plane was taxiing down the runway and Mitch checked Kelly's seatbelt.

"I'm kind of scared," she confessed.

He took her hand.

Shay dampened her fingers on her tongue and smoothed Hank's cowlick. "I want you to be nice to Kelly," she said as the arrival of Flight 703 was announced over the airport PA system.

Hank scooted away, his dignity ruffled. "Mom, don't spit on me anymore," he complained. "I look good enough already."

Shay laughed. "I'm soooooo sorry!"

The plane landed and, after several minutes, the passengers began to stream in through the gate, most carrying brightly wrapped packages and wearing home-for-the-holiday smiles. Mitch and Kelly appeared just when Shay was beginning to worry that they'd been left behind.

Kelly pulled at a little string and the Santa Claus face pinned to her coat glowed with light. "Look, Hank!"

Hank tried his best to be blasé, but he was obviously fascinated by the plastic Santa and its flashing red nose.

"I brought you one just like it," Kelly assured him.

Shay could feel Mitch's eyes on her face, but it was a moment before she'd shored up her knees enough to risk looking into them. She wondered what he'd say when he found out that he wasn't involved with a modern woman at all, but one who wanted a time-out, who would willingly trade her career for babies and Cub Scout meetings and love in the afternoon.

Maybe he wouldn't even want a woman like that. Maybe— "Shay."

She realized that she'd been staring at Kelly's pin and made herself meet Mitch's gaze. Her throat was constricted and though her lips moved, she couldn't make a sound.

"I know my nose doesn't light up," he said with a teasing note in his voice, "but surely I'm more interesting than a plastic Santa Claus."

Shay found her voice. It was deeper than usual and full of strange little catches. "You're definitely more interesting than a plastic Santa Claus," she agreed. "But we won't make any rash statements about the nose until after Marvin and Jeannie's Christmas party."

He laughed and kissed her hungrily, but then they both remembered the children and the airport full of people and they drew apart.

"Yuk," said Hank, but his protest lacked true conviction.

Ivy's face glowed as she turned, displaying her dress for Shay. It was a beautiful white gown with tiny crystal beads stitched to the full, flowing skirt and the fitted bodice. Because this was a Christmas wedding, the hem, neckline and cuffs boasted a snowy trimming of faux fur.

Shay's gown, like Kelly's, was of floor-length red velvet, also trimmed with fur. In lieu of flowers, the attendants would carry matching muffs with sprigs of holly attached.

"We look beautiful!" Kelly piped out, admiring herself in the mirror of the little dressing room at the back of the church.

Ivy laughed and her joy brought a pretty apricot flush to her cheeks. "We do, don't we?"

There were still a few tinsel halos and shepherds' robes lying about from the Christmas program that had been held earlier and Shay gathered them up just for something to do to pass the time. It wasn't her wedding, but she was almost as excited and nervous as if it had been.

Ivy's mother, an attractive if somewhat icy woman, came in, followed closely by Mitch. It was obvious that Elizabeth was trying to ignore her stepson, but Shay couldn't. He looked so handsome in his dark tuxedo that she almost gasped.

He gave Shay a wink over Elizabeth's rigidly coiffed champagne-blond head and then turned his attention to Ivy. Elizabeth winced at his wolf-whistle, but Ivy glowed.

"We look beautiful, don't we, Daddy?"

Mitch crouched to look into Kelly's face. "Yes, indeed, you do."

"You shouldn't have just walked in here that way," Elizabeth fretted, speaking to Mitch but not looking at him. "They might have been dressing."

Mitch wagged a finger in her face. "Peace on earth, Elizabeth. Good will toward men."

To the surprise of everyone, Elizabeth permitted herself a faltering smile. "You are just like your father," she said. Shay hoped that Mitch had noticed the love in Elizabeth's face when she mentioned his father.

"Merry Christmas, Elizabeth," he said gently, and then he kissed Ivy's cheek and left the room.

There were tears glistening in Ivy's eyes as she looked at her mother. "Thank you, Mama," she said quietly.

"Pish-posh, all I did was speak to the man," Elizabeth replied, and then she was fussing with Ivy's skirts and straightening her veil.

Minutes later, Kelly led the way up the aisle of the candlelit church. Shay followed, smiling when she spotted Marvin and Jeannie. As she passed Alice, the old dickens winked at her.

There was a hush in the crowded sanctuary as Ivy appeared in the rear doorway, her face hidden by a veil that caught sparkles of candlelight. Mitch stood at her side, and he looked as comfortable in a tux as he did in the blue jeans and T-shirts he usually wore.

The organ struck the first chord of the wedding march and there was a rustling sound as the guests rose. Everyone else was looking at Ivy, of course, but Shay's eyes would not leave the man who would give away the bride.

For Shay, the ceremony passed in a shimmering haze. The holy words were spoken and Shay heard them in snatches, adding her own silent commentary. "For better or worse." *Let it be better.* "For richer or poorer." *No problem there. These two already have IRAs.* "In sickness and in health." *Please, they're both so beautiful.* "Till death do you part." *They'll grow old together—I want your word on that, God.* "I now pronounce you man and wife, you may kiss the bride." *My feet hurt. Is this thing almost over?*

It was over. Triumphant music filled the church and the bride and groom went down the aisle together, each with an arm around the other. Kelly followed, on cue, but the best man had to give Shay a little tug to get her in motion.

Snow was wafting slowly down from the night sky as Ivy

and Todd got into their limousine and raced away toward the restaurant where their reception was being held.

Hank pulled at Shay's skirt. "Mom? If nobody's at home when Santa Claus gets there, will he still leave presents?"

Shay bent and kissed the top of his head. "Don't you worry, tiger. He'll definitely leave presents."

"That's easy for you to say," Mitch muttered into her ear. "Where did you say all that stuff was hidden?"

"On the big shelf over the cellar stairs," Shay whispered back.

"I'll meet you at the reception," Mitch said after he'd helped Shay and Alice into Shay's van. Hank and Kelly were in the backseat giving voice to the visions that would later dance in their heads.

"He's tall for an elf," Alice commented as Mitch walked away and got into his own car.

A few hours later, when Hank and Kelly were both sound asleep on beds Mitch had improvised for them by putting chairs together, Ivy and Todd left the reception with the customary fanfare, the guests throwing rice, God throwing snow.

"Did you set the presents out?" Shay whispered to Mitch.

He touched the tip of her nose. "Yes. And I filled Hank's stocking."

The other wedding guests were all putting on their coats and the sight gave Shay a sad feeling. It was Christmas eve and she wished that she could share the last magical minutes of the night with Mitch. It would have been fun to set out presents and fill stockings together, talking in Santa Claus whispers....

"I'll see you tomorrow," Mitch said gently. It seemed that he had read her thoughts, that he shared them.

After dropping Alice off at her apartment—like Mitch and Kelly, she would spend Christmas day at Shay's house—Shay ushered her sleepy son out of the car and up the front walk to the door. The porch light was burning bright and she blessed Mitch for remembering to leave it on as she rummaged through her purse for her keys.

The tinsel on the Christmas tree shimmered in the dim light as Shay passed it, and snow still wafted past the windows. She put Hank to bed and returned to the living room, switching on the small lamp on the desk.

Hank's toys had been carefully arranged under the tree, his new skateboard, his electric train, his baseball glove. His stocking, resting on the sofa because there was no mantelpiece, bulged with candy canes and jacks, rubber balls and decks of cards. Shay had shopped for all these things herself, but it seemed to her that there were a few more packages than there should have been.

She took a closer look and found that four enormous presents, all tagged with Hank's name, had been added to the loot. Smiling to herself, she shut out the light and went into her room.

Santa had visited there, too, it seemed. Her bed was heaped with gifts wrapped in silver paper and tied with gossamer ribbons. Shay's heart beat a little faster as she crept closer to the bed, feeling the wonder, the magic, that is usually reserved for children.

Some of the packages were large, and some were small. Shay shook them, one by one, and the biggest one made a whispery sound inside its box. She lifted a corner of the foil lid but couldn't see a thing.

Should she or shouldn't she?

She tried to distract herself by stacking the gifts and carrying them out to the Christmas tree. She would open her presents in the morning, she decided firmly, when Hank opened his. When Mitch and Kelly and Alice were all there to share in the fun.

Resolutely, Shay washed her face, brushed her teeth and put on her warmest flannel nightgown. She tossed back the covers and started to get into bed, only to find a tiny red stocking lying on the sheet.

She upended it and a small, black velvet box tumbled out, along with a note. Shay's fingers trembled as she opened the paper and read, "I want your body. Love, Santa."

She was smiling and crying, both at once, as she opened the velvet box. Inside it was a beautiful sapphire ring, the stone encircled by diamonds.

On impulse, she grabbed for the phone on her beside table and punched out Mitch's number. He sounded wide awake when he answered.

"It's beautiful," she said.

There was a smile in his voice. "You're beautiful," he countered.

Shay willed him to say that the ring was an engagement ring, but he didn't. She wasn't going to get out of proposing, it appeared. "I left your present with Mrs. Carraway," she said, admiring the flash of the beautiful stones. "I asked her to put it in the library, beside the TV."

"That's intriguing," Mitch answered. "I'll get it and call you back."

Shay's heart was in her throat. In order to withstand the wait, she scampered out to the living room and snatched up the big present that had made her so curious.

Chapter Fifteen

The package was sitting near the TV set in the library. Mitch smiled as he picked it up and turned it over in his hands, savoring not the gift itself, but the thought of the woman who had given it. After some time, he tore away the wrapping; by the shape, he had expected a CD, but he saw now that Shay's present was a homemade DVD instead.

His lips curved into a grin. The woman was full of surprises.

He slid the DVD into the player and pressed the proper buttons and, as he settled himself on the library couch, Shay's face loomed on the television screen. "Oh, Lord," she muttered, "I think it's going already."

Mitch chuckled.

The camera's shift from telephoto to wide angle was dizzying; Mitch felt as though he'd been flung backward through a tunnel. Shay was fully visible, standing in front of a gigantic cardboard rainbow and looking very nervous.

"I love you," Mitch mumbled to her image.

The cardboard rainbow toppled over, and Shay blushed as she bent to pick it up. "You'll have to be patient," said the screen Shay. "I rented this camera and I don't know how to work it."

He heard Alice say, off-camera, "I'll be going now. Good luck, dear." A door clicked shut.

The rainbow threatened to fall again and Shay steadied it before going on. The pace of her living room production picked up speed.

"Mitch Prescott!" she crowed so suddenly and so volubly that he started. "Do I have a deal for you!"

Mitch leaned forward on the couch because the picture on the screen seemed blurry. He told himself that the video camera must have been out of focus.

"We all know that rainbows are a symbol of hope," Shay went on with an enthusiasm that would have put Marvin Reese to shame. She thumped the rainbow in question and it toppled to the floor again; part of Shay's TV set and the end of her sofa came into view. Resolutely she wrestled the prop back into place. "But rainbows can get a bit ragged, can't they?"

Mitch almost expected a toll-free number to appear on the screen, along with an order to have his credit card information ready. He grinned and rubbed his eyes with a thumb and forefinger.

"I'm offering you a brand-new rainbow, Mitch Prescott," Shay went on, in a gentle voice. Then, suddenly, she made him jump again. "But wait!" she cried. "There's still more!"

Mitch leaned forward.

"With this rainbow—" this time she held on to it with one hand while thumping it for emphasis with the other "—you get one wife, guaranteed to love you always. Yes, that's right! Even if you get bored and go back to doing dangerous things and writing books about nasty people, this wife will still love you. She'll laugh with you, she'll cry with you, and if worse comes to worst, she'll even fold your socks. Call now, because a woman this good won't last long! She's ready to deal!"

Shay left the rainbow to its own devices and came closer to the camera, peering into the lens. "You wanted a proposal and this is it. Will you marry me, Mitch?"

Mitch was overwhelmed with a crazy tangle of emotions; one by one, he unwound them, defined them. There was love, of course; he felt a tenderness so deep that it was almost wounding. There was admiration, there was humor, there was gratitude. He knew, perhaps better than anyone else could have, what it had cost Shay to lay all her emotional cards on the table.

The screen went blank, then the menu options popped back up. He left the couch, pressed the play button and watched the movie again, this time standing, his arms folded across his chest as if to brace himself against some tidal wave of emotion.

Shay felt downright dissolute, waking up in a faux-mink coat, curled up around the telephone as though it were a teddy bear.

Mitch hadn't called. Surely he'd seen the DVD by now, but he hadn't called.

Shay sat up and squinted at the clock on her bedside table. It was five-fifteen. No point in going back to sleep; Hank would be up and ready to rip into the presents at any moment.

She lay back on her pillows, setting the phone away from her. Her hands came to rest in the deep, lush fur of the coat and tears smarted in her eyes. Maybe Mitch didn't see her as wife material after all. Maybe she was more of a kept woman, a bird in a gilded cage.

Shay bounded off the bed, tore off the fur coat and flung it across the room. Then, in just her flannel nightgown, she padded out into the living room to turn up the thermostat and light the tree. She had just turned away from the cof-feemaker when she heard Hank's first squeal of delight.

When Shay reached the living room, her son was whiz-zing over the linoleum on his new skateboard. She couldn't help smiling. "Hank Kendall, get off that thing!" she or-dered, a mother to the end.

"I suppose we can't open presents until Grammie gets here," he threw out as he came to a crashing stop against the far wall.

"You suppose right, fella."

Hank was beaming as he left the skateboard behind to crouch in front of the tree and examine his electric train. "This is going to be a great Christmas, Mom!"

Shay leaned against the jamb of the kitchen doorway, her smile a bit shaky now. She'd bared her soul to Mitch Prescott, like a fool, and he hadn't even bothered to call. Sure, it was going to be a great Christmas. "I'll get break-fast started." She waggled a motherly finger at her son. "You content yourself with the Santa Claus things and whatever might be in your stocking, young man. No pres-ent-peeking allowed!"

The doorbell rang fifteen minutes later and Shay greeted a package-laden Alice.

"Look, Grammie!" Hank crowed, delighted, as his elec-tric train raced around its track, whistle tooting. "Look!"

Alice laughed and rumpled her great-grandson's red-brown hair, but it was obvious that she had noticed Shay's mood. She placed her packages under the tree, took off her coat and bright blue knitted hat and joined Shay in the kitchen.

Shay was thumping dishes and pans around as she set the table for breakfast.

"What's the matter, Shay?" Alice asked. The look in her eyes indicated that she already knew the answer.

"He gave me a mink coat!" Shay exclaimed, slamming down a platter of sausage links.

"I always said that man was a waster," Alice mocked in a wry whisper.

Shay was not about to be amused. "It's some kind of sick game. I made an absolute fool of myself proposing to him—"

"I take it he's had an opportunity to watch the commercial?"

"He's had all night!" Suddenly tears began to stream down Shay's cheeks. "Oh, Alice, he's going to say no!"

Alice shook her head. "I doubt that very much, Shay. Mitch loves you."

"Then why hasn't he called? Why isn't he here?"

"He probably wants to accept in person, Shay." At the protest brewing on Shay's lips, Alice raised both hands in a command of silence. "The man has a little girl, and it *is* six o'clock on Christmas morning, you know. Give him a chance to wade through the wrapping paper, at least!"

Shay was comforted, if grudgingly so. "I still think he should have called," she muttered.

"Let Mitch have this time with his daughter, Shay," Alice said gently. "It's probably the first Christmas he's spent with Kelly since the divorce."

Chagrined, Shay nodded. "Breakfast is ready," she said.

Except for the stack of gifts Mitch had left, Santa Claus–style, on Shay's bed the night before, all the presents had been opened. The living room looked like the landscape of some strange wrapping-paper planet.

Shay was gathering up the papers and stuffing them into a garbage bag when the doorbell rang. A sense of sweet alarm surged through her as Hank left his electric train to answer.

"That stuff you gave me was really neat!" the little boy whooped, and his face glowed as Mitch lifted him up into his arms and ruffled his hair.

"I'm glad you liked it," was the quiet answer.

Kelly came shyly past her father, holding the doll that had been her gift from Shay. A beautiful, delicate fairy, complete with silvery wings and wand, the doll was well suited to its ladylike owner. "Thank you very much," the little girl said, looking up at Shay with Mitch's eyes.

Shay forgot her own nervousness and smiled at Kelly. "You're welcome, sweetheart."

Alice, who had been quietly reading a book she had received as a gift, suddenly leaped out of her rocking chair, the warmth of her smile taking in both Kelly and Hank.

"Let's go and see how that turkey of ours is coming along, shall we?"

The children followed Alice into the kitchen.

"Crafty old dickens," Mitch muttered, watching Alice's spry departing figure with a smile in his eyes.

Shay suddenly felt shy, like a teenager who has just asked a boy to a Sadie Hawkins dance. She just stood there, in the middle of a mountain range of Christmas paper, the garbage bag in one hand, stricken to silence.

Mitch seemed similarly afflicted.

Alice finally intervened. "Get on with it," she coaxed from the kitchen doorway. "I can't keep these kids interested in a turkey forever, you know!"

The spell was broken. Mitch laughed and so did Shay, but her nervousness drove her back to her paper gathering.

Mitch waded through the stuff to stop her by gripping both her wrists in his hands. "Shay."

She looked up into his face, her chin quivering, and thought that if he turned down her proposal, she'd die. She'd surely die.

"Where did you get that rainbow?" he asked softly.

Shay was incensed that he could ask such a stupid question when she was standing there in terrible suspense. "I made it myself," she finally replied through tight lips.

He pried the garbage bag from one of her hands and a wad of paper from the other. "I love you," he said.

Shay thought of the mink coat lying on her bedroom floor, the sapphire ring on her finger, the stack of elegantly wrapped gifts tucked beneath the Christmas tree. "I will not be your mistress, Mitch Prescott," she said in a firm whisper.

Puzzlement darkened his eyes to a deeper shade of brown. "My what?"

"You heard me. If we're going to be together at all, we're going to be married."

One of his hands rose to cup her face. His skin was cold from the crisp Christmas-morning weather outside, and yet his touch was unbelievably warm. "I'm ready to deal," he said, and the light in his eyes was mischievous.

Shay's heart was hammering against her rib cage. "Are you saying yes, or what?"

"Of course I'm saying yes."

Shay's relief was of such intensity that it embarrassed her, coloring her cheeks. Her eyes snapped. "It so happens, Mr. Prescott, that there are a few conditions."

"Such as?" he crooned the words, his thumb moving

along Shay's jawline and setting waves of heat rolling beneath her skin.

Shay swallowed hard. "I feel so foolish."

He kissed her, just nibbling at her lips, at once calming her and exciting her in a very devastating way. "You, the rainbow mender? Foolish? Never."

"I worked very hard to start my catering business," she blurted out. There was more to say, but Shay's courage failed her.

"I understand."

Shay forced herself to go on. "I don't think you do, Mitch. I—I thought it was what I wanted, but—"

Mitch arched one eyebrow. "But?"

"But it isn't. Not for now, anyway. Mitch, I want to take a time-out. I want to let Barbara and Louise run the business for a while. For now, I'd just like to be your wife and Hank's mother."

His lips twitched slightly. "Why was that so hard to say?" he asked, and he was holding Shay close now, so close that she could feel the beat of his heart through his coat.

"I guess I thought you were going to be horrified, or something," Shay mused aloud. "Most women of today…"

"You are not 'most women,' Shay." He cupped his hand under her chin and made her look at him. "I hope you kept that cardboard rainbow."

Shay was puzzled. "It's in the utility room. Why would you want a paper rainbow?"

Mitch ran a finger along her jawline again, setting her aquiver. "For the rainy days, Shay. There will be a few of those, you know."

She understood then, and she smiled. "We'll have our quarrels, I suppose."

"Quarrels? We'll have wars, Shay." The brown eyes twinkled. "But we'll have a good time negotiating the peace treaties."

Shay laughed and snuggled closer to him. "Ummm. I like the sound of that."

He swatted her bottom with one hand. "You would, you shameless vixen!" His whisper sent an aching heat all through her, and so did his gentle nip at her earlobe.

The tropical sun was hot, shimmering on the white sands of the secluded Mexican beach, dancing golden on water of so keen a blue that just looking at it made Shay's breath catch in her throat.

"Mitch?"

He was sitting on the small terrace outside their hotel room, his feet up on the railing, a man with five long minutes of marriage behind him. He looked back over one shoulder and laughed. "It's a little warm for that, isn't it?"

Shay ran her hands down the front of the mink coat he'd given her for Christmas. "It's New Year's day," she answered. "That means it's cold at home."

"Your logic, once again, escapes me."

Gulls and other seabirds squawked in the silence; it was the time of siesta and most of Mexico seemed to be asleep. Shay yawned and opened her coat.

Mitch, the sophisticate, the man of adventure, actually gasped. His eyes moved over Shay's naked body with quiet hunger, leaving a fever in their wake. He rose slowly from his chair and came toward her, pressing her back into the shadowy coolness of their room. "Mrs. Prescott," he muttered. "You are about to have the loving of your life."

She slid the coat back from her shoulders, allowed it to slip sensuously down her back and arms to the floor, where it lay in a lush, sumptuous pool. "Call now," she purred. "A wife this good can't last long."

As if bewitched, Mitch stepped closer. His throat moved, but he seemed incapable of anything more than the guttural growl he gave when she began unbuttoning his shirt.

Shay undressed her husband very slowly, pausing now and then to touch a taut masculine nipple with the tip of her tongue or tangle a finger in the hair on his chest. His groans of pleasure excited her to greater devilment.

Mitch bore her mischief as long as he could, then, with gentle force, he pressed her to the bed. He lay beside her for a time, caressing her breasts, her stomach, her thighs and even the backs of her knees. And when he had set her afire, he began kissing all those same places.

Shay's triumph became need; she twisted and tossed on the satin comforter that covered their marriage bed, she whimpered as he loved her, tasted her, tormented her.

Only when she pleaded did he take her.

Nine months and ten minutes later, as Mitch liked to say, Robert Mitchell Prescott was born.

Epilogue

It had been one hell of a fight; the rafters were still shaking.

Glumly, Mitch climbed the steps leading to the attic and opened the door. He flipped a switch and the huge room was bathed in light.

There were cobwebs everywhere and for a moment Mitch hesitated, then grew angry all over again.

It wasn't as though he intended to do anything really dangerous, after all. He wouldn't be tangling with Nazis or Klan members or hit men. This book was about racecar drivers, dammit!

He sat down on the top step, his chin in his hands. Okay, so he'd told Shay that he was through writing adventure books and now he was about to go back on his word, however indirectly. Hadn't she told him herself that she'd love him even if he did that?

Mitch gave a long sigh. He loved Shay, needed her,

depended on her in more ways than he dared to admit. And yet he'd just spent half an hour hollering at her, and she'd hollered back, with typical spirit.

Mitch was glad that Hank and the baby were with Alice that day. The uproar might have traumatized them both.

After a long time, he stood up and went into the attic.

Shay sat in one corner of the library sofa, her eyes puffy from crying, her throat raw. She couldn't believe that she'd yelled those awful things at Mitch. He was her husband, the father of her son, and she loved him more than she had on her wedding day, more with every passing minute.

She hugged herself. She'd known that Mitch would eventually want to write again, once the scars on his spirit had had time to heal. She'd known it, even without being warned by both Alice and Ivan, Mitch's agent.

Shay snatched a tissue from the box on her lap and blew her nose. Loudly. She supposed she should be grateful that Mitch was only planning to drive racecars; knowing him, he might have parachuted into Central America or slipped into some country where journalists were greeted with guns.

She rested her hands on her still-flat stomach, where a new baby was growing. She'd wanted to tell Mitch, use it to hold him to a quiet life of building condominiums with Todd Simmons, but that wouldn't have been fair. She sniffled again and reached for another tissue.

If she insisted that Mitch stay, he would give in. Shay knew that. But he would be miserable and there would be more fights. Gradually the great love they shared would be worn away.

The telephone rang and, because it was Mrs. Carraway's day off, Shay answered. The voice on the other end of the line was Garrett's.

"Hi'ya, Amazon," he said.

Shay burst into tears.

"What is it?" Garrett asked softly when the spate of grief was over.

Feeling like an absolute fool, Shay explained. The book about Rosamond had been published under Mitch's real name, so that much of his career was no longer a secret.

Garrett waited until Shay had told him all her fears of seeing Mitch crash in a burning racecar on some faraway track and there was a gentle reprimand in his voice when he spoke. "If you wanted to go back to your catering business, you'd do it, wouldn't you, even if it made Mitch mad?"

"That's hardly the same thing! I made cheeseballs, Garrett. I didn't race around some speedway, taking my life in my hands!"

"It *is* the same thing, Shay."

Shay dabbed at her face with a wad of tissue. "I know, I know. But I love him, Garrett."

"Enough to let him be himself?"

"Yes," Shay answered after a long time. "But that doesn't mean I have to like it."

Garrett chuckled. "I guess I called at a bad time. I'll get back to you later, sweetheart. Keep the faith."

Shay might have protested, but for the strange bumping-and-thumping sound coming from the stairway. "If you were calling about this year's camping trip, Hank is all for it."

Garrett promised to call again and hung up.

"Shay?"

She turned on the sofa to see Mitch leaning against one side of the library doorway. Despite his attempt at nonchalance, he looked wan and haggard and Shay felt a painful tightening in her heart. But fear for him made her voice cool. "Yes?"

"I won't go if it's that important to you. I'll write a novel or something."

Shay felt all broken and raw inside. "You'll only be racing for two or three weeks, won't you? Actually driving the cars, I mean?"

She thought she saw hope leap in the depths of his dark, dark eyes. "Three weeks at the most," he promised hoarsely.

"I'll hate every minute of it. I love you, Mitch."

He disappeared around the corner, came back in a moment dragging a very large and very dusty cardboard rainbow. A shower of glued-on glitter fell from the colorful arch as Mitch pulled it across the room and propped it against his desk.

"I think this is one of those rainy days we talked about," he said.

Shay felt tears sting her eyes. It was late July and the sun was shining, but Mitch was right. She held out her arms to him and he came to her, drawing her close, burying his face in the warm curve of her neck.

"I love you," he said.

Shay tangled the fingers of one hand in his hair. It was dusty from his foraging expedition in the attic. "And I love you. Too much to keep you here if that's not what you want."

"You could go with me." His hand was working its way under her sweater, cupping one breast, not to give passion but to take comfort.

"Of course I'll go."

Mitch lifted his face from her neck, let his forehead rest against hers. His fingers continued to caress her breast, after dislodging her bra. "Thank you," he said.

"I'd better get at least a dedication out of this," Shay

warned. "I don't exactly enjoy standing around racetracks with my heart stuffed into my sinuses, you know."

Mitch had found her nipple and his fingers shaped it gently. "My other books were dedicated to you. Why would this one be different?"

Shay was kneeling on the sofa now, her forehead still touching Mitch's. He had dedicated her mother's book to her, and the one about Alan Roget, too. She couldn't for the life of her remember what he'd said in those dedications, though. She groaned softly with the pleasure he could so easily arouse in her. "Is this the part where we work out a treaty?"

Mitch chuckled. "Yes." Deftly, he unfastened the catch of her bra, freeing her breasts, catching first one and then the other in the warm, teasing strength of his hand. With his other hand, he caressed her.

"Clearly, sir," she managed to say. "It isn't a treaty you want, but a full surrender."

He lifted her sweater high enough to bare one of her breasts and bent to take a tantalizing nip at its throbbing peak. "How astute you are," he muttered, his breath warm against her flesh.

Shay trembled. They were, after all, in the library. It was the middle of the day and anyone could walk in. "Mitch," she protested. "Alice—the kids—"

Mitch circled her nipple with the tip of his tongue, then got up to close and lock the library doors.

* * * * *

THE MIRACLE BABY

Janice Kay Johnson

JANICE KAY JOHNSON

The author of more than sixty books for children and adults, Janice Kay Johnson writes Harlequin Superromance novels about love and family—about the way generations connect and the power our earliest experiences have on us throughout life. Her 2007 novel *Snowbound* won a RITA® Award from Romance Writers of America for Best Contemporary Series Romance. A former librarian, Janice raised two daughters in a small rural town.

Chapter One

"Are you Mr. Nathan McCabe?"

The man who stood on Nathan's front porch was young, sandy-haired, a little soft around the middle. His face was unfamiliar, but pleasant enough. Your average Joe.

"That's right," Nathan agreed a little warily, his hand gripping the open door. Salesmen didn't know your name.

The man extended a card. "Richard Clayton, private investigator."

Nathan took the card. It was plain, but the paper was heavyweight, expensive, the print engraved. His wariness edged into apprehension.

"What can I do for you?" he asked.

The P.I. cleared his throat. "Mr. McCabe, did you have a brother named Robin?"

Rob. Sometimes he could almost forget the part of himself he'd lost with the estrangement. Being reminded was a jolt.

"I have a brother named Robin." What could admitting that much hurt? "Did he hire you?"

The first real emotion showed on that bland face. "Hire me? You're not aware…?"

"Aware of what?" Nathan asked sharply.

Unexpected compassion added a few lines to the man's face. "I'm sorry, Mr. McCabe. It's your brother's widow who hired me to find you. I'm afraid he's dead."

Dead? Rob? Shock held Nate still, unseeing. Dead? How could his brother be dead without his knowing?

Images flashed through his mind with scattergun speed: the boy, cheeks still childishly round, beguiling their kindergarten teacher; Rob, maybe ten, on the pitcher's mound; hanging upside down from the top bunk in their bedroom, tongue out and eyes crossed; lounging against his locker in high school, grinning lazily at some girl; the twenty-one-year-old, wiping blood from his nose and snarling. This last image was sharp, though fifteen years old. They hadn't seen each other since. Fifteen years, and Nathan didn't have to wonder what his brother had looked like before he died. All he had to do was glance in a mirror.

"How long ago?" he asked numbly.

"Three years. I'm sorry. I—"

"How?" Nathan's teeth were set. "How did he die?"

"I…" The P.I. retreated a step. "I'm not quite sure. Mrs. McCabe didn't say."

Mrs. McCabe. Rob had married and Nathan had never known. He couldn't picture his brother standing at the altar, gaze held by one woman. Couldn't imagine him saying, "I do," and meaning it. Lifting the veil and kissing her, sweeping her across a threshold, staying faithful, maybe changing diapers or coaching a Little League team. Making a marriage work, when Nathan couldn't.

Fifteen years. He kept bumping up against it. A big chunk of his lifetime. They'd been so young when he'd broken his brother's nose and walked away without looking back. Their parting wasn't supposed to be permanent, whatever he'd said at the time. Nathan had always figured Rob would give him some time to cool off, then come find him. Alone on Christmas Eve this year, Nathan had started thinking maybe it was time *he* did the finding. But even then, it had been too late.

Nathan closed his eyes for a moment, let the pain rip open a wound he'd thought long healed. He rubbed a hand over his face.

"If he died three years ago, why does she want to find me now?"

The P.I.'s unmemorable face would be forever engraved in Nathan's memory, stuck in his mental photo album. The poor SOB hadn't even known he was to be the bearer of the worst tidings.

He was talking, and with difficulty Nathan latched on to his words. A daughter. Something about a daughter, eleven years old. *Rob's daughter.*

He interrupted. "Do you have a picture?"

He'd caught the P.I. off guard. "Yes, I… Right here." He groped in one pocket of his jacket, then the other. "Mrs. McCabe thought…"

"A picture would soften me?"

"Yes. No. That is…"

Nathan took the photo and tuned the man out. It was a school picture, like those that came with Christmas cards, friends showing him in the faces of their children how quickly the years were passing. The girl wore a denim dress with an embroidered neckline and she was smiling uncertainly. Nathan knew her eyes, big and dark; they were Rob's—and his own.

But, good God, her hair wasn't an inch long, dark and fine, revealing the shape of her skull. And she was ghost pale, and thin. He was reminded of pictures he'd seen of concentration-camp survivors.

He lifted a shocked gaze to Richard Clayton, P.I. "What's wrong with her?"

"Leukemia," Clayton said bluntly. "She needs a bone-marrow transplant. Mrs. McCabe isn't a suitable donor, and the National Bone Marrow Donor Registry hasn't found one. Because you and Amanda's father were twins, the chances are excellent that your tissue is a match."

As he absorbed the news, Nathan lowered his gaze to the picture again. Rob's daughter. His niece. Maybe dying for lack of her father.

"What do I need to do?" he asked simply.

Beth ran the vacuum cleaner down the hall. Ahead of her, bobtailed Calvin, an orange kitten, darted into Mandy's bedroom and no doubt under the bed. Behind Beth, Calvin's sister Polly chased the vacuum cord. From the same litter, with the same upbringing, and one was terrified by the vacuum cleaner while the other apparently thought it was just a big noisy mouse. Was there a gene for courage?

Was there one for leukemia?

She turned into her daughter's bedroom and ran the vacuum over the carpet while she tried not to look around, not to think. But her effort was as useless today as it was every other day. Mandy was doing well right now, to all appearances a normal preteen. In front of her, Beth pretended; alone, she had no defense against her fear. With a sigh she switched off the vacuum cleaner.

In the sudden silence Beth stood in the middle of

Mandy's bedroom and gave way to the knowing, to the terror. The room was too neat—books in alphabetical order, spines perfectly lined up, dresser drawers and closet doors shut. And Beth knew that inside them the shoes and the socks and dresses and jeans would be stacked and hung in order just as perfectly, sorted by color or sometimes by a mysterious system all Mandy's own. Even her bulletin board was ordered: school pictures of her friends marching along the bottom, all held in place by the same-color thumbtacks; awards and ribbons just above them held by tacks of a different color; and in the upper third of the board a tidy line of odd tidbits—a dried bunch of flowers, a piece of lace, one earring, a newspaper photo of the middle-school boys' soccer team and a Garfield cartoon. It was as though Mandy thought she could save herself by imposing order on her world.

Exactly at the center of her desk was her journal, the cover marbled paper, the spine navy blue leather. Mandy left it there every day, never hiding it as Beth suspected most girls did with their diaries. Was her openness an act of trust? Or a way of begging her mother to peek into her heart and see her fears?

So far, Beth hadn't let herself. Every day, she resisted the terrible temptation. A girl's diary should be private. If Mandy handed it to her, she'd read it. Until then, she had to give her daughter the freedom to confide the unspeakable.

Beth blinked hard to clear the mist from her eyes. When she realized her nose was running, too, she mumbled, "Oh, damn. Why did I have to start?"

She was in the bathroom blowing her nose when a knock sounded on the front door. Her forehead crinkled. Funny, she hadn't heard the UPS truck pull in. Oh, well, maybe she'd still had the vacuum running. Fortunately she had the half-dozen shipments of jam packed and ready to go. She tossed the tissue into the wastebasket and hurried to answer the door.

"Hi, I'm all set—" When she saw the tall dark-haired man standing on her porch, shock snatched her breath and her voice with it. Rob. Oh, God, her dead husband was within arm's reach. Clutching the door frame, she whispered his name.

He moved his shoulders uncomfortably. "No, I'm Nathan McCabe. Rob's brother."

Still she sagged against the door, staring. She'd known Rob had a twin, had even hired the private investigator to find him, but somehow she'd never dreamed that he would *be* Rob all over again. The hair, wavy and short and silky, those prominent cheekbones, the dark slash of brows over brown eyes, the thin hard mouth. Her unbelieving gaze searched his face for some difference, anything she could fasten on to convince herself that he wasn't Rob, that Rob hadn't found a way to come back to her.

He flushed under her stare, something her supremely confident husband would never have done. But still…

His clothes. She seized on it. Rob would never have chosen anything as conservative as a gray suit, white shirt and narrow maroon tie. Yet that suit jacket would have hung just the same way from her husband's shoulders had he worn it. Even this man's hands, tanned, large and half-curled into fists, could have been Rob's. She made another strangled sound.

"I'm sorry," he said quietly. "I didn't think. I should have let Clayton warn you."

She lifted her gaze back to his face. "He found you?"

"Yeah. I thought you'd be pleased."

"Pleased." She sounded and felt blank, too stunned for rational thought.

He made that uneasy movement with his shoulders again. "Clayton said you needed me."

Understanding flooded back and with it embarrassment. She pressed hands to her hot cheeks. "Nathan. Your name's Nathan."

His eyes met hers. "Rob called me Nate."

"I know." Of course she did. "Is…is that what you go by?"

"Rob and our parents were the only ones who called me that."

"Family," she said softly.

The grooves on each side of his mouth deepened. "Yeah."

"We would have been family."

"We *are* family," he said with quiet intensity.

Beth shook her head, not in rejection of the idea, but in astonishment. He was here because she needed him. He was family.

She let out a long breath. "I'm sorry. Come in. I've been rude. It's just…"

"We look so much alike. I understand. I suppose it's… unnerving."

He stepped past her and she gave a small shiver. "He said you were identical twins. But somehow I thought after all these years there would be differences."

"There probably are. Were." Just inside the living room he stood silent for a moment, his back to her. "I didn't know he was dead."

"I'm sorry," Beth said again. "I should have tried to find you then. But that's when Mandy got sick. I…I just couldn't deal with everything. It was easy to convince myself you wouldn't care."

"We were twins. A lot came between us, but no matter

what, we were tied together." He faced her and his mouth twisted. "I can't believe he's dead."

"Please, sit down." She moved to the couch and curled up on one end, watching him sit stiffly in the worn wing chair she kept meaning to reupholster.

"How?" His voice was hoarse. "How did he die?"

She looked down at her hands. "A car accident. He always drove too fast. He had this red Corvette he really loved."

"He always wanted one." Nathan's dark eyes became unfocused as he saw a past that Rob hadn't shared with her.

She nodded, even though he probably didn't see her. "I was glad when we could afford it. We don't get to fulfill that many dreams. Now I'd give anything to take it back. Maybe if he'd been driving a different car he wouldn't have been going so fast. All he was doing was coming home from work. Just a normal commute." She fell silent, remembering that night.

In January darkness fell early. The roads had been icy, but Rob was such a good driver, even if he did go too fast sometimes. His reflexes were quick, his instincts sure. Though he'd promised to be home by five o'clock, she hadn't worried until six came and went. She'd called his office and gotten no reply. She'd been standing at the front window, looking at the dark driveway, willing Rob to appear, when a pair of headlights turned in. A giddy burst of relief had told her how worried she'd been. And then fear had trickled into her chest, for almost immediately she'd realized that the headlights weren't right, didn't look like the Corvette's. She'd moved out onto the porch, hugging herself against the cold, and it was then she'd seen it was a police car. The trooper had climbed out and come slowly, heavily, toward her.

Remembering, Beth gave another small shiver and heard her husband's brother say, "Are you all right?"

She shook her head, attempting to clear it of memories. "Our insurance rates were horrendous. When I asked Rob to slow down, he'd just laugh. He'd never had an accident, just tickets for speeding. I told him if he needed an adrenaline rush, he should take up skydiving. It would have been safer."

"Did he…" Nathan cleared his throat. "Did he hit anybody else?"

"Oh, yeah." She was staring straight ahead, that video still playing for her. "A van driven by a mother with her two kids. The road was icy and the Corvette apparently went into a skid and crossed the center line. Rob died instantly. The mother had some broken bones, but thank God she recovered. The kids were in car seats and weren't hurt at all. If they had been…" She pressed her lips together.

"It wouldn't have been your fault," he said quietly.

"Maybe not, but it felt like it was."

Their eyes met, held; for a second she'd have sworn the world narrowed to the two of them. Then she squeezed her eyes shut just long enough to blot out the memories.

Almost composed, Beth looked from his hands, spread on the smooth gray fabric of his slacks, back to his face. *Don't think about Rob,* she told herself. *He's here because of Mandy; nothing else matters.* "Mr. Clayton told you about my daughter?"

Nathan leaned forward. "He said she has leukemia. He showed me a picture."

"Yes." She bit her lip. "She's doing fine right now, but doctors give her only two or three years unless she has a bone-marrow transplant. We can't find a donor who matches. Would you be willing?"

"That's why I'm here." He frowned. "Isn't hers the usual

childhood leukemia? I thought doctors were doing wonders with chemotherapy."

"They are." Her throat wanted to close, which surprised her. She and Mandy had lived with the bogeyman for so long now; she'd explained the illness over and over again to teachers and principals and the parents of Mandy's friends. Why was it hard now to describe the monster inside her child?

Somehow she kept her voice steady. "Mandy—Amanda—has a more unusual form of leukemia for children that's difficult to treat. It was such a shock. She started having stomach cramps. We thought she had the flu. A week later she felt better and went back to school. But then the cramps started again. She was in agony. Of course, I took her to the doctor." Beth looked down to find that she was wringing her hands. With an effort she separated them.

"That must have been frightening."

She let out a breath in a laugh that held no humor. "Terrifying is a better word. When I was a child, my best friend died of leukemia. They couldn't do anything then. She just…came home until she was too sick, then went into the hospital to die. To have Mandy get it, too…" *Why?* she cried inside. *Dear God, why her?*

Nathan stirred, as though he would have liked to come over to her. Or was he longing to bolt, instead? Beth had discovered that many people were so uncomfortable with the subject they avoided her.

"Mandy had lumps, too, around her ankles. She'd noticed them and just…shrugged them off, I guess. She was only eight. As soon as she was diagnosed, they started chemotherapy. She lost all her hair and was horribly sick. She responded well, though. But the doctors warned us that this form of leukemia is essentially incurable without a transplant. All they could do was buy time."

"When was this?"

She scrubbed at suddenly wet cheeks. "Three years ago."

"Then Rob was alive...?"

"No." Oh, how angry she'd been at him! "He'd been dead a month when she got sick."

He made a sound in his throat. "Did you have anyone to...?"

"Friends." She tried to smile. "Strangers. People were wonderful. I don't think I cooked a meal for six months. Casserole dishes just...appeared."

His dark eyes didn't waver. "Then what happened?"

"We couldn't find a donor. I have such a small family, and none of us comes close. The donor registry hasn't found anyone. A year and a half ago, Mandy got really sick again." Beth fought for composure. "This time the doctors used both chemotherapy and radiation. If...if she gets that sick again, she might be too weak to survive the procedure. She desperately needs the bone-marrow transplant."

"Was she sure to match either Rob or you?"

"No." Did she sound as helpless as she felt? Beth wondered. "A patient can have a large family and not be a close enough match with any of them. But the odds are a lot better with you than they would be with someone unrelated. Then the odds become something like one in twenty thousand."

He rose as though he couldn't bear to sit any longer. "I'll do anything."

She stood slowly, her eyes blurred. "Thank you," she whispered.

He came around the end of the coffee table, this man who looked so much like her husband. There he stopped, as though unsure what to do or uncertain of her reaction. If he'd opened his arms, she would have stepped into them, laid her head against his chest, accepted his strength and comfort. It was disquieting to know how easily she could have accepted almost anything from him, a total stranger. She didn't like to think she would have pretended he was Rob.

This man's eyes were unreadable, dark, but he lifted a hand and carefully brushed away the tears from her cheek. The gesture was heart-stoppingly intimate, and yet innocent. Any adult might do the same to a hurt child.

"I..." Her voice was high, breathless. "I'd better call the hospital. Make...make arrangements."

He cleared his throat and stepped back. "I can go anytime."

She blinked at the reminder of everyday details, and was a little ashamed she hadn't asked any questions about his life. Not even where he lived.

"Do you live around Seattle? Or did you fly in?"

"Flew. I'm from Portland."

"Maybe they could still do the blood test today. You haven't checked into a hotel already, have you? I have an extra bedroom."

He shook his head immediately. "I'm afraid I can't stay overnight. Not this time. I have an early-morning meeting back in Portland."

She wondered if he'd planned it that way to give himself an escape. Would they ever see him again after the procedure? Did it matter? she asked herself impatiently. He was here now; that was what counted.

"Um...would you like a cup of coffee? Or anything else?"

"Thank you," he said, "but no."

"Then excuse me for a moment."

"Mrs. McCabe?" His voice stopped her in the doorway. She turned. "Yes?"

"Clayton didn't tell me your name. He kept calling you the widow."

"Beth." She actually smiled, if tremulously. "I'm Beth McCabe."

The touch of his dark eyes was as palpable as a knuckle brushing her cheek. "Beth. Beth and Mandy."

"Does it feel strange?" She flattened her hand against the door frame. "To be here like this when you didn't even know we existed?"

"Very strange," he admitted, "but right."

She gave a small nod and left him in her living room. In her office she sat down at the enormous rolltop desk, reached for the phone—and suddenly felt herself trembling all over. She squeezed her hands into fists and closed her eyes. It was just reaction—the shock of finding her husband's double on her doorstep and the knowledge that he could be the gift of life to Mandy.

She knew she was crying again, but didn't care. He'd come without hesitation. He was willing. For the first time in a long while, she had hope.

The house was too silent after his brother's widow left the room. Feeling the tension in his neck and back, Nathan listened for her footsteps or her voice. Nothing. It was as though she'd never existed, as though he'd imagined finding her. He began to pace.

A few strides took him from the Oriental rug onto hardwood floor. The old-fashioned, high-ceilinged parlor had the tall sashed windows typical of the time the house was built—between 1910 and 1920, he guessed. Lacy curtains hung open. He glanced out one side window at fields of some kind of vine—probably berry—twining along wire supports. A handsome wooden sign out at the road had said Tillicum Creek Farm. He supposed the fields went with the house. But surely, he thought, frowning, Beth wasn't farming alone.

All the while, he knew his speculation was no more than an attempt to distract himself from the framed photographs lovingly displayed on the fireplace mantel. He'd noticed them the moment he stepped in the room. They exerted a force that both repelled and drew him. It was the pull that was winning.

He had pictures of Rob, too, a couple of boxes of albums that had been faithfully kept by his mother, stashed in a seldom opened closet. He'd gone straight to the closet when he closed the door on Richard Clayton, P.I. When he pulled the albums out of the box and flipped them open, he'd found only the kid his brother had been: cheeky, smart-mouthed, too charismatic for his own damned good. His twin. That part of himself he'd savagely excised. None were of the man Rob had become. He had cried finally, howls of agony he'd kept corked tightly inside for too many years. With the knowledge of Rob's death, the seal had failed, and the poison of his bitterness and loneliness poured out. It was the most terrible night of his life, worse than discovering how his brother had betrayed him, worse than their fight, worse than losing his parents or his wife's leaving him.

And now he would be confronted with the man his brother had become. Bracing himself, Nathan approached the fireplace. Rob was there all right, in half a dozen photos, grinning in that crooked lazy way women always had found irresistible. Nathan gripped the edge of the mantel, feeling as though the wind had been kicked out of him. Bracing himself hadn't worked. He tried to look away from the photographs until he could control his reaction, but his hunger to see his brother's face was too great. In the sea of pain, Nathan was vaguely aware of surprise: Rob hadn't changed very much from Nathan's memory of him, which didn't gibe with Rob's having been a married man with a child. Maybe the change was all on the inside.

In only a couple of the photos was he alone; the others were either family portraits or home snapshots. In one he had a dark-haired toddler on his shoulders. She was clutching Daddy's hair and grinning, heels drumming his chest, if Nathan was any judge. In another Rob wore a suit, the solemnity spoiled by the tie, which sported a bold Van Gogh sunset. This time Amanda must have been seven or eight; she stood proudly beside him in patent-leather shoes and a pretty dress with a pleated skirt and a big fat bow on one shoulder. They looked uncannily alike, despite the gender and age difference. They *belonged* together. How could Rob be gone?

But the ones he found himself most reluctant to look at were those that included Beth, the studio portraits. In them, they were the perfect family: broad-shouldered handsome man hovering protectively over his delicate wife and cute daughter. Rob's expression seemed to hold a little smugness; *I've got it all,* Nathan imagined him saying. As a kid Rob would have added, *And you don't.*

Nathan swore under his breath and muttered, "Grow up." He wasn't talking to his brother. He was shocked to discover how much competitiveness he still felt, even amidst his grief. No wonder he'd been a failure as a husband! No wonder he couldn't bring himself to forgive the person who had once been the most important in the world to him. He was corroded inside by the acid of his resentment.

Right now most of it had to do with Beth McCabe, the woman Rob had married. Didn't it figure that, at least in the looks department, she was exactly what had always attracted Nathan more than his brother? Curly blond hair— not the gold of a shiny new wedding ring, but something paler, softer, a shimmer instead of a glitter. Creamy skin with a few unexpected freckles on her small nose. Mist-gray eyes that were candid and uncomfortably percep-tive. A small-boned build that looked fragile but probably wasn't. He'd noticed her short unpainted nails, seen a few scratches on her hands. Her clothes didn't match the china-doll image, either: she wore snug, faded denim jeans with a Madras cotton shirt knotted around her slender waist, outlining small but shapely breasts.

Rob had always liked flashier women, ones with big tits and pouty lips and invitation in their eyes. Which hadn't stopped him from pursuing the ones with a quieter kind of beauty once he'd noticed his brother's interest. It had been his life's work to demonstrate that anything Nathan could have or do, he could have or do, too.

Nathan focused on his brother's grin again and could have sworn it had become a taunt from the past.

"What the hell is the matter with me?" he said aloud, backing away from the mantel. Good God, did he still hate Rob after all this time? Maybe his brother never had been the one with the problem. Maybe *he* was.

Before he had a chance to pursue the disquieting thought he heard the front door slam, quick footsteps and a girl's voice. "Hey, Mom, what are you doing—" She broke off suddenly, obviously noticing there was a man in the living room. His back was still to her. "Oh, sorry. I didn't know anybody was here."

Nathan turned to face her with damn near as much re-luctance as he'd approached the family portrait gallery. He shouldn't have come like this, taken them by surprise.

He got what he expected and deserved. The skinny curly-haired girl first flushed, then paled. In a clogged voice she said, "Daddy?"

He felt lower than lice. Nothing like replaying this scene, and with a child even more vulnerable than her mother.

"No," he said quickly. "No, I'm not your father. I know I look like him. We were twins. I'm his brother."

She did nothing but stare from those huge dark eyes for a long unnerving moment. Then she said tentatively, "Are you Uncle Nate?"

He wasn't sure which part hit him harder, the "Uncle" or the "Nate." Rob's name for him.

"Yeah. That's me."

"Daddy…" She pressed her lips together. "Daddy used to talk about you sometimes."

"Did he have anything good to say?" Nate cringed inwardly at his question. Did he sound like he was begging? *Throw me a crumb. Tell me my brother remembered me with some affection.*

"Well, of course!" Her smile was unexpectedly merry in that solemn little face. "He used to tell me about things you guys did together. You know. Pranks." The smile dimmed a little. "He said he hadn't had as much fun since."

That part had hurt her feelings, Nathan could tell. He wanted to tell her the pranks hadn't been fun at all, though probably they'd started out that way. But he could hardly say, "Your dad lied. He liked cruel pranks."

He settled for, "Twins can pull things off that no one else can."

"I wish I had one," she said wistfully.

This pang was closer to a knife stabbing in his chest. If she had a twin, she could be cured of leukemia. She had to be thinking that.

"It has its downside. Sometimes…" He hesitated, then said what he'd never admitted aloud, "Sometimes you're not sure whether you exist at all alone."

Her eyes were disconcertingly intense. It was a relief when, after a moment, she ducked her head and hunched her shoulders awkwardly. "Uh, do you know where my mom is?"

"She went off to make a phone call."

"Oh." Her head lifted and she offered him a polite smile. "Excuse me. I'll go tell her I'm home."

"Sure."

She turned and walked right into her mother, who came through the doorway. Amanda gasped, and Beth gave her a hug. "Sorry. I sneaked up on you." Though her tone was light, Beth's gaze went straight to him, and he saw the wariness in it. "Did you meet your uncle Nathan?"

"Uncle Nate. That's what Daddy always called him."

Always. Had Rob talked about him often? Missed him? Nathan had a disorienting sense of the ground shifting under his feet. All these years he'd done his damnedest not to think about his brother. Someday they'd forgive and forget. But what was the hurry? Apart from Nathan, his mirror image, maybe Rob would quit feeling as if he had to prove himself over and over. Maybe he'd find contentment.

Well, to all appearances he had. With luck he'd been freed to remember Nathan with fondness.

Mother and daughter were staring at him, he realized suddenly. He'd been silent too long, missed something. "I'm sorry," he said.

Nobody repeated whatever it was. Amanda suddenly frowned. "Why is Uncle Nate here now?"

The alarm in Beth's eyes was clear, as was her dilemma. Did she tell the truth and, perhaps falsely, raise her daughter's hopes? Or lie?

He had no idea how much his niece knew about her illness. *His niece.* Already he couldn't bear to think of her dying. If he hadn't seen that school picture, which must have been taken a few months ago, he might not have believed in her illness. Her hair was several inches longer now and curly, a halo surrounding a piquant face that was all cheekbones and high forehead and big eyes. She was thin, but no more so than many girls her age who had barely begun developing. Her mother had probably looked much the same, only her curls would have been silky pale, instead of fine and dark.

If she'd meant to lie, Beth shouldn't have hesitated as long as she did.

Amanda stepped away from her and lifted her chin. "It has something to do with my leukemia, doesn't it?"

Beth visibly gathered herself. "Yes," she said gently. "He's here to have his blood tested to find out whether he might be a suitable bone-marrow donor."

Mandy went completely still, unblinking. Then she focused on his face, gave a small nod and said politely, "Thank you." She turned to her mother. "May I get a snack?"

"Of course you can." Lines formed on Beth's brow as she watched her daughter leave the room, composure undented.

Nathan waited for a moment. Then he asked in a low voice, "Is she afraid of the transplant?"

He had never seen a woman look as vulnerable as Beth McCabe did at that moment. "Do you know," she said, "I don't have the slightest idea?"

"She doesn't talk to you?" he asked incredulously.

She clasped her hands together as though she was praying. "On any other subject, yes. On this one...she listens and nods and asks questions when she doesn't understand something. Usually she answers a direct question. But as close as we've always been, I truly don't know how frightened she is. I think..." Her voice broke. "It's as if she senses my fear and doesn't want to burden me with hers."

He nodded and shoved his fisted hands into his pants

pockets. It was the only way he could figure to keep himself from pulling her into his arms. They didn't know each other well enough for that, even if he felt as though they did. Or maybe he only wished they did.

"When do they want me at the hospital?" he asked with unplanned brusqueness.

She gave her head a shake, as though she could rid herself of sad thoughts like a dog shaking off water droplets. "Now, if you want to go. It's in Seattle, at Children's Hospital. At least you're going against rush-hour traffic. You can make it in forty-five minutes."

"How long until they know whether I'm a match?"

"A while, unfortunately. Next week sometime. The doctor guessed Thursday." Beth smiled wanly. "You wouldn't believe how slowly time can crawl. Or how little sleep you can exist on."

He knew damn well that he wouldn't sleep much tonight, either. No more than he had last night. Then he'd had only his brother's ghost to torment him. Now, Amanda, slender and too grave, would stand beside her father to stare reproachfully at him in his waking nightmares.

She and her mother needed him, and he hated like hell knowing that his ability to play the hero was no more in his control than tomorrow's weather.

Yeah, he told himself, *and if you do turn out to be the hero, it's only because you're a carbon copy of Rob.* A humbling thought.

"I'm on my way, then," he said.

"We…we'd really like to get to know you." Her gray eyes were anxious. "Will you come for a longer visit soon? As I said, I have an extra bedroom. Maybe you could spend a weekend."

"You're sure? It wouldn't upset Amanda?"

"Are you kidding?" Beth actually reached out and

squeezed his arm. "You're the next best thing to having her dad back again. You'd be good for her."

He almost wished he hadn't given himself an out, that he *was* coming back here tonight. But he'd figured it would be easier for everyone if he didn't have the option of hanging around.

"If you mean it, I could come next week. Say, Thursday morning." He'd rather be here when she got the news, good or bad. Maybe especially if it was bad. "I could stay until Friday afternoon."

She smiled, for a fleeting moment radiant, letting him glimpse what she would look like freed from her ever-present fear. "Bless you. We'll look forward to it. It'll give Mandy something to think about." Something besides the blood test was what she meant.

He nodded and let Beth walk him to his rental car. On the way down the long bumpy lane, he allowed himself a wry smile. They needed him, all right. He was "the next best thing" to having Rob back again.

He guessed his little brother by one minute had won another round.

But when Nathan glanced in his rearview mirror, he saw that the smaller figure of Rob's daughter had come out onto the porch to join her mother in staring after his car. He was instantly ashamed of the pettiness of his thoughts.

Only one person counted here. Amanda McCabe. Rob's daughter and his niece. Whatever anger had lain between the brothers, on this they'd be united, Nathan felt suddenly sure. He hoped there was somebody up there listening when he prayed that his blood was Mandy's salvation, since Rob couldn't be here.

Chapter Two

Nathan was virtually useless at work that week. All the
memories he'd repressed these past fifteen years stole back
one at a time. They came at unexpected moments, one
catching at him like a sharp nail tearing skin, another poking like a little boy jabbing him with a stick, yet another
making him smile before he clenched his teeth in agony.
The memories slipped into his dreams, and he woke twice
with a face wet with tears. Moments of distraction, of real
attention to the life taking place right in front of him, were
sliced short by the knife edge of a name, a face. He jogged
each morning from habit, but even then the pain of his
brother's death gripped him like a side ache.

He didn't understand the extent of his grief. He hadn't
seen Rob for so many years, hardly even thought of him.
He'd even believed he hated his brother. Curiously, terrify-
ingly, his dreams filled in those lost years. He was at Rob's
wedding, watching his brother lift the veil, kiss his bride.

Somehow, Amanda was the flower girl. Another night, Rob drove up in his brand-new red Corvette, eager to show it off. They went for a drive, and the road was icy. In the middle of a long skid, Nathan woke up to his own muffled shout. God almighty. He'd seen through the windshield of the van they were about to hit head-on. Beth was driving and Amanda was in the passenger seat.

There were other, more innocuous dreams. Rob sitting beside their parents at Nathan's college graduation. At the other end of the rope, belaying Nathan, on a climb up Three Fingers.

Under the onslaught only one thought held Nathan together: Rob's daughter needed him.

And Beth was right. Nathan hadn't known time could slow down to the point where waiting for the clock to move forward a minute was like waiting for the next drip from a leaky faucet. He'd sneak glances at his watch during meetings, then find out he'd missed half of what went on. As Monday passed, then Tuesday, his tension rose, like the jagged energy too much caffeine gave to an exhausted man. Finally, Tuesday evening he couldn't stand it. He called.

"No word yet," Beth told him in an upbeat voice, which meant her daughter was nearby. "But Mandy's doing great. She got straight A's this quarter."

"Hey." He felt absurdly pleased, as though his genes had helped make her smart. "Can I talk to her?"

"You bet."

A second later, "Uncle Nate?"

"Congratulations on the 4.0. You and your mom celebrating?"

"She took me to Baskin Robbins for an ice-cream sundae. It was really good."

"You deserved it." When she didn't say anything, he continued, "May I speak to your mom again?" After Beth came back on, Nathan asked, "Any chance I can move my visit up to tomorrow? I have to see some people not far from you. It'd be late afternoon, probably just in time for dinner. I'd like to take you and Mandy out."

Her voice warmed even further. "Tomorrow would be great. Mandy keeps asking about you, and I have to admit how little I know. But why don't we plan on eating here? You won't want to turn around and head back into the city. We can go out another time. Thursday, if you can stay that long."

"Done," he agreed. They broke off the connection, and he immediately dialed another number. Maybe he really should try to set up a meeting at R.E.I.

"Do you have a family, Beth?" Though he was speaking to her mother, Nathan smiled across the dinner table at Amanda, who ducked her head shyly.

"A brother, but we're not close. He's a geologist for a petroleum company. He's been in Saudi Arabia for a couple of years, although he did fly home…" She hesitated and glanced at her daughter.

Nathan could finish the sentence. *He did fly home when Mandy got sick the last time.* His blood must not have been a match, either.

"I still see my stepfather occasionally and we talk often," she continued, "but my mother passed away some years ago. Lung cancer. She smoked."

Nathan grunted. "My father, too. Emphysema got him."

"Yes, Rob mentioned it." Her gaze flitted nervously from his and she made a production out of buttering a roll.

Mandy announced suddenly, "I want to be a doctor when I grow up." Her tone was defiant and he knew why. Unlike most kids, she had no certainty that she would grow up.

"Good for you," Nathan said. "I used to say the same, until I discovered how much I hated my college chemistry course."

Beth's eyes met his. "So what did you do?"

"Majored in business, worked a few years for Eddie Bauer, then I started my own company, Mount Hood Sporting Goods. We manufacture small tents, sleeping bags, climbing equipment. Stuff for serious outdoorsmen."

"Why, we have a couple of your sleeping bags." Expression arrested, Beth let her fork clatter onto her plate. "One of them was Rob's! Did he know…?"

Grief, sudden and strangling, tightened around his chest. What if Rob had known? What if he'd bought the sleeping bags *because* he'd known? As a—oh, hell—a kind of connection to his lost brother?

"I don't suppose he did." Beth wasn't the one Nathan was trying to convince. "We're based in Portland. Unless he read about the company in the business section of the newspaper, I can't imagine how he would have stumbled on my name."

"He talked about you quite a bit, you know." She hadn't picked up her fork. Tiny creases formed between her brows. "Didn't you ever…oh, wonder about him? What he was doing?"

"Of course I wondered." Anger edged his tone, though it wasn't directed at her. "I even thought… Damn." He swallowed hard. "Lately I'd been thinking I ought to try to find him." And kept putting it off. Now to learn Rob had been dead these last few years…

"Rob talked about hunting for you, too."

"It wouldn't have been hard," he said shortly. "I didn't hide."

Her voice cooled. "I encouraged him. But he didn't think you'd want to see him."

She didn't like him because he'd hurt her husband. He couldn't blame her. At the moment, knowing what his temper and pride had cost him, he didn't like himself, either.

It was sure as hell too late to discover he missed his twin.

Out of his peripheral vision, Nathan saw Amanda watching him anxiously. He laid down his knife and fork. Curiosity provoked the question, but a desire to reassure the girl made him school his voice to be pleasantly inquiring—no more, no less.

"What did Rob do? He always intended to go to law school. Said he had a golden tongue, could talk anybody into anything."

Beth wrinkled her nose. "He talked me into marrying him, and we'd only met a month before."

A bitter memory surfaced briefly before Nathan could shove it under again. His tone was sardonic. "He'd have been another Clarence Darrow if juries were all made up of women."

"Because we're all open to suggestion?" she asked tartly.

"Only Rob's."

Amanda was turning her head to follow the conversation as though it were a tennis match. "Who's Clarence Darrow?"

"A famous trial lawyer."

"Oh." She thought it over. "You mean, Dad talked women into—" She broke off abruptly, her cheeks flushing crimson.

"In high school, your father always dated the prettiest girls," Nathan said, smiling at her. "I never could figure out where I went wrong."

"Maybe he dressed cooler." Amanda sounded teenage-wise, although she was only eleven. "Or hung out with more popular kids. Sometimes girls like guys for really dumb reasons."

His grin this time was genuine. "Right. It had to have been his clothes. Or maybe because he wore his hair longer. I had to cut mine to be on the wrestling team."

"Dad was really cool, though," Amanda said. "He drove a red Corvette. All my friends wished *their* dads were like him."

Nathan glanced at the girl's mother, catching a flash of pain in her eyes, but she hid it quickly.

Before Amanda could remember that her father's red Corvette had killed him, Nathan said, "You look like him. Especially when he was your age. Except we were both shrimps."

"You mean, you were shorter than all the girls in fifth grade?" she asked incredulously.

"Yep. My ego has never recovered."

She digested that. "But if I look like Dad, that must mean I look like you, too."

He exchanged a silent glance with her mother. This time Beth said easily, "I really can see a resemblance to your uncle Nathan."

"Uncle Nate," Amanda corrected her.

Beth looked from his face to her daughter's and back again. "It's partly your coloring, but...oh, there's something about the shape of your face. And your nose."

"But I look kind of like you, too, don't I?" Amanda sounded suddenly anxious.

Nathan gave her a teasing smile. "The pretty part comes from your mom."

"But I'm not pretty," she said gloomily. "I'm shaped like a stick and my hair's so dumb and short, and Mom says I have to get glasses."

"By the time the boys are worth looking at," Beth said, "I promise I'll let you get contacts."

He felt another twist in his gut. Having a conversation with his niece was like crossing an unstable snowfield. The future was everything to most kids Amanda's age, but she had to live with the knowledge that she might not have one.

How the hell did Beth manage to talk about next year and the year after and the one after that as though they were certainties? If he hurt for Amanda, what must her mother feel? Yet she was able to quietly express her faith over and over again, just by assuming that Amanda would be around to need contacts and braces and a bra. Someday Amanda would know how lucky she had been.

If she had that someday.

Had Rob known how lucky he was? Nathan tried to imagine his brother sitting in this chair, presiding over the family dinner, listening to Amanda chatter about school, then his wife relating tidbits of her day. The picture just wouldn't develop, like a Polaroid snapshot still murky.

Maybe she saw his discomfort, because Beth steered the conversation to generalities. Next thing he knew, mother and daughter both stood and started clearing the table. "Coffee?" Beth asked.

He pushed back his chair. "Thanks. Can I help?"

"Your next visit." Her smile looked a little forced. "Tonight you're a guest."

By the time the coffee was ready, Amanda had gone upstairs to do her homework. Beth brought his cup and a mug of herbal tea for herself out to the living room. She kicked off her shoes and curled up on one end of the sofa.

Before she could think up yet another innocuous topic, he asked, "What kind of work *did* Rob do?"

"Sales. He was a regional sales rep for an electronics company. He majored in business, too."

Damned if Nathan didn't feel a surge of resentment. One more thing he hadn't been permitted to do alone. His twin had echoed him in that, too.

But the resentment was mild, a shadow of the raw fury that had driven them apart. Rob couldn't possibly have copied him deliberately. The fact that they'd taken the same path in the last two years of college was just another reminder of how much a person's nature was determined by genes. He and his brother had been alike because they couldn't help it; hell, maybe he was attracted to Rob's widow because he was programmed to be just like his twin. Maybe their lifelong battle to be unique individuals had been doomed from the beginning, because physiologically they *were* identical.

Her soft voice interrupted his brooding. "Why does that upset you?"

He became aware that he was frowning in Beth's general direction, his coffee untouched. He raked his fingers through his hair. "Was I glowering at you? Sorry."

"Actually I had the sense you'd forgotten I was here."

He grimaced. "That's even worse."

"I don't take offense so easily." Her gaze was serene, though he wondered how much effort it took for her to give that impression. "I know this isn't easy for you. I'm all the more grateful that you were willing to come."

"How could I not?" He resisted the urge to stand up and pace. "She's my niece, for God's sake."

"But you didn't know her."

"I wish I had. I wish meeting her hadn't taken something like this." It swamped him then, a fact he couldn't quite believe. Couldn't quite accept. His throat closed and his eyes burned.

Dead. His brother was dead. They were part of each other, however far separated. Rob couldn't be dead.

Her voice entered his grief like a gentle touch. "He was a wonderful father. Silly sometimes. Like a little boy. He'd play games for hours with Mandy, give her rides on his back. He coached her soccer team, even took off work sometimes to go on school field trips. The mothers teased him, because he was usually the only father." She fell silent then, and he looked up expecting to see tears, but instead, she was smiling, her thoughts obviously faraway.

So Rob had grown up. Or else his boyishness had let him do one thing—maybe the most important thing—right: be a loving father.

Beth was still gazing at a past he couldn't see, and now he saw the shimmer in her eyes though she still smiled. His own grief eased even as he saw hers and realized that Rob had done more than one thing right. If he hadn't, his wife wouldn't still mourn him. Funny, Nathan thought, how he could feel such pride at the same time jealousy ground a hole in his chest, like a piton pounded into rock.

Beth suddenly stood, blinking rapidly. "I...I'd better check on Mandy. If you want to watch TV..."

She needed to get away. He was just as eager to gain some breathing space to try to understand all these emotions buffeting him. Grief should be simple. Why the hell did everything feel so complicated?

"No," he said, rising, too. "I think I'll just read in bed for a while, if that's all right."

"Really, you don't have to hurry." But she didn't quite manage to hide her relief.

"It's been a long day," he said.

She half turned, head bowed, so that he saw only the curve of her cheek and the long graceful line of her neck below curls bundled into a knot at her nape. "And tomorrow…" Her voice ached. "Oh, tomorrow will seem endless. Until they call."

And he'd thought the last week was bad. "You've gone through this before." Why hadn't he realized what an agony his appearance was putting her through?

She gave him one haunted look. "Each time I really believe…" The words caught on a hiccuping breath. "And each time it's harder."

"I understand."

She looked so damned fragile that primitive urge to shelter her grabbed him by the throat again. Once more, he had to remind himself he was the last man who ought to take her into his arms, even if comfort was his only objective. How must she feel looking at him, seeing her husband and knowing what her eyes told her was only an illusion?

But Beth stunned him. "Thank you again," she whispered. So quickly he might almost have imagined it she came to him, brushed her lips against his cheek and hurried from the room.

He stood stock-still, breathing in an insubstantial scent that reminded him of ripe berries in the sun, and cursed the fact that she was his brother's widow.

Mandy sat on her bed, legs crossed, and listened to the murmur of voices drifting upstairs. She knew they must be talking about her, and about Dad.

It was so bizarre that Dad and Uncle Nate had gotten so mad at each other they didn't want to be brothers anymore. And they were twins! One of Mandy's friends, April, had an identical twin sister. Even though April and Samantha had other friends, it was obvious they were always each other's best friend. In the cafeteria once, April got really upset, and it turned out that at that exact same moment

Samantha, who'd gone ahead out to recess, had broken her arm jumping from a swing. Everybody thought it was really weird, but cool. Mandy wondered if Uncle Nate and her dad had ever felt each other's pain like that. When Dad died, had Uncle Nate hurt without knowing why?

What would it be like to have someone who knew you that well? She dropped her binder on the floor and flopped on her stomach on the bed. She dreamed sometimes that she had a twin. It wasn't just that her twin would have the right blood antigens to save her. What she wanted most was someone who could understand how *she* felt. For a while she did; her first time in the hospital for chemo, she'd shared a room with another girl her age who had leukemia, too. After the nurses turned the lights out, they'd talk, not having to see each other's faces or put on any kind of act. They'd wondered whether death would hurt, whether there really was heaven or hell. They promised each other that if one died, she would try to come back long enough to tell the other.

"Unless—" Jessica's voice had come from the darkness "—it's really awful. Then I don't think I want to know ahead."

"Me, neither," Mandy said.

Jessica left the hospital two weeks before Mandy. She lived in eastern Washington, so they couldn't see each other, but they wrote and phoned. Then Jessica got sick again and came back to Children's Hospital. Mandy saw her once. Jessica had IVs and oxygen and she was bruised-looking, and Mandy knew she was dying. Jessica grabbed her hand and said, "I'll keep my promise if I can. So if you get a note or dream about me or something, it's really me. Okay?"

Jessica died the next day, but she never came to Mandy, unless it was in a dream Mandy didn't remember when she woke up. That scared her, because it meant either that dying really was horrible, or that Jessica was just gone—that there wasn't any soul or spirit or anything left that could keep a promise. It scared Mandy most that there might be nothing at all left of her when she died.

Her next time in the hospital, her roommate was only six, and Mandy had to reassure her. She couldn't talk about dying. Now she was really alone. Children's Hospital had counselors, but they didn't really know her. Mom always pretended that things would be fine. Once, a long time ago, when Mandy asked her what she thought dying would be like, Mom jumped to her feet and said, "You're not dying! I won't let you!" She'd sounded mad, but she'd also had tears sparkling in her eyes. Mandy hadn't asked her again.

Now she rolled onto her back and gazed up at the poster she had taped to her ceiling. Maybe Uncle Nate's blood would turn out to be right. Before, they hadn't had anybody from Dad's side of the family to test. And he was Dad's twin. The odds must be pretty good, right? She examined her feelings and discovered she was hopeful. She pictured the feeling as a little bubble lodged in her chest. A bubble, because it was shimmery and iridescent and it wanted to float upward where she couldn't ignore it. But also a bubble because it could be popped so easily. The tiniest pinprick and it would be gone—snap!—just like Jessica was gone.

She sniffed and realized her cheeks were wet. She never cried anymore. She never let herself think about Jessica, either.

Footsteps on the stairs warned her that Mom was coming. Mandy sat up quickly, wiped her eyes, then bent over and grabbed her binder and pencil. By the time Mom stepped into her bedroom, Mandy was studying the next math problem.

"How's it going, kiddo?" her mother asked.

"Okay."

"Need any help?"

Mandy shrugged. "Not really."

Mom sat on the edge of the bed and pushed her bangs back from her forehead. "Are you almost done? It's bedtime."

"I don't really have to do this. I can finish it in class. I'll go brush my teeth now." She jumped up. "Will you tuck me in?"

"You bet." Mom smiled at her. "So what do you think of your uncle?"

Mandy sat back down. She didn't mind talking about him. "I like Uncle Nate." She thought for a moment. "He listens when you talk to him. You know what I mean?"

"Uh-huh. He's quieter than your father. Not really like him, if you can forget his looks."

Mandy frowned. "Do you think we'll ever see him again? I mean, now that they've tested his blood?"

"He did come back. I'll bet he does again. Anyway, if he matches, you'll see him in the hospital." Mom smiled, like she was suggesting a trip to the zoo or something. "Maybe you could share a room."

"They wouldn't let me." Mandy knew Mom was just joking, but she argued, anyway. "In case he had a cold or something."

"They won't let me touch you, either." Mom reached out and gave her a quick fierce hug.

Mandy didn't draw back. With her face buried in the crook of Mom's shoulder, she mumbled, "Do you think he *will* match?"

"The chances are pretty good, but…you know he may not, don't you?" Mom kissed the top of her head.

"Yeah, it's okay. I know."

They didn't talk any more about it. Mom didn't say whether she thought Uncle Nate would want to come back just to visit, whether he really felt like her uncle. She thought maybe he would. He smiled at her like he meant it, not fakey like some adults. Mandy wished she knew what they'd said downstairs.

After Mom tucked the covers around her and turned out the light, leaving only the soft glow from the hall, Mandy thought, *I don't want to die. Please, God, make Uncle Nate be right. Make him my miracle.*

Waiting was the worst part. Each time they had hope of a close match, Beth wished she could just *know,* even if the news was bad. She'd rather not be given hope at all if she was always to be disappointed.

In the morning she woke Mandy, then got herself dressed. The house was quiet, the door to the spare bedroom closed. She'd awakened once during the night and seen light under his door. Maybe he'd read late. She assumed he was still asleep, but downstairs she found a note on the kitchen counter. "Gone jogging," it said in bold script. "N."

Mandy ate her usual breakfast of cold cereal with a sliced banana, got dressed, grabbed the lunch Beth had made and started out the front door. Halfway down the porch steps, she turned.

"Mom, will you call me at school if…if…"

"Of course I will!" Beth set her cup of coffee down on the porch railing and moved to Mandy to give her another hug. "But we may not hear until late afternoon."

"Okay." Her daughter looked unnaturally mature and solemn again. "I know that."

"Mandy—" She heard the squeal of brakes and looked up. Through a stand of alders clothed in spring green she saw the yellow of the school bus. "There's the bus. You'd better run."

Mandy did, her book bag bumping on her back. Like everything else she did, it was enough to send a shaft of "what if" deep into her mother's heart. She'd played soccer before she became sick the first time. At least she could run now, but the doctor had vetoed sports. He didn't want her to get that tired.

Even after the school bus had lumbered down the road, belching exhaust, and disappeared around a curve, Beth stayed on the front porch. She sat down on the top step, sipped her coffee and gazed at her kingdom.

The fields were weeded and the canes pruned and tied up. They'd be blooming soon, and the sunny acres would hum from the bees feasting. Then the berries would form, small and green, growing and blushing until they were fat and red or blue and sweet. That was when the hard work started.

In just five years she'd built this run-down farm into a business—Tillicum Creek Jams and Preserves. She grew most of her own raspberries and strawberries and blueberries, the last on huge bushes that grew happily in the low wet land down by the creek. She bought blackberries, boysenberries and gooseberries from other local farmers. The barn, now bright red with white trim, housed the kitchen where the jam was made and the shelves where sugar and pectin and empty jars were replaced by labeled jam, stored until shipped to gourmet kitchen shops and fine restaurants. Just last year she'd added a mail-order business that was more successful than her most optimistic projections and made tiny inroads on her mounting debt to hospitals and doctors and pharmacies. Thank God for Rob's life insurance, and for the increasing popularity of her jam. The first few years she'd managed mostly alone, with some seasonal help. Now she had one full-time employee year-round. Several others signed on to prune and weed and, during the season, make three to four thousand pounds of jam a week.

The business was to have been hers and Rob's together. Her skill in the garden and kitchen was to be allied with his in marketing. Someday he'd be able to quit his job, they'd dreamed. Because he traveled so much, she'd done most of what it took to start Tillicum Creek Jams herself, from designing a distinctive label to contacting potential outlets.

Now she was glad she'd proved herself before he died, that she hadn't lost a business partner, as well as a husband. Her ability to cope on her own had been tested severely enough by Mandy's illness. For a short while it had even turned her mourning into bitterness, because Rob's cocky refusal to admit he was mortal meant he wasn't here now that he was really needed.

But Rob's brother was. As though her thoughts had summoned him, she caught a flash of color through the alders and made out the figure of a man running along their country lane. A moment later he turned into her long driveway and slowed to a walk, head down as he shook his arms to loosen tight shoulders.

Despite the chilliness of the morning, he wore a bright red basketball jersey that bared broad shoulders, tanned and muscular. Sacky black sweatpants rode low on his hips. His dark hair was damp and matted to his head. While she watched, he lifted the hem of the jersey and wiped beads of sweat from his face. She caught a glimpse of flat stomach and reacted on some visceral level. Only because he reminded her of Rob, she told herself, and was uncomfortable with that realization.

Or perhaps her sexual awareness had more to do with

the last-ditch plan she'd had in mind from the moment she'd hired the private investigator.

Nathan lifted his head and saw her sitting on the porch steps. His eyes narrowed for a flicker, but his face remained impassive.

Some days she'd still have been in her bathrobe. But today, in his honor she'd showered and dressed before she'd even gone downstairs. One of the pleasures of the self-employed was that dressing meant jeans, no socks and an oversize flannel shirt with the too-long sleeves rolled up. She'd used a clip to confine her hair, although she could feel escaped curls on her neck.

"Morning," he said. "They haven't called?"

She shook her head. "It's a little early. If I don't hear from them by late afternoon, I'll phone them."

He grunted and bent over to do some stretches.

"What would you like for breakfast?" she asked.

"I can make my own." He began rolling his upper body from the waist.

"I don't mind."

He stopped, hands on his hips, and lifted a dark brow. "I'm still a guest?"

"Until your next visit."

"Ah. In that case, I'll take hash browns, an omelet, English muffins." He smiled, deepening the crease in one cheek. "Actually, I usually have cold cereal at home."

"I haven't eaten yet myself," Beth said. "I was thinking of making scrambled eggs and toast. You can try out my jam."

He nodded toward the field. "These are yours, then?"

"Uh-huh. Those are raspberries. Strawberries beyond the barn, blueberries down by the creek."

"Do you sell them?" he asked, contemplating the acres of vines tied to wires strung between split-wood supports.

"I make jam." She smiled at his expression. "It's a business. Tillicum Creek Jams and Preserves. We're small still, but doing well. I don't suppose you've heard of us…"

"Actually, I buy your jam. Usually the raspberry. Beats the hell out of the grocery-store brands. I should have caught on when I saw your sign." He nodded toward the road, his eyes holding new respect. "Was Rob involved?"

"He gave me advice. We had in mind that eventually, if the business took off the way we hoped, he'd be able to quit his job and take over the sales part of Tillicum Creek."

"I take it that didn't happen soon enough."

"No." She watched him walk in a circle to cool off, her thoughts casting circles of their own. "It occurs to me," she said, "that I didn't ask much about your life. My only excuse is that having a sick child makes you single-minded. Are you…are you married? Do you have kids of your own?"

"No, and no. I was married once, divorced after a couple of years. Fortunately we didn't have children."

Words came she hadn't intended to say. "Do you ever miss…?"

"Yeah." Nathan shot her an unreadable look. "I always pictured myself with a wife and a house and children by this age. It's…ironic that Rob had it all and I didn't."

She smiled a little wryly. "Yes, he always said he hadn't planned to marry. We laughed about it."

Something flashed in his eyes and then was gone. "Well—" Nathan wiped his forehead again "—let me take a quick shower, and then breakfast sounds great."

The meal was oddly companionable. They talked about the news on the front page of the *Seattle Times,* argued amiably about a few recent movies and avoided the painful subject that had brought him here: Amanda.

After breakfast Beth gave him a tour of the barn, from the commercial kitchen where she sterilized jars and boiled jam in thirty-gallon steel vats, to the workbench where labels were wrapped around the distinctively designed jars.

"My office is in the house. That's where I make my phone calls and do correspondence. I have one full-time person, but Julie's on vacation right now. We're in the lull before summer. During berry season I have a couple of extra employees."

He studied her catalog and they compared experiences in their respective businesses. It was all so pleasant, so involving, she could almost forget what they were waiting for.

Twice the phone rang and her heart jumped sickeningly, but neither call was from the hospital. Aloud, Beth considered going grocery shopping, although the truth was that nothing short of a tow truck could have hauled her out of earshot of the telephone. Nathan insisted on taking a list and going for her, which left her with nothing to do but dust bookcases that didn't need it and scrub a bathtub that already sparkled. She knew she couldn't concentrate on work; if she'd tried, she would have fouled up orders. And she couldn't do nothing; she'd go crazy. She kept reminding herself that the call might not come today at all. It might be tomorrow or even, conceivably, not until Monday.

Nathan was back, still carrying grocery bags into the kitchen, when the phone rang again. Beth glanced at the clock. Two.

She felt dizzy when she picked up the receiver. Her voice cracked. "Hello?"

"Mrs. McCabe? This is Dr. Simonson at Children's."

"Yes?" If her life had depended on it, she couldn't have gotten more than that one word out.

Across the kitchen, her eyes met Nathan's. Somehow she communicated her panic and hope, because he came to her side, reached out and gripped her shoulder. The warmth and strength of his hand were obscurely comforting, although her entire being was focused on the voice in her ear.

"My news isn't good, Mrs. McCabe. I'm sorry. We were all hopeful, but I'm afraid not enough markers in Mr. McCabe's blood match Amanda's to make him a potential donor. We'll have to continue our hunt through the registry."

She said something—she hoped it was appropriate—before gently replacing the receiver in its cradle. Her breath came out in a long trembling sigh, and the hand on her shoulder tightened.

"No?" he asked roughly.

She closed her eyes and shook her head. His arms came around her, and she laid her cheek on his chest. For a moment all she could do was lean against him, hear the thud of his heart, feel his chest rise and fall with each breath, feel his arms holding her tightly.

Oh, God, she couldn't bear it. To have found someone so closely related to Amanda, to have hoped again... In anguish her mind skipped to the thought of her daughter bounding off the school bus and running down the driveway. How would she tell Mandy? Could she sound cheerful and promise that other treatments would be enough? Would she be doing Mandy any favor when they both knew that Nathan McCabe might have been her last chance?

No, she thought, going very still. Not her last chance. Mandy had one other. If her Uncle Nate would agree.

Beth straightened and stepped back; Nathan released her, his hands falling to his sides.

"There's one other thing you could do," she said, hearing as if from a distance her own calmness and determination. "If you would."

"Name it." His eyes were dark and intense, his mouth set grimly.

"Father a baby for me."

Chapter Three

Nathan stared at Beth. Good God, had she just suggested they have sex? He couldn't have heard right. "What did you say?"

She clasped her hands before her and said in the tone of one who'd memorized a speech, "If Rob and I'd had another child, the odds are one in four that he or she would be a match for Mandy. Normally—" she drew a deep breath "—I couldn't change the fact that we didn't have another baby. But because you and he were identical twins, I can."

He dug his fingers into his hair and gave it a yank. Maybe a little pain would wake him up.

"Let me get this straight. You want me to pretend I'm Rob and provide some sperm."

Her teeth worried her lower lip. "Well, I…I wouldn't have put it that way, but…yes."

He swore and turned his back to her. Hands flat on the tiled kitchen counter, he leaned on braced arms, shaking his head. God almighty. It was crazy. *She* was crazy.

And he was scum to have felt a knife-thrust of pure sexual longing at the very idea.

He was breathing as if he'd just finished a ten-kilometer race. Clenching his teeth, he slowed his breathing and blanked out the image of Beth McCabe, ripe with his child. Then he turned and faced her.

"My...participation aside, you can't have thought this through. In the first place, the odds are three to one that the baby *won't* be a match. Then what? Do you try again?"

Her face was so white the scattering of freckles stood out. "If I have to," she said steadily.

"What about the baby?" He made his tone brutal. "Do you discard him because he didn't measure up and hope for more success the next time?"

She flinched, but her voice was fierce. "I would love any baby of mine no matter what! Do you think I'd even suggest this if I wasn't sure of that? If...if I lose Mandy, another child would give me a reason to live. And for her sake, how can I not try? What kind of mother would I be?"

He didn't want to be impressed by her arguments, to feel himself swayed. He wanted to keep thinking she was crazy. Most of all, he didn't want to envy his brother all over again for having been lucky enough to have her.

Hoarsely he said, "How the hell would we handle custody?"

"We wouldn't." Her gray eyes glittered. "I'm not asking you to be a real father. We don't even know each other! All I'm asking is that you donate sperm. I don't expect anything else from you. You can walk away. I'm perfectly capable of supporting two children."

He stared incredulously. "You want me to have a baby and take no responsibility?"

"These are hardly normal circumstances."

"You can say that again," Nathan muttered. "Lady, you're nuts."

Her chin came up another notch. "Because I'm willing to do anything to save my daughter's life?"

If Amanda were his, wouldn't he do the same? He shook his head again. "I can't believe we're even talking about this."

"Other people have done it." She was pleading now. "They've done it and succeeded. And you can't tell me it's any worse than a lot of the other reasons people have children."

He'd heard some of those reasons. His administrative assistant had had a baby because she thought it would bring her and her husband closer together. They were divorced now and she was raising her son alone. Or how about the people who wanted to make sure someone would take care of them in their old age? Or the ones who just loved babies, forgetting that they become teenagers? At least Beth McCabe's motives were unselfish.

But what would his be?

If he'd thought things were complicated before, he hadn't known what complicated was.

"I have to think about this," he said.

"That's all I'm asking right now." Her voice had softened; she stretched a hand out to him. "Will you stay tonight?"

For a stunned second he thought again that she was inviting him into her bed. And, God help him, he didn't know if he could have refused her. She was beautiful: slim and strong, with emotional depths that darkened the mist gray of her eyes to the deep shades of dusk. Her curls looked as silky fine as her daughter's, completely suited to the delicacy of her cheek and jaw and sweep of throat. Under that shirt she'd be as delicate. For the first time in his life, Nathan wanted something that had belonged to his brother.

Before he could do anything incredibly stupid, reason asserted itself. He was a goddamned fool. She didn't want him under her covers; she wanted him to stay as a guest. She wanted him to have time to learn to love her daughter, so it would become impossible for him to deny mother and child the one thing they needed of him.

And that sure as hell wasn't her husband's double mounting Beth in bed.

His voice sounded like gravel scraping a metal surface. "What time is it?"

"Um…" She looked oddly dazed, and he realized this conversation was as bizarre for her as it was for him. "Three-thirty. Mandy'll be home anytime." That note of pleading was in her voice again.

If he left now he could probably get a commuter flight for the short hop from Seattle to Portland. But he wouldn't be home until late. His assistant had cleared his calendar. Why not stay another night and satisfy his hunger to learn more about Rob and his family?

"I'll stay." He cleared his throat. "If I won't be inconveniencing you."

"Don't be silly." Her cheeks were pink now and she was suddenly bustling around, putting away groceries, which meant her eyes didn't have to meet his. "Even if…if nothing comes of it, Mandy and I are delighted to have had a chance to get to know you. Maybe, wherever Rob is, he sees you here."

Nathan almost laughed, although the sound would have been harsh. Rob wasn't smiling down from heaven or scowling up from hell. No, if he knew, he'd manage to come back one way or another so he could make damn sure he wasn't one-upped. Rob had never let Nathan get the last word in, throw the longest pass, buy the best gift. It didn't require any stretch to figure out how he would have felt about his brother being the last one to impregnate his wife. He'd accomplish an immaculate conception before he'd let Nathan's sperm reach her womb.

But this wasn't the time to remind Beth McCabe that her husband hadn't just loved his brother, he'd hated him.

Nathan made a noncommittal noise in his throat. "Why don't I take you two out to dinner tonight? I'd like to return your hospitality."

She turned to face him, back against the tile edging of the countertop. "My hospitality is nothing—nothing!— compared to what you were willing to do for Mandy."

"Willing doesn't cut it," he said roughly. "I can't help her."

"Yes, you can."

He couldn't look away from Beth, even though he knew he was being reeled in. "If I agreed, you'd have to share custody. I wouldn't disappear."

The pause was infinitesimal before she nodded. "That's fine. We'll make it work somehow."

"We'll *be* family. You won't be able to change that."

He heard the change in verb tense; he wasn't talking *if* anymore, but *will*.

She gazed back at him, not with the intensity of a hypnotist, but with the unwilling fascination of the one *being* hypnotized. "I understand," she whispered.

"The baby will be mine, not Rob's."

She wrenched her gaze away and he saw her mouth tremble. "I never—" She broke off, took a deep breath, controlled her voice. "I never was going to pretend the baby was Rob's. Those are your words, not mine."

"All right." He hated the hard edge to his voice. "I'll do it, so long as you understand my conditions."

Now her eyes were huge. "I do."

"Then how do you want to go about it?"

She opened her mouth—and then shut it when they both heard the sound of the front door opening and slamming, and Mandy's call, "I'm home!"

"We're in the kitchen!" Beth called back. She lowered her voice. "I don't want her to hear anything about this."

He saw her gird herself and wondered, like a coward, whether he should leave her alone to give the bad news to Mandy. But it was too late; the skinny eleven-year-old already stood in the kitchen doorway, her gaze darting from her uncle to her mother and back again.

"It was no, wasn't it?"

Her mother took a couple of quick steps, but Mandy retreated, vanishing from his sight into the front hall. "Just tell me," the girl said.

From where he stood, Nathan could only see Beth's back, but the compassion and pain in her voice sliced into his chest like a surgeon's scalpel. "It was no. He doesn't match. We're back where we started. Just remember that you're feeling well. One of the drugs they used on you is a new one. Who knows? Maybe you won't even need the transplant. And we still have time."

He expected an outburst of emotion: angry words, sobs, feet thundering up the stairs. But Mandy spoke with the quiet resignation of someone three times her age. "Right, Mom. I might be that one in a hundred or whatever it was. Or maybe they will find somebody. Don't worry."

"Sweetheart—"

"I have homework. I'd better get started."

He caught a glimpse of her trudging up the stairs, a small figure who couldn't even cry about her own fate.

Beth turned to face him, her mouth trembling. "Can we...can we talk about this later? After Mandy's gone to bed? Right now I just want…" She pressed her hands to her cheeks. "I just want…" Her voice shattered.

He took a step toward her, ready to draw her back into his arms, but she retreated, just as her daughter had done from her.

"I'm sorry," she whispered. "I just…I need to be alone." And she turned and fled.

Nathan waited until she was out of sight, then swore bitterly. Some savior *he* was. They'd have been better off if he hadn't appeared in their lives to give them hope.

Unless, a voice in his head reminded him, he was more of a success as a father than he'd been as a brother.

Amanda waited until she heard her mother's bedroom door shut, then she crept down the stairs. Uncle Nate was still in the kitchen, but his back was to her and she was sure he didn't hear the creak of that second-to-the-bottom step, or else he would have turned. She slipped out the front door, then hurried around the house and down the sloping field toward the creek. She crossed it by stepping on the flat rocks Dad had set in place to form a small dam, which made a deep enough water hole to wade and splash in. On the other side was her refuge: a huge old weeping willow. The branches parted like lace curtains to let her inside.

Her heart was slamming against her ribs. She huddled with her back to the trunk, surrounded by pale wavering green light.

Mom had said she and Dad bought the house because of this tree. When Mom was a little girl, she'd had a willow tree, and the room inside its green walls was her special place. She wanted that for Mandy.

Nobody ever bothered her here. She didn't even know if Mom knew she came here.

Mandy stared sightlessly at the shifting curtain of long

narrow leaves, thinking about the conversation she'd overheard. She hadn't meant to eavesdrop, but she'd come into the house from school so quietly they hadn't known she was there until she tiptoed back to the door and opened and shut it again, this time noisily.

What if Mom really had a new baby? Would Mandy have to share her willow tree?

Babies couldn't even walk until they were a year old, she knew from seeing her friend Kayla's baby brother. So it would be a long time before she had a sister or brother toddling behind her, demanding to be included.

That part didn't sound so bad, anyway. What really scared her was the reason Mom wanted to have the baby. She'd never wanted another kid before. Mandy bet Mom had told Uncle Nate they should have the baby so it could become a donor. But what if that was a lie? Or at least, kind of a lie? What if Mom really wanted the baby to replace her, Mandy, because she was going to die?

Her chin rested on her knees and she felt the hot tears running down her cheeks. She hardly ever cried anymore! She should be happy, instead of sad that Mom might not have to be lonely when she died!

It was just… She sniffed and wiped her nose on her sleeve. She'd discovered there was something worse than leaving an empty space when you were gone, worse than there being *nothing* where you'd been. It was that space being filled by someone else, so you weren't only gone, pretty soon you were forgotten. Maybe not *totally*—after all, she still thought about Sylvester, their gray cat who'd died last summer of old age. But not very often, especially not since she and Mom had brought home Calvin and Polly from the animal shelter. Already sometimes she'd be snuggling Polly under the covers, the warm furry body curled against hers, and she'd try to remember whether Sylvester felt any different or maybe what his purr sounded like, and she couldn't, because her memories had gotten all tangled up with the present. Had his fur been softer? Had he rubbed his face hard against hers the way Calvin did? It bothered her that she wasn't sure.

That was partly what she was crying about right now. Because if she couldn't remember, maybe her mother wouldn't be able to, either. Maybe babies all felt the same in your arms; maybe Mom would forget what Mandy's laughter sounded like, because she was hearing her new little girl's.

If only, Mandy thought, she had someone to talk to!

"Jessica," she whispered, "where are you?"

In the dark bedroom, Beth stood for a moment above her sleeping daughter, listening to the quiet even breathing. In the crook of Mandy's knees, their black-and-white kitten slept, as well. Beth knew that sometimes Mandy pretended to be asleep when she checked on her. But tonight was the real thing: her face was utterly relaxed, her fingers that had started the night clutching her beloved blanket were uncurled now. She looked so peaceful, so defenseless. Beth leaned over and very softly kissed her daughter's temple.

Then she stroked her fingers down Polly's thin back and heard the astonishingly powerful purr start automatically. Perhaps it would give Mandy sweet dreams.

She slipped out of the room and pulled the door almost closed behind her, leaving a crack for Polly to escape if she needed her litter box or was in the mood for a midnight wrestle with her brother.

Downstairs, Beth stopped in the living-room doorway. Nathan was sprawled in the wing chair, feet on the ottoman. From this angle, she couldn't see his face, only the unruly dark hair and the bulk of his shoulder and those long lean legs. How many times had she seen the same scene?

Something in her went very still as past overlaid present. If she took a step forward, he'd turn his head and smile, that lazy charming smile that had never failed to soften her heart. "How's Sleeping Beauty?" he'd ask. "Do I need to go give her a kiss?"

How like him that was! He was forever magical to his daughter.

She took a step into the living room, then another, and he turned his head, but not lazily as Rob would have. Instead, the movement was sharp, contained, and the dark eyes that focused unerringly on her face were wary and penetrating. The anxiety that had coiled inside her relaxed, leaving her feeling foolish; this wasn't Rob, however much they looked alike. She knew that.

"Asleep?" Nathan asked, his deep voice a little rougher than his brother's, making her wonder how his unshaven chin would feel under her palm.

"Uh-huh." She sat on one end of the couch and curled her legs beneath her. She hardly ever sat any other way. But tonight the outward relaxation was a pose. *Can we talk about this later?* she'd said. *After Mandy's gone to bed?* Well, now was later.

Beth looked with near envy at the mug of steaming coffee he cradled in his big hands. She had enough trouble sleeping these days without having tea or coffee so late, but she could have made herbal tea. If nothing else, it would have given her something to do with her hands.

"Have you, um, thought any more about it?" she asked. "I mean, about—"

"I know what you mean." He sounded abrupt. No longer looking at her, he leaned his head against the high back of the chair. "Hard not to."

"Yes." She studied her hands, traced a scratch across the palm of one with a finger. "I suppose it's…a little unusual."

"Yeah, you could say that."

When he didn't add more, she sneaked a glance at him. He was watching her now, and her own gaze nervously flitted away. "You haven't…changed your mind?" Beth was exasperated to hear how timid she sounded. She'd asked him boldly enough in the first place; why was she so nervous now?

He muttered something under his breath that she suspected was an obscenity. "No," he finally said, voice flat. "Good God, how can I look at Amanda and not do anything I can?"

"I'm glad you don't still think I'm nuts."

For the first time a hint of humor entered his dark eyes. "Did I say that?"

She found herself smiling. "Well, maybe I am, but I'm willing to do it, anyway."

"Yeah, me, too, I guess." He took his feet from the ottoman and planted them on the floor, then leaned forward. "Have you talked to the doctor about this?"

"You mean, Mandy's doctor? No."

"I meant yours."

In her heart, she'd known exactly what he meant. *Then how do you want to go about it?* His words, spoken earlier in the kitchen, were felt and heard more powerfully now, like an earthquake that rolled underground to tremble the earth far from its point of origin.

"No," she said carefully, not looking at him. "I haven't yet."

"Will your insurance pay for this?"

Still she evaded his gaze. "I doubt it. It's not medically necessary—not for me, anyway."

He sat silent for a moment. "Is the expense a problem?"

Did he sound annoyed? "I wasn't asking you to pay for it," she said quickly. "I just thought…" Oh, God, why was this so hard to say? But she didn't need to ask God. She knew the answer, and she finished in a rush, "I just thought maybe we could do it the old-fashioned way. If we slept together just once, at the right time of the month…" She trailed off again, unable to complete the sentence. *Slept together.* What a terrible euphemism.

The stirring in her belly when she looked at him, as she couldn't help doing, the way her mind kept flashing on images of the two of them in her big soft bed upstairs, made her wonder: was she really suggesting this only to be thrifty?

"The old-fashioned way?" he repeated, staring at her with utter blankness, as though what she had just suggested was unthinkable. Repugnant.

Her words tumbled over themselves. "Not if you don't find me at all attractive, of course. I mean, I know it wouldn't work if you didn't…" Oh, Lord, now she was bright red. And she was trying so hard to sound as if she didn't mind an admission that he found her physically unappealing!

Emotion flashed in his eyes, clenched the muscles of his jaw. If he'd been Rob, she would have known what he was thinking. But this man was a stranger, however familiar that face.

"Damn it!" He rose to his feet and glared down at her. "Are you imagining that you can have Rob back for a night or two? Well, get this straight, lady! I'm not Rob! Summon a ghost if you want him back! Just don't expect me to be it!"

Angry, she stood, too. With an effort she kept her voice down. "I have never for a minute pretended you were Rob, and I never will! All right, it was a dumb suggestion, but it didn't have anything to do with him!" Didn't it? she had to ask herself, only to decide she'd have to think about it later. "I only wanted—" to have someone hold her close? "—to avoid a ridiculous charge for something so easy. That's all." *Yeah, right!* murmured a mocking voice from her subconscious.

He frowned at her again, and she could see that she'd caught him off guard. "Isn't Mandy's illness covered by insurance?"

"Not all of it. Not at first." Damn it, this wasn't any of his business. Or was it, considering the link they would now have? "We'd just switched medical plans," she explained reluctantly. "They covered most of her care, but not some of the first bills. The worst part is, they won't pay for the bone-marrow transplant. Fortunately Rob had life insurance, enough for us to squeak through, but I have to save it all for that. And when Rob died, my business hadn't reached a point where it could support us."

"They'd let a kid die rather than cover something that's done as routinely as bone-marrow transplants?" Nathan sounded as incredulous as she'd felt when her insurance agent first rendered the company's decision.

"They said they couldn't make an exception for one child. They said the plan would have to be more expensive to the insured if it covered extras like that. *Extras.*" She uttered the word with loathing. "They pointed out that I knew what was covered and what wasn't when I chose their plan."

He swore.

She gave a twisted smile. "I'm lucky, because I *can* pay for the procedure. Most people can't. You hear those pleas for donations and I always wonder if they got enough. Can you imagine seeing your child die because you're lacking forty thousand dollars? Or twenty, or even five? It must happen."

The compassion in his eyes was almost more than she could bear.

"So you see," Beth said, "why I suggested something so crazy. But you're right." She tried hard to sound brisk, positive. "The doctor it is." She started toward the doorway.

"Beth—"

"No." She barely glanced over her shoulder. "We should keep it impersonal."

"We can't keep a baby impersonal. *Our* baby."

She stopped, one hand on the cool wood of the door frame. "That's a little different."

"Is it?" His tone was odd, confusing her.

She couldn't afford to be confused. Only the goal was allowed to count: Mandy's salvation.

"Yes," she said firmly. "People do it all the time, after divorces. They share a child and both love him or her without feeling anything for each other. We can do it, too."

He didn't agree or argue; he just watched her with an expression as odd as his tone. What was he thinking?

"Good night," she said briskly. "Feel free to watch TV if you'd like, or raid the refrigerator."

"I have to leave first thing in the morning."

She'd almost whisked out of sight. Now she had to pause again, look back. "I know."

He cleared his throat. "You'll let me know when you need me? When the, uh, best time is?"

Best time. When she was most fertile. When his seed, implanted in her womb, would find an egg ready to receive it. At the thought, yearning, warm and exciting, spread throughout her belly. It was maternal, not sexual, she tried to tell herself, but it felt uncomfortably the same.

She imagined herself on the examining table at the

doctor's office, thighs parted to receive some cold instrument. And how must Nathan feel, knowing he had to arouse himself sexually to provide the seed? Somehow, she hadn't realized quite what she was asking.

"I think…" She groped for a date, feeling absurdly self-conscious to be discussing something so intimate. "Maybe two weeks from now? If…if that's good for you?"

His look held irony. "I'll make it good for me."

The double meaning, which she suspected he'd used deliberately, made her cheeks hotter.

"I'll call after I talk to the doctor."

"You do that."

She fled then, after murmuring something about seeing him in the morning. She peeked at Mandy once more, then went on to her own bedroom, where she got ready for bed in a flurry. Once she was curled alone in the queen-size bed, she squeezed her eyes shut and willed sleep to come.

It absolutely refused. All she could think about was how she'd feel right this minute if Nathan McCabe *had* agreed to father her child "the old-fashioned way." It wasn't something they could have done quickly and put behind them. Tonight wasn't the right time of the month. No, she would have had the next two weeks to anticipate his visit, to imagine over and over what it would be like, making love—no, having sex—with the stranger who lived in a body she knew so well.

But the quality of sex, she guessed, wasn't determined by the shape or size of any part of a man's body. No, it was determined by his sensitivity, his kindness, his sense of humor. *And* by the depth of feeling he had for the woman. Which was where she would have lost out.

Obviously he hadn't been interested at all, or he wouldn't have turned her down flat. She ought to be glad he had, glad that their future relationship wasn't to be complicated as it would inevitably have been if they'd shared a bed.

But, staring into the darkness, she had to admit the truth: she had wanted to find out whether it would be different with him. Maybe whether what she'd had with Rob was once in a lifetime for her. Did that make her despicable?

And most of all, she had wanted their baby to be conceived in the warm dark intimacy of her bed, in a moment of real emotion, even if it was only passion. Not with her staring up at a fluorescent light, the paper on the examining table crinkling under her, her feet held awkwardly in cold metal stirrups.

Could a miracle happen that way? she wondered with a shiver.

Chapter Four

Left alone in a somewhat unusual examining room, Nathan looked with distaste at the TV. A selection of ten pornographic movies was available for his...viewing pleasure. Should he prefer it, several copies of popular magazines containing pictures of naked women were neatly stacked on a shelf. Everything a man should need to get aroused.

Then, of course, there was the cup in which he'd been instructed to deposit the semen. Assuming he could get inspired to produce any. The nurse, a heavy cheerful woman, had told him not to worry if he had trouble; sometimes men needed to come back several times before they could relax enough to perform. Her word, not his.

"There is something just a tiny bit intimidating about this, isn't there?" she'd added with a chuckle just before she shut the door, leaving him alone.

Intimidating. Good God. He prowled across the room and back, the tiny, starkly lit confines making him feel claustrophobic. Hell, he'd never been interested in pornography. Photographs of naked women whose breasts looked like they'd been pumped full of helium left him cold. The women who attracted him had little in common with the nude models in those magazines, and they sure as hell wouldn't be appearing in any X-rated movie.

Take Beth McCabe. Her combination of delicacy and toughness had an allure that could captivate a man both in the bedroom and outside it. He could as easily picture her pruning vines in the fields as he could lying back against her pillows in a cotton nightgown all the more seductive for its simplicity.

He almost groaned at the last image. If he wasn't such a damned fool, he would know exactly what her gown hid, and whether her sheets were plain cotton or printed with dainty flowers. She'd be waiting for him, the bedclothes clutched to her chin, her eyes huge and apprehensive. That soft mouth might be trembling as he gently pried the covers from her grasp and peeled them back to allow his hands to cup her pretty breasts. He would bend forward and capture her mouth, stilling the trembling. He'd coax a response until she shyly reached for him, until her legs parted and she made soft needy sounds….

He did groan this time and then glanced ruefully down to see that his fantasy had done what no erotic video could accomplish: aroused him until he ached with wanting.

He wanted to smash his fist against something in anger and frustration. He could have had her. It didn't have to be a fantasy.

Sure, he could have had her. But what he never would have known was whom *she* was having: him or Rob. And damned if he was going to play his brother in any woman's sex games, even Beth McCabe's.

But that didn't mean he couldn't dream a little. He closed his eyes and reached for his zipper.

Beth tried to read the murder mystery she'd brought, but comprehension eluded her. After a while she set it down and picked up a magazine from the selection fanned open on an end table in the waiting room. She'd only been here an hour, but it felt like forever. Other women sat briefly on the soft teal armchairs, then were ushered by the nurse into examining rooms. After a while, they left. Beth just sat.

Not that she was bored. How could she be? Her heart took a little jump every time the nurse appeared, then sank like a rock when another name was called; her palms were so damp she had to wipe them surreptitiously on her jeans every few minutes. Her stomach seemed to have climbed into her throat, where it lodged uncomfortably. She felt as if she was in an airplane, ready to leap out and parachute down for the first time.

She must be certifiably nuts, she decided. What had seemed like a good idea was appearing more and more bizarre. She hardly knew this man, and here she was waiting to be impregnated with his sperm? All this, because the baby might—might!—have bone marrow compatible with Mandy's?

Twice she opened her wallet and flipped through several photos of her daughter, to remind herself of what was important. In one, Mandy was pale, her hair cropped, her eyes huge and dark in that white face. Both times, Beth felt steadied; her heartbeat calmed, her stomach settled, tension leached out of her muscles.

Five minutes later she was as scared as ever.

She knew Nathan had showed up; she'd asked when she got here. So now he was in some room trying to do his part.

The part he refused to accomplish with her, because she didn't attract him.

She tried not to think about him or what he was doing right this minute. But images kept creeping into her mind, like tiny movements in her peripheral vision. If she lowered her guard, they assumed the impact of the huge screen in a movie theater. The trouble was, his resemblance to Rob allowed her mind to fill in the details. She *knew* what Nathan McCabe looked like nude, plus or minus a tan or a scar.

And she hated the idea of him turned on by watching some big-busted bimbo on a TV screen, when she left him cold.

The violence of her feelings didn't make sense. He was a stranger. Why did she care what turned him on?

Well, duh, she thought, in imitation of her daughter. He *did* look just like Rob. Sure, she'd been a widow for three years. But Nathan's looks had brought back fading images of Rob, sharpening them. Like any other woman, she would have been jealous if she'd found out her husband was having an affair. That was all that was wrong today. She was transferring rational feelings about Rob to his look-alike brother.

Only...she didn't buy it.

She *knew* Nathan wasn't Rob. Their facial features might be alike, but the moment Nathan moved or spoke, the resemblance faded. He was quieter, more intense, more perceptive. And it had stung more than she liked to admit to know that, even in a good cause, he couldn't bring himself to share her bed.

"Mrs. McCabe."

Her heart jumped again. She let the magazine drop from nerveless fingers and rose to her feet.

The nurse was smiling. "We're ready for you now."

Oh, God. That meant he'd… She shied away from this particular image, but even in absentia, it sent an odd quiver from her heart down to her belly. Beth was honest enough with herself to acknowledge that the feeling was sexual, as were the shivery yearning cramps between her legs. However clinical the method, his seed was about to impregnate her. Her body knew it on a level that was purely sexual.

If all went well, she would soon be carrying Nathan McCabe's child in her womb.

Please, God, she thought, *never let me regret what I'm doing.* She clutched her purse and book so tightly her fingers hurt and followed the nurse.

"Congratulations, Mrs. McCabe." Her doctor, an attractive black woman close to her own age, beamed at her. "You're definitely pregnant."

Relief made Beth dizzy. She hadn't been wrong. "Thank God!" she breathed.

But right behind was a wave of apprehension. There was no getting out of this now. She couldn't change her mind. And she especially couldn't change it when, at five months, an amniocentesis would be performed and the baby's tissue typed. She would know then whether the baby she carried could save Mandy. And if it couldn't…well, she'd promised herself she would welcome this second child no matter what. Now she silently renewed the vow, her hand splayed protectively over her belly.

The doctor was glancing through her chart. "You're not a smoker, I see, so we don't have to worry about that. I recommend you avoid alcohol altogether, even a glass of wine or a beer."

Beth nodded dutifully.

Dr. Williams wrote her out a prescription for prenatal vitamins and they discussed diet. It was all so ordinary—so much like the last time she'd gotten pregnant, when she had a husband. Not, however, at her side, Beth recalled; she'd wanted to surprise him.

She drove home almost in a dreamlike state. She would have to tell Mandy, of course. The cowardly side of her wanted to wait until her pregnancy became obvious. Or perhaps it was her compassionate side. This time they didn't have a week or ten days to wait before they would find out whether the news was good or bad; they'd have four more months. Wouldn't it be cruel to tell Mandy about the pregnancy now and give her hope?

She'd have to tell Nathan, too. He wouldn't be needed again. He would surely be pleased about that, at least.

Almost home, Beth felt her exhilaration ebb, leaving an emotion she couldn't name. Her stomach felt hollow, her chest squeezed by an invisible hand. It wasn't nervousness, not quite. After all, what did she have to be nervous about? No matter the outcome, she would do the same thing again, make the same decision. Nor was what she felt the tension of waiting; she knew it well, that sense of time blockish and slow, like a river jammed by chunks of ice.

She turned the van into her driveway, past the sign that usually gave her a flash of pride. Today she hardly saw it. Outside the barn she stopped the van, but didn't get out.

Damn it, she wanted to cry and she didn't even know why! She gripped the steering wheel and breathed slowly, in through her nose, out through her mouth.

For a woman, finding out she was pregnant was a momentous occasion. That was all that was wrong with her, she decided. That, and the sudden awareness of how alone she was. She didn't have the excitement ahead of breaking the news to her husband, of rejoicing and planning and dreaming with someone else who cared as much as she did. Even if she decided to tell her daughter, Mandy was too young to lean on. Beth knew she would battle her queasy stomach alone, nap alone, go to the hospital alone when the time came.

She was lonely.

She sighed, thought about lunch, decided against it when her stomach lurched uncertainly. She'd known she was pregnant two days ago when she poured her morning bowl of cereal, took one mouthful and had to run to the bathroom. Beth only hoped her stomach tolerated the smell of jam cooking. Otherwise, she'd be in big trouble.

Through the intercom, his assistant announced crisply, "Mrs. McCabe is on line one."

"Thanks," Nathan said, wondering briefly whether Beth's last name had Jennifer speculating about the caller's identity. He picked up the phone and punched in the line.

"Beth. Nathan here."

"Hi." She sounded faraway, uncertain. "Is this a bad time?"

"No. I'm just doing paperwork."

"Oh." She drew an audible breath. "I wanted to call you while Mandy was at school. I'm pregnant."

The bluntness of it crushed the breath from his chest. He just sat there, receiver in hand, and waited to get his wind back. She was pregnant. Beth McCabe, with the silky curls, the soft mouth, the uncomfortably perceptive eyes, carrying a baby. His baby. Not Rob's, as she probably wished. In one way it didn't seem real. In another... He gritted his teeth on the jolt of sexual hunger she had a talent for awakening.

"Congratulations." His voice came out harsh, abrupt. "That was quick."

"Yes." A pause. "I'm due February fifth."

"And you won't know until then."

"Actually, I will. The doctor will do an amniocentesis at five months. She can do tissue typing at the same time."

Because of her age, his assistant had had the procedure, to make sure her baby didn't have Down syndrome. They had told Jennifer then that her child would be a boy. Beth would learn not just if she carried a healthy boy or girl, but whether he or she would be Mandy's savior.

If Nathan had any say in it, she wouldn't be alone when she found out.

"Does Mandy—?" He stopped. "You wouldn't be calling me while she's in school if she knew."

"I'll have to tell her eventually, of course, but…" Beth went quiet, then said in a voice so low he barely heard her, "I don't want her to hope too much. If I can wait until almost five months…"

"You can get the news over with, good or bad." He made a rough sound in his throat. "How is she?"

"She's doing fine. She ought to be able to hold out."

"I hope so." The words weren't a platitude. Although not a churchgoing man, he was praying.

"Yes. Well. I won't keep you."

She was trying to end the conversation. His hand tightened on the receiver. "How are you feeling?"

"Good. Just a little tired, which is perfectly normal."

"No morning sickness?"

"A little. But it doesn't last long."

"You're not going to be able to work as many hours, are you?" He didn't like the picture he suddenly saw of her slaving over those stainless-steel vats, the jam bubbling and the kitchen hot. How heavy were the flats of berries and the boxes of jam ready for shipment? Would she pick berries out in the summer sun?

"Women generally do," Beth said tartly.

"You mean, the European serfs did. Women who put

in long hours now are usually in an office, not doing farm work and heavy lifting." He was scowling. "You should hire an extra employee."

She didn't answer for a moment; he was afraid she'd hung up on him. But finally she said evasively, "I'll think about it."

She probably couldn't afford another employee. Would she take money from him? Nathan had a pretty good idea what the answer to that question was.

"I'll be up in Seattle again next week." It was news to him; impulse seemed to have taken over. "I'll get a hotel room, but I was hoping to see you and Mandy."

"You're welcome to stay with us if you'd like."

He scowled again, hearing the change in her tone. He hadn't realized how slow and heavy her voice had been until he heard it lighten.

"You're sure?"

"We'd love to have you." If she didn't mean it, she was a hell of a liar. "Mandy talks about you a lot."

What about you? he wanted to ask. Did she think about him? Look forward to seeing him again? Or did he remind her too much of Rob?

"Great," he said too heartily. "I'll plan on it. Uh, let's see…" He reached for his date book, deciphered his brief scrawls. What could be jettisoned? "Tuesday through Thursday?"

"Wonderful," she said. "You can see Tillicum Creek Jams in full operation. Strawberries and blueberries are both ripening now."

"Maybe I should stay longer. I could pick berries."

Unexpectedly she laughed, the sound unfettered, a child's giggle. "The owner of Mount Hood Sporting Goods picking strawberries? Do you have any idea how back-breaking it can be?"

"Yeah, I picked berries summers when I was a teenager. You'll be getting experienced help."

"You *must* have better things to do!"

"Like?"

"Ohh…" She drew the word out, and he pictured her pursed lips. "Make important decisions. Plan advertising campaigns. Glare at incompetent employees. Talk about quality assurance and employee morale."

"We just finished planning our upcoming advertising campaign. I have no incompetent employees, morale is just fine, thank you, and I've already assured quality." Damn, but he was enjoying himself. "Did I forget anything?"

"Important decisions." Laughter rippled through her voice.

"I can make them in Seattle."

"Oh, in that case, I'll be sure we save a few rows of berries just for you." That voice, a little husky, amused, intimate, made him crave her presence.

"Then I'll see you Tuesday afternoon."

He hung up and punched the intercom. "Jennifer, will you come in here?"

His assistant was going to love juggling his schedule yet again.

Beth straightened and pressed one hand to her lower back. She blinked sweat from her eyes and looked down at her basket, only half-full with fat red berries. She'd finish filling it and then stop for lunch.

On this June day no leaves stirred on the alders that fronted the road; the air, sharp with the scent of crushed berries, hung still and warm over the fields. A lawn mower growled, the sound muted by distance. Closer was the hum of bees pollinating the raspberries.

Reluctantly Beth crouched again and began deftly

plucking the ripe strawberries from the plants. The ache in her lower back intensified, but when Evan, a college boy who worked here summers, paused in the next row and asked if she was okay, she managed an almost convincing "Sure. It's just so darned humid I feel like I'm working in slow motion."

She didn't remember this back ache from her first pregnancy. Of course, then she hadn't done farm labor. She and Rob had lived in a condo in Edmonds, north of Seattle on Puget Sound. She'd been an administrative assistant at a software manufacturer. Even minor manual tasks like copying were done by someone lower in the hierarchy. What's more, she'd been eleven—no, twelve—years younger.

Making herself continue picking, Beth wondered if she could somehow afford another worker. She hadn't taken Nathan's suggestion seriously before. She was used to hard work. But now…

She hardly saw the level rising in her basket, so preoccupied was she by her review of her mental spreadsheet. Expenses here, income there. There ought to be some extra in late June— No, she remembered another bill. She couldn't possibly pay another wage, she thought, feeling the familiar spurt of panic. Her business had gotten where it was because she'd been willing to put long hours into it. Anything she couldn't afford to pay someone else to do, she did herself. With no cushion of savings and a baby on the way, this was hardly the moment for her to become a lady of leisure. If only she didn't feel so tired!

She straightened again and wiped sweat from her forehead, her hands stained red. The sound of a car engine, rare on her quiet country road at this time of day, made her turn. An unfamiliar blue sedan had slowed and was pulling into her driveway. Hope, even excitement, tingled through her veins.

Heaving her now full basket to her hip, she carried it to the pickup truck that was parked between the fields. Beth set it on the tailgate and followed the dusty footpath between rows of raspberry vines, which seemed to vibrate, so covered were they with bees.

As she approached, a man got out of the car and stretched. Nathan. Beth was astonished and disquieted by the strength of her pleasure. He was visiting for a few days. So what? He was her brother-in-law; the only thing really personal between them was the baby.

But when he smiled at her, the slow quiet grin that didn't remind her at all of Rob, her heart lightened and she felt better than she had all day.

"I didn't expect you so early."

"I had no reason to go into the office." His broad shoulders moved in an easy shrug. "Caught a nine-o'clock flight."

"I was just going to stop for lunch." With his gaze moving over her, Beth was suddenly, acutely aware of how filthy she was. And how little she wore. As the day warmed, she'd rolled her khaki shorts up as high as they'd go and tied her sleeveless cotton shirt under her breasts. Her hair was bundled back in a red scarf, which she'd yanked off a couple of times to wipe the sweat from her eyes. It would be silly to take a shower, then go back out and get dirty all over again, but she was tempted.

"I'll make lunch." Darned if he wasn't frowning at her. "You should rest."

"I'm not sick, you know."

"You may not show yet—" his gaze touched her bare midriff "—but that doesn't mean you shouldn't take care of yourself."

It was childish to feel rebellious, but she couldn't seem

to help it. Who the heck was he to approve or disapprove of how she ran her life?

"You're not my father." At least she didn't stick out her tongue at him.

"No, but I am the baby's father," he said sharply.

Just the reminder was enough to make her feel warmth and tingling between her legs. She'd never imagined that carrying Nathan's baby would make her body so determined to know him sexually. She could only hope the reaction disappeared as time went on. Otherwise, how could she stand the next twenty years?

She crossed her arms, half-protectively. "You aren't really worried about him. Her."

"No." This time his dark eyes didn't waver from hers. His voice had softened. "It's you I'm worried about."

Her defiance evaporated. "I'm fine. Just a little tired."

"You're sure?" He searched her face and she saw something unexpected in his eyes. Something vulnerable.

She felt a guilty twinge. "Sometimes my back aches," she admitted.

His frown returned. "Go wash up and sit down. I'll make sandwiches, or whatever you want."

"Thank you." She felt absurdly shy. "I might take a shower."

"Go ahead." He jerked his head toward the house. "I'll grab my suitcase and follow."

"I was going to make an egg-salad sandwich. I hard-boiled some eggs. If you'd like something else…"

"This time I'm not a guest." He went around to the trunk. "I like egg salad. I know how to make it. It'll be waiting when you come down."

She looked back toward the field, where her workers were heading toward their cars or the shade of the big maple to have their lunches. They didn't need her standing over them. This afternoon, she'd cook jam, instead of picking strawberries. At least then she wouldn't have to bend over.

The trunk of the car slammed. Nathan held a suitcase and a smaller traveling bag. "Why are you still standing here?" he asked gruffly.

Beth held up both hands. "I'm going, I'm going."

Three-quarters of an hour later Nathan had begun to worry. He'd heard the shower turned off twenty-five minutes ago. It had been followed by the hum of a hair dryer. Since then...nothing. What the hell was she doing?

Maybe she'd slipped on the wet floor. Or fainted. Did pregnant women faint? He had no idea.

The sandwiches were made, sliced in half diagonally and stacked artistically on a plate. He'd poured himself juice and Beth milk—he had the vague idea that pregnant women were supposed to drink plenty of milk.

Okay. He'd go find out what was keeping her. All he had to figure out was which door led to her bedroom.

In the upstairs hall, he hesitated. The guest room, where he'd earlier dumped his suitcases and changed clothes, was the first on the left. He knocked on the door across the hall. When no one answered, he cautiously opened it. Stuffed animals and dolls were packed cozily on a shelf above a white-painted student desk. Posters of teen idols masked a good part of the floral wallpaper. Mandy's room.

His knock on the next door brought no response, either. This time when he opened it a crack, he saw Beth right away. She lay curled on her side on the bed, head on her lace-edged pillow, eyes closed. A fuzzy blue robe gaped open at her neck.

Alarm pulsed through him. Maybe she *had* fainted. Soundlessly he pushed the door all the way open and crossed the carpeted floor to the bed, one of those affairs with posts that tapered gracefully to finials near the ceiling. He gave a wild glance through another door, which stood open to a bathroom. Beside the claw-footed tub, surrounded by a shower curtain, was a heap of clothes.

Holding his breath, he listened for hers. It came, a deep sigh, then a resumption of even slow breaths. The strength of his relief made him feel like an idiot. What—had he really thought she was dead?

But why hadn't she let him know she was going to take a nap?

She murmured just then and rolled onto her back. He stood transfixed, feeling like a lecher but unable to look away from the curve of a creamy breast and the shadow of a nipple almost exposed. He was sweating as he stared down at her. With a near physical effort, he wrenched his gaze inch by inch from her breast, but nothing else he saw made him cool down any. Her throat was pale and graceful. This close, he could see every tiny freckle on her nose and cheeks. Her mouth was soft, the lower lip full. Her lashes were fans of spun gold against her delicate skin. She *had* dried her hair; the curls looked so springy he was sure a lock would curl around his finger if he just reached out. One arm was flung above her head in a pose of innocent abandon. The sleeve of the robe had fallen back to reveal a narrow wrist, veined in blue.

Nathan groaned, the sound recalling him to some sense of decency. What was he—a Peeping Tom? Good God, what if she woke up and found him gaping at her?

With another painful effort, he stepped back. His palms tingled. He could *feel* her breast, just rounded enough to fill his hand, the skin softer than anything he'd ever touched. The bones of her shoulder would be fragile, her waist slender. If that robe fell all the way open, would he see curls as

gold as those on her head? The image had him clenching
his teeth and backing up another few steps until he bumped
into the open door.

At least from here he couldn't see her breast anymore.
He finally noticed that one of her feet, pink and clean from
the shower, touched the carpet. It was as though she'd sat
on the edge of the bed, then thought, *I'll just put my head
down for a minute.*

"I'm fine. Just a little tired," she'd said.

More than a little, he thought now. She'd needed a nap
and been too stubborn to take one. She was the boss here;
who was going to tell her what to do, even if it was for her
own good? Mandy? One of her seasonal berry pickers?

And he'd bet his next year's company profits that she
hadn't told a soul but him she was pregnant. She wouldn't
want someone to let it slip to Mandy. No, she'd forge on,
pretending nothing was any different. She'd only told him
because she'd had to! Otherwise, he'd have shown up at that
damn clinic again to put himself through the humiliation
of coming in a cup.

For now, Nathan decided, he'd let her sleep, even if she
was annoyed at him later. But he didn't like the idea of not
being here in the future, especially these next couple of
months, when berry season would be at its height and she
was bound to push herself beyond any sensible limits.

Downstairs he ate two sandwiches and gulped the juice
before heading outside. He'd take her place picking this
afternoon and maybe tomorrow. After that…well, hell,
maybe he could get up here for a couple days every week
or so.

Or— He stopped dead, aware that the other workers,
gathering again after the break, had turned to stare at him.
Or why not rent a place up here? He could do a good part
of his business by email and phone. What traveling was

required he could do just as well out of Sea-Tac Airport as he could from Portland International. Maybe every other week he could go to Portland for two or three days.

Beth would try to talk him out of it, he knew. She'd regard his presence as interference. But damn it, he had rights and responsibilities as the father of the child she carried. A baby was a pretty abstract idea. At the moment he was more concerned about Beth. But he didn't have to tell her that.

Yeah. He liked it. He had confidence he could arrange things so that he was around enough to make life easier on Beth.

For the moment Nathan shoved the more mundane concerns—how to handle specific obligations—out of the way and headed toward the pickers.

"Hi," he said, nodding. "I'm Nathan McCabe, Beth's brother-in-law. She's not feeling too well, so I'm going to help out."

The pause was noticeable. Most of them, if not all, hadn't known she *had* a brother-in-law. Two looked startled; they must have been around long enough to have met Rob. But none of them would quibble as long as he was ready to work.

A chorus of names came back at him. A college-age stud looked him over. "You ever done this before?"

"Yeah, summers when I was your age."

The kid nodded, as though begrudging him any credit, and pointed to one row. "She left off about halfway down. Take a basket and go for it."

He'd do that. Now and for as many days as he could manage. It was the least he owed the mother of his unborn son or daughter, even if the circumstances were a little bizarre.

Chapter Five

When Mandy arrived home on the school bus, she dropped her book bag on the front porch and went out to the field. She automatically scanned the pickers. No Mom. Maybe she was making jam. Mandy was about to turn back when she saw Uncle Nate. Cool!

He was pretty grungy, and his dark hair, a little longer than hers, was matted with sweat. Even so, she thought it suited him.

When he heard her coming, he looked up with one eyebrow raised. Then he grinned, a flash of white teeth in a dirty face streaked with strawberry juice.

"How come you're working?" Mandy asked, squatting next to him. She plucked a big fat berry and bit it off just below the stem. Her tongue caught a squirt of juice trying to trickle down her chin.

"Your mom won't let me stay unless I earn my keep."

She gave him a look. "Yeah, right."

He grimaced. "Actually, I'm hiding out here because she's mad at me."

"What did you do?" she asked with interest. Mom hardly ever got mad at her.

He kept picking, his hands quick and sure. "When she came in for lunch, she fell asleep. I didn't wake her up. Mea culpa."

"What's that mean?"

She liked the way the crease in his cheek got deeper when he smiled. "I'm at fault. Guilty as charged."

Mandy frowned. "But *she's* the one who fell asleep."

"Try telling her that," Uncle Nate muttered.

"You're kidding, aren't you?" It wasn't quite a question. She frowned again. "Why did she fall asleep?"

He paused, still squatting, and rested his elbows on his knees. "Would you believe she was so excited about my visit she couldn't sleep last night?"

Mandy thought about it. "No."

He pretended she'd stabbed him, clasping his hand to his heart. "Are you telling me you slept like a baby, too? You weren't the slightest bit excited, either?"

Mandy didn't see any reason not to tell the truth. "I was kind of," she admitted. "I like having you here."

His smile was different this time. Not teasing at all. "I like being here. I wish I'd known about you and your mom a long time ago. I...feel like I've missed out. Your dad and I were idiots."

"What did you fight about?"

He picked without speaking for a minute. Then he paused and looked up at her. "I can't tell you about our last fight. It's...adult. But really, it was just the last straw. We'd spent years competing. I used to tell myself it was all your dad, that he'd never let me succeed at anything without him doing it, too, and better if he could. But I guess maybe

I was doing the same without realizing it. Probably both of us were uncomfortable with the fact that we looked so much alike and had similar abilities. You get to be a teenager and you need to know who you are, what makes you special. We'd look at each other, and we weren't sure."

Mandy listened, frowning. "I can see why you'd feel that way," she said gravely. "I'm not a teenager yet, but already everything seems really confusing, you know? But at least I don't have a..." She'd been going to say "twin," but she changed her mind. "An echo."

"An echo," he repeated, and she could tell he was thinking about it. "Yeah. Our trouble was, we both wanted to know who was making the original sound and who was only echoing it."

"Dad was really competitive." She wrinkled her nose. "I remember Mom getting mad at him in the car. He acted like he thought all the other drivers were racing him. He always had to get away from stoplights before the other cars. Or be the fastest on the freeway."

His face was fading from her memory—or it had been until Uncle Nate came—but most of what she did remember about her father was good. Comforting. So it was hard to think back to something that had scared her a little, like him driving too fast.

"Yeah, he was always kind of a show-off," Uncle Nate said. "I wasn't. But then I resented it when he got more attention. What we should have done was go in different directions—me into something where I'd get attention without asking for it, Rob into drama or radio or car racing." He grinned. "He should have been an Indy 500 driver."

"Maybe that was your parents' fault."

He shot her a look of surprise. "Maybe."

"What were they like?" When Dad died, she was too young to care much about grandparents who were already dead and whom she'd never met. And now Dad wasn't around to ask.

Somebody shouted a question and Uncle Nate waved a hand. To her he said, "How about we talk about them this evening? Right now, I'm falling behind."

"Okay," Mandy agreed. "I'd better go do my homework. Is Mom in the house?"

"No, she's making jam in the barn."

Mandy nodded. "Bye."

"Hey," he called after her. "I like your glasses."

She made a face over her shoulder. She *hated* wearing glasses.

Pushing them up on her nose, she went to the barn so Mom would know she was home. The whole barn smelled sweet, like the taste in Mandy's mouth. Mom was in the kitchen ladling jam from a huge vat into jars. She was frowning and muttering to herself, and jam dripped down the side of the jar in her hand.

She *was* mad.

"Hi, Mom," Mandy said carefully, pretending she hadn't noticed.

"Sweetie." Her mother smiled and blew upward to puff her bangs from her damp forehead. "Have a good day?"

It was so hot in here Mandy was already backing toward the door. "Sure. Did you remember I have drama tonight?"

Mom's eyes widened. "Drama? Oh, Lord. Dinner should already be on. I'll finish up here as quick as I can."

"If I'm late or can't go, that's okay." Mandy didn't want to sound disappointed. Because of being sick, she knew she took more of her mother's time and energy than most kids did. But she really loved her drama class. It was the only time she could completely forget herself and, for a little while, be someone else. Maybe she was a show-off, too, like her dad.

She didn't mind being like him.

"No, we'll manage." Mom wiped off the jam jar and grabbed an empty one, then the ladle. "Your uncle Nate's here."

"I know. I talked to him." Mandy shifted her backpack from one shoulder to the other. "Maybe he could take me tonight."

Mom glanced at her. "Would you like that?"

"He could watch for the last half hour."

"I'll bet he'd enjoy that."

"Will you let me ask him?" Mandy bit her lip. "That way, I can tell if he doesn't really want to."

Mom tried to smile. "Okay."

"I could have told him and Dad apart right away," Mandy said. She wasn't exactly sure what she meant by that, but it seemed important to say.

Her mother only nodded. "Me, too. It seems funny when they look so much alike, doesn't it?"

At the dinner table, Beth could hardly bring herself to meet Nathan's eyes. She'd thrown a temper tantrum today, something she didn't remember ever doing before.

She'd awakened feeling drugged, her arms heavy, her eyelids leaden. Her thoughts moved as slowly as her body. Why was she lying on the bed in her robe? She rolled to one side and stared without understanding at the clock. Three. In the morning? But she had her robe on. Sunlight lay in a warm golden band across the floor.

And then she remembered. She'd come in for lunch, taken a shower and laid down for just a minute. Three hours ago.

But surely Nathan would have woken her up. He knew she had to be back out to work.

She dressed and hurried downstairs to find a note on the kitchen table. *Sandwich and milk in the fridge. I'm out picking.*

Beth had stormed out to the field and told him he had no business deciding whether or not she would put in a full day of work. She'd all but stamped her foot and yelled, "So there!"

Dark eyes opaque, he'd listened until she wound down, then said tersely, "You wouldn't have fallen asleep if you hadn't needed the extra rest. If you're going to do this, you can't afford to be a fool."

Flushed, she looked around to see that they had an audience, although, thank God, she doubted anyone could have caught their words. She set her teeth and marched back to the barn, where one of her helpers was already rinsing berries.

She hadn't seen Nathan since, although half an hour ago she'd heard him come into the house and then the shower running. Now they sat across the table from each other, Mandy serving as a buffer.

He wasn't looking at Beth, either. He listened as Mandy told him about her drama class, offered by the Seattle Children's Theatre Drama School.

"My teacher is in a production right now at the Seattle Rep. It's not a play for kids, so I haven't seen it, but she thinks she's going to be in *Peter Pan* at the Intiman. Mom says we can go to that."

Beth hadn't heard Mandy chatter with such animation in a long while. Nathan was making all the appropriate responses and looking like he meant them.

"Anyway, my class is tonight, and I wondered if, um, you could take me. The teacher lets parents watch the last half hour." All of a sudden she was fiddling with her fork and only stealing sidelong glances at him.

Beth was going to kill him if he said no.

He offered her daughter one of those quick rare smiles. "I'd like that—if your mom doesn't mind."

"I'd be delighted," Beth said offhandedly. "If you can take her, I'd have some extra time to catch up on laundry and clean the kitchen."

His eyes met hers. "Don't you ever sit down and relax? Watch TV? Read?"

"Of course I do!" she snapped.

Mandy's anxiety showed in her too-thin face.

Nathan noticed, too, because he smiled again at Mandy. "Your mom makes me feel lazy. I can't keep up with her."

"You mean, you couldn't nap for three hours like I did?" Beth could have kicked herself the minute the words were out. She sounded so petty, so unpleasant. It was that damn smile that had done it, she acknowledged unhappily. She was jealous of her own daughter.

He gave Beth a brief unreadable look, then said, "Everybody's entitled."

She hated that deliberately courteous tone, which made it plain who interested him: Mandy. He had to get along with her to be allowed to visit her daughter.

Enjoying feeling sorry for yourself? her inner voice asked.

Yes! she answered, before a spark of humor let her see the idiocy of her pique. Nathan had been just as nice to her as he'd been to Mandy until she indulged in her little fit today. The funny thing was, she didn't even know why she'd been so angry. For Pete's sake, the man had gone out and done her job so she could sleep!

She automatically put a bite of lasagna into her mouth,

tuning out whatever Nathan and Mandy were talking about.

She always woke up grumpy from naps, one reason she never took them. But still… Beth thought back to the way her heart had cramped in anger when she read the note. No, she amended slowly, not anger. Panic. She hadn't liked the idea that he was taking care of her. That implied a loss of control, which was scary. She didn't want to depend on anyone. She wanted to cope all on her own.

Why? she asked herself, but this time she had no answer.

"Cool!" Mandy bounced in her chair. "You're really moving?"

Moving? Beth turned a wary gaze on Nathan. "What did you say?"

"Would you please pass the garlic bread?" he asked Mandy before glancing at Beth with that same courteous blank expression. "I'm going to rent a place up here. Probably a little south, closer to the airport, but near enough to you so that I can be here if you need me."

Once again irrational panic fluttered in her chest. "But your office is in Portland."

If he noticed the way her voice rose, he ignored it. "I only go in a day or two a week, anyway. The rest of the time I'm either traveling or I work from home. With my computer I can get almost anything done remotely."

"You must have friends, a health club, favorite restaurants." Beth tried hard to think of everything he might miss. "Why uproot yourself?"

Betrayingly his gaze shifted lower to where he might have seen her belly if the table hadn't blocked his view. "I don't know that I have roots there." He shrugged, meeting her eyes again. "Seattle will be just as convenient."

Given her daughter's presence, what could she say but

"Just so you don't feel some kind of...obligation. We've been doing fine on our own."

One of his dark brows rose, the merest twitch, but enough to signal his skepticism and arouse her rage. She'd hit the nail on the head: he'd decided they needed him. She was working too hard, and poor sick little Mandy was languishing for lack of a father figure. He was some kind of demiGod, condescending to sweep in and save them.

Just wait until Mandy goes to bed, Beth thought, lips tightening. Then she'd tell him what he could do with his patronage.

Too bad she couldn't tell him what to do with his sperm. Yet even as she had the thought, her hand moved to her abdomen. Even if this child did entitle Nathan to some rights she'd rather deny him, she wouldn't change what she'd done. The baby they would share had restored her hope.

Nathan put the last pan in the cupboard beside the built-in range and closed the door. The kitchen still looked uninhabited. The whole place did. He'd rented the town house furnished, the mostly neutral colors obviously chosen to be acceptable to any tenant, even if they didn't excite anyone. He'd brought some stuff from Portland, but not everything, because he'd decided to keep his condo there. He'd be spending nights down there often enough to make it handy. And while this seemed like a good idea right now, he could easily find himself unwelcome at Beth McCabe's. Regular reminders that this residence was temporary might not be a bad idea.

After all, she'd made it plain enough that she didn't want him around as often as he had in mind. The minute Mandy had gone to bed, she'd told him so. One remark struck below the belt.

"You're the one who suggested I was inviting you to stand in for Rob. Isn't that what you're trying to do?"

Was it? Hell, yeah, he intended to help out his brother's widow and daughter. If he'd known about their existence and Rob's death sooner, Beth wouldn't have had to struggle alone these past three years.

But was he, on another level, trying to step into his brother's shoes? The question made him uncomfortable. Rob might even consider that Nathan was evening the score, tit for tat. Nathan wanted to believe his motives were nobler than that, but how could he be sure?

He muttered a curse and headed into the spare bedroom, which he was converting to an office. With his things just half-unpacked, it bore more of his stamp than the rest of the town house. The computer was already set up, the printer plugged in. On the white walls, he'd hung a couple of favorite photos, blown up and framed simply in black metal. One showed autumn leaves, pale yellow and vivid gold, lingering on an aspen tree. Those already fallen floated in a small stream and clogged a natural dam of tumbled boulders. The other photograph was the classic of Mount Shuksan, with its reflection cast on the still lake. Not original, but evocative. He could almost smell the huckleberries, feel the sharp chill of the water, breathe the crisp air.

It had been too long since he'd done any climbing. Even hiking. He thought back to the previous summer. He'd climbed Mount Hood a couple of times. He and his buddy Matt had vowed to climb Constance in the Olympic Mountains, but their free weekends never coincided. He couldn't even remember the last time he'd talked to Matt. It had been weeks. Hell, probably months. Too long. And Nathan considered Matt his best friend.

Remembering Beth's mock concern about his pulling up roots, Nathan snorted. He hadn't put any down. If he were honest with himself, his condo in Portland was damn near as arid as this rented place. Did he ever really think of it as home? "My place," he tended to call it, which was even how he thought of it. He owned it, he lived there, but when he thought *home,* what flashed in his mind was the neat white bungalow where he'd grown up, not so far from here. Home had been Bremerton, on the other side of the sound. It was a navy town; his dad had been a welder working on destroyers and the occasional aircraft carrier. Dad had been a beer-drinking, chain-smoking veteran, proud because his boys were smarter than he was. Mom had never worked—Dad wouldn't let her—for dinner might not have been on the table every day at five-thirty when he walked in the door.

Funny that in the light of memory, Mom's personality had a clarity and individuality Dad's didn't. Volunteering was okay with Dad, and by God she volunteered. Friends of the Library, Room Mother, PTA. When she joined an organization, she ended up running it. She ran her household just as efficiently. She'd have made a hell of a CEO, something Dad's ego could never have stood.

Nathan sat down in his padded office chair and stared unseeingly at the blank computer screen. Mom would have been disgusted if she'd known he and Rob had let a quarrel end their relationship. "Remember," she used to tell them, with a brisk nod, "nobody will ever know you or understand you the way your brother does."

But then, he'd long ago realized Mom was partly responsible for the way things had turned out. She had believed in competition. She was constantly pitting her twin sons against each other. He could see her now, in her housedress, arms crossed. "Which one of you can fold the laundry the fastest?" She'd be sure to add, "And do it right."

They'd done it fast and right, but one of them would

end up humiliated. He had to win back his self-esteem doing the next chore. Neighbors must have wondered why their lawn was always the most closely mowed, the most neatly raked. And in the meantime those McCabe boys had maintained straight A's and gone out for baseball, football and basketball. Always the same sports, except for the one spring when Nathan tried wrestling, instead of baseball.

They'd parted ways only when Rob stuck his head under the hood of a car and when Nathan swung a fifty-pound pack on his back and headed up into the Olympic Mountains. Some of the sense of freedom and joy he found there, he'd come to realize, was from the severing of the bond, which sometimes felt like the physical joining of Siamese twins. Probably Rob's pleasure in fast cars was partly made up of the same relief.

Nathan swore again and pushed back his chair. Hell. Wasn't it enough that he grieved for his brother? Did he have to understand the past, too? What was done was done. They'd each made a life separate from the other. Rob's had ended sooner than it should have. Nathan was doing what his mother had taught him was right: fulfilling the responsibility one brother had taken on. But he wasn't trying to do it better. Even if he'd wanted to, he couldn't. Beth McCabe had loved Rob, and no gratitude she came to feel for Nathan would ever equal that.

Sometimes she wanted to scream at him to stay away, if only his being here wasn't, God help her, such a relief. She was so *tired* this time around. The nausea, too, wore her down. There were days she didn't think she could bear the smell of cooking jam another minute. That rich sweet smell had always meant success to her, security, strength. The recipes were hers, the result of endless experimenting.

When she tasted a batch of raspberry jam, the experience was sensual. But now…now, it was just work.

The summer was already setting heat records for the Northwest. That was good for the berries, which were ripening early and sweet. For a pregnant woman, it was sheer misery. She had two fans set up in the barn kitchen, but all they did was stir the muggy air around. She took showers twice a day, but she was sweating before she could even towel-dry. She dreamed of installing air-conditioning, but it was an unnecessary expense they couldn't afford.

She wanted to blame the heat for her insomnia, too, but was too honest. Heat did rise, making the upstairs of the old house too warm even after night fell. But with her windows flung open and the ceiling fan whirling, cooler air soon whispered over her skin as she lay sprawled on the crisp cotton sheet, covers flung to one side.

It was other things keeping her awake. Things like her conscience, which had stayed silent until she'd made an irrevocable decision but now was whispering questions.

Won't you be angry at this baby if he's not a close enough match to Mandy? How can you be sure you'll really love him, no matter what?

Firing up at someone else was easy enough; being one-hundred-percent, never-look-back sure in her own heart and mind was another matter. She lay in bed and splayed her hands over her belly. It was flat and smooth, without even a small swelling to convince her that she was really pregnant, that this wasn't all a dream or a nightmare. She touched her breasts, too, but even they weren't more sensitive yet.

"I'm pregnant," she whispered, and didn't altogether believe it. Except for the tiredness. And the nausea. And the confirmation from the doctor. But she needed that flutter inside, that shiver of life separate from herself, to settle her internal debate.

Of course she'd done the right thing. How could she have done less? But Beth wanted desperately to feel an attachment to the baby she carried, a love as powerful and protective as that she felt for Mandy. Only then could she silence the voices that expressed her deepest fears.

Nathan insisted on accompanying her the next time she saw her obstetrician. Half a dozen times she tried telling him he really didn't need to come. She was fine; the appointment was routine; even most husbands didn't go in the early months.

"Maybe so," he'd agree, "but their responsibility is pretty firmly established. Mine isn't. I'm here for you, and I'm here for my son or daughter. I want you to be sure of that."

I don't care! she wanted to cry, but it was a lie. She was scared of being alone this time around. Probably every parent fouled up sometimes, but when you were all your child had, panic was never very far away. She blamed herself for those times when Mandy looked at her with eyes older than her own, when Mandy said, "I'm fine, Mom. No, I don't want to talk about it. Really. Don't worry." When had her own daughter quit telling her what she felt? If only she knew what she'd done or said that was wrong, she could undo it. But she had no idea. And now she was proposing to raise another child, as though she'd become an expert. What if Mandy fell ill again while she had a baby crying nights? She was doing this for Mandy, but who would she choose then? Without Nathan, she might have to leave the baby with a hired sitter while she spent nights at the hospital. Or stay home with the baby, leaving Mandy alone in the hospital.

She needed him, but that didn't have to mean she gave up all her privacy. He wasn't her husband, even if he looked like he was.

She had to keep reminding herself of that, because when she lay in bed drifting toward sleep, she'd find herself reaching out for Rob, a pleasant ache between her thighs. They hadn't made love in such a long time. But he was here now, his weight settling on the edge of the bed. Surely he was as hungry for her as she was for him—

Beth jolted awake. Almost awake. *Rob,* she cried inside, and then knew. He was dead. Oh, God. She wasn't dreaming about Rob at all. The man sitting on the side of the bed wasn't smiling insouciently, his teeth flashing white even in the moonlight; the line of his mouth was grim. As he pulled his sweater over his head, she saw that the puckered scar bisecting her husband's belly, a legacy of a motorcycle accident, was missing.

She shot bolt upright and he faded. But she'd *seen* him! Beth squeezed her eyes shut and tried to slow her breathing. No. Nathan McCabe hadn't been in her bedroom only a moment ago, any more than he'd been there the other nights she'd had similar dreams. Her subconscious was confused, that was all. Thank God he didn't know. And thank God, she thought guiltily, Rob couldn't know.

In the morning Beth felt heavy-eyed and sluggish. Leaning against the counter as she waited for water to boil, wanting coffee and knowing she'd settle for herbal tea, she watched Mandy eat her cereal at the kitchen table. Jean shorts showed long legs so skinny the knees were knobby. Her elbows stuck out awkwardly. Despite the sun, she was still too pale. Fear cramped in Beth, as familiar as every other daily emotion. Even if your child was cured, how long did it take until the dread and fear quit stabbing a reminder of your helplessness, of what you might lose? Or did they ever?

Mandy looked up. If she saw what her mother tried to hide, she didn't comment. "When are you going to take me to Kayla's? I should call her."

Last week Beth had asked Kayla's mother if she'd have Mandy over today.

Mandy had no idea her mother had a doctor appointment. Now Beth said, "As soon as I've had breakfast."

"Okay." Mandy set her cereal bowl in the sink. "I have to go get my swimsuit and put sunscreen lotion on and stuff."

Mandy swung between awkwardness and grace. Today she pounded up the stairs, sounding like a teenage boy in size-twelve Reeboks.

The phone rang just as Beth was sitting down with her toast and tea, all her stomach seemed able to handle these days.

"Hello?"

"What time shall I pick you up?" Nathan asked without preamble.

A flash of anger had her saying more sharply than she normally would have allowed herself, "You shouldn't. You're not my husband. Please quit acting as if you are." *Please quit encouraging me to dream about you as if you are.*

The silence was long enough, thick enough, to have her opening her mouth to apologize. She didn't have a chance.

"I've been having trouble believing I'm really going to be a father." His voice was toneless. "I thought, if I heard the heartbeat…" He didn't finish. "It had nothing to do with you."

There was a soft click and Beth realized he'd hung up.

She slammed down the receiver and fought the urge to burst into tears. She would not feel guilty. He was the one trying to take Rob's place, and she wouldn't let him! Next thing she knew he *would* be sitting on the edge of her bed looking at her, not tenderly, but grimly, as though she was a burden.

No, she thought, staring blindly at her dry toast. He would never sit on the edge of her bed. She'd offered him the chance and he'd refused. He didn't want what had been Rob's. Didn't want her. She was the one confused, not him.

She should apologize at least. Maybe let him go with her to the doctor. What would it hurt? But she didn't reach for the telephone. Her emotions were too muddled for her to deal with his, as well. Later, she decided. They had time enough to come to terms—seven months, to be exact. And by then surely—please, God!—this child inside her would be real, a person, and she would be able to look at her baby's father and know he wasn't Rob.

Chapter Six

Damned if he wasn't going to cry. Nathan blinked hard and inhaled through his mouth. Around him other adults, probably all parents, stirred. A baby started to babble and the mother murmured nonsense in a singsong voice. But he didn't look away from the pale, dark-eyed girl sitting facing the audience, hands clasped in her lap.

Mandy was doing a monologue from *The Diary of Anne Frank*. It was a poignant little speech in which she was wishing herself out of the attic that had hidden the family for two long years. Soft, wistful, her voice ached with youth and dreams and resignation. Mandy *was* Anne, the Jewish girl who would die of fever in a concentration camp.

When she finished and bowed her head, the long moment of silence told Nathan he wasn't alone in being moved by her performance. Then the small audience erupted into applause. The teacher of the drama class rushed forward.

"Amanda, that was wonderful. I almost cried."

Nathan gave a quick surreptitious swipe to the corners of his eyes. The power of her performance and the sting her illness gave it was being supplanted by pride, enough to clog his throat.

Mandy quietly crossed to the chairs at the side of the room where the other members of the class awaited their turns. A younger boy had collected some props and taken her place. Just before she sat down, she put her glasses back on and looked toward Nathan. It both hurt and gratified him to see the need for approval in her eyes. His approval.

He grinned and offered her a thumbs-up, and was warmed by the quick smile that gave her face an elfin charm.

The woman beside him leaned over and whispered, "Your daughter is very talented. Does she have an agent?"

"She hasn't done that much acting yet," he returned in a low voice. He ought to tell her that Mandy wasn't his daughter, but he allowed himself the indulgence of pretending, if only for the evening.

After the class was over, he hugged Mandy. "You're incredible," he told her. "The woman who sat beside me thinks you ought to have an agent."

"Really?" Mandy brightened. "You mean, so I can do commercials and stuff?"

"I guess."

"That'd be cool." She thought about it. "Except this kid who was in my class last year went to lots of auditions. He said you'd sit for hours sometimes, and then you could tell they weren't even listening to you when it was your turn. He got one or two parts, but it didn't sound worth it. I mean, he couldn't play soccer or baseball or anything because of auditions."

Nathan breathed in the night air and opened the passenger door for her. Other car doors were slamming, tail-lights flashing. "You'd have to want it pretty bad."

She plopped inside and reached for the seat belt. "Yeah." Face dimly illuminated by the roof light and the yellow parking-lot lamps, she was quiet long enough that he almost closed the door. But suddenly she added in a false bright tone, "Maybe someday I'd like to do it. I don't know."

His heart contracted. He'd discovered that what he wanted most in life was for Mandy to be able to talk about the future with real hope, to believe that she *had* a future. He'd have given her his own if he could. Maybe, in a way, that was what he was doing, becoming a father for her sake.

Rob, he thought again, *did you know how lucky you were?*

He was beginning to suspect that his brother had indeed known. Nathan was spending a hell of a lot of night hours wishing he could do it all differently, have a chance to see Rob as a man he would have liked.

But then came an insidious thought. He would also have had to see Beth happily married to his brother.

By the time he'd reached his own side of the car, he had squelched his turmoil, shoved it back down and slammed the lid, like a hamper full of dirty laundry that had to be washed sooner or later, but not now.

Trouble was, now never seemed like the right time.

He and Mandy chatted on the way home, just an easy conversation with comfortable silences, as though they'd known each other all their lives. It was August, and tonight was her second-to-last acting class of the summer session. Next week was the final performance of the monologues they'd worked on all summer; tonight had been a rehearsal. Parents could come to either or both. Mandy had decided he could come tonight, her mom next week. He could go next week, too, she'd added hopefully.

Unspoken was what they all knew or at least suspected: Beth would rather he didn't. She was avoiding him. Even Mandy had to have noticed. Oh, he saw Beth, but mostly in passing. She'd suggest someplace he might take Mandy. An errand he could do for them, since he was determined to be helpful. Sometimes she took naps when he was there.

Damned if that wasn't worse torture than her presence. She'd go up the stairs and close her door, and eventually only silence would come from up there. Nathan would picture himself climbing the stairs the way he had the other time, easing open her bedroom door, stepping inside. She'd be curled on her side as she'd been that afternoon, her fuzzy blue gown gaping open. Below the golden tan of her throat, her breasts would be pale. If he slipped a finger into the opening of the gown, he'd be able to ease it aside. Just another inch, and he'd see her nipple. And, God, he wanted to see it, as he'd never wanted anything in his life. Almost, he amended. Next to Mandy being cured.

When Beth was awake, her face held so much wariness he clung to the vision of it in sleep. Gold lashes, tiny freckles, mouth soft. It looked younger than she must be. Sweet. Pretty. Kissable.

And she was probably dreaming about Rob. The knowledge was like an icy clump of snow falling on his head. She had loved his brother. Still loved his brother. Nathan looked just like Rob. Wasn't Rob.

He knew he couldn't have her, tried to make himself quit dreaming he could. Good God, even if by some miracle she claimed to fall in love with him, how would he ever know whom she imagined she was going to bed with?

Tonight he almost didn't go in with Mandy, but when he failed to turn off the ignition, she grabbed his hand

and begged, "Will you come and tell Mom how I did? Please?"

What could he say? "You just want me to puff up your ego," he grumbled, but in a way that let her know he was kidding. He turned off the car and got out, looking across the roof at her. "Next week, your mother'll see for herself that you're going to be a star. Assuming she's never noticed any dramatics around the house."

Mandy dragged him up the porch steps. "You mean, like me pretending I hate something I really don't?"

"Yeah. Like that."

"You mean, like lie?"

"Uh—" he held open the front door for her "—exaggerate."

"Would I do that?" She raised shocked eyes to him.

"Yeah." He poked her. "You're pretty good, too."

Her grin was unaffectedly childlike, a couple of crooked front teeth making him think about braces and contact lenses to replace those detested glasses. God willing, she'd need both.

"Mom!" she bellowed.

Her mother appeared from the kitchen, a half-grown black-and-white cat draped over her shoulder. "Polly is determined to help me wash the dishes."

Damn, she looked good. Three months pregnant, and still she could wear snug jeans and a short sleeveless shirt. Her hair was held up by a clip, but pale curls were slipping out all around her face.

Mandy took the seemingly boneless animal from her mother. "She likes water."

Beth wrinkled her nose at the cat. "There's something about her staring in the toilet every time I flush it…"

"That shows she's intelligent," Mandy said confidently. "I mean, just think, she's trying to figure out where all that water is going and then why it comes rushing back."

So far Beth had ignored Nathan, but now her eyes met his in amusement over her daughter's head. For just a second she'd forgotten he threatened her. Upset her.

"Yeah, well," he drawled, "if Polly has an IQ of 150, Calvin's is about eighty-five. The other day, he was so busy watching a bird he fell off the porch railing into a lilac bush. Should've seen him slink away."

Eyes alight with laughter, Beth said, "It could have been worse. He might have fallen in a rosebush. Then more than his dignity would have been damaged."

Nathan tried for an easy grin. "I don't think he has any dignity."

"Of course he does!" Mandy declared indignantly. "He's like a little kid, that's all. Kids aren't supposed to be dignified."

"More like a teenager," her mother muttered.

"Speaking of teenagers," Nathan said, "I seem to remember that somebody around here has a birthday coming up."

"Two somebodies, actually," his niece told him with a sly look at her mother. "My birthday is on the twentieth, Mom's on the twenty-fourth."

Beth rolled her eyes at Mandy. "I'm doing my best to forget it."

"Oh, come on," Nathan said, "it can't be that bad." He leaned an elbow on the stair banister. "What is it? Thirty-three? Thirty-four?"

The scrunched-up nose reminded him of a nearly identical expression Mandy sometimes made.

"Thirty-five."

"Hey, I'll hit the big four-0 long before you will."

She blinked; a shadow crossed her face. "You will, won't you?"

Damn it, he'd screwed up. His birthday meant Rob's birthday. But Rob wouldn't make the big four-0.

"By the time you're forty," he said lightly, "you may have a famous actress for a daughter. She's dynamite."

The shadow disappeared. As clear as a high mountain stream, Beth's eyes fastened on his. "She's good, isn't she?"

She hadn't asked him to come any farther into the house and sit down, but at least they were talking. Well, he might kill it here, but one reason for his involvement in their lives was to share remembrances of his brother. "Yeah. Did you know Rob was in high-school drama? He wasn't half-bad."

"Really?" Mandy's eyes widened.

"Darn right. Let's see. He played Scrooge in *A Christmas Carol* in our senior year and, um, the King of Siam in *The King and I*. He was a real ham."

"You know, he never said." Beth's voice was soft. "I suppose the subject didn't come up. Mandy wasn't acting yet—" She stopped. "What are we standing here for? Would you like a cup of coffee?"

"Wouldn't mind," he agreed casually.

Of course that meant he had to continue to talk about Rob, dredging up every memory of those three or four high-school plays that had given his brother another chance to be the center of attention. Rob wouldn't have acted if he couldn't have had the starring roles. Nathan didn't tell Beth or Mandy that. The second he ran out of recollections, Mandy popped to her feet. "I'm gonna get ready for bed. Thank you for taking me tonight, Uncle Nathan. Night, Mom."

Two-thirds of his coffee was left. Nathan hesitated, then put his cup down and started to get to his feet.

Beth's glance shied away from him, but she said, "You don't have to hurry off."

He raised an eyebrow. One surprise after another. He'd have sworn Mandy was trying to leave them alone, except he couldn't figure why she'd do that. Now Beth wasn't politely pushing him out the door as she normally did, either.

When she didn't say anything, he did. "You've raised a nice kid."

"She is, isn't she?" Beth's eyes, shimmering with emotion that needn't be named, met his. "Have you noticed she's developing?"

Developing? Blankly, Nathan thought, developing what? Then it clicked. "Oh. Yeah." Mandy's breasts weren't much yet, but he had noticed her self-consciousness. "That's normal, isn't it?" he asked. "She's almost twelve." Fifth, sixth grade, he seemed to remember that was when he really became aware of breasts, presumably because that was when the girls began to get them. His awareness had fueled a few wet dreams.

Unconscious of his detour into personal history, Beth nodded. "Uh-huh. One of her friends is already—" Beth's hands sketched a somewhat improbable Playboy-bunny bosom "—and she's been menstruating for ages." She closed her eyes with a snap, and a tinge of pink ran along her cheeks. "I'm sorry. I forget, you haven't had kids or... Am I embarrassing you?"

"Nah." He let his amusement show, not the clutch of longing her friendliness awakened. "I do know the facts of life. Even if my one venture into parenthood didn't require a hell of a lot of knowledge."

Now she was truly blushing. Primly she said, "I'm sure the nurse must have given you instructions."

"I think she did." A grin pulled at the corner of his

mouth. "I just didn't take them in. I was too stunned by the, uh, circumstances."

"Well, I did give you an alternative…" Horror made her mouth form an O. She hadn't meant that to slip out.

He rubbed the back of his neck. "You know why I turned you down."

She didn't seem to have heard him. "It was dumb of me." She was trying to sound cheerful, uncaring, but her tone was forced. "I don't even know what kind of woman attracts you! Maybe it's buxom redheads. I mean, if you'd agreed to my proposition just to be kind, think how humiliating it could have been for both of us."

His eyes narrowed. Damned if she hadn't decided that he couldn't have gotten it up. Since she was so unattractive. The irony made him franker than he should have been for his self-preservation.

"Actually Rob and I had pretty similar tastes in women." More irony. Which wasn't why his voice roughened. "Under other circumstances, I'd have given a lot to go up to your bedroom with you."

She looked shocked and…flattered? Good God, had she really believed he'd turned her down because he didn't find her sexy?

Her tongue touched her lips. Nervously, no doubt, but he felt a jolt of pure hunger. She spoke gravely. "Did anybody ever tell you you're chivalrous?"

He swore and stood up, looming over her. "I didn't say that to be nice. I said it because it's the truth. You're Rob's widow. If you weren't—" His turn to put the brakes on. Probably too late.

She rose to her feet, too, slowly, never looking away from him. "If…if it weren't for Rob, maybe…"

He sucked in a breath and squeezed his eyes shut. "I shouldn't have said that."

"No." She was being painfully honest. He wished she'd quit. "I've been thinking the same thing. I'm confused. It's just…I can't be sure which of my feelings are for Rob and which are for you."

Nathan forced himself to open his eyes and say levelly, "A little confusion is natural. I make you think about him."

"Sometimes—" she bowed her head, exposing the long line of her neck "—I have dreams…"

He had a feeling he knew what kind. God, why was she telling him this? He'd started it, he thought, appalled. Why hadn't he kept his damned mouth shut? He'd been better off not guessing that she felt some of the same turmoil he did. Now he'd lie awake nights wondering if she was thinking about him, dreaming about him, her nipples hardening for him.

Or for Rob.

"I'd better go." He blundered backward. "I hope I haven't made you more uncomfortable around me."

"No." Her sigh sounded unconscious. "I think maybe it needed to be said. I've been rude. Hiding because I didn't know how to deal with the things I've felt."

Things. Like what? he wanted to ask. Did her heart speed up when he was around? Did she feel a quiver in her belly? Did she have to busy her hands to keep from touching him? Or was she just talking about dreams of Rob, only she wasn't sure it wasn't him, instead?

He shrugged. "We're in a strange spot. Not just because of Rob. Because of…" He gestured at her belly.

Her hands spread protectively over it. The sight sent a lurch of pure desire through him.

"That's true." Her eyes were softer than he'd seen them in weeks. "Maybe we've cleared the air."

Had they? Oh, hell, maybe he could pretend. Maybe

pretense would even become reality. Maybe eventually he could feel brotherly toward her.

Yeah, an inner voice mocked, *not in* your *dreams.*

"Are you feeling okay?" he asked awkwardly.

"Still nauseated," she admitted. "But it ought to pass soon. Otherwise, I'm fine."

He nodded. She didn't mention the tiredness, but he knew she still battled that, too. At least she'd listened to common sense and took naps when she could manage it. And berry season was winding down.

She seemed to be eyeing him carefully. "I...I have a doctor's appointment tomorrow."

Surprise coursed through him. He schooled his voice to be noncommittal. "Yeah?"

"If you'd like to come..."

Only the gravel in his voice betrayed his emotions. "Do you mean that?"

"I was a pig last month."

"This isn't exactly a toy we have to share."

"That's probably not a half-bad description," Beth said wryly. "We do need to learn to share. Or maybe *I* need to learn."

"We'll work it out." He cleared his throat. "What time?"

The night was cooler. In her dark bedroom Beth stood at the window looking out at the fields. A cloud cover—maybe rain tomorrow?—hid the moon. She couldn't see anything. Still, she let the air drift over her body until she felt goose bumps rise. Then she slipped into bed, poking a cat—Calvin, she decided, from the sound of the purr—out of the way with one foot.

Surely she would sleep better tonight. She almost hugged herself with pleasure because of her talk with Nathan. They should have done that long ago. She'd let her belief that he didn't want her rankle, had resented it for some absurd reason. Because of Rob, she supposed; it was as though Rob had reappeared and didn't want her anymore.

Everything was because of Rob, including her reawakened sexual longings. But maybe those would fade, if she could get to be friends with Nathan. They'd move past any stirrings between them. They were a man and a woman, so it was confusing to be thrust so much together, to be bound the way they would be forever by their child.

But she felt optimistic tonight. He'd go to the doctor with her tomorrow, and she'd feel nothing inappropriate. She had been selfish. He, too, should have the thrill of hearing their baby's heartbeat.

She closed her eyes and pictured him—Nathan, not Rob. A tanned strong neck. Lean forearms with prominent veins and tendons and only a light dusting of hair. Though not bulky, big-shouldered. Leaner than her husband, she thought; Rob had thought running was boring.

Immediately she realized she was comparing them again, standing one beside the other, hunting for differences. Tonight she wouldn't do it. *Picture Nathan alone,* she told herself.

Heavy brows, and eyes that were a little hooded. Cheekbones to die for, and a mouth that was all the sexier for being rather unsmiling. Beth felt a pang of guilt, because Rob had always been grinning and teasing and flirting, but she ignored it. *Nathan,* she reminded herself. Not Rob.

Short wavy hair he did his best to subdue. Steady quiet eyes. Emotions suppressed, ghosts behind those eyes, flickering sometimes in a cheek muscle, but rarely overt. She tried to imagine him angry, really angry, or shouting with laughter or—

A wave of heat washed through her. "Oh, God," she moaned. "What am I doing?"

Arousing herself apparently. Forgetting they were going to be friends. Remembering the grit in his voice when he'd said, "Under other circumstances, I'd have given a lot to go up to your bedroom with you." And, "You're Rob's widow. If you weren't…"

If she wasn't, she'd want him. She *did* want him. She admitted that much to herself. No question, no hesitation. He turned her on.

But how much was memory, because her husband had turned her on, too, and how much was the present? How much was Nathan?

She was terribly afraid that sooner or later she'd have to find out. But how?

As it turned out, she didn't sleep better, not with such thoughts tumbling about in her head. Her unease wasn't improved by having to lie to Mandy come morning about what she'd be doing while Mandy went swimming with her friend Barbara.

"Oh, just a pile of paperwork…" She pretended to think. "I might run to the grocery store, so if you call and can't reach me, don't worry."

Mandy gazed at her without blinking for a moment that stretched a little too long, then gave a small nod. "Okay." She cocked her head. "I hear a car. That must be Barbara's mom."

Don't let it be Nathan, Beth prayed. *Don't let him have decided to come early.* "Sunscreen lotion," she said. "If you stay long, don't forget to put more on."

Her daughter curled her lip. "Mom, I'm not dumb."

A glance out the window reassured Beth that the car in front was indeed Barbara's mother's minivan. "No, you're just a kid." Mandy accepted Beth's hug with more grace than she sometimes did. "Kids are dumb. They don't get smart until they turn twenty-five."

Real indignation sounded this time. "Mom!"

She laughed. "Just kidding. Have fun."

Not until Mandy darted out the door, slamming it behind her, did Beth let out a sigh. How would Mandy feel when she learned Beth had been hiding something as central to their lives as a pregnancy? Would she ever trust her again?

Nathan showed up precisely on time, which she should have expected. He was well aware, after all, that Mandy wouldn't know where her mother was going today. Beth had offered to meet him at the doctor's office, but he'd shaken his head.

"I'd rather drive you. It'll give us time to talk."

She'd agreed; after all, they were going to be friends, right? Maybe, she thought hopefully, there was something to the saying that familiarity breeds contempt. She'd rather feel contempt than…whatever it was she did feel.

She couldn't quite work up anything approaching contempt this morning, however, not with him looking as good as he did in faded jeans, boots and a cream-colored shirt. He paused beside his car and gazed up at the house, that brooding face unreadable. Nor did his expression change when she came out onto the porch, though he nodded and said, "'Morning."

Beth felt unaccountably shy. "Hi. I'm all set."

He came around and opened her car door. "Where's Mandy?"

"Swimming with a friend."

He frowned. "She's taken lessons?"

Touched rather than offended by his concern, she smiled. "Yes. She won't drown."

He slammed the door, came around and got in behind the wheel. He reached for the keys, then turned to look at her, instead. "It's just that she's so frail."

"I know," Beth said softly.

"You're better at this than I am."

"No. I worry all the time."

He saw in her eyes that it was the truth, and he nodded. A moment later he started the engine.

They didn't talk about Mandy again, or last night's conversation, or their dreams, or even the baby. She was grateful when he said, "Looks like we're getting a big order from a sporting-goods chain back East. We're going to have to bump up production."

She congratulated him, encouraged him to talk, even discussed some marketing efforts of her own. All the while, she couldn't seem to tear her eyes from his hands. At the moment they were competently wrapped around the steering wheel. Every once in a while, as traffic slowed or sped up, he'd reach over to change gears, nearly brushing her thigh.

His hands were large, tanned, the nails clipped short. Pure male in their size and strength and bluntness, they made her feel safe.

Startled by the thought, she wondered where it had come from. Safe? She wasn't exactly in danger. Mandy was, but Nathan McCabe couldn't save her with brute strength or gentleness or determination.

Maybe not, but something in the sight of his hand every time he rested it on Mandy's thin shoulder cramped Beth's heart. She could easily picture him cradling a baby in those hands, too, dwarfing the small body even as he protected it. He'd scarcely touched her, yet Beth knew in every fiber what his hands would feel like on her.

And not because she knew Rob's touch. His had been different, she thought, looking away at last, gazing blindly out her side window as the car crossed the Evergreen Point Bridge. Rob hadn't been physical the way his brother was.

His hands had been thinner, better cared for, the nails smooth, his fingertips uncalloused. He'd hated the hard labor when she'd coaxed him to help tie up the long whippy canes of the raspberries or plant rows of strawberries. Only under the hood of a car was he willing to get really dirty or take a chance of scraping a knuckle.

More differences. She might end up like the mother of twins she knew who'd confessed that her two girls hardly looked alike to her and was always surprised when others confused them. Beth was pretty sure that if Nathan and Rob were both standing in front of her, she'd know one from the other immediately. So why was her dreaming mind so muddled?

She started to give Nathan directions to the clinic before remembering that he'd been there, and why. If he noticed her embarrassment, he didn't comment.

Her doctor's office was situated in a trendy area of Seattle with expensive shops, busy sidewalks and scant parking. Fortunately the clinic had its own small lot. Inside, the middle-aged receptionist, Margaret, was saying hello to Beth when her eyes traveled to Nathan. They widened and she sucked in a breath.

"Mr. McCabe?" she whispered.

Oh, Lord. Dr. Williams had delivered Mandy, and the receptionist had worked here then. She'd known Rob. Beth recalled that she *wasn't* here the day the sperm was implanted. Without knowing the circumstances, no wonder she looked so shocked.

"My brother-in-law," Beth said hastily. "He's Mr. McCabe, too."

"Nathan." He held out a hand. "We were twins."

Margaret shook it, while she pressed her other hand to her chest. "I'm terribly sorry! I thought I was seeing a ghost!"

"No problem." But the crease between his brows had deepened, and Beth had the impression he was bothered by being mistaken even momentarily for Rob.

The nurse who called Beth's name was new, so she chatted under the apparent impression that they were married as she ushered them in. She checked Beth's weight and blood pressure—"Just dandy!" she chirped—before leaving them in an examining room and promising that Dr. Williams would be in shortly.

Beth would have sworn the room had shrunk since she was last here. Waiting alone was one thing; who cared if there wasn't space to do a pirouette? The stark decor and lack of window always had her feeling vaguely claustrophobic, but nothing like today. Today she wanted to bolt. Nathan's shoulders seemed several inches wider even than usual; he towered over her as she perched on the end of the examining table. What on earth had possessed her to invite him?

Maybe her panic showed on her face, because he turned abruptly away. She sensed, though, that his reason for retreating was instantly forgotten when he noticed a chart on the wall showing the fetus at different stages.

"He looks like a baby," he said suddenly.

"He? Oh." She touched her stomach. "You mean ours."

"Yeah. That picture says three months. That's what you are, right?"

"Yes," she told his back.

"Somehow I didn't think—" He stopped.

She had to swallow to hold down a tide of emotion. "It's…it's hard to believe, isn't it?"

He turned toward her again. She wanted to launch herself into his arms, cry a few tears against his chest; she didn't know why. She was actually scooting forward when the door swung open and Dr. Williams hustled in.

"Sorry to keep you waiting." Her dark eyes studied Nathan. "Mr. McCabe, good to meet you. I'm glad to see you here."

"Why?" he asked.

Another doctor might have been taken aback by his blunt question; Dr. Williams just raised an eyebrow and replied with equal bluntness, "Because it bodes well for your involvement once the baby is born."

His mouth lifted in a half smile. "I'll be there."

"Good." The doctor turned to Beth. "How're you feeling?"

Beth answered the usual questions while she lay back on the crinkly paper and let Dr. Williams lift her shirt. She had a flashback to the insemination, when she had stared at the same poster on the ceiling and imagined the man who now stood only a few feet away, his eyes fixed with seeming fascination on her bare belly.

The doctor's hands deftly probed. "The fetus should be about three inches long at this stage," she said. "Weighing maybe an ounce. Fingers and toes all formed. A twelve-week fetus even has fingerprints. If we could look, we'd see what sex your baby is."

Nathan hadn't moved, just stared. He didn't even appear to notice that Beth was watching him, not the doctor.

"Well, let's find that heartbeat," Dr. Williams announced, pulling her stethoscope from around her neck.

Listening intently, she paused, moved the bell-shaped diaphragm a few inches on Beth's abdomen, paused again. At last she smiled. "There we go. Steady and brisk. Mr. McCabe, would you care to hear your child's heartbeat?"

"Yeah." His voice was gravelly, as Beth was learning it always was when he felt a powerful emotion. "I'd care to."

He took a couple of steps forward and bent his head to place the tips of the stethoscope in his ears. He was so close Beth could see the blunt dark fan of his lashes against his cheeks, a tic at the corner of his mouth, the whorls of his ear and the lines beside his eyes. He went completely still, not even breathing.

At last he lifted a stunned gaze. "Incredible," he murmured.

"It is, isn't it?" Dr. Williams matter-of-factly took the stethoscope from him and pulled Beth's shirt down over her midriff. "Well, Beth, I'll see you in another month. Looks like things are going just as they should be. You ought to find the nausea disappearing in these next few weeks."

She nodded. "It did last time."

From the corner of her eye, she saw Nathan step back. The doctor breezed out a moment later and Beth sat up.

"That's it?" Nathan asked, voice still husky.

"I told you it was routine."

"Maybe for you. Not for me."

"Well…it's not as if I've been through this half a dozen times." Glad it was over, she retrieved her purse and slipped by him when he held open the door for her.

He waited while she made another appointment, then suggested, "How about some lunch?"

"I should get home…."

"Why? Mandy's not due back yet, is she?"

"Well, no."

"Then?"

A date. It felt like a first date, and with the father of her unborn baby. *Stop this!* Beth told herself sharply. He was being polite. They were supposed to become friends.

Nonetheless, when she agreed with a casual-sounding

"Why not?" she felt reckless, a little excited. And when his hand, steering her out the door, touched her lower back, heat settled between her legs.

She couldn't regret having been married to Rob, she thought desperately. She'd loved him. They'd had good years together, and Mandy. She *was* his widow. So how could she be letting herself feel these things for Rob's brother?

Chapter Seven

"Happy birthday, dear Amanda," everyone sang, "happy birthday to you!"

Mandy's tears blurred the faces around the table; she had to sniff. The five friends she'd invited to her party grinned at her. Uncle Nate was snapping pictures while Mom, who'd carried the cake from the kitchen, stood beaming to one side.

Gazing down at the twelve flickering candles, Mandy took a deep breath, made her wish and then blew. Everybody clapped because she'd blown them all out. That meant her wish would come true, right?

Maybe. The hope was like the wisps of smoke still rising from the candles even as Mom pulled them from the cake. Her wishes other years hadn't exactly come true, but they hadn't *not* come true, either. She was alive, wasn't she? Maybe Mom was right and the last chemotherapy really *had* made her better. Maybe the baby... She wouldn't let herself think about that.

"Big piece?" Mom asked her. She held the knife poised above the lemon yellow cake.

"Yeah, and I want lots of ice cream," Mandy said.

Uncle Nate put down the camera and started scooping vanilla ice cream onto the plates as Mom handed them to him. For a second he looked just like Dad. Well, she guessed he always looked like Dad, but just not quite as much as now, or at least she wasn't aware of it. But she'd sat in this same chair her last birthday that Dad was alive— her eighth, she decided, counting back. She squinted until today's party almost blended into the one she remembered, when Dad had teased her friends and slapped big helpings of ice cream onto their slices of cake. Pink cake; she'd been really into princesses and fairies and stuff like that then. Kid stuff. Kayla and April and Samantha had been at that party, too, she was pretty sure. They'd been friends a long time.

By her ninth birthday, Dad was dead and Mandy was in the hospital. The doctors had let Mom bring a cake in, and they'd all gathered around and sung "Happy Birthday" to her. Her only friend there was Jessica, in the next bed. She had a piece of birthday cake, too.

Mandy shook away the memories. She wouldn't think about Jessica, not today. This was her birthday, for Pete's sake! She was celebrating. Now she was a teenager. Well, almost a teenager.

Uncle Nate left after he'd had a piece of cake. She gave him a hard squeeze around the waist and whispered, "Thank you." His present had been tickets to a Broadway musical coming to the 5th Avenue Theatre in Seattle. Four tickets, so she could take a friend and Mom could come, too.

He gave her a big smile and said, "Happy birthday, kiddo."

She and her friends spread their sleeping bags on blown-up air mattresses in front of the TV in the family room. She'd chosen two movies, which happened to have cute boys in them. The girls whispered and giggled, and later Mom brought them popcorn and soda.

At first, after the lights went off, they talked about starting middle school and what it would be like to have so many different teachers and classrooms and whether the eighth-grade boys would be any more grown-up than the ones their own age that they'd been stuck with forever.

It was later, when the whispers were getting further apart, that Barbara's voice came softly to Mandy. "You're not sick anymore, right?"

Mandy hadn't told her friends that her leukemia was incurable without the transplant. "I guess not," she said, trying to sound careless. "I might still have that bone-marrow transplant, if the doctors can ever find anyone whose blood matches mine."

"Why?" Kayla asked.

Mandy gave the easiest answer. "Just to be sure."

"Oh," another girl murmured.

Into the silence Mandy said, "Do you ever think about dying? I mean, just not being here? Like not ever turning thirteen?"

An answer was a long time coming. Finally April said sleepily, "I don't like to think about it. That'd mean I'd never be able to date, or drive a car, or kiss a boy, or..."

Barbara flopped over onto her stomach. "I don't want to kiss a boy. If anyone ever kissed me, it'd probably be somebody like Brian Robb."

They all squealed. Brian was this total nerd. He practically fell over his feet he was so big and clumsy. Mandy guessed he wasn't dumb or anything, but he always tried to be funny and he wasn't. Besides, he had big lips. She shuddered.

Somehow the other girls were talking about boys again and especially about kissing. Death wasn't real to them, not the way it was to her. They didn't know about the plaques lining the hallway at Children's Hospital, each with the name of a child who'd died. She couldn't talk to any of them, any more than she could to Mom.

Jessica popped into her mind again and she knew why. One night in the hospital Jessica had whispered to Mandy, "I used to say I never wanted to get breasts."

"They're gross, aren't they?" Mandy had agreed. She'd only been eight years old then; she couldn't imagine wanting blobs bobbing up and down on her chest when she ran or jumped.

After a long pause Jessica said in a low voice, "Yeah, but I really, really didn't want them. I think I was trying to give God an order."

"I bet he doesn't take that kind of order." Mandy frowned, staring at the light showing under the door. "Or maybe any kind of order."

Jessica was silent a long time. She sounded funny, kind of choked up, when she whispered, "I hope not."

I hope not? It took Mandy a second to realize what Jessica was afraid of. She was afraid she'd wished so hard not to get breasts God was giving her that wish. The only way He could keep her from getting the breasts was not to let her grow up.

"I bet lots of girls wish they wouldn't get breasts," she'd told Jessica. "God doesn't pay any attention to dumb little-kid wishes like that."

Jessica hadn't said anything else. Mandy'd almost forgotten the conversation. It had come back to her one day not very long ago when she'd been staring at her naked body in the mirror after her shower. She was getting hair and boobs and everything. It partly *was* gross and partly kind of exciting. Life *had* to be more exciting when you got to be a real teenager. And she wanted to grow up. She didn't just assume she would, like most kids probably did. She wanted it with an active passionate hunger that beat along with her heart. She wished Jessica had made it to being twelve years old, too. That she'd gotten breasts, so she could see that God wouldn't be so cruel.

Only, He *had* been, because Jessica didn't get to grow up. What Mandy didn't understand was why. Why Jessica? Why did some of the kids leave the hospital and never look back? Why was she still alive?

She wished she knew if there was a God at all.

"Jessica," she whispered, but nobody answered. Her friends were asleep, and Jessica never *had* answered once she was gone.

"Cool! We never come to the zoo," Mandy exclaimed in satisfaction.

"Now that's not true," Beth protested. "We just haven't come *this* summer." Or last summer, she remembered; Mandy had been too sick.

Nathan eased the car into a slot in the zoo parking lot and turned off the engine. "I haven't been to a zoo in years."

"They've changed," Beth told him. "The animals aren't in little cages looking miserable anymore. Wait'll you see the lion enclosure and the elephants. Oh, and the wolves."

"I like the prairie dogs," Mandy contributed, already out of the car. In defiance of her mother's insistence that she wear a hat to keep from getting sunburned, her baseball cap was on backward. She looked boyish and gangly and cute.

Beth decided not to make an issue of the hat for now. After all, her daughter, like herself, was slathered with sunscreen. And she had to be protective about some things. It was just hard knowing when to quit.

They paid and entered. Mandy stopped immediately. "Can I climb the tree?"

Other kids already were. The huge fir spread its wide ancient branches parallel to the ground. A toddler bounced delightedly on one thick branch crying, "Giddyap, giddyap!" while her father supported her. Boys dared each other to go higher.

Nathan said, "Sure. Want a boost?"

Beth opened her mouth automatically to argue, then shut it. Right now Mandy was as well as she might ever be. No reason she couldn't climb a tree.

Beth reached out and touched a branch, the bark worn smooth by the scrape of countless jeans and tennis shoes. Helped up by her uncle Nate, Mandy clambered gingerly around, her smile as joyous as the toddler's. Suddenly she jumped, hitting the ground hard and falling to her hands and knees.

Beth gasped, but Mandy hopped up and said, "Come on. I want to see the giraffes."

They wandered from the African safari, where giraffes, antelopes and zebras grazed together, to the glass-fronted enclosure where lions sunned themselves on rocks only feet away. One lioness prowled at the edge of a pool, her eyes on something beneath the water's surface. She moved much like Calvin and Polly, with that boneless grace, yet each enormous paw was bigger than either kitten's whole body.

Mandy reached out and squeezed Beth's hand. Beth felt

Nathan standing behind her, so close his warmth enfolded her. It took her back, this tableau.

Family. She and Rob and Mandy used to come to the Woodland Park Zoo three or four times a year, sometimes even in the winter, and wandered just like this. Coming here was never Rob's idea. He'd always groan and say, "But we were just there!" But if she and Mandy decided to go alone, he'd be waiting at the car, and once here he'd always be standing just behind her or boosting Mandy onto his shoulders so she could see better.

"Look!" Mandy cried now.

Beth's attention returned abruptly to the lioness. She caught the animal in midleap, then watched as it hit the water with a huge splash. As quickly, the lioness vaulted back onto the bank, a large fish flopping in her great jaws. The lioness gave her head a shake, the fish went still, and she crouched with her back to the glass to devour her prey.

Mandy chattered excitedly about the successful hunt even as they moved on to see the otters and the mountain goats, the elk and timber wolves. As Beth strolled across the grass, she watched Mandy and Nathan up ahead. Her daughter's cap was still on backward, her legs long and skinny beneath her cutoffs. Beside her, Nathan wore faded denim jeans and a dark green T-shirt that emphasized the breadth of his shoulders. Dark glasses partly masked his expressions.

They reached the enclosure with the wallaroos, and he and Mandy propped their elbows on the low fence. He threw back his head and laughed at something she said, the flash of teeth awakening his guarded face to a charm that matched Rob's. Maybe that was why Beth felt the odd lurch in the vicinity of her heart.

Or maybe not, she admitted with a private sigh. The

sight of him had been giving her pleasure all morning; he moved with a grace as contained as the big cats', as sure and even arrogant. She imagined him in the mountains, hefting a heavy pack easily or feeling his way surefootedly up a rock face. She was agonizingly conscious of the play of muscles and tendons when he lifted a hand to snatch off Mandy's hat and ruffle her hair. A play of muscles and tendons so like Rob's.

Or was it?

She shook her head, annoyed at her confusion. At first, she'd seen Nathan as a reflection of her husband, a shadow. When he lifted an eyebrow, she'd see Rob doing the same. Now she'd find herself thinking, *Rob did that,* and then wasn't positive he had. Maybe she'd seen the same expression on Nathan's face before and was mixing that up with her memories of her husband.

She reached them, and they both turned naturally to include her. "Slowpoke," Nathan teased. When Mandy hurried inside to see the wallaroos more closely, he lowered his voice. "Feel okay?"

"Yep. Except I'm as hungry as that lion."

"You want sushi, too?"

She made a face at him, her dark mood vanishing. "A hot dog will do very nicely, thank you. And a snow cone. I saw someone with one."

His smile this time was lazy and more than charming. Sexy. "You're a cheap date."

"We'll make you take us someplace really expensive for dinner before that 5th Avenue musical," she promised, feeling suddenly lighthearted. "I'll show you how cheap I am."

As casually as though he did it every day, Nathan laid an arm across her shoulders. "Is that a threat?"

She caught a scent of pure male, felt the weight of his

arm, the heat of his body. Her voice sounded a little husky to her ears. "Depends on how prosperous you're feeling."

"I've never had a family to spend money on before. You know I'd be willing to help with everyday expenses."

She was both touched and made uneasy. He'd inserted himself so deftly, so relentlessly, into their lives she could scarcely turn around anymore without finding him there, or some reminder of him. What if she decided she didn't *want* him around all the time? What if these confusing feelings really began to frighten her? How would she say, *Go away?* How would she keep Mandy from being hurt?

He must have felt her stiffen, because his arm dropped and he gave her an unreadable look before moving ahead to rejoin Mandy. Beth was annoyed with herself to realize she felt bereft, even a little jealous again of Mandy's easy relationship with him. And his with her. Beth wondered whether Mandy, too, was seeing her father in him. Did she ever get at all confused, or did she, because of her age, just not remember Rob as well as her mother did?

"I see a concession stand," Nathan said. "How about if we eat in the shade of that tree?" He pointed.

"Yeah, and then we can go in the nocturnal house," Mandy replied eagerly. "The snakes are in there, too."

"And the cockroaches." Beth shuddered.

"They have a display of cockroaches?" Nathan sounded incredulous.

"Behind glass." She couldn't help another shudder. "Heaps and heaps of them. Huge ones. They give me the creeps. I'll take a rattlesnake any day."

"I'm not too crazy about snakes," he confessed. "I, uh, hike reluctantly in rattlesnake country."

A crafty look crossed Mandy's face.

"No," Beth told her. "Don't even think it."

Nathan turned. "Think what?"

"Mo-om. I wouldn't do something like that."

"Like what?" he asked again.

Beth ignored him. "If you hadn't been thinking it, Amanda McCabe, you wouldn't know what I'm talking about."

"I wouldn't have *really* scared him," Mandy said sulkily.

"You have a snake," he said.

"Just a pretend one."

"And it's extraordinarily realistic," Beth said severely. "This charming child put it in the vat where I make jam, out in the barn. I just about had a heart attack."

"I'd have had one." He proceeded to poke fun at himself as he told a story about meeting an enormous rattlesnake on a trail in Baja, California. "A cliff going up on one side, dropping into the ocean on the other," Nathan said. "No way around. He was all coiled up, his tail rattling."

"Maybe it was *her* tail," Beth said.

"Nasty as it sounded, you're probably right," he agreed, then grinned as she poked him.

They took their hot dogs and pop to a shady spot and sprawled on the grass, Nathan on his side, head propped on his hand. Beth's gaze kept wandering down his body to places where his jeans were especially worn, and she had to repeatedly yank herself in. Damn it, she wished he'd sit up, not loll there like a man lazily lying on his bed watching a woman undress.

She swallowed hard. Where had *that* come from? All he was doing was relaxing and telling a story. About snakes.

"I waited all afternoon," he told them. "Once I tried poking it with a stick, but all it did was coil tighter and rattle until it sounded like a tornado whipping the sagebrush. So I just moseyed back a little, gave him—her—plenty of space, but it just kept those cold eyes fixed on me."

Her own eyes wide, Mandy leaned forward. "So what'd you *do?*"

"Retraced my steps, walked a couple of miles across rough country until I hit a road and hitched a ride with a truckload of Mexican laborers."

Amused, Beth asked, "And did you admit to them why you were on the road with your thumb out?"

There was that smile again, the one that sent a shiver down her spine. "You kidding? I implied, in my limited Spanish, that a bandit had held me up. Even though I'd been lucky enough to get away, I figured he'd be waiting for me down the trail."

His story ended, Mandy began crumbling her bun and feeding the birds waiting for handouts. Nathan rolled onto his back and closed his eyes. Contentedly Beth watched her daughter. Mandy looked as happy as she'd ever seen her.

In part that was because of the man whose breaths slowed and deepened even as the tension left his face. His forearms were lean and brown; his fingers were splayed on his flat belly. Beth let herself look her fill, from his strong brown neck to his crossed ankles and the worn running shoes on his size-eleven feet.

She was amused and intrigued by the shoes. Nathan ran a sporting-goods manufacturing company; shouldn't he always wear the latest in high-tech running shoes and space-age material? His business suits looked well made and pretty sharp, but most of the clothes she'd seen him in appeared to be old friends, far from the cutting edge of sporting apparel.

She was glad. As uninterested as she was in fashion, she wouldn't have felt comfortable with a man who fussed his hair and showed off sculpted thigh muscles. She found more than enough to enjoy in the way the faded denim hugged his narrow hips and long legs.

Beth wanted, with a fierceness that shook her, to sit astride his hips. She wanted him to roll over and pin her down, take off those dark glasses so she could see the intensity in his eyes. She wanted that big hand on her breast, that grim mouth to capture hers. She wanted—

With a near physical wrench, she closed her eyes and averted her face. Why him? she wondered in despair. Why not one of the other men who, in the past couple of years, had suggested dinner or dancing or a show? Why the one man for whom her emotions would inevitably be so complicated?

Damn you, Rob, why did you have to die? She struggled to picture her husband. A moment of passion, tenderness, the kind of intensity with which Nathan would make love to a woman. She saw Rob bending his head, but he was laughing, teasing, coaxing. All she could remember was lighthearted lovemaking. Had he ever slammed into her, his emotions raw? Had he ever completely lost control? Had she ever *wanted* him to? Why was she wondering now why she hadn't felt a bone-deep need to see him utterly vulnerable to her alone?

Her memory had to be faulty. She'd loved Rob. She was happy with him. She'd enjoyed his touch, his teasing, the way he made everything fun. She must have seen stark emotion on his face, heard aching need in his voice. She was just forgetting, which gave her a panicky sense that she had to scrabble for everything she did remember, clutch it tight or else it, too, would be gone.

That had to be the need that drew her to Rob's brother. *Just be smart,* Beth told herself. *Now that you recognize these feelings for what they are, you can ignore them. They'll go away.*

She opened her eyes, faced him. He had rolled onto

his side again, his head propped on his elbow, and was watching her.

She said the first thing that came to mind. "Rob..." Her voice died.

His mouth hardened. "I'm not Rob."

"I know. I didn't mean..."

"What did you mean?"

Beth had no idea. "I don't know," she admitted. "I was... thinking about him."

He grunted and rose fluidly to his feet. "I suppose I stepped into his shoes today."

"No." Less gracefully she scrambled up. "No, it's not the same at all. I... I've been doing a lot of thinking lately. Maybe because..." Mandy was coming toward them, so Beth made a quick gesture toward her belly.

"Just don't confuse us."

The grit in his voice reminded her of how bitterly the brothers had once quarreled. She'd give a great deal to know what they'd fought about. She knew better than to ask right now.

"Look, they're giving pony rides," Mandy said, bouncing on her toes when she reached them. "I wish I weren't too big."

"I'd forgotten how much you loved them." Beth didn't look toward Nathan. "Do you remember the neighbor who had a horse? They were always offering you rides, but you were scared to be so high off the ground. The ponies here are such miniature ones."

"It embarrassed Dad when I got scared," Mandy blurted. Her eyes widened, as though the memory took her by surprise. "I guess...I guess he was so brave he wanted me to be, too."

"Reckless, you mean," Beth muttered. "It was some kind of macho thing. I'm glad he didn't infect you with it."

"Can girls be macho?" her daughter asked.

"Darn right! Some women seem determined to be as stupid as men."

The clearing of a masculine throat reminded her of Nathan's presence.

"Present company excepted," Beth added, flushing a little.

"Thank you," he said dryly. "But, Mandy, let me tell you something I've realized recently. Your dad was like that because our mother pushed us to be competitive. We always had to do everything better than everybody else, faster. We had to win. She didn't want to hear excuses. We weren't allowed to cry. So, yeah, women can be like that. And it wasn't your dad's fault he was."

Mandy's gaze was grave. "But you're not."

"Yeah." A muscle in his jaw worked. "Yeah, I am. Just in a different way. I don't speed behind the wheel of a car. Instead, I've been a workaholic the past fifteen years. Success was more important than anything. And, uh—" he moved his shoulders uneasily "—your dad and I wouldn't have stayed mad at each other so long if we weren't both stubborn. If he'd admitted he was wrong, or if I had, that would have meant losing. Neither of us could do that."

Mandy's brow creased beneath the backward baseball cap. "But—" She stopped.

"Yeah. It was stupid as hell, wasn't it?"

"I think it was sad," she told him.

He grimaced. "Just remember, you never embarrassed your dad. Not really. He wasn't that big an idiot. I'll bet you were the sun and moon to him."

"He said I was his princess."

Nathan smiled crookedly. "Same thing."

"Has anybody ever been *your* sun and moon?" she asked artlessly.

He was silent for a moment as they walked, his face closed. "Oh, a time or two I thought a woman was," he finally said. "There was a girl in college." The memory didn't seem to be a happy one. "And I was married some years ago. Not for long. Julianne got tired of my schedule and my—" He broke off abruptly.

"Did you call her darling?" Mandy asked next. She'd been listening avidly. "Or...or baby or sweetie?"

"Mandy!" Beth gave her daughter a quelling look.

"It's okay." Nathan grinned at Mandy. "Maybe a man'll call you 'nosy babe' someday."

Unrepentant, she made a face. "Nobody tells me anything if I don't ask."

"True enough. Okay. I seem to recall referring to my wife as Jewel. That's as romantic as I got."

"That's not bad," Mandy told him kindly.

His tone was dry. "Thank you."

"Daddy called Mom—"

"Don't you dare," Beth interrupted.

"Berry pie," her indiscreet daughter continued blithely. "He used to call her sugar pie, but then after she started making jam, he changed it."

Beth poked Mandy with her elbow. "It was a joke. He didn't call me that..."

"...at more romantic moments?" Nathan suggested when she didn't finish.

She flushed.

"Shall we let your mom off the hook?" he asked Mandy.

"Or out of the pie!" She giggled hysterically and scampered ahead when Beth made a lunge for her.

Nathan said quietly, "You're not upset with her, are you?"

Beth assumed an air of dignity. "I'd put up with any humiliation to see her laugh like that."

"Good." The smile he gave her was warm, friendly, uncomplicated. He reached out and took her hand. "Let's go see the gorillas."

Sweetness pierced her at the feel of that big hand enveloping hers, tugging her along. If only his gesture were more than friendly—

No! She clamped down on the thought. Thank God his gesture was only friendly. Because if Nathan ever laid a hand on her in passion, she had no idea how she would react.

Chapter Eight

Nobody had come in response to the doorbell. Nathan lifted his hand and knocked firmly. Mandy must be home; he'd passed the school bus out on the road.

The knock echoed. He repeated it. Still no one came. His anticipation seeping into disappointment, Nathan turned and surveyed the fields, as tidy as when he'd first seen them last spring. The raspberries had already been pruned and tied up. He'd helped with the job, which had proved simple enough, but damned unpleasant. This year's canes, drying up, had to be unwound from the wire supports and cut off at the base, then hauled in bundles to a low spot behind the barn where Beth let them compost. It had been hot and airless between the rows when he crouched to snip canes. Sweating more than he did in a ten-K race, he couldn't bear to wear a long-sleeved shirt, which meant he'd ended up with scratches all over his forearms.

He loosened his tie. Maybe Beth and Mandy were in the

barn. He crossed the yard and entered the shadowy stuffy interior through the half-open door. A rustle came from a heap of straw to one side, which Beth used for mulching. Polly was flinging around an already dead mouse and then pouncing on it again. She snatched it up and uttered a small growl when she saw him looking.

"It's all yours," he told her. He raised his voice. "Anyone here?"

Silence. He found the kitchen dim and still, everything spotlessly clean. The back of the barn was lined with rows of shelving units, filled to near capacity now with the summer's bounty. Some of the jars were boxed, others still single, the distinctive shape and the labels too classy for the concrete floor and open rafters and scent of hay and long-aged manure.

Well, hell. He'd made a trip out here for nothing. He should have called. He'd come on impulse after flying in to Sea-Tac Airport. He'd been away for almost a week on business, the longest he'd gone without seeing Beth and Mandy since the P.I. had found him. On the road he'd caught himself thinking about them all the time, wondering what they were doing that minute, how Mandy liked middle school now that the first week's excitement had worn off, whether Beth ever thought about him. At night especially, trying to sleep in hotel beds, he pictured her curled up in hers, hair tousled, bare arms and shoulders golden from the sun, her window flung wide to let in the quiet sounds of night in the country. Sometimes his imagination left him more restless; other times it soothed him to sleep, as though he'd had to see them vividly to be sure Beth and Mandy would still be there, waiting when he got home.

When he'd pulled in, he'd half expected the front door to crash open and Mandy to pelt down the porch steps to fling herself into his arms. Beth would be close behind, shyly welcoming. Right. Father coming home from work, circa 1950s, he told himself dryly. Norman Rockwell. Only, he wasn't the father. This wasn't his home.

Even if it felt like it.

Nathan wandered out of the barn, then on impulse went around to the back. From here a dirt track led down to the creek. Mandy had dragged him down there once. At this time of year, the water must be low, maybe only deep enough for wading. Between blueberry bushes whose leaves were turning yellow, he caught a glimpse of green coolness: a sparkle of water, alder leaves flashing green-silver in a faint breeze, lush tangled grass. And something else: a red shirt, a shimmer of pale gold hair. Beth.

Nathan moved without thinking, each step kicking up a puff of dust. A hot summer had stretched into a dry autumn. School had started two weeks ago. On the trees along the road, leaves were turning color already. They'd be falling, brittle and brown, in no time.

He didn't call out a greeting. Mandy would probably see him coming, anyway. If not, he wouldn't mind a moment to savor the sight of Beth before she spotted him. Maybe that made him a voyeur, but what the hell. He seldom saw her completely relaxed, unguarded. He made her wary, just as she made him.

Beth stood in the middle of the creek. She wore khaki shorts, rolled up several times and just showing beneath a sacky red T-shirt. The water rippled around her calves. Her legs, slim and tanned, seemed to go on forever. That was about all he could see of her. Her back was to him, her head bowed as she stared down into the water with great concentration, like a child hunting for pollywogs.

"Hi," he said at last, huskily.

She whirled and slipped, just catching herself from falling. Her mouth trembled, and either she'd splashed herself in the face, or she was on the verge of tears. Tears, Nathan decided, seeing the strain in her wide gray eyes.

"You...you scared me."

"I'm sorry. I knocked and, uh, nobody came, and then I saw a flash of red down here." He felt as though he were walking on loose talus, the boulders rocking under his feet. They'd made progress, he'd have sworn they had, and yet now she radiated distress at the sight of him.

"It's...it's okay." She hugged herself. "I, um, I was just thinking. Pretty hard, I guess. I should've heard you coming."

Not for the first time, he wished she had a dog, instead of two half-grown cats. With her and Mandy here alone...

"Where's Mandy?" he asked, looking around.

"Oh—" Beth's smile was forced "—she went to a friend's place. Barbara's. Barbara just got a puppy. Mandy'll be home by five. I can have her call you."

Nathan nodded.

"Did you have a good trip?"

So, she'd noticed he was gone. But she wasn't suggesting he stay for dinner.

"Yeah," he said quietly. *No,* he wanted to tell her, *I was homesick.* He nodded toward a sort of pool where the water was deeper. "Were you going swimming?"

She bent over and trailed her fingers in the ripples. The curve of her neck and cheek moved him almost unbearably. "I don't know." This smile wasn't any better. "It's hot in the house. I just thought... I come down here sometimes. It's sort of Mandy's place. She doesn't know I use it, too."

"The creek?"

"And under the willow. In there, I feel...enfolded by the tree. Did she show you?"

"No. The creek was higher, and I was dressed about like I am today."

He had the sense she was really looking at him for the first time. "You're a stick-in-the-mud. Why don't you take off your shoes and come in?"

What the hell. He sat down on the grass and unlaced his dress shoes, pulled off his socks, started rolling up his slacks. Knowing Beth was watching him was enough to make his fingers fumble.

"All right." He wriggled his toes in the grass, then stood. "Ready or not."

"Not." She said it so softly he knew he wasn't meant to hear.

He didn't have to hear it. He'd already known. Nonetheless, he stepped into the chill water and waded gingerly toward her. He hadn't rolled his pants up far enough. They were already wet.

When he was an arm's reach from her, Nathan said quietly, "Mandy's not sick, is she?"

"No." She put up a hand and pushed at her hair, tumbling as always from the giant clip on the back of her head. "Nothing's wrong. Not really."

"Not really?"

Beth sucked in a breath, closed her eyes. Her lashes sparkled like rays of sunlight, and he realized tears trembled on them.

"I don't know what's wrong with me," she whispered. "I'm strong. I've always been strong." Her lashes abruptly swept upward, and she stared fiercely at him. "I've started a business and done a damn good job. Rob died and I didn't fall apart. Mandy got sick and I coped. I've done just fine! So what is it now? Why do I keep crying?"

"Hormones—"

"It's not hormones!" she snapped. "It's...it's you!"

His brows drew together. "What the hell are you talking about?"

"You'd make it easy for me to be weak, wouldn't you? You'd offer your strong shoulder, take care of Mandy, probably run my business. Well, I don't like it!"

She might as well have slugged him in the stomach. Numbly he said, "You don't want me here at all."

"I didn't say that!" Her eyes glittered up at him.

"Then what did you say?" Feeling sick, he hung on to an even tone by his fingernails.

Her face worked. "I'm just... I'm afraid sometimes."

"Of me." He ran a hand over his face. "God."

"No." Beth scrubbed her own cheeks. "I didn't mean it."

"Didn't you?"

Beneath the tan and the sprinkling of freckles, her face was pale. "I'm afraid of myself."

He swore softly. "Because you want to lean your head on my shoulder."

She gave a quick nod.

His throat damn near closed. "I'm here."

"Yes. I know." She didn't move.

He didn't dare. Could only wait her out.

"This morning..." Beth's voice faltered. "I was getting dressed. Mandy walked in on me."

What the hell...? Then he understood. "You're starting to show."

Wordlessly she lifted her shirt. She hadn't been able to get her shorts zipped all the way up or buttoned. The gentle swell of pale belly was another kick in his gut.

"She...she looked straight at my stomach."

"Did you say anything?"

Beth let the shirt fall. "Something dumb about eating too much. And I laughed! Oh, God. What's she going to say when I tell her?"

"You're doing it for her!"

"Yes." Beth swallowed a sob. "Yes, of course I am."

"Then what are you so worried about?"

Beth gave him an incredulous look. "Oh, only ten or twelve things. What do you *think* I'm worried about?"

He didn't let her divert him. "Telling Mandy. You're afraid she's going to feel angry or threatened or…" He spread his hands. "But I don't get it. She's a sensible kid. Why would she feel more threatened than any other child who finds out she's going to have a baby brother or sister?"

Beth closed her eyes. "Because I'm not married. Because I lied to her. Because this all might be pointless."

He got it at last. "Because you might have to say, 'I'm pregnant and I did it for you, but the baby's blood isn't compatible with yours.'"

"Yeah." Her mouth twisted and she looked away.

"Why don't you just tell her now?" he suggested gently. "Before she figures it out herself. Before you have the amniocentesis."

A distinct sniff came from Beth's direction. "I know you're right. It's just that I want to save her from…"

"Hope?"

"False hope."

"Maybe she doesn't need protecting. Maybe it scares her more when you try to pretend everything is great."

Her gaze sliced like a switchblade. "You think I should take her down to the funeral home and let her choose her own casket?"

"Damn it," he said, "you know that's not what I meant! But do you ever talk about the possibility that everything might *not* be great?"

"She's too young to think about death!"

"But not too young to die."

He felt like a bastard when she clapped a hand to her

mouth and he heard the tearing sound of a suppressed sob. He took a step toward her and brought his foot down on a sharp rock. He muttered a curse. "Can we get out?"

He half expected her to suggest he depart and never come back. Instead, her shoulders slumped, and she turned and waded toward the far bank, where the strands of narrow green willow leaves hung like a curtain. Beth parted them and stepped onto the grassy bank. Nathan followed, unsure if he was expected to, but knowing he didn't want to leave Beth alone right now.

Inside was another world, a cavern under the sea, washed in pale green light that eddied like water chased by golden fingers of sunlight. But for the ripple of the creek and the whisper of breeze in the willow, the silence was near complete, the sense of separation and security curiously comforting.

"Like a womb," he murmured.

He hadn't meant her to hear him, but she nodded. "It is, isn't it? I know Mandy spends hours here."

"And you?"

"Oh, I come down once in a while." Her voice was hushed. "I grew up on a farm. We had a tree and a creek just like this. It was my hideaway. I wanted Mandy to have one."

"Rob and I had a treehouse," Nathan offered. "Nothing fancy. Dad helped a little, but we did most of the work ourselves. We used to look down on people's heads and think they didn't know we were there. There's something... godlike about that."

"And kids feel so powerless."

"Yeah."

Beth's eyes met his directly. "Mandy most of all. How can she help it when she's so vulnerable?"

He let out a breath. "I was wrong, what I said out there.

I'm sure you've talked to her about being sick and dying and everything else. I shouldn't assume, just because you're usually upbeat—"

"I haven't." Abruptly she sat, wrapping her arms around her knees. Her bent head muffled her words.

He stared at her. "Never?"

Beth shook her head without lifting it. She was barely audible. "At first I just couldn't! She wanted to, but it seemed…oh, like acknowledging it might really happen." She looked up at last, eyes damp and beseeching. "And then later…Mandy wouldn't talk to me. I mean, I haven't sat down and said, 'We're going to talk about dying.' But when I try to find out what she's worrying about or thinking, she puts me off. She does see a counselor at the hospital, and I've assumed…"

He dropped to his knees in front of her. "Quit blaming yourself," he said almost harshly. "Your reaction was normal. You probably didn't want to start crying in front of her."

"I should have pushed the issue later," she said dully. "I should have insisted she talk to me."

His mouth twisted. "Remember what you said about kids feeling powerless? If you'd intruded on her privacy, Mandy would have lost what little control over her life she has."

"Yes, but—"

"Mandy loves you. When she really needs to talk, she'll come to you."

Her eyes glistened like windowpanes on a rainy day. "You sound so sure."

Nathan gently wiped tears from her cheek. "She teases you. That's when I really hear her love."

She tilted her head to press her cheek against the back of his hand. "You always know what to say, don't you?"

His laugh grated. "You and I would've gotten along better if I were so damned tactful."

"I think," Beth whispered, "our troubles have more to do with…with *this*—" she touched her open mouth to his hand "—than with anything either of us has said."

He groaned and with both hands cupped her face, his touch rough. "Beth…"

Her gray eyes were hauntingly beautiful, her lips trembling. "Would you…would you kiss me?"

A surge of near agonizing hunger rocked him. He didn't give himself time to think. He pulled her up to meet him and crushed her mouth with his. She came eagerly, her lips parting, her breath warm and taste sweet.

Exhilaration rushed through him and he lost the power to think, could only feel. Her shoulders were as fine-boned as he'd dreamed, her back as narrow and supple. Her mouth was so damned soft, her throaty murmur intoxicating. He plunged his fingers into her hair, and the silky curls wrapped around them as though unwilling to release him.

His tongue plunged into her mouth, and hers met it. She nipped at his lower lip as he growled words of praise and desire and coaxing. His hands shook as he lifted that oversize T-shirt and pulled it over her head. He didn't give her time to react to the air on her skin, to protest. His mouth captured hers again and he bore her backward until she lay beneath him in the long grass.

He felt like a madman, need shoving him along as if he had a hand planted in the middle of his back. He'd die if he wasn't inside her in the next minute. She was his woman. She grew his seed, carried his baby. He undid the catch of her bra as he strung kisses down her throat, feeling the frenzied beat of her pulse. For one moment he lifted his head to gaze hungrily at her breasts, as pale as milk and delicately veined in blue. Her nipples were swollen, peaked for him to draw into his mouth.

Her skin was as soft as it looked. She gave a small cry when he kissed her breast, rubbed his cheek against her nipple, then stroked it with his tongue. She reached up and gripped his hair as he drew her nipple into his mouth and sucked strongly.

His loosened tie fell across her other breast. He ripped it from his neck, tore open the front of his shirt. He laid his hand over the mound of her belly and remembered the quick fluttering heartbeat. *His child.* Carried in her womb.

Beth's hands flattened on his bare chest; for a moment, stunned, he thought she was pushing him away. But then she made a wondering sound in her throat and her hands slipped higher to knead his shoulder muscles. *Ah, God.*

He lifted his head again to look at her, neck arched, eyes foggy with passion, lips curved softly, curls loose and shimmery as the slender tree branches swayed and parted to let in narrow bands of sunlight. She was the picture of sensuality. Wanton. So why the hell did his chest tighten?

Because he wanted her eyes focused on *him.* Not gazing dreamily at nothing as her breasts rose and fell enticingly with each breath. Damn it, he wanted to know who she saw in her mind's eye!

"Beth…" he said huskily.

She made a murmured response.

Rob. Had she said Rob's name? His skin chilled and he rolled away from her, swearing.

Beth sat up, crossing her arms over her breasts. "What… what's wrong?"

He clenched his teeth and stared straight up at the canopy of willow. "I'm not Rob."

"I know you're not!" Her cheeks flushed.

"You just said 'Rob.'" His brother's name scraped his throat.

"I didn't!" She shot to her feet, Botticelli's Venus stepping from a seashell, curls tumbling around her white shoulders, arms protecting her bare breasts. "I didn't say anything! I just made a noise!"

He laid his forearm across his face. "It sure as hell sounded like—"

"It wasn't! But you can think what you damn well please!"

The rustle of clothing as she pulled on her T-shirt, the swish of branches, a splash and one muttered profanity, and she was gone. He lay there, eyes closed, and imagined her snatching up her sandals from the bank and then stalking up the hill without putting them on. That straight slender back, the proud angle of her head, those shining curls… His whole body clenched in anguish. God, he'd had her beneath him, skin as silky as he'd dreamed, breasts small but soft, her hips pushing up against his hand. And he'd blown it.

A groan tore from his chest. Why the hell couldn't he just have taken what was offered? She probably *hadn't* said "Rob." The sound had been rough and throaty, maybe no more than a wordless response to her own name. And he'd gone off the deep end. If she'd been any other woman…

But she wasn't. She was his brother's widow. He would not, could not, play Rob in her fantasies. Anyone else, but not Rob. Not his brother, who one too many times had played him, Nathan.

He had to know. He wanted Beth as he'd never wanted a woman in his life. He might even love her. But his instincts had been right from the beginning. He wasn't his brother.

Until he was sure she knew that, he had to do a better job of keeping his hands off her.

What had she almost done? Beth curled into a ball on her bed, knees drawn up and arms squeezing herself. Oh God, oh God. *Had* she said "Rob"?

But she hadn't been *thinking* about Rob! She hadn't been thinking anything, only feeling.

Feeling a familiar rush of desire, the melting warmth running to her toes and fingers, the deep sense of urgency, the sweet tightening in her belly. But it wasn't familiar, she realized in shock, her eyes snapping open. Not familiar at all. The hunger in her blood was stronger, more desperate, than anything she'd felt before.

Yes, but maybe that was only because she'd been celibate for more than three years. She'd missed the closeness and gentle satisfaction of making love with her husband. Oh, how often she'd reached for him at first! Half-asleep, she couldn't understand why his side of the bed was empty. But as the months had stretched into a year, she'd become accustomed to being alone at night; after so long, she'd hardly been consciously aware of her loneliness. But surely, surely, her fierce response to Nathan's kisses and touch today could be explained by all those empty nights.

She made a small whimpering sound. Did she *want* that to be the explanation? Nathan hadn't mattered, only her own need?

And—oh, Lord, this was the part that really mattered— had she been pretending he was Rob?

But how could she have when Nathan's kisses and touch were so different? She had felt that difference with every fiber. It had excited her, she admitted, his intensity firing the urgency that had made her so quickly want sex, not just delicious foreplay. She had wanted him inside her right then. She had *needed* him.

And it wasn't Rob she needed. Not then, not now.

But she'd loved Rob! Beth thought in panic. How could she feel these things for his brother? She moaned again. What if Nathan had come into their lives when Rob was still alive? Would she still have been attracted, betraying her husband secretly, in thought if not in action?

Stiffly she uncurled herself and rolled onto her back, staring up at the ceiling as she faced the bleak knowledge that she would almost rather have discovered she was pretending today. For that, she could have forgiven herself.

Chapter Nine

Mandy gave the glider a push and turned the page of her book. It was a second before she realized she'd heard a footstep. She looked up to find Mom had just come out onto the porch.

"I need to talk to you." Her mother sounded totally serious, the way she did when something bad had happened.

As quickly as her heartbeat sped up, fear raced through Mandy. She'd been for her regular checkup last week. The weird white blood cells must be multiplying again, shutting out the red ones. Her feet quit pushing and the glider stilled. She gave a small nod. "Okay."

Mom crossed the porch and sat down beside her. Calvin stood up on the railing, arched his back and stretched like a Halloween cat, then hopped onto Mom's lap. Somehow he'd become Mom's cat, and Polly was Mandy's.

Stroking Calvin's back as though unaware she was doing it, Mom gave a push and they began to swing. But she didn't say anything, and when Mandy stole a glance at her, her lips were tight.

After a moment she sighed. "Maybe I should have told you this a long time ago. I hope you'll understand why I didn't."

"But I only went…" Mandy trailed off, puzzled.

"Went?"

"Well, I thought… I mean, I did just have the blood test."

Mom gave a soft cry. "No, no. I haven't heard results. And you're feeling fine, aren't you? It's nothing like that. I'm sorry, I didn't think."

"That's okay." Mandy shrugged awkwardly. "But if you don't want to talk about me being sick…" Then it hit her. She'd wondered how long her mother thought she could hide her stomach. Jeez, even Mandy's friends were going to notice pretty soon.

"This is something else." Mom nibbled on her lower lip. "Although I'm doing it because of you."

"I know."

"The thing is…" Mom had continued talking as though she hadn't heard Mandy, but suddenly her head shot up. "You know what?"

"I know you're pregnant," Mandy said calmly. "And I know why. I heard you and Uncle Nate talking about it."

"When?"

"I don't know." She shrugged again, looking down at the book that still lay open in her lap. "A long time ago. When you were trying to get him to be the father."

Mom's breath whooshed out of her. "You've known since last spring?" she whispered.

Mandy pushed her glasses up. "Yeah."

"And you didn't say anything?"

She told the truth. "I figured if you didn't, I wouldn't."

"Oh, honey..." Mom moved to put an arm around her. Mandy stiffened and Mom's arm dropped. "You don't understand why I didn't tell you."

"I guess you didn't think it was my business." Some of her resentment leaked into her voice.

"Of course it's your business!" Mom sounded indignant.

Yeah, right, Mandy thought. *Then why didn't you tell me?*

As though she'd heard her, Mom said, "I didn't want you to worry. Or...or hope. Like you did when we found Uncle Nate and thought he might have the right kind of blood."

Mandy didn't believe her. Hoping for something wasn't that bad. It was better than *not* hoping. What she thought was that Mom had given up after Uncle Nate wasn't a match. If Mom thought she, Mandy, was going to die, then it made sense for her to have another baby, didn't it? That way she wouldn't be left all alone.

Mandy tried not to mind. Or not too much, anyway. She didn't doubt her mother's love. Mom had loved Dad, too. Think how awful it would be for her, with Dad and her only kid both dead. So if Mom had another baby, it wouldn't be as bad for her. She wouldn't be as lonely.

Only, Mandy felt even lonelier and more frightened to know that her mother wouldn't miss her as much, that she'd be busy cooing at some baby and teaching him his colors and to read and to swing. Maybe the willow tree would be his.

Knowing how much Mom would grieve for her had been one way Mandy reassured herself that dying wouldn't be like God zapping her and saying, "You're gone. You never existed." If she was really, really missed, that meant some part of her spirit was still here, right? But if she wasn't really, really missed...

Mandy's stomach clenched. She didn't want to talk about it. She just nodded. "It's okay," she said again.

"The thing is, I'll have an amniocentesis in about a month. That's when they stick a needle into my stomach and take out some of the fluid. They can tell if the baby is healthy then. But they can also do tissue typing."

Interested for the first time, Mandy frowned. "You mean, we'll know then? A long time before the baby is born?"

"Yes."

"The baby might not be right."

"No. The chances are one in four. But those aren't bad odds."

"I guess not." Mandy hesitated. She felt like her mother was waiting for something. Finally, using her most polite voice, she said, "It's cool you'd do this for me. Thank you."

Mom's hands were wringing together in her lap. "I'd do anything for you."

Mandy's heart cramped. *Then don't have this baby.* "I know."

Although her face was averted, she felt her mother's searching look. "You won't worry too much?" Mom asked.

"No." She pretended to find her place in her book. "I just don't let myself think about stuff like that."

"Smart girl." Mom kissed her cheek and stood up, dumping Calvin off her lap. "I go to bed worrying about whether I'll remember in the morning to cut my toenails or buy peanut butter at the store. I'm glad you didn't inherit my neurotic tendencies."

Mandy watched Calvin hop back up on the porch railing and begin cleaning himself. "Maybe I'm like Dad."

"He certainly didn't worry," Mom agreed dryly, and left her alone.

Mandy closed her book, not even glancing to see what page she was on.

I worry, too, she'd wanted to say to Mom. *I worry all the time. I'm scared.* She couldn't figure out why she didn't say it. If only she could, Mom would hold her tight and promise she'd get better. She could cry, and feel her tears wetting someone else's skin. She wouldn't be so terribly alone, the way she was when she cried into her pillow at night.

But the words just wouldn't come out. She'd trained them so well to stay unsaid that they didn't even struggle to say themselves anymore. It was easier to keep things to herself. Probably, she reminded herself, it wouldn't do any good to say those things, anyway. She made people uncomfortable. Or angry, like Mom had been that once. Jessica was the only one who'd understood.

After a long while Mandy sighed. Maybe this baby brother—she didn't know why, but she thought it was a boy—*would* be compatible. She'd rather hope than not. It wasn't *impossible* that he could save her.

If he did, just think how awful she'd feel for ever having hated his guts.

If Nathan had been any other man, Beth knew darn well she'd have done the cowardly thing and called to tell him she didn't want to see him again. Given who he was, she couldn't do that. Mandy needed him.

But she couldn't imagine what they'd say to each other the next time he came over. Especially if Mandy was there. How could they pretend nothing had happened?

The day after her talk with Mandy—no, not with—the day after she'd talked *to* Mandy, Beth went to Nathan's

condominium. She'd never been there; he always came
to see them, not the other way around. But they needed
to be alone if they were to be honest with each other, and
she'd rather be away from the house she'd shared with Rob.
Away from the photographs on the mantel, the stool he'd
sat on in the kitchen to watch her cook, the porch glider
he'd bought for Beth's thirtieth birthday. Nate's place would
be…neutral.

She called and asked if he'd be home and have time for
her to stop by. Sounding only momentarily surprised and
then matter-of-fact, he suggested eleven o'clock. Now, she
was here on his doorstep, hand raised to press the bell.

She felt a little queasy for the first time in at least a
month. Not morning sickness. Nervousness. Taking a deep
breath, she rang the doorbell.

He opened the door so quickly she wondered if he'd
seen her park in front and been waiting. His hair was damp
from the shower, and he wore charcoal-gray slacks and a
white shirt, unbuttoned at the collar and cuffs. The sight of
the dress shirt and the tanned V at his neck sent a quiver
through her. The last time she's seen him, he'd worn a white
shirt just like that one. When he'd pulled it open, she'd laid
her hands against the hard muscles of his chest, felt the
heavy pounding of his heart, the warmth of his skin.

Don't think about it, she told herself. *Block it out.*

His dark gaze flicked to her stomach before returning
to her face. He did that every time he saw her, she realized
with some remote part of her mind. It was as though he was
checking to make sure she was still pregnant. Apparently
reassured, he nodded and stood back.

The condo—well, really a town house—was upscale,
from its elegant tiled entry to thick blond carpet in the
living room and a bay window in the dining room. For all
that, it was lifeless, she saw in one surprised look. Colors

were neutral, the furniture could have come from a hotel room, and the walls were undecorated. He hadn't troubled to make it a home. He obviously felt as if he was just passing through. Her stomach took a panicky dip. She'd become used to his presence in their lives! Did he intend to disappear again, once he was satisfied she could manage?

"Would you like coffee? Tea?" The groove in one of his cheeks deepened. "No, you've given up caffeine, haven't you? Can I get you something else?"

"No. Thank you. I just thought—" she hesitated "—we ought to talk."

His gaze lowered for an instant again. "You're all right?"

Beth nodded. "I, um, told Mandy." Now, where had that come from? She wasn't supposed to be here to confide in him. But when he relaxed perceptibly, she thought her instinct had been sound. *Instinct?* an inner voice murmured. *Try cowardice.*

"And?" He gestured her toward a seat on the leather sofa, sinfully soft. She wasn't quite the shape of a hippopotamus yet, but she was still going to have to struggle to get up again. In the matching chair, he leaned back, his pose relaxed. Nevertheless, she felt the tension radiating from him. If she touched him—

Don't you dare think it.

"She already knew." Beth smiled, one of those smiles that hid painful emotions. "She overheard us talking last spring. She's known all along."

"And she didn't say anything?" He sounded incredulous.

"She figured if I didn't, she wouldn't. I quote."

He shook his head. "She's twelve going on thirty."

Beth squeezed her hands together. "You'd be justified in saying I told you so."

His eyes met hers. "You had good cause for keeping quiet."

"Maybe not so good."

"Hindsight is easy."

If only he wouldn't be so decent, so uncritical, so...sexy. Unreasonably annoyed, she stiffened her resolve.

"I really came about what happened at the creek. It wasn't such a good idea."

He closed his eyes for a moment and kneaded the back of his neck. "I was a jerk. I suppose I'm paranoid."

"I didn't say 'Rob.'" It seemed important to convince him.

He grimaced. "Yeah. Later I realized—"

"I wasn't thinking 'Rob,' either."

"Weren't you?" He sat forward, elbows braced on his knees. The intensity in his eyes cut through any pretense.

"No." She had to look away. "At least... No. I couldn't have been."

"But you're not sure." His tone was hard.

Her chin shot up. "I was married for ten years. I haven't made love to a man since Rob died. Is it unnatural that he'd come to mind the first time I..." Her throat clogged.

He swore under his breath. "Put that way, no. God. No, of course it isn't."

"Are you the kind of man who only wants a woman who's untouched?" She said it acidly, refusing to acknowledge the sharp pain lodged behind her breastbone. "Or is it only being untouched by your brother that matters?"

Nathan rose to his feet and crossed to the window to stare out at the parking lot. His neck and back were rigid. "I knew Mandy wasn't an immaculate conception."

Her question came without conscious thought. "Why do you hate Rob so much?" She knew suddenly, with some shock, that this was why she'd come. To hear the answer to this one question.

"Does it matter?"

"Yes." She looked down to where her hand stroked the buttery soft leather. "I assume, because of Mandy and the baby, you and I will have a relationship of sorts for a long time to come. It's obviously complicated by your feelings for Rob."

How stiff she sounded! Even stuffy. But how else could she have phrased it? What else could she have said? *Sometimes I think I'm falling in love with you, and I need to know whether you feel anything for me, or whether it all has to do with Rob.*

With a rough sound, Nathan turned to face her. His face, usually imperturbable, showed harshness and sorrow and a thousand other tangled emotions.

"All right. We competed." He chopped off each word. "Everything—every goddamned thing—was a competition. Our mother encouraged it. But Rob—" Nathan closed his eyes momentarily "—Rob had this incredible compulsion to best me at everything we did. Nothing could be mine alone. If I did it, he did it, too. Preferably better. If I had one, he had to have one, too." His eyes burned into hers. "I'm not trying to excuse myself, Beth. Maybe I was just as bad. Maybe if I'd *let* him beat me often enough, he'd have been satisfied. But I was too driven to do that."

"You were twins," she whispered. "Didn't you love each other?"

His face worked. "Yeah. Of course we did. We always knew what the other one was thinking. We stuck together. Other people never would have guessed—"

"That you were both fighting so hard to be individuals," Beth said softly. "Separate."

Composed again, he looked at her without expression. "Got it in one." He shrugged. "That's the story."

She ached with a terrible muddle of feelings: sadness at what they'd lost, at what *all* of them had lost, regret that it was too late to mend the brothers' rift, and most of all, anger at their mother, who, whatever her intentions, had sown such bitterness.

"No," she said. "You didn't tell me the ending. Something must have happened. Something more."

"It was a long time coming."

"I want to know."

He swore and turned away again, then abruptly swung back to face her. His face held, not the anger she'd expected to see, but an expression more akin to pity. "You don't. It'll taint your memory of Rob."

The queasiness returned full force. Her husband had had his flaws; he was sometimes lazy, content to coast on his charm, maybe even a little selfish. She knew he wasn't perfect. But what could he have done that was so terrible even his twin brother wanted nothing to do with him?

"You've already tainted it," she said flatly. "If I don't know, I'll always wonder. That's worse."

The lines carved in Nathan's cheeks and forehead aged him, made him look weary. "I never intended—"

"I know. But it's too late to go back."

"Maybe it wasn't even so bad. Rob thought it was a joke. I'd been packing away resentment for years. His little joke brought it to a head."

Joke? She stared at him. "He didn't…murder somebody or rape a woman or…"

"Murder, no. Rape, maybe." Nathan let out a heavy breath. "Oh, hell. It's just a sordid episode I've never told anyone about. I had a girlfriend in college. I was pretty serious about her. One day she mentioned how wild the sex had been the night before." He paused. "Trouble was, I hadn't been with her. Rob knew I was busy."

"Oh, no," Beth breathed. She saw it with stark clarity, Rob borrowing one of his brother's shirts or jackets—or had they dressed enough alike he hadn't even had to do that? Knocking on the girl's door, playing a game. Only, he should have been old enough to know it wasn't a game.

"Oh, yeah." Nathan sat back down. With a grimace he continued, "I confronted Rob. He admitted it was him. Turned out, he'd pretended to be me half a dozen times. She never had a clue. He was damned good at it. To him, it was a grand joke. When we were kids, we thought it was funny to trick people. What was any different about this?"

Shock made her voice thin, thready. "What did you do?"

"I punched him. He broke my nose. I transferred to another college. I never saw him again."

"Did you...did you tell *her?*"

He shook his head. "What was the point? She took birth-control pills. Rob was healthy. We broke up not too much later."

"Because of what happened?"

Nathan looked away. "Yeah. I'm not proud of myself. I couldn't quit wondering which of us she'd preferred."

"What he did...it was *sick.*" She spoke with astonishment and loathing. Nathan was right. Her memory of Rob *would* be tainted. It *was* tainted. How could he have?

"We'd both asked her out. She turned him down. But if I had something, he had to have it, too. Most twins are fulfilled by the relationship. Rob was tormented by it."

"Thanks to your mother."

"Maybe." Nathan let out a long breath. "But maybe not. Maybe it was innate. Kids are born with needs their parents haven't created. Hell, maybe I took up too much space in

her womb, and he hated me by the time we were born."
He laughed without humor. "I beat him at that, too. I was
born one minute ahead of him. When we were about eight,
I made a big deal out of being the *older* brother. I had all
the sensitivity of a rockfall."

"According to Mandy, no boys have any sensitivity."

His smile was wry. "She's probably right."

"Thank God boys grow up," Beth said thoughtfully.

"Some boys."

"Would you ever have forgiven him?" She flushed at
her abruptness. "If...if he had called you when I told him
he should?"

"I hope so." He eyes held bleak honesty. "I don't know."

"I think...I think he changed."

Roughly Nathan said, "I have no doubt he did. All I
have to do is look at you and Mandy. He made you happy.
Somehow he learned to deserve you."

"I wish..."

"I wish, too." He cleared his throat.

For a moment they sat in silence. Beth wondered why
she hadn't doubted Nathan's story. Shouldn't she have automatically leapt to Rob's defense? Couldn't Nathan have
gotten it wrong, somehow misunderstood? What if the girl
had thought it was kinky fun to have sex with both brothers and had slipped up talking to Nathan? Rob might have
been trying to shield Nathan from the hurt....

But she didn't believe it. Nathan's story rang true. And
she had always known that Rob felt guilty for whatever had
happened. He'd missed his brother desperately, but he'd
steadfastly refused to try to find him. Shame, she thought,
had made him feel he deserved a loneliness she'd never
altogether understood, because she didn't have a twin. Rob
hadn't believed Nathan would forgive him. And she knew
now why he'd refused to tell her about the fight.

Feeling numb, she stood up. "I should go now. But first—" she bit her lip "—first I have to say what I came to say."

He stood, too, and she had the sense of him bracing himself, although he only waited.

"I sort of…came on to you the other day." Her cheeks warmed. "I know it was my fault. I also know that for us to act on…on any kind of attraction we feel would be a big mistake. For Mandy, you've taken her dad's place. She needs you. So if things didn't work out between us, that might make it impossible for us to all be together. I don't want that to happen." She hesitated, nibbling again on her lip. "Can…can we just be friends?"

"Friends." He repeated the word with no intonation, as though he didn't understand its meaning.

Anxiously she said, "Like we have been."

Nathan took a step toward her. "My feelings are a little more than friendly."

Beth retreated. "We've been doing just fine. Until the other day."

"And that was so bad?"

"No." She pressed her lips together. "No, of course not. But you don't believe I'm not seeing Rob every time I look at you, and I'm…" She hesitated.

"You're not sure." He'd made it not a question. His expression had closed. Shutters down.

Well, to hell with him. She lifted her chin. "All right. I'm not sure."

"Then *friends* it'll be." The sardonic emphasis told her what he thought of their chances of being buddies, but she couldn't blame him. She *was* the one who'd ignited the bonfire the other day.

He escorted her to the door, nodded goodbye and was already buttoning his cuffs as he shut it. While walking to her car and then driving home, Beth reminded herself over and over again of all the good reasons they shouldn't make love, shouldn't risk falling in love, shouldn't risk a blowup that would break Mandy's heart.

Friends. We can be friends.

They tried. They even succeeded up to a point.

Nathan came over nearly as often as before. Mandy seemed not to notice any special tension between her mother and her uncle. Maybe, Beth thought ruefully, that was because it had been there from the very beginning.

The last weekend in September Nathan took Beth and Mandy on a short hike to the ice caves at the foot of Big Four, a magnificent mountain with small, easily accessible glaciers. The trail, just over a mile long, crossed a crystal-clear river tumbling over rocks, then rose on switchbacks through deep woods. Moss coated tree trunks and draped from branches. Ferns, their fronds edged with brown after the hot summer and dry September, clambered over decomposing stumps and brushed the trail.

Mandy skipped ahead, her skinny legs letting her bound like a fawn. Around every turn of the trail, she'd either wait impatiently or start back to meet them.

"Look!" she said. "That whole line of trees is growing out of the one that fell down."

"It's called a nurse log," Nathan told her. "As it rots and crumbles, seeds take root and it provides the nutrients they need to grow. Eventually it composts altogether and enriches the forest floor. That's why a forest that's logged every fifty years is so much poorer."

"This is cool!" Mandy declared, and hurried ahead again.

"Well, she's sure got energy," Beth said, half rueful.

This pregnancy was still making her tired, although she'd gotten over the worst of it along with the nausea.

"Yeah. You've never taken her hiking before?"

"We did some when she was younger, but after she got sick…"

"This one is short enough not to tire her."

She made a face. "Or me?"

His mouth tilted into a genuine smile. "Or you."

The rest of the day was more relaxed. They ate their picnic lunch sitting on a huge rock. Mandy ran and slid on the snowfields, falling and giggling as she soaked her jeans. The sun warm on her face, Beth watched with the most positive feeling of contentment she'd known in a long time. Mandy looked so healthy, so *normal*. It was hard to imagine that she could be sick. But maybe, just maybe, this pregnancy would provide the insurance she needed. As though the baby had read her mind, Beth felt fluttery movements in her abdomen.

Eventually they scrambled up over a narrow rocky ridge and stood in the mouth of a cave formed by melting glacier ice. The air was frigid, and the only sound was the dripping of water. Toward the back of the cool dark natural cathedral, sunlight fell through an opening in the ice as if through a stained-glass window.

"Oh, it's so beautiful!" Mandy cried. "Can we go in?"

"You read the signs." Beth nodded toward one posted at the opening. "It's not safe. I remember reading just last year about a couple of guys who got trapped when a cave collapsed."

"Oh, poop." Mandy wrinkled her nose. "It looks safe."

"It probably is, but why take a chance?"

Mandy gave her a look that previewed the teenage years. "Sometimes," she said, as though her mother were an idiot, "it's worth taking risks." She turned and walked away.

Beside her Nathan said nothing, and Beth could only pray he hadn't noticed the double meaning in Mandy's words.

Sometimes it is worth taking risks, Beth silently agreed. *But sometimes they're too great.*

Or had she been turned into a coward because she had to live constantly with the fear of losing her daughter?

She followed Nathan out of the mouth of the cave, picking her way carefully on the water-slick rocky footing. Internally she continued the debate. She had someone else to think about, too, she reminded herself, a baby whose face and personality and name she didn't know, but who was becoming increasingly real to her nonetheless.

She touched her stomach and wondered what the child would think, when he or she was Mandy's age, about the admittedly bizarre conception and the arrangement between the mother and father. Or would Nathan still be around?

But she knew the answer to that. Nathan took his responsibilities seriously. He'd be a good father, even if it meant she had to share custody.

Think how easy it would be, an insidious voice murmured, *if you got married. Mandy would be thrilled, and your financial problems would be at an end. And it isn't as though you aren't attracted to each other.*

Ahead of her Nathan paused just then and held out a hand to help her down a short scramble. Right, Beth thought, looking from his big brown hand to his broad shoulders and his face, handsome and somehow quite different from Rob's, it wasn't as though she wasn't attracted to him.

But children and good sex weren't basis enough for a marriage. Children grew up. Sex with any one person lost its novelty. Look at celebrities. As soon as the excitement wore off, they got divorced. No, there had to be more: real liking, a shared sense of humor, commitment. And love.

But love could only come when they exorcised Rob's ghost. As Nathan's hand closed on hers and she accepted its support, she suddenly saw his face, not courteous and even friendly as it was now, but contorted with emotion as he told her what his brother had done to him. Her heart squeezed painfully with the loss of the hope she must secretly have been nursing. What were the chances Nathan could ever forget that she had loved Rob first?

Chapter Ten

"Damn it!" Nathan exclaimed. Didn't that woman have any sense? Five months pregnant, and she was hefting boxes heavy enough to break her back!

He leapt out of his car and covered the fifty yards to the barn in long strides. "Let me take that."

"It's okay," she said blithely. "I've got it. If you want to help, there's more—"

He snatched the box from her arms and almost sagged under the weight of it. Straightening, he growled, "Where to?"

"Front porch steps." She rushed after him. "I'm perfectly capable of carrying it!"

Nathan didn't say a word until he'd set the box down on the bottom step as carefully as though it contained eggs. Then he straightened to face her.

"You're pregnant," he said tautly. "You shouldn't be lifting or carrying anything heavy."

Her cheeks flushed with indignation. "I have a business to run! What's more, five months pregnant does not constitute a disability! Lots of pregnant women work, not all at desk jobs."

His jaw muscles ached. "But you have more at stake than most. Or have you forgotten?"

Her eyes narrowed and she snapped, "Don't be insulting. If that's all you came for..."

"It's not." He rubbed a hand over the back of his neck, belatedly recognizing that she had reason to be annoyed, however stupid her insistence on playing part-time longshoreman. "I'm sorry. I didn't mean to sound dictatorial."

"How *did* you mean to sound?" she asked tartly.

"Concerned."

"Concern duly noted." Her gaze didn't soften. "Why *are* you here?"

Because I didn't want to go home. Because this is home. "To finish my Monopoly game with Mandy. Is she here?"

"She's in her bedroom." Obviously grudging, Beth said, "I guess you can stay for dinner if you'd like."

"How about if I go pick up a pizza?"

She planted her hands on her hips. "Are you trying to appease me?"

Standing there like that, eyes sparking and chin defiant, she looked cute. Pretty. Sexy. Her pale curls were even more tousled than usual, as they might be when she awakened mornings. The pink in her cheeks was flattering to the delicate lines of her face. Her combative stare meant he didn't dare lower his gaze, but he was acutely aware of the ripe swell of her belly and the fact that her breasts were fuller than they used to be. Her position thrust them out.

Hell, these days, he was *always* acutely aware of her

belly and breasts and long graceful neck and the softness of her lower lip. Every time he saw her—and all too often when he didn't—he remembered her taste and feel and small muffled sounds.

Appease her? He couldn't afford not to.

"Yep," he admitted, trying to sound a hell of a lot more free and easy than he felt with his groin tightening.

She thought about it. "Okay," she said at last. "And I'll let you help carry some of the boxes."

He had no intention of allowing her to pick up even one. On her long packing table in the barn he found a dozen ready to go.

"Do you ship every day?" he asked.

"More like twice a week. And Julie is usually here to help." She wrinkled her nose. "She's almost as bad as you are."

"You told her you're pregnant."

She glanced down at her stomach. "This is one secret that's impossible to keep."

"Good."

She sealed a box with packing tape, then pushed it at him. "Let me finish with these last couple, then I'll help you. The UPS truck should be here any minute."

Orders didn't work. He'd try begging. "Let me carry them. Please. I'd feel better."

Her eyes met his gravely. After a moment she nodded. "Okay. This time." She reached for the tape again, but her hand stilled. "Thank you."

"No problem."

"I wouldn't say that." Her lashes lowered and she stared fixedly at the brown carton she made no move to tape closed. "You're here so often. You must have given up vacations and time with friends and…" She let out a small sigh and her lashes swept up so that she could search his face with disquieting intensity. "You must have had a life before us."

Pride or truth? It was no contest. "Not much of one," he admitted gruffly. "Yeah, I have friends, but hell, most of 'em are married and too busy coaching their kids' Little League teams to be free to climb Mount Olympus. I, uh—" he rotated his shoulders uneasily "—mostly worked. Seventy, eighty hours a week sometimes. When I was in Portland the other day, my assistant congratulated me for loosening up. I have you and Mandy to thank for that."

Her brow creased. "I think you're trying to make me feel better."

"I enjoy being here." His sincerity sounded closer to fervency.

Her eyes, shadowed here in the barn, contemplated him for another long moment. "Okay," she said at last with a nod, "I'll let it slide. Probably because I'm too glad you're here to be noble."

His heart lifted like a kite catching the wind. He felt foolish to be as excited as he'd been at the age of ten when his parents announced the family was going to Disneyland. But Beth had never before come right out and said she was happy he was around. He'd guessed she was when he showed up with dinner and saw her tiredness washed away by relief, or when she asked him to drive Mandy somewhere and he agreed, or even, sometimes, when he and Mandy were goofing around and Mandy's laugh rang out, clear and uncomplicated. But she hadn't *said* it, and the words felt good.

Now, he thought wryly, if only she'd confess that she wanted him to kiss her and needed him desperately! He grunted. In his dreams. Hoisting the next box of jam destined for—he glanced at the label—a gourmet-food store in San Rafael, California, he said, "Be right back."

Done packaging, she closed up the barn and they walked to the house together, Nathan with the last box on his shoulder. The brown UPS truck was just pulling into the driveway at a speed that sent dust billowing.

In seconds the driver had sunnily greeted them, slapped on labels, loaded the pile into the truck and was tearing back down the driveway.

Nathan shook his head in admiration. "I should hire him."

"They're always in a hurry. And he already had the shipping info. I'm hooked up by computer."

"Still…" The truck was gone.

She gave a sudden mischievous smile. "I offered him a job last year. He turned me down. The pay I offered was lousy."

He grinned. "Lucky he didn't report you to his bosses. Maybe they'd have refused to ship your merchandise."

Her smile deepened. "I'm afraid he thought I was joking. You should have heard him laugh. Minimum wage sounds so puny it *is* a joke."

On the porch she sank onto the glider, instead of continuing into the house. He didn't push his luck by plunking himself down next to her. Instead, he half sat on the railing, watching as she idly swung. Her lips still curved; even her eyes held a smile. He wanted her with sudden ferocity. He did his damnedest to hide the way his muscles clenched.

But still she saw enough to make her smile fade and her gaze become wary. He was silently cursing himself when her expression changed yet again.

"Oh!" she exclaimed, her mouth rounding in surprise. She laid her hands over her belly and pressed.

He shot to his feet. "Is something wrong?"

"No. Oh, no." This smile was incredibly gentle and her

eyes had softened. "He—she—just did some gymnastics. A tumbling run, I think."

His hunger found a new channel. He couldn't tear his eyes from her belly where her slender hands were splayed. He wanted to feel the life inside her. His seed. His baby. He wanted to lift her shirt out of the way and lay his own hand there, or even his cheek, until his son or daughter stirred again. He wanted to say, "Hi, kid. This is your dad. Hope it's going okay in there."

He swallowed hard, the silence roaring in his ears. He was probably scaring her again. Here they'd finally laughed together, and he was ruining it because he wanted more.

"Nathan." She spoke just above a whisper. "Would you, um, would you like to feel him move? I think you can if you put your hand here."

He wrenched his gaze up. "Do you mean it?" he asked hoarsely.

"Well, of course!" She took a deep breath. "If you won't be embarrassed."

She stopped the glider and he sat next to her, so close his thigh pressed hers. He reached out a hand that shook, and she took it in hers and spread it on her belly. Nathan closed his eyes, all his concentration focused on the point of contact. He felt the slight rise and fall as she breathed, but nothing else.

After a moment he cleared his throat. "Nothing's happening."

"It will."

He waited. Still no movement.

"Over here," she murmured, taking his hand again. She lifted her shirt and this time laid his hand on her bare skin.

Silk and warmth and unexpected firmness. She was so close he felt her breath. He could have bent his head and kissed her breast. Hammered by a barrage of sensations, he wondered how he could bear this.

And then her belly jumped under his hand. Astonished, he lifted his gaze. Beth was smiling. "You felt him?"

More movement shivered beneath the surface, like a fish disturbing a quiet pool.

"Later," she said softly, "little knobs will poke out. Fingers or toes or elbows. Or I'll be able to feel his hiccups. And he'll be able to hear our voices."

"Amazing." Incredible joy expanded like a helium balloon. "He's really in there. Alive."

"Already a person." The gentle curve of her mouth, the misty softness of her eyes, almost undid him. "Our son or daughter."

Her stomach jerked again and she laughed with quiet pleasure. He was going to kiss her. He had to kiss her. He couldn't survive another moment without touching and tasting her mouth, sharing her breath.

Her eyes widened, her smile faded, but he saw no wariness, no pulling back. She studied him solemnly as he bent his head, brushed her tremulous lips with his own, groaned—

A huge sob erupted behind him. "Please!" Mandy cried from only feet away. "Please don't have a baby!"

Earlier, before Uncle Nate had come by, Mandy was lying facedown on her bed trailing her fingers along the floor for Polly to pounce on. She didn't feel very good; her nose was stuffed up and she was tired. She should tell Mom; both times when she'd gotten sick with leukemia, it had started with stomachaches. For Jessica, it had been a runny nose and fever. The first time it had happened, nobody had guessed anything was wrong for weeks and weeks, because everyone thought she just had a cold. Of course, she and Jessica had different kinds of leukemia, but maybe this time Mandy's was showing itself with different symptoms. At the very least, the doctors would put her on an antibiotic, so she wouldn't get an infection. The maintenance drugs she took weakened her immune system.

But she didn't want to tell Mom. Mandy rolled onto her back and stared up at the ceiling. Her mother already thought she was dying. Maybe if she didn't tell anybody, it would all be over quicker. Mom could feel sad for a while, then be happy with the new baby.

But Mandy bet Uncle Nate would miss her. He came mostly to see her. She was almost sure he did. Two nights ago they'd played Monopoly for *hours* and still weren't finished the game. She had hotels on Boardwalk and Park Place, and he had them on the green Pacific, Pennsylvania and North Carolina Avenues. Plus, she owned Marvin Gardens and Atlantic and Ventnor Avenues. He was really cool to play with. Most of her friends sulked when they were losing and they wanted to give up right away. Or, if *she* was losing, they'd feel sorry for her and want to excuse rent she owed so she wouldn't have to drop out of the game. Either way was no fun. Uncle Nate was like a shark. She bet he'd take her last penny without feeling the least bit apologetic. But he also just got more determined when things didn't look good for him. Now that they were evenly enough matched, she bet this game would go on for days. Maybe, she thought hopefully, he'd come over this evening, although he hadn't promised to.

Tires crunched in the gravel out front, and she rolled off her bed to peer out the window. It *was* him. She was about to race downstairs to meet him, but he'd jumped out of his car and was heading toward the barn, not the house. He grabbed this big box out of Mom's hands even though Mom didn't want him to, and she trailed after him looking irritated. Mandy couldn't hear what they were saying, but they seemed to be arguing. After a moment, though, they went back to the barn.

She stayed at the window, watching as Uncle Nate carried a whole bunch of boxes of jam to the front. When he was done, he'd come in. She knew he would. Usually he came in first to say hi to her, even if he had to talk to Mom about something.

But the UPS truck came and went, and she didn't hear the screen door slam. What were they *doing?* She blew her nose, so he and Mom wouldn't be able to tell she was congested. Then she sat on the edge of her bed again and stroked Polly, who blinked sleepily up at her. Polly's eyes glowed emerald green, even when they were half-closed. Mandy could stare into them for ages they were such an incredible color, and so deep, like this fishing pool on the Sauk River that Mandy remembered seeing with her dad. Sometimes she almost thought she could tip forward and fall into Polly's unblinking cat eyes and sink without a trace. Sometimes she almost wanted to.

The house was completely quiet. No voices floated up the stairs, no doors slammed, no footsteps creaked on the stairs or in the hall downstairs. What were they doing?

Finally she had to find out, even though she was hurt that Uncle Nate hadn't come in. Had Mom been really mad at him? Maybe he'd left. But Mandy looked and saw his car still sitting right in front of the house. So she gave Polly one last stroke and slipped out of her room and down the stairs.

The living room and kitchen were empty. Mom's study was, too. Maybe they were still out in the barn. Mandy was hesitating in the hall when she heard the rumble of a man's voice. On the porch, then.

She opened the screen so quietly they didn't hear her

come out. They didn't see her, either. Uncle Nate sat right next to Mom on the glider. As Mandy watched, Mom lifted his hand under her shirt, onto her stomach. A second later his head shot up.

"You felt him?" Mom was talking like it was the most incredible thing on earth. "Later," she said, "little knobs will poke out. Fingers or toes or elbows. Or I'll be able to feel his hiccups. And he'll be able to hear our voices."

"Amazing. He's really in there. Alive." Uncle Nate's voice had a wondering note. He'd never sounded that way about anything Mandy had done. And it wasn't like the baby had *done* anything yet, Mandy thought resentfully.

"Already a person," Mom said. "Our son or daughter."

What am I? Mandy wanted to wail. *Just some kid who won't be around to be a bother much longer?* Her fingers curled into fists so tight they hurt. Look at them! They were…they were like a family, only without her. They had a baby—together—and Uncle Nate was going to kiss Mom. Pain burned in Mandy's chest. He was here to see Mom. Probably he never *had* come to see her.

"Please!" The words were torn from her. "Please don't have a baby!"

Uncle Nate swung to face her; Mom, hand pressed to her mouth, half rose to her feet. "Mandy!"

"I won't leave you!" Hot tears poured down her face and she could hardly see Mom and Uncle Nate. "I promise I won't die! I promise, I promise, I promise! We don't need any baby!"

Uncle Nate got to her first. His arms crushed her into a hug and she sobbed against his stomach. Then she felt Mom's hands on her shoulders, turning her.

"Sweetheart!" Mom framed Mandy's face with her hands and tilted it up. "Of course you won't die! We're not having a baby to *replace* you! Is that what you think?"

She nodded dumbly, tears running down her cheeks and mucus down her upper lip.

"Amanda McCabe, I love you more than anything or anybody in the world." Mom's voice broke. "Don't you know that?"

She did, kind of. But the baby would be Mom's, too, and she'd love him more than anything or anybody in the world, too, wouldn't she? More than *anybody* might mean more than her, Mandy.

"We don't need him," she mumbled, sniffing.

"Mandy..." Mom looked so...so hopeless, as though she didn't know what to say or do. Mandy had never seen her like that before. Mom *always* said positive things and acted as if she was never out of control. A big sigh made her shoulders sag. "I think we'd better talk."

Mandy couldn't quit crying. Tears rolled down her cheeks and into her mouth and dripped off her chin. She nodded convulsively and hiccuped. Behind her the screen door slammed and a second later Uncle Nate thrust a tissue at her.

Mandy snatched the tissue and buried her face in it. The horrible snuffling sounds that came out humiliated her. She'd made such a fool of herself! She'd never done anything like this!

She found herself ensconced on the glider with Mom. A few feet away Uncle Nate leaned against the porch railing, arms crossed, his brows drawn ferociously together. He was so tall, rearing over them. Mandy couldn't meet his eyes. He must think she was some kind of idiot.

Mom spoke in her gentlest voice. "Mandy, love, why didn't you *say* anything before?"

Through the humiliation and the terror and the tears, her original resentment lifted its head. "What good would it have done?" she cried. "You didn't give *me* any choice! You just went and did it. So why should we talk about it?"

"Sometimes parents have to make decisions their kids don't agree with. But when I have to do that, I always hope you'll listen to my reasons. Don't I listen to you?"

"Only when you want to." Mandy blew her nose again. "Otherwise, you don't ask my opinion so you don't have to listen."

Mom flinched. "Okay, you're scared I'll love this baby more than I love you. That's not...unnatural. Most only children feel that way when they find out they're going to have a brother or sister. But do any of your friends' mothers love them less because there're other kids in the family?"

Mandy hunched her shoulders wretchedly. "Kayla couldn't take that art class, even though she's a really great artist and she desperately wanted to, because her brother already had football. Remember?"

"That's time, not love."

"If you really love somebody, you'd have time for them."

"There are parents who work two jobs just to pay the bills. Does that mean they don't love their children?"

Misery burned in Mandy's chest. "No," she whispered.

"Mandy," her mother said, "I love you. I promised I wouldn't let you die. I'll do anything to keep that promise. One thing I can do, thanks to your Uncle Nate, is give you one more good chance to have a bone-marrow donor." Her eyes were fierce, unblinking. "This baby—" she put her hand on her belly "—is your best chance yet. If he's not compatible, I'll get pregnant again." She spaced the next words out, her intensity making each hard and pure. "I will do anything for you."

Mesmerized by her mother's glittering eyes, Mandy felt

shame flush her cheeks. She did know that. She always had. She opened her mouth and tried to speak, but her mother swept on.

"I will do this even if it makes you jealous. I'll do it even though I know I'll love this baby just as passionately as I love you, and that might hurt you. But I will *never*—" her voice shook "—love you any less than I did the day you were born, and any less than I do today. Do you understand?"

Fresh tears gushed so fast Mandy thought her body must be wringing itself out. "Yes!" she wailed.

"Oh, honey." Mom wrapped her arms around her. "Oh, honey, I'm so sorry you've been feeling this way. I was an idiot for not telling you. I was trying to save you from worrying, and look what I did! Shh, don't cry so hard. You'll make yourself sick. Shh." She kept murmuring as Mandy sobbed. Mom's arms were tight, and the glider began a gentle movement that was obscurely comforting.

It seemed like forever before her tears slowed and finally stopped. Mom's shirt under her cheek was soaked. Mandy knew what she looked like when she'd been crying: her face blotched red, her nose running, her eyes swollen practically shut. She couldn't lift her head, not with Uncle Nate still standing there watching. He must despise her!

After a moment her mother murmured something and handed Mandy some more tissues. He must have got them from the house, she realized. Turned away from him, she blew her nose again and mopped her cheeks and then defiantly looked up.

He was smiling at her, his mouth kind of crooked so she could tell he was sad underneath. "You know," he said, "the only reason *I* agreed to have this baby was you. I guess I'm starting to like the idea of being a father, but no more than I like the idea of…well, standing in for Rob with you.

This sister or brother you're going to have can't take your place with me. By the time he's old enough to take me on in Monopoly, you'll be grown-up and off at college."

It was true the baby wouldn't be able to do stuff like play games. A little bit cheered, Mandy mumbled, "It's okay if you don't like me as much. I mean, he *will* be yours."

This time he grinned, and she could see that what she'd guessed was true, it really was. He did love her. Even if he hadn't come into the house today to say hello to her first. He reached out and ruffled her bangs. "As far as I'm concerned, kiddo," he said gruffly, "you're mine, too."

"Oh," she said shyly. "I…I'm glad you're here, Uncle Nate."

After that he insisted he had to go. Mom didn't argue and even Mandy didn't. She felt shaky and clingy and…oh, about five years old, not twelve. Just for now, she wanted her mother and nobody else.

She laid her head against her mother's breast and closed her eyes. Neither of them moved until after Uncle Nate's car was gone.

Then Mom let out a little puff of breath against Mandy's hair. "Do you worry all the time about dying?"

Mandy didn't say anything for a long time. It was hard to. She was out of practice. Would Mom get mad again? Or tell her she was silly? But all the tears had left her feeling weak and oddly calm.

"Pretty much." She rubbed her cheek against her mother. She loved her mother's softness and smell and the quiet beat of her heart. "Well, not all the time. Not so much in the day. I mean, mostly I'm busy. But at night…" She let her words hang.

Mom's breath caught raggedly. "But why, *why,* haven't you ever said anything? To think of you alone in your bedroom worrying about dying…"

"I guess I thought—" Mandy hesitated "—you wouldn't understand if I asked you about dying. Or—" she tried not to sound as though she minded "—you'd get mad and tell me I'm not going to die."

Mom was silent for a few heartbeats. Then her arms tightened convulsively and she bowed her head against Mandy's. "I did that once, didn't I?" she asked, choking up.

Mandy didn't answer. Mom distinctly sniffed before answering her own question. "I did. I…I just wasn't ready. I couldn't bear to think…" Her voice broke.

Tears had begun to seep from Mandy's eyes onto Mom's shirt again. "I know," she whispered.

"But that was so long ago." Mom straightened, taking her arms from around Mandy and turning her to face her. Her face was wet, too. "I've tried to talk to you, over and over. Hundreds of times! Did you really think I'd get mad if you asked again?"

Had she? Confusion momentarily clouded Mandy's thoughts. That was what she'd always told herself—that Mom would get mad. But it wasn't really true, she saw now. "I guess," she said slowly, "I didn't want to tell you how scared I was. I didn't want you to tell me you were scared, too."

Brow wrinkling, Mom stared at her. "It made you feel safer if I didn't admit I was scared? I don't understand."

Mandy looked down. In a rush she said, "Because if you weren't scared, I didn't really have to be. Even if sometimes I was."

Mom made a little gasping sound. Her fingers squeezed Mandy's upper arms. Then she hugged her again. Against Mandy's hair she murmured, "You're braver than I'll ever be. You've been afraid for *years,* and you kept quiet." Mandy felt her swallow. "Oh, honey."

Not now, but tonight when she went to bed, Mandy thought, she would talk to her mother about dying and whether there would be heaven or nothingness, or maybe you got reincarnated as a person or a cat or a bug. Some gross bug. She'd thought about that before. She never stepped on even an ant if she could help it. But right now she felt too much at peace to talk about dying.

She lay quietly against her mother for a long while, until her neck started to hurt from being in such an awkward position. When she stirred, Mom let her go.

Mandy sat up. "Mom. Can *I* feel the baby move?"

Mom looked so surprised Mandy hunched her shoulders. "It's okay. It's no big deal. I just…I heard you talking and—"

"Of course you can!" Mom laughed, although her eyes were puffy, too, and she had to sniff again. "I never suggested it because I thought you were happier pretending I wasn't pregnant. But…oh, it's such a funny feeling. Let's see." She jiggled a little and then sat still, an inward-looking expression on her face. "Is he still— There!" She gripped Mandy's hand and laid it on her stomach under her shirt. Her stomach felt hard. And then it jerked, went still, then rippled, all without Mom moving a muscle. Mandy pulled her hand back.

"Hey!"

"You just met your brother or sister," Mom said solemnly.

Mandy got goose bumps. "Weird," she whispered.

"Yeah, it is, when you think about it." Mom's expression changed. "Kiddo, you need a bath. Your face is a mess. Look at you, your nose is still running! Come on." She eased to her feet, drawing Mandy with her.

"Mom—"

"We can talk more later, can't we? Aren't you starved? Why don't I put on dinner while you—"

"Mom, listen to me for a minute!"

Her mother froze, her mouth still forming an O.

Mandy took a deep breath. "Mom, I've got a cold. Or something." She waited for the panic, the dread, the rush for a thermometer and a warm sweater and the car keys.

But Mom only reached out and touched her forehead and frowned slightly. "So you do! Oh, dear, it'll mean an antibiotic. Heck, I'll go see if whoever's on call at the hospital can phone one to Howard's Drugs."

Mom was pretending. She must be. Because she, Mandy, had told her she didn't want to know when Mom was scared.

"But they'll have to see me…"

"Oh, I doubt it." Mom gently pushed her to go ahead. "Remember, you just had your blood workup. And *everybody* gets colds."

The knot in Mandy's chest loosened. "But…but when I got sick…"

"I know." Mom kissed her on top of her head and let the screen door close behind them. "But you get colds, too. I used to always get scared. I guess you noticed, huh? But I don't think this time the leukemia could possibly have come back that fast. And don't I remember you saying something about Barbara missing school because she had a cold?"

"Oh, yeah. Yeah!" Mandy bounced on her toes, then gave a hop. "Cool! I thought…"

"…you were dying."

Mandy realized Mom was teasing her. Incredible! Her giggle felt good. "Yeah! Thanks, Mom." She bounced again. "I'm gonna go take a bath, okay?"

"Okay."

Mandy poured bubble bath under the running water. When the tub was full, she sank into the hot water feeling as light and shimmery as the bubbles. It wasn't dying she thought about or her throat getting raw, but the funny way her mother's stomach had shifted under her hand. She closed her eyes and pictured a baby—a really tiny baby—doing a somersault. Or maybe finning around inside Mom like she was doing now in the bathtub.

She smiled and sank lower in the water until the bubbles tickled her chin.

Chapter Eleven

Beth hated hospital waiting rooms. They smelled alike. They *felt* alike, however homey the decor. Dozens of magazines through which people leafed without ever taking in a word. A television that chattered on one wall, unheard. A view of a parking lot. Comfortable chairs that nobody relaxed in. Tension, fear, like the fume rising from new carpeting.

This time, Beth thought semihysterically, at least she hadn't a child dying down the hall. She was only waiting to hear the result of her amniocentesis. Only a verdict on her unborn baby's health—and Mandy's future. That was all.

She drummed her fingers on the smooth oak arm of her chair, then rose to gaze out the window at the people hurrying to and from cars. Her appointment had been twenty minutes ago. Why the delay? Did it mean bad news?

Of course it didn't! Doctors were *always* behind. There'd

been times she'd had the first appointment of the day and found the doctor already late. They had emergencies. Patients in hospital beds. Rounds. Consultations. Her appointment was routine. It could wait.

She crumpled back into the chair. *But* I *can't wait!* she cried inside. If the doctor had a grain of sensitivity, he had to know how anxious she was! Anxious. What a mild word. One was anxious about going to the dentist. Anxious when a distributor called to complain that a major order was overdue. Anxious for a check to arrive.

No, she was flat-out terrified.

"Mrs. McCabe?"

She shot to her feet, clutching her purse. "Yes?"

The nurse smiled pleasantly. "Dr. Simonson is ready to see you."

Beth's feet rooted to the floor. *But I'm not ready!* she thought in panic, fully aware of the absurdity of her reaction. He was going to steal her hope and present her with the truth, however crushing, instead.

"Oh. Fine." She shifted her purse unnecessarily from hand to hand, touched one palm to her stomach in an instinctive need for reassurance and was answered by a stir within.

The nurse waited in the doorway. "If you'll follow me?"

"Yes. Of course." She must look like an idiot, standing here frozen. Somehow her feet came unstuck; she was walking down the wide hospital corridor, into his office.

How the man could make a career of treating young cancer patients, she had never understood. Despite advances in treatment, he must lose so many! But Dr. Simonson was perhaps forty and had specialized in juvenile oncology from the beginning. When he was ten, his brother died of leukemia, he had told her once. The loss had fired him to devote his life to defeating that particular enemy. He was big, with hands that should have been clumsy. Carrot-red hair was receding without it appearing to trouble him. His blue eyes usually twinkled, although she had seen him cry once. She and Mandy both loved him, as much as you can love someone with such terrible power.

White lab coat rumpled as always, he leapt up, smiling, to shake her hand. She sank again into a chair, this time in front of his desk. He perched on the edge of it and started talking immediately. Things looked good with the baby, he said; she heard him from some great distance. Did she want to know if it was a girl or boy?

Beth stared mutely up at him. He understood, for the impish twinkle in his eyes blazed into wholehearted joy.

"The baby is going to be compatible," Dr. Simonson said quietly. "I think we have a perfect match."

Compatible. He'd said compatible. She couldn't have misunderstood, could she?

He seized her hands. "Did you hear me, Beth? I had questions in my mind about your doing this, but damned if it wasn't justified. This baby is going to be Mandy's miracle."

The first tears rolled down her cheeks. Otherwise, she seemed paralyzed. "Dear God," she whispered. "You're *sure?*"

"Sure as we can be." He snatched up a lab report from his desk and began talking, but not a word penetrated.

She'd won. She'd kept her promise to Mandy. This child inside her was Mandy's miracle. Suddenly she had to bury her face in her hands. Tears dripped between her fingers.

Thank you. If You're listening, thank you.

She could, of course, have had company during her torturous wait. Nathan would have come with her; in fact, lately he'd been asking with exasperating insistence when she was to have her amniocentesis. She had managed to be vague without exactly refusing to answer.

She hardly even knew why she had been so fixed on coming alone. She'd known only that, if the news was bad, she wanted to crawl into hiding all by herself. She didn't want comfort, not even a shoulder to cry on. She alone had fought to conceive this baby; if the baby's tissue had proved not to be compatible with Mandy's, Beth needed to deal alone with the knowledge before she accepted or gave sympathy.

But, oh, he was compatible. *He.* She knew that now, too; her baby was a boy. She wanted suddenly, desperately, not to be standing alone in a hospital corridor.

Other people passed without even glancing at her, some with an air of urgency and tension, others, like a pair of off-duty nurses, laughing. An orderly pushing an empty wheelchair gave her a vague smile and she almost grabbed him and said, "I'm going to have a baby boy! And he's going to save my daughter's life!" But she saw that his mind was somewhere else and she let him pass.

She wished she could tell Mandy, but she'd have to wait until four, when her daughter got home from school. Her watch said one fifty-three. Two hours and seven minutes seemed like forever.

Nathan. Beth's mind fastened onto the name and the image of the man, tall, quiet, dark. Nathan would want to know almost as much as she had. He might be angry because she'd come alone, but he'd forget it quickly enough. Eager now, Beth hurried toward the exit.

Behind the wheel of her car she sat for a moment, imagining the moment when she told Mandy. It was tempting to call her at school, but some news was too emotionally laden to hear in a crowd. Only two hours.

How would Mandy react? Beth wondered. Before the explosion a week ago, she probably would have given a small collected nod, then retreated to her room. Now? If her daughter tried, Beth knew better than to let her get away with it. They would talk, even if that meant crying, too.

Beth drove to Nathan's in a daze. She glanced at herself in the rearview mirror and saw her own foolish smile. Amazingly, unbelievably, Mandy actually had a donor. All she had to do was stay healthy until he was old enough. The impossible, the bucket of gold at the end of the rainbow, the Holy Grail, was theirs. She'd hoped so many times. Prayed. Railed at God. And now... She touched her stomach and laughed out loud.

His car was in its slot, thank heaven. What if she'd had to go home and contain herself for the entire two hours, not having a soul to tell? She might have had to wake her brother up in the middle of the night in Saudi Arabia.

When Nathan flung the door open, he had a cell phone to one ear and was shoving his free hand through his hair. "Yeah?" he snapped, before he saw who was on his doorstep. "No, no, not you," he said into the phone as his gaze and Beth's held. "Listen," he added brusquely, "something's come up. I'll get back to you." Without waiting for a reply, he turned the phone off.

"Is something wrong?" Nathan asked.

She was taking in the sight of him in those same, baggy black sweatpants—she recognized the tear in one knee— and a Stanford University T-shirt.

"Stanford. You transferred to Stanford after you and Rob fought."

"Huh?" He glanced down at his T-shirt. "Oh. Yeah. What difference does it make?"

When he backed up she stepped over the threshold.

"What?" he asked roughly. "You have news. Damn it, is it good or bad?"

"I had my amniocentesis." Inexplicably, tears ran down her face again. "It's a boy. The baby, I mean."

"A boy." Wonder showed briefly in his eyes. It was chased away almost immediately. "He doesn't match. Oh, my God, Beth…" He reached clumsily for her.

"No! Wait!" She held out both hands to fend him off. "He does! Dr. Simonson says he's a match!"

Nathan froze. "Then why are you crying?"

"I don't know!" she wailed, and tumbled into his arms.

He laughed and swung her off her feet. "Damn, Beth! You're sure? *They're* sure?"

Through her tears, she told him, "Dr. Simonson seemed positive. He called the baby Mandy's miracle."

Nathan's arms loosened and he stilled. "Mandy's miracle. Incredible." Voice ebullient, he added, "You were right. *You're* the miracle worker."

"Without you…"

"My part was pretty minor," he said dryly. "Stud service."

She looked up into his face, her eyes drenched with tears but her gaze grave. "Only you would have done. If you hadn't come when I contacted you, and if you hadn't agreed to become a father…"

He didn't seem to be listening. "Have you told Mandy yet?"

She shook her head. "You're first."

"What's she going to say?"

"I don't know." Beth was silent for a moment, suddenly aware that Nathan's arms were still around her, that if only he tipped his head, their mouths could meet. "Last week

Mandy admitted that she thinks about dying all the time. Especially at night."

His hands reached up and threaded through her hair. "Now she can quit."

The skin on his neck was smooth and brown, his jaw clean-shaven. Swallowing, Beth said, "This isn't as easy as a pill she can pop. The doctor wants to do the transplant when the baby is six months old. That's almost a year away. She has to stay strong that long. Even if we get that far, there are still risks. They have to kill all her bone-marrow cells, you know. And then sometimes the body rejects a transplant."

Silent for a long moment, his emotions plain in his eyes, he said at last, "How have you stood it all these years?"

"What else could I do?" she asked simply.

"I wish I'd been here." His jaw worked. "You shouldn't have been alone."

Now that she wasn't, Beth couldn't understand why she'd wanted to be today. Nathan would have held her hand in the waiting room. His strength might have lessened her fear.

"You don't have to be alone," he murmured, uncannily echoing her thoughts. "Not again."

A second later his mouth touched hers, as delicately as if he was handling a ripe tender berry. She closed her eyes and felt the sweetness burst inside her, freeing a tide of longing and gratitude and— No, not love, surely not love! But, oh, his lips were so gentle, so affectionate, coaxing her to feel impossible things. His big hands framing her face were just as gentle, his thumbs drawing circles on her temples and cheekbones and over her closed eyes. Passion was curiously absent from this kiss; with his mouth, Nathan conveyed admiration and congratulation and joy. Friendship.

The wrench in her heart told her she wanted more.

Abruptly his mouth left hers and he turned her in his arms, until they wrapped around her from behind. He pressed her to him; she discovered that passion had not, after all, been altogether absent, because he was aroused. But he didn't cup her breasts or nibble her neck. Instead, his hands splayed open over her belly.

"A boy," he murmured against her hair, and she heard again that wonder. But there was something more. He sounded choked, as though... A tear, wet and hot, slid down her neck, and she understood that he hadn't wanted her to see him cry. "Thank God. Without Mandy—" He stopped, audibly swallowed, continued in a painfully gritty voice, "I was afraid he couldn't help her, and we'd love him, but we'd blame him, too."

Her eyes burned with new tears. "No. We wouldn't have. We'd have loved him for what he was, just like I love Mandy. Nathan McCabe, you're not the kind of man who'd ask a baby to be responsible for someone else's fate."

"He is, though."

"Inadvertently. But it's a...a blessing." She struggled to explain. "A gift. Not something he had to be."

"I hope you're right." Nathan was silent for a moment. "Are you going to name him after Rob?"

"No. Oh, no!" The idea was instantly repugant to her. "He's not Rob's baby. He's yours. I...I thought of Patrick, after your father." It was hard to speak at all normally with his body and hands on her so intimately. "What do you think?"

"I like Patrick," Nathan said huskily. "What was *your* father's name?"

"Joe. Joseph."

"Patrick Joseph McCabe. Has a nice ring to it."

"Mmm-hmm." She could hardly think with his hands still wrapped around her waist.

"I don't feel him moving."

"No. I think he sleeps when I'm up and around."

"The better to plague you at night."

"Yes."

Nathan took a deep breath and lifted his hands from her belly. They shook, and he curled them into fists as he stepped back from her.

Beth sniffed and slowly turned to face him. He'd swiped away any betraying tears, but his eyes were reddened. He didn't seem to have any more idea what to say than she did. They looked at each other, Beth feeling as awkward as a fifteen-year-old alone for the first time with the boy she had a crush on.

"I…I'd better go." She took a step toward the door, assuming Nathan would move out of her way. "Mandy will be home soon."

He stayed blocking her path. "Can we celebrate? How about dinner tonight? Somewhere really fancy. Or would Mandy hate that?"

Beth seized on the subject of her daughter. "Are you kidding? She's twelve. Twelve-year-olds like to feel glamorous. She'll be sure she looks at least fourteen."

His mouth tilted into that heart-stopping smile. "I'll tell her so. Six o'clock?" Some of the emotion left his face. "Unless you'd rather be alone with her this evening. It's your celebration."

"Ours," she said firmly. "Six sounds great."

He walked her out to her car and opened the door for her, as if she was too fragile to make it on her own. Beth slipped in behind the wheel. Hand still on the door, Nathan gazed down at her.

"You know I'd have gone with you."

She stared fixedly ahead. "Yes. You offered."

"Then why the hell go through it alone?" Suddenly he

was scowling. "Don't you have a friend who'd have gone with you if you didn't want me?"

"I didn't want anybody." It was Nathan she'd thought of first after Mandy. She had never considered asking anyone else.

"You can be damned stubborn," he informed her.

"I know," Beth said with unaccustomed meekness. "I felt…like *I* should take responsibility. It was my idea, such a drastic step, and the chances still only one in four. I thought… I was afraid…"

A thoughtful scrutiny had replaced the scowl. "Afraid he wouldn't be compatible."

"Yes." Now she stared down at her lap. "I was so scared. Sometimes it's easier to pretend to yourself than to other people."

"I'm sorry." His voice held that husky note again. "I shouldn't chew you out. It was your decision."

But she'd hurt him, she guessed, by leaving him out. "I came straight here," she said.

He only raised an eyebrow. "Would you have, if the news had been bad?" Without waiting for her answer he nodded goodbye and slammed her door.

She almost rolled down her window and lied. "Yes. Of course I would have." Or was it a lie? But she didn't know, hadn't the slightest idea what she'd have done, where she'd have gone. The willow tree? Her bed, like a child who had no place else as refuge? Or maybe she would have gone to Nathan, who'd have understood as no one else could. Who, she saw now, loved Mandy. Perhaps not quite with a mother's ferocity, but with nearly a father's.

She made it home with fifteen or twenty minutes to spare before Mandy arrived. Not that she could make any use whatsoever of the time. She tried sitting on the glider and found herself jumping back to her feet. She sat on the railing and swung her legs, moved to the porch steps, paced. Finally she grabbed her garden gloves and cleaned up the flower beds to each side of the steps, deadheading October asters and gathering armfuls of brown foliage from earlier perennials. The rose was past; already it was forming hips that by Christmas would be glossy ornaments hanging from the bare thorny arms of the climber.

The rumble of the school bus in the distance brought her to her feet. It squealed to a stop down the road where the Jameson kids got off, lumbered to a start again and finally appeared through the alders, which had lost most of their leaves. She waited in unbearable suspense as the bus slowed and stopped again, the doors opened, and Mandy finally hopped out, turning to wave at her friends as the bus struggled up to speed again. Then Mandy began poking her way down the driveway, kicking at yellow leaves.

Beth couldn't stand it. She moved to meet her daughter, first strolling as though she had no particular reason, then faster and faster until she was running.

Mandy lifted her head. "Mom?"

Beth reached her like a whirlwind. Thank God she was laughing instead of crying, as she grabbed Mandy's shoulders and twirled her around until they were both dizzy.

Mandy pulled away and backed up, staggering a little when her foot hit uneven ground, but not seeming to notice. "Mom?" Her voice was thready. "Why are you acting like this?"

"He matches." Beth began to tremble all over. "You finally have a donor."

"He…" Her daughter's gaze darted to her stomach. "You mean, *him?*"

"Your brother. Patrick Joseph McCabe."

"It's a boy?" Mandy stared at her mother, eyes wide and dark. Stunned.

"Yep. Our miracle."

"You…you'd tell me the truth if he didn't match, wouldn't you?" Mandy's face was too old. "You wouldn't lie to make me feel better?"

"I have never lied about your illness," Beth said with quiet intensity. "I never will. We have our miracle."

Mandy's tears came with a child's suddenness, belying her too-wise eyes. Her backpack dropped with a thud to the ground, and she sobbed against her mother's shoulder as though hope had been snatched away, not given to her. But with the memory of her own tears, Beth understood.

They dried up eventually, with sniffles, blown nose and a few fresh bursts. Beth carried Mandy's pack and they walked slowly up the drive, brown leaves crackling and disintegrating underfoot. Soon it would be raining, and then snow might come, and Christmas, and a new year. And in February, a baby. A miracle.

"Mom?"

"Mmm?"

They reached the porch steps and Mandy plopped down. Beth followed suit and waited.

"Does this mean I'll get well for sure?"

If Beth hadn't sworn always to be honest, she might have lied now. But Mandy had faced too much unblinkingly not to deserve the truth.

"Well, first you have to stay healthy until Patrick's old enough to do the transplant. And the radiation needed to kill your own cells is risky, and there's always a small chance your body will reject the transplanted marrow."

Mandy stared ahead, thinking it over. After a moment she nodded. "You won't blame Patrick if it doesn't work, will you?"

Somebody might just as well have chopped Beth's heart in two. "No," she said tremulously. "We'll love him no matter what, I promise. He's…he's already a person to me."

Mandy scooted over a few inches until her hip bumped her mother's. "I'm going to be a good big sister. He'll never be sorry for what he had to go through for me."

"No." Beth could just get the words out. "No, I don't think he'll ever be sorry."

Mandy laid her head against her mother's shoulder. "He might hate knowing you had him only for…for some cells. Maybe you should lie."

"I don't like to lie," Beth said, "but this time you might be right."

They sat in peaceful silence. After a while Beth said lazily, "Nathan is going to take us out to dinner. To celebrate."

"Cool." Mandy didn't move. "Mom?"

"Mmm?"

"Can I buy a bra?"

"A bra?" Eyebrows lifted, Beth turned her head. "What on earth does that have to do with anything?"

"It's just that…well, you can see my nipples. When I wear anything tight. It's embarrassing!"

"Then I guess it's time," Beth agreed. "To tell you the truth, I'd noticed."

"Bras must be awfully uncomfortable." Mandy scrunched up her nose. "Why do we have to hide our breasts? *Boys* don't hide their chests."

"No, and very nice they are to look at, too."

"Mo-om!"

"Hey, I'm single. I can look, can't I?"

Mandy rolled her eyes. "Just don't look when my friends can see you, okay?"

"Deal." Beth stood up. "Whaddaya say we start gussying ourselves up? We're going fancy tonight."

"Can I wear that dress?" her daughter asked eagerly.

"That dress" was a hand-me-down from Beth's brother's daughter. Apparently their social circles and private schools in Saudi required even preteens to dress to the nines. This particular dress was black and gold and…well, sexy. Mandy had been praying for an appropriate occasion to wear it; Beth had been praying she'd get too tall before one arose. But seeing the hope in her daughter's dark eyes, she didn't have a qualm about capitulating.

"Why not?"

Mandy let out an ecstatic breath. "Thank you, thank you, thank you!"

"Just don't outshine me, okay?"

On her feet Mandy gazed critically at her mother. "But do you have anything really pretty that fits? I mean, since you're pregnant?"

Beth's eyes widened and she looked down at herself. "I don't know! I didn't think… Oh, no, what'll I do?"

"Uncle Nate will understand," her daughter said kindly.

"I don't want understanding!" Beth wailed, scrambling to her feet.

Mandy eyed her with a peculiar expression. "What *do* you want?"

Beth gulped. With what she considered quick wits, she said haughtily, "Admiration. Adulation. Awe would be okay. But I'd settle for not sticking out like a sore thumb."

"Oh." Mandy's face cleared. "Well, you're not *that* fat yet. You must have something."

She did, thank God, she found after an investigation of her closet. When she tugged the slinky teal sheath on, it fit all too snugly over her breasts and belly, but the black velvet jacket hid the overabundance of some parts of her body. And her legs still looked good, she decided, pirouetting in front of her mirror.

Half an hour later she opened the door to Nathan. He, of course, was heart-stoppingly handsome in a dark suit. The severity of the white shirtfront was the right foil for the angular, almost harsh lines of his face.

"Beautiful," he murmured to Beth, his eyes warm. His gaze went past her at the sound of Mandy clattering down the stairs. Beth, too, turned to look. The little girl wasn't quite gone, but close enough. The dress enhanced her slight curves and plunged at the neck, leaving a long sweep of white neck. Her dark hair was fastened on the crown of her head with a gold clip. Her eyes shone, her cheeks bloomed, and she was both ungainly and astonishingly graceful. Duckling and swan at the same time. Growing up, the way Beth had dreamed she would.

Beth couldn't have said a word to save her life. Fortunately Nathan said it for her.

"Sweetheart, what happened to your thirteenth and fourteenth birthdays? You decide to bypass them? You're going to break all the boys' hearts."

Mandy grinned, though she sounded anxious. "I really and truly look okay?"

"You take my breath away." He added quietly, "I'm glad for you, kiddo. I cried when your mom told me."

"Did you really?" She blinked as though to prevent new tears. "I did, too."

"Come here." He held out his arms.

Mandy launched herself into them. After a second he held out an arm for Beth, and blinking fiercely to save her makeup, she went.

When they separated a moment later, they all had the same foolish smiles on their faces.

"Group hugs," Mandy said with satisfaction, "are the best kind."

"That was my first, but I think I'd have to agree." Very

formally Nathan held out one elbow for Beth, the other for Mandy. "Ladies, shall we?"

Beth had never been happier than she was that evening. Only once did they put into words the source of the well-spring of joy that had them all laughing at next to nothing, that made the food ambrosia and the surroundings perfection.

Nathan made a toast, his glass of champagne gently touching theirs of sparkling cider. "To Mandy," he said. "And Patrick."

"To miracles," Beth said, her eyes meeting first Mandy's, then his.

"To Mom," Mandy contributed solemnly. "And to Uncle Nate."

They all drank, equally solemnly. And then Mandy said, "Just think. If Patrick was already born, we couldn't have brought him tonight. We'd have had to leave him with a babysitter! So this is best, huh?"

"Darn right," Nathan said. "Anyway, once he's born, we probably won't want to go anywhere. We'll be too busy sitting around the crib or cradle or whatever at home, ex-claiming about how cute he is when he cries or spits up his milk or does something incredible like roll over."

From the experience of friends having little brothers and sisters, Mandy informed him how long it was before Patrick would roll over or do anything else really interesting. "They don't even *smile* for, like, six weeks or something. Babies are really pretty boring."

"But this one will be ours," Nathan pointed out.

Ours. Her heart ought to be numb by now, Beth thought, but the sharp stab she'd just felt showed that it wasn't. *Home.* He'd said *we'll* all sit around at home, hadn't he?

Today she'd been given what she wanted most in the

world. Maybe it was selfish to ask for more, and so soon. But she couldn't seem to help it.

For the first time she let herself dream. Was it possible they could be a family? That Nathan could love her, as well as Patrick and Mandy? That it could quit mattering to all of them that he and Rob had been twins?

Chapter Twelve

In the next two and a half months, Beth's optimism wilted. Not that Nathan wasn't there, wasn't solicitous, wasn't friendly. He was. They had Thanksgiving together, celebrated Christmas as a family. Nathan found out when she regularly sent shipments of jam and managed to be around to carry the boxes. He called, he stopped by, he brought dinner, took them out to dinner, drove Mandy to drama and attended her school play. He was a devoted uncle/father figure. He was Beth's best friend. But that was all.

Occasionally she imagined she saw heat in his eyes when she touched him casually or looked up to find him watching her across a room. But he never, not once, acted on his desire—if he still felt any and she wasn't just seeing things.

And they never talked about Rob.

As far as the desire went…well, she didn't *feel* very desirable. Somehow with this pregnancy, she'd expanded faster and farther than when she carried Mandy. Now, at eight months along, she couldn't decide whether she more closely resembled a whale or a hippopotamus. Probably a hippo, she thought ruefully, looking at her bulging white stomach rising above the bubbles in her bath. Hippos didn't float. She was pretty sure she wouldn't, either. Who could blame a man for not lusting after this body?

The business about Rob, though, was something else again. It had taken her a while to notice that Rob's name rarely came up anymore. Those first few months, Nathan had made a point of talking about his brother, especially for Mandy's benefit. When Mandy asked questions, he still answered them without seeming uncomfortable, but he never spontaneously reminisced as he once had. *Did you know Rob was the quarterback of our high-school football team?* Or, *Did Rob ever tell you about the time he backed the car into the neighbor's fence, and we propped it up until a winter storm blew it over? Did you know Rob had childhood asthma?*

Just the other night Mandy was insisting she'd been really, really ugly in about fourth grade, and she dragged Uncle Nate to the fireplace mantel to see her school picture from that year. Out of curiosity Beth had followed them. Nathan looked at Mandy's photo, but his eyes never strayed to any of the other framed pictures standing along the mantel. He had to have *worked* at not looking.

Apparently he'd decided that the way to deal with his feelings about his brother was to pretend Rob never had existed. Beth couldn't imagine that, in the long term, his avoidance would work. One of these days that buried resentment was going to boil over. And there was no way they could have any kind of romantic relationship without him accepting that she'd once loved and been married to his brother.

Not, she had to admit, that Nathan gave any sign of *wanting* a romantic relationship. Beth made a face and slumped lower in the tub.

A moment later she sighed, reached for the towel and carefully got to her feet. She dried her arms and breasts and back, then lifted one foot to the rim of the bathtub and bent over to pat her leg dry.

That was when she saw the blood trickling down her thigh and staining the bathwater.

Some days he figured he was a gutless wonder. On others Nathan convinced himself he was being sensible, maybe even gentlemanly. Hell, noble.

Wait until she had the baby, he told himself. Five, six, eight months pregnant, she couldn't possibly be interested in love and marriage. She was dealing with enough already. Let her have the baby, see that he really would be a devoted father, get used to the idea that he *was* Patrick Joseph Mc-Cabe's father. By that time, maybe she wouldn't see Rob anymore when she looked at him.

Then a bad day, like today, would come, and he'd know in his heart that he wasn't waiting for Beth. His feelings were the stumbling block. He didn't have the guts to put her to the test. Looking up at him that day back in September, her eyes cloudy with passion, she probably hadn't said "Rob." But what if the next time she did? What if she was *thinking* Rob? Damn. What if she still wanted Rob? Nathan shoved his chair back from his computer and squeezed his eyes shut. How would he ever know?

How could he stand not knowing?

When the phone rang he didn't pick it up. Let the machine handle the call. He kept the answering machine in the living room so his concentration wouldn't be broken when he was involved in something. This time, ignoring the murmur of his own voice from the other room, he rubbed his temples and tried to focus on the columns of figures on the screen.

He was damned lucky he'd built a strong company and had people working for him who knew what the hell they were doing. He'd sure as God left them alone to do it lately. He should be traveling more than he was, but every time he got on an airplane, he felt uneasy. What if something went wrong with the pregnancy? What if Beth went into labor early? What if Mandy got sick? He didn't like knowing that no neighbor was within shouting distance, didn't like the narrow winding road separating their house from the nearest medical clinic. It was January now, and thus far the winter had been relatively dry for the Pacific Northwest, but what if a storm dumped eight inches of snow on the ground? Or the rain froze into black ice? He'd seen to it that Beth had snow tires on her car, but he still wasn't happy. He could have concentrated a hundred times better if he'd been there instead of—

A tremulous quality to the voice murmuring in place of his own on the answering machine wrenched Nathan from his brooding. Swearing, he snatched up the receiver.

"Beth?"

"Nathan?" She gave a sobbing breath that sounded like relief. "You *are* home."

"I was working." Alarm masqueraded as brusqueness. "What's wrong? You're not in labor, are you?"

She seemed to withdraw. "No, I… Oh, I can manage alone. I just…"

Manage alone. He gritted his teeth. Her confidence in him overwhelmed him. Brusque this time from irritation—or was it hurt?—he said shortly, "You don't have to. If you need me, I can come right away."

The tremble returned to her soft voice. "Are you sure?"

He surged to his feet and roared, "Goddamn it, Beth, what's wrong?"

Silence chastened him. And then, shakily, she said, "I'm bleeding." A sniffle came over the line. "Nathan, I'm scared. What if…?"

Pure terror tore a hole in his stomach like an ulcer. With an effort he spoke gently. "Have you called the doctor?"

"She wants me to come in. I…I was just getting dressed."

Nathan gave a wild glance at his watch as he groped for his car keys in his pocket. "I'm twenty-five minutes away. Shouldn't you have an ambulance?"

"My bleeding isn't that heavy. She wants to see me, but she said it's not necessarily an emergency."

He could tell Beth didn't believe the reassurance any more than he did. "I'm going out the door right now," he said steadily. "You know my cell-phone number if you need me. If things get worse, you call an ambulance. I'll be there as quick as I can." And to hell with any speed traps along the way.

Every traffic light turned red just as he got to it. Every grandfather out to drive the little woman to the grocery store cruised down the road at twenty-five miles an hour. Kids on bikes swerved from the shoulder into lanes of traffic. Nathan's knuckles were white on the steering wheel. He used language he'd forgotten he knew. He was saved only by frequent desperate looks at his watch, which told him he was making good time, despite everything. He took the swooping curves of her country road as if behind the wheel of a sports car. The tires skidded and spit out gravel when he accelerated down her driveway and slammed to a stop.

He half expected to find her lying in a pool of blood on the kitchen floor. Relief uncramped a fraction of his tension when she opened the front door before he could mount the stairs. Her curly hair was disciplined with a clip. She looked composed, pretty. She even wore makeup, for God's sake. The contrast to the nightmarish images that had kept his foot heavy on the accelerator couldn't have been greater. Why the hell had she scared him?

Then he noticed her pallor, the shadows beneath her eyes, the fear in her eyes. And he saw the bag she carried.

Her gaze followed his. "I packed a few things just in case…"

He nodded tightly and took it from her. Although she moved confidently, he held her elbow as she descended the porch steps. Normally, as he opened the passenger-side door of the car and eased her in as carefully as he might have a new piece of furniture he didn't want to scratch, she would have been protesting that she didn't break. Today, she only gave him a shaky smile. Now she knew that she did break.

He broke more speed records getting her to the clinic. The nurse whisked Beth right in. When he started to follow, the nurse said, "Why don't you wait here, sir. The doctor will do an examination, then we'll come get you. I promise."

So he had to suffer the agony of watching Beth disappear through the door. Then he looked helplessly around. What was he supposed to do? Chat with another restless father-to-be? Trip the five-year-old who was running laps and zooming like an airplane? Sit and read *People* magazine? He didn't give a damn which celebrity was divorcing her husband. Right this minute he didn't give a damn about the state of the economy, either, which was featured on the cover of *Newsweek*. He made himself sit down, but he didn't even reach for a magazine.

What were they doing to her? How heavily was she

bleeding? Would they hospitalize her? God, was she losing the baby? A fierce protest rose in his throat, had him gripping the arms of the chair until his hands ached.

His son. And what if Beth was in danger? And Mandy—how could they tell Mandy if the worst happened?

Mandy. Nathan looked at his watch again with new alarm. No, they were okay. It'd be two hours until she got off the school bus. They'd know something by then. If necessary, he would leave Beth to go pick up Mandy.

The nurse appeared and smiled at him. As he shot to his feet, she said, "Mr. McCabe? You can come back now."

She showed him into an empty room. Briskly she bundled up the crumpled paper on the examining table, but not before he saw some bright red bloodstains.

"Mrs. McCabe has gone downstairs to have an ultrasound," she said brightly. "Dr. Williams wanted to speak to you briefly, and then perhaps you'd prefer to wait out in front. It may be half an hour. You could even go get a cup of coffee."

He didn't say anything. She bustled out as cheerily as she'd led him in, leaving the door open. Fortunately Dr. Williams entered almost immediately.

Without preamble she said, "I suspect a condition called *placenta previa,* in which the placenta is partially over the cervix. Bleeding at this stage can signal the separation of the placenta, which is far more serious, but Mrs. McCabe has no tenderness, no rigidity in her abdominal wall. We're taking a closer look right now with an ultrasound."

"Is she losing the baby?" he asked hoarsely.

"I don't believe so." Compassion made the doctor's tone less brisk than the other times he'd come here with Beth. "Besides, if necessary, we can do a cesarean section at this point. I'd prefer she hold on for at least another couple weeks, though."

Hold on. Nathan felt even more helpless. "How?"

"Bed rest," she said succinctly. "Maybe hospitalization. Home if she has enough help."

"She's got it."

"That's what I wanted to hear." Dr. Williams gave him a rare approving smile. "Would you prefer to wait in here?"

"Thanks."

The moment she quietly closed the door behind her, his legs collapsed, dumping him in the hard plastic chair. He was glad to be alone.

The half hour he waited was the longest of his life. Up to this point, he thought grimly. Beth hadn't asked him to take childbirth classes with her, which meant he'd be excluded when she had the baby. What if she was in labor for twelve hours? Would he have to pace a waiting room? The prospect was so appalling he gritted his teeth. He'd rather be the one suffering in the delivery room.

When the door opened, Nathan got to his feet. Dr. Williams and Beth came in together. Beth's face was pale and solemn, her eyes still frightened. When he reached out a hand, she slipped hers into it and squeezed back when he gripped tightly. Together they faced the doctor.

"My guess was right," she said. "The placenta is only partially blocking the cervix. It does mean we'll have to do a C-section when the time comes. But what we need to focus on now is sustaining your pregnancy as long as possible, Beth. Your bleeding is relatively minor and intermittent. I think, if you're willing to go to bed for the next few weeks, you can make it close to full term."

The shock on Beth's face told Nathan she hadn't been forewarned.

"Weeks?" she repeated. "Spend almost a *month* in bed?"

"You can get up. We won't tie you down. Bed *rest* is

what we call it. But no lifting, no housework, no shopping, no jogging. For the most part I want you resting in bed. Indulge yourself. Read, watch TV, snooze. If you do too much and start bleeding again, I'll have to hospitalize you."

"A month?"

"If all goes well." Dr. Williams's tone wasn't without sympathy, but she was still matter-of-fact. "The indulgence doesn't carry over to food unfortunately. No heart-shaped boxes of chocolate. Weight gain hasn't been a problem for you, but without exercise, you'll have to be especially careful."

Beth dropped into a chair as abruptly as Nathan had earlier, her legs apparently giving way. She still held on to his hand.

"But…I can't do nothing! Mandy's only twelve." Beth looked from the doctor to Nathan and back as she begged for understanding. "She can't clean house and cook dinner and do the laundry and… I do have an assistant who I guess can handle the business for a few weeks, but… I have a life!" she wailed.

Nathan figured it was time to contribute to this discussion. "I'll clean house and cook dinner and do the laundry. I can give Julie a hand with the jam, too, if she needs it."

Beth stared at him. "But how can you? You have your own business! This is crazy." She turned beseeching eyes on the doctor. "There has to be another way."

"There isn't." The doctor's warm brown eyes didn't waver. "The baby's welfare has to come first, however tough that is for a while."

Beth was still in shock when Nathan ushered her out to the car a few minutes later after having agreed to bring her back in a couple of days. Sooner, if she began bleeding again or had any discomfort.

"We'll keep a close watch on her," had been Dr. Williams's last words.

Damn right they would. He'd take her home, wait until Mandy was there, then go to his condo and pack. He could use Beth's computer to keep in touch with his office, but somebody else would have to handle the trip to Arizona and New Mexico scheduled for the week after next. Already mentally shuffling schedules and duties, he only listened with half an ear to Beth's desperate objections.

"You're going to move *in?*"

"Mmm," he agreed absently.

"But...but..."

Waiting at a red light, Nathan turned his head. "You have a problem with that?"

"I can hire someone." She waved her hands. "You don't have to drop everything."

"I won't. I'll use your office if that's okay. I presume the housework isn't a full-time job."

"You may be surprised. Especially—" she scrunched up her nose "—if you have to wait on me hand and foot."

"Are you going to be demanding?" he asked, feeling his first trace of amusement that day.

"What I'm going to do is go nuts," she said gloomily.

"You can keep up on paperwork."

"There's hardly any at this time of year." Beth sounded as sulky as Mandy in a bad mood.

"Hey, look on the bright side. What if this were June?"

She moaned and flopped back against the headrest. He let her brood the rest of the way home.

She didn't, however, take it well when he tried to help her up the front porch steps. "I can walk!" she snapped.

"Oh, this is going to be a fun month," he muttered, releasing her elbow.

In front of him Beth abruptly stopped. He waited a couple of steps below her. She was entitled to be angry, he figured; fear often came out that way. And she sure as hell had plenty to be afraid of.

She took a deep breath and turned to face him. No anger. Instead, tears streaked her cheeks. "I'm sorry. I'm being awful." Her voice rose into a wail. "And you're being so nice!"

"Ah, damn," he said, taking that next step and wrapping his arms around her. She stood enough higher that her face ended up buried in the crook of his neck and shoulder, instead of leaning against his chest. He felt the tears, hot and wet, against his bare skin; felt the quivers of sobs shake her swollen body.

When at last she looked up, her eyes were red and puffy and her nose was running. Which was a hell of a time for him to feel love rock him so hard he'd have stepped backward into space if he hadn't still been holding her.

"I *am* sorry," Beth repeated. "I'll be good. Dr. Williams was right. Nothing matters but the baby. And here I am sulking because I have to laze around. You're the one who's giving up everything to take care of us!"

"I'm not giving up anything," he said roughly. "For now, you guys are my only family. I've been worrying about you, anyway. Now I have an excuse to be right here where I want to be."

She sniffed one more time, then flung her arms around him again and gave him a quick hard hug. He felt her lips move against his neck, heard a murmur, but his ears wouldn't take in what she said. It couldn't have been "I love you." Or if it was, she didn't mean it the way he wanted her to. Friends loved each other. Family members loved each other. She was just grateful to Mandy's uncle Nate for being a good guy and helping out. She didn't mean "I love you" the way he felt it.

And that hurt like nothing had since his brother's betrayal.

Mandy thought it was cool having Uncle Nate living with them.

At first she'd been scared about Mom's losing the baby. Here she'd gotten used to the idea of having a brother. Patrick Joseph McCabe. Patrick. That was what she planned to call him. Not Pat or Joey or anything else cutesy. Patrick. She could close her eyes and picture him, dark-haired and dark-eyed like her, toddling after her like Kayla's little brother followed his big sister. Mandy could hold him, chunky and round, and he'd grin up at her without teeth. Eventually she'd teach him stuff. Like how to whistle and how to read and how to pump on the swing. She didn't want him never to be.

Even as frightened as she was, Mandy didn't let herself think about the other reason she desperately wanted him to be born. It seemed so selfish, as if she was the only one who mattered. So she just blanked her mind to it. Only, that didn't completely work. She knew that underneath, the selfish motive was still there.

But after a few days, when Mom and the baby seemed okay, Mandy started thinking how much fun it was to have Uncle Nate here. He made easy dinners, like pancakes, or macaroni and cheese, or sloppy joes. Mom rolled her eyes and asked how anyone could have lived alone all these years and not learned to cook. Mandy liked the dinners better than some of the stuff Mom got out of cookbooks, but she didn't say so where Mom could hear.

Uncle Nate teased Mandy a lot, and he played games with her and helped her with her homework. Once her social-studies teacher got mad because nobody was paying attention, and she said that everyone in the class had to write, "I will be courteous and listen to Mrs. Curtis when she speaks" three hundred times as homework. But Mandy *had* been listening! It was so unfair. And humiliating, treating them like little kids. Uncle Nate agreed, and he copied her handwriting and wrote half the sentences for her. How many parents would have done that?

Sometimes they all played a game together, Mom propped against pillows and Uncle Nate sitting on one side of her on the bed and Mandy on the other. They'd open the game board on Mom's lap—well, really her legs, since she didn't exactly have a lap anymore. That worked okay until she got up to go to the bathroom, which she had to do *constantly*. Uncle Nate teased her that it would be easier to wear a diaper. He was funny lots of the time. He made Mom laugh.

It was while they were playing TriBond one night that Mandy got her idea. Mom was scowling as she tried to decide what Superfly, The Body and The Macho Man had in common. Mandy happened to look at Uncle Nate, who was watching Mom. His mouth had this little smile, and his eyes were sort of soft and moony, and it hit Mandy: he was in love with Mom!

"Japanese horror movies," Mom finally decided.

"Nope," Uncle Nate said. "Professional wrestlers."

Mom made this awful face. "Superfly?"

"Yup. Dignity is not a component of professional wrestling."

"I guess not," Mom mumbled. "Okay, Mr. Know-it-all, it's your turn."

Mandy read the three things that had something in common. "A map, a fish and a weight-loss clinic."

"I know that one!" Mom gave a little bounce, which

made their markers on the board slide. "Sorry, sorry." She put them all back in place.

"A map and a fish." Uncle Nate stared into space.

This time, Mom watched *him*. Mandy couldn't quite decide whether she was looking moony, too, or just normal. He *was* really cute. Mom must have been in love with Dad a long time ago. And since Uncle Nate looked a lot like Dad, why couldn't she fall in love with him, too?

If they got married, Uncle Nate would stay, always and always. He'd be Mandy's stepfather.

"Scales!" he suddenly said triumphantly.

"Huh?" Mandy looked down at the card in her hand. "Oh. Yeah. You get to roll again."

Later she kept thinking about them, married. She could be a bridesmaid, or maybe even the maid of honor, if kids were allowed. Mom could wear white lace, and Uncle Nate a black tuxedo, and Mandy wouldn't even mind if they went away for a honeymoon, not when it meant Uncle Nate would come back with Mom forever. What would she call him? she wondered dreamily that night as she waited to fall asleep. Would she still call him Uncle Nate? Or just his first name, like some kids did with stepparents? Or... Well, not Dad. Somehow that seemed disloyal, even if she was having a harder and harder time remembering her father. Uncle Nate's face had gotten in the way. It was him she saw now when she tried to picture Dad.

Sometimes that made her feel guilty, too, just like her secret thoughts about Patrick, but then she remembered how much Dad had talked about Uncle Nate, and she convinced herself Dad would like knowing his twin brother was here, doing things with her and helping Mom out. And if Mom married him, it wasn't like she'd *chosen* Uncle Nate, instead of Dad. Dad was *dead*. Gone. All her friends thought it was romantic that Mom never dated; they said it must mean she was mourning him still. Probably, they thought, she'd mourn him for the rest of her life, and he'd be waiting for her up in heaven. But Mandy wasn't so sure. Mom didn't *act* like she was still grieving. Once, about a year ago, Mandy had asked her why she didn't date, and Mom had looked surprised.

"I don't know anybody I want to date." She'd shrugged. "And I'm busy. I don't feel the need."

Mandy had nodded. That was kind of what she'd guessed. She and Mom were okay by themselves, except for when Mandy was really sick. Why would they want some strange man around?

But Uncle Nate was different. Mandy wanted him around. What she couldn't figure was any way to push things along, except for thinking of reasons—like playing games—for him to be in Mom's bedroom every evening. Or keeping him away from Mom when she started to get grumpy about having to lie there and do nothing. Or, once in a while, when Mom was depressed and didn't want to bother doing anything to her hair or putting makeup on, Mandy encouraged her. If he saw her looking really awful, Uncle Nate might lose interest.

Mandy wouldn't have minded if these weeks could have gone on and on. She knew Uncle Nate was taking Mom to see the doctor really often, and that Mom would have to be cut open to have the baby out, instead of having him the normal way. But she thought Mom or Uncle Nate would at least give her some notice.

Instead, she was called from her prealgebra class to the office one day. The vice principal was waiting for her.

He smiled. "Amanda, I have good news for you."

She thought about an essay she'd entered in a national contest. But hers wasn't that good. It couldn't have won, could it?

"Your uncle Nathan just called. He wanted you to know your mom has had her baby. He's a boy, and they're both doing fine."

Mandy just stared. Patrick was already born? Had Mom and Uncle Nate known last night that today was the day? Why hadn't they told her?

"Your uncle says he'll pick you up from school, so you can go directly to the hospital. He guessed you might want to meet your new brother."

Her new brother. Excitement suddenly fizzed through Mandy. Maybe she could hold him today. And she already knew how to change diapers and that you had to support a baby's head. Kayla had shown her. She could take care of Patrick while Mom napped and stuff. This was going to be so cool!

Uncle Nate came really fast. Mandy was waiting just inside the door. She wanted to run out and hop in the car, but, no, he had to come in and fill out a stupid form releasing her. By that time, she was practically hopping up and down.

"Let's go!"

He grinned when she grabbed his hand and tugged him toward the door. "You're the one who told me babies don't do anything exciting for at least six weeks."

"Yeah, but I want to see if he looks like me. And if he has all his toes, and what color his eyes are." She swallowed. "And if Mom's okay."

Uncle Nate's arm snaked out to give her a boa-constricting hug. "Your mother is doing just great. She looks as proud as if she'd just painted a masterpiece."

"Well, she kind of did."

"Hey." He pretended to be offended. "*I* wielded a brush, too, you know."

"Yeah," Mandy said interestedly, "I've been wondering about that. I mean, *how…*"

"Don't ask."

Mandy had the feeling he meant it. He had a weird expression on his face, like he was remembering something really depressing. She was pretty sure he and Mom hadn't had sex, so how had they done it? It couldn't have been much fun. Maybe she could ask her health teacher how people make babies if they didn't want to go to bed together.

Once they got to the hospital, all she could think about was her brother. Patrick Joseph McCabe. She knew he couldn't smile, but maybe he'd—well, *look* at her at least, as though he knew they meant something to each other.

She kept having to hurry Uncle Nate, and the elevator took forever. But at last the doors crept open, and ahead was a sign that said Maternity.

"Shall we go by the nursery first?" Uncle Nate suggested.

It turned out to be this bright room surrounded with glass. Inside were rows of bassinets. Most were empty. Only a few babies slept in theirs, and she could hardly see them. The littlest ones had tiny knit caps covering most of their heads, and they were all swaddled up in blankets so she could just barely see their red, scrunched faces in between.

"Where is he?" she whispered.

"Not here," Uncle Nate said. "He must be up with your mom."

Mandy bounced on the balls of her feet. "Where's *she?*"

"Just down the hall."

Mandy was dying to see Patrick. And Mom. But when Uncle Nate turned into one of the rooms down the hall, Mandy hesitated on the threshold. She felt…shy. Maybe a little scared. What if Mom had changed? This was a big deal, having a baby. And what if she, Mandy, thought Patrick was ugly, or hated him on sight? What if he was going to save her life, and she didn't like him?

The first bed was empty. Beyond the curtain, Mom called, "Mandy? Where are you?"

She edged around it. The head of Mom's bed was lifted, so she could sit up and still lean against the pillows. She wore a flannel nightgown that Mandy had never seen before. But she was smiling, and her cheeks were pink, and she held out her arms.

"I could hardly wait until you got here!"

Mandy flew over and closed her eyes against sudden tears while Mom hugged her.

"So, what do you think?" Mom asked.

Mandy opened her eyes and eased back. Patrick was nestled against Mom's side. He wasn't quite asleep, but almost, his fist pressed against his mouth. He definitely had ten fingers, though they were really, really tiny. And his eyes—well, she couldn't tell what color they were. They had a vague look, as if he couldn't see much of anything.

She bent over and touched the back of his hand. He jerked and rocked his head toward her. "Hi, Patrick," she whispered. "I'm Mandy."

He frowned, but instead of being offended, she giggled. He was a person, not a doll. Eventually he'd learn to like her, and do what she told him to do.

Suddenly she had the strangest feeling in her chest, as though she could hardly breathe. It was partly a good feeling, and partly a scary one.

He was a real person, not just an idea. Her little brother. And he was going to have to do something that, no matter what Mom said, she was sure would hurt. What if later, when he found out what they'd made him do, he was mad at her?

Mandy took a deep breath. *I'll make it up to you,* she told him silently. *I'll be the best big sister ever. I promise.*

Chapter Thirteen

When Nathan brought Mandy, Patrick and Beth home, he had every intention of staying. He wondered how long it would be before Beth noticed he still occupied the spare bedroom. Even as he carried her suitcase up the stairs, he waited for her to ask why his wasn't packed. She'd say thanks and goodbye nicely and send him on his way. But instead, right behind him, she paused in the doorway of her bedroom. "Oh! The crib looks beautiful! You even set up the bumper pads."

The white-painted crib stood within a few feet of Beth's bed. The crib's bedding, in sunshine yellow and sky blue, added a vivid note to her pale yellow bedroom, cheerful despite February's gray light coming through the windows.

"I did that part," Mandy told her, crowding in, too. "Uncle Nate couldn't figure out where the ties went."

Beth flashed him a teasing smile. "And this is the man responsible for manufacturing mountain tents. Can you set up your own?"

"I could have figured out how it worked," he said with dignity. "Mandy just beat me to it."

"I put the sheet on, too," the twelve-year-old said. "I thought that was the cutest one."

"Me, too." Her mother smiled at her. Then she glanced down at the small bundle in her arms. "Well. Shall we try it out? It looks like Patrick has no intention of waking up."

Nathan held out his arms. "Let me. You shouldn't bend over for a few days."

He had to give her credit. However she felt about him, she'd so far been unstintingly generous in sharing their son. She handed Patrick to him without hesitation.

Nathan eased the receiving blanket back from Patrick's face, set in the fierce scowl that appeared to be his usual sleeping—and often waking—expression. Despite the fact that his scrunched-up face was also red and wrinkly and flaking, and that his dark hair stuck up in sweaty tufts like marsh grass, Nathan was immediately pierced by a love so sweet it made his chest hurt. He was still baffled by the powerfully protective, triumphant, tender feelings that had gripped him from the moment he first saw his son.

Gently Nathan laid him in the crib on his back and tucked the thin blanket around him. Then, like idiots, they all stood around the crib and raptly watched Patrick Joseph McCabe sleep.

After a moment Nathan looked up. Beth's fingers were curled around the top rail as she smiled softly down at her newborn. She was as achingly beautiful as a Renaissance Madonna, if more fragile. No woman who'd just had surgery ought to be so clear-eyed, so glowing. Pale hair curled around her face, creamy with only a hint of the gold the summer sun had lent her. Her breasts were fuller, although her neck and arms were as slender as ever.

It had been bad enough remembering the shadowy cleft

of her breasts from that day he'd come on her napping. Bad enough to remember the way she'd shuddered when he'd kissed them. It was far worse now that he was forced several times a day to see the ripe pale swell of one, even the brown aureole and nipple before she deftly slipped it into Patrick's mouth. Lucky Patrick.

Good God, he thought, half ruefully and half grimly, this was hardly the time to be getting sexually stimulated. What if Mandy noticed? He wrenched his gaze from Beth's breasts to her face—only to find that she was watching him now, not Patrick. Her eyes had darkened and her cheeks flushed a delicate pink. They stared at each other for an endless moment during which he cursed himself for giving her good reason not to want him living in her house.

But she could only be guessing about his thoughts. *Say something,* Nathan told himself. *Make her wonder.*

He had to clear his throat first. "Shall we let him sleep?"

Her eyes flickered at the distraction. "I suppose we should."

Nobody moved except Patrick, who grunted and jerked and frowned more fiercely.

"Do you want me to close the blinds?" Mandy whispered.

"It doesn't look like *he* cares." Her attention no longer on Nathan, Beth wrinkled her nose. "Besides, I don't know if I want him to sleep that well. I'm afraid he envisions being nocturnal."

"You mean, he'll scream all night," Mandy said knowledgeably.

"Right." Her mother made another face. "Last night the nurses helped out. Tonight I can't push a button and summon someone who's being paid to be wide awake and cheerful."

To hell with it. He might as well declare his intentions right now. "I'll get up with him, too," Nathan said, as though his presence were a given. "Surely he doesn't need to be fed every time he wakes up."

Beth's eyes widened. But before she could say anything, Patrick grunted again and squirmed deeper under his blanket. Beth made shooing motions at his audience. They all tiptoed out into the hall.

She turned to him and said quietly, "You mean, you haven't already gratefully packed your suitcase?"

"You just had surgery. You still need help."

Her chin was up, her gaze level. "We could manage."

Mandy was watching them anxiously, he noted out of the corner of his eye. To her mother he said evenly, "You shouldn't have to manage. Mandy and I can handle the meals and housework for a while. You should rest."

Her favorite word. "All I've done is rest!"

Mandy jumped in. "Yeah, but staying in bed makes a person weak, Mom. You always told me that when I couldn't figure out why I was so shaky. And you've been in bed for *weeks*."

One second the issue hung in the balance, their gazes warring and her pride on the line; the next she blinked and held up both hands. "So I have. Okay, okay! Pamper me. Adore me. I don't mind."

Wouldn't he like to, Nathan thought. But unfortunately she wasn't looking at him, and her tone was teasing.

"How about a cup of tea right now?" he asked.

Her laughing eyes met his, jolting him back into a heightened—no pun intended—state of physical awareness. "Certainly, sir. You may serve it in the parlor."

"Come into my parlor, said the spider to the fly," Nathan murmured.

Her mouth remained curved, but her eyes had gone serious on him. "Now's your chance to run away," she suggested for all the world as though she was still teasing.

Another anxious glance from Mandy told Nathan that *she* wasn't fooled, either.

"I'll worry about the sticky web when it wraps around me," he said, holding Beth's gaze just long enough to see how she reacted. Then, satisfied, he draped an arm around Mandy's shoulder. "Come on, kiddo. A life of service awaits us."

She ought to be grateful he'd stayed.

She *was* grateful. Sometimes. Like this morning, when her son's fire-engine wail dragged her eyes open to the murky gray light of dawn, and a bleary glance at her clock told her she'd only been asleep for an hour this time. She thought she might die if she couldn't sleep just a little longer, but the wailing went on and she was just bracing herself to get out of bed no matter how wretched she felt when Patrick abruptly quit crying. She didn't even have to hear the soft creak of the rocking chair to know Nathan had come. She *felt* him in the room, no matter how silently he moved. Prying open leaden eyelids again, she could just make him out, bare-chested, cuddling their son and humming so low that it was no more than a murmur to her ears. His presence, that hum, the creak of the chair, all soothed her as much as they did Patrick, and she slept again for a few more precious hours.

But when she awoke later, she couldn't believe that she was letting this man wearing nothing but pajama bottoms come into her bedroom during the night whenever he pleased, and that she slept right through his visits. Or, worse, was comforted by them.

During the day she'd become absurdly shy with him. In return he was formal, even distant. Gone were the laughter and easiness of the last weeks of her pregnancy, when he'd sat on her bed and played board games on her lap. Letting it get to her now made her feel like a fool; okay, he'd been almost a total stranger when she asked him to father her baby, but he wasn't anymore. They were friends, at least, weren't they?

They'd be better friends if he wouldn't watch so fixedly when she nursed Patrick. Like now. She sat on one end of the couch, legs curled under her, Patrick lying lengthwise along her arm, mouth firmly attached to her breast. Nathan sat on the other end of the couch. Because he was so close, she was being as discreet as she could manage; she'd arranged her shirt so that he couldn't possibly have caught more than a fleeting glimpse of her breast before Patrick latched on. He wouldn't have seen even that much if he'd really been watching the TV news, his ostensible reason for lounging only a few feet away from her. But he wasn't, any more than she was. She could feel his eyes on her, and she knew that if she looked up she would see them, narrowed, intense, dark. Disquieting, making it hard, suddenly, for her to breathe.

What was she supposed to do? Cry, "Don't look at me that way?" Lurk behind closed bedroom doors every time she nursed Patrick? Damn it, this was her own home, and she was sick to death of her bedroom!

Besides… *Okay, admit it,* she ordered herself, pretending to watch the anchor chat about a stalemated Congress. *You like knowing Nathan's watching you. It turns you on.*

That was what was really getting to her. It wasn't him, it was *her.* She wanted him. Fiercely, hungrily, sweetly.

Every nerve in her body seemed to be aware of him, like a radio tuned to only one airwave.

She sighed and felt Nathan stir two cushions down the couch from her. And no wonder. Congress might have warranted the sigh; the bouncy commercial currently on for dishwashing detergent didn't. She transferred her gaze from the television to the fuzzy top of Patrick's head. His sucking was slowing, his eyes had drifted shut. Soon his mouth would slip from her breast, and she would have to ease him up to her shoulder and refasten her bra at the same time. In her heart, she knew she might dawdle just the tiniest bit with the bra clasp.

She was pathetic. A woman who'd had a baby only three weeks before—and had a fresh incision in her stomach— shouldn't be, however subtly, trying to seduce a man. Or letting herself be seduced. She wasn't sure which was happening. All she knew was, if Nathan beckoned, she'd want to go more than she'd ever wanted anything.

With momentary humor Beth amended the thought: she'd go during those rare times she'd had enough sleep to feel human. In the murky light of dawn, even Nathan's bare chest didn't incite passion, only…comfort. Beth frowned a little. There was that word again, an odd one to use to describe your feelings for a man you were in love with.

And, oh, she was in love with him. For the first time she admitted it, knew it, accepted it. She loved Nathan McCabe. Not Rob. She no longer thought of him when she looked at Nathan; Nathan didn't even remind her of Rob anymore. In fact, the other day when she'd glanced at the photographs on the mantel, for a second she'd been startled, not because Nathan looked like Rob, but because Rob looked like Nathan.

When she thought about Rob at all, it was with fondness, a pallid emotion. What had once been love had eroded, the edges worn away until it was like a small smooth stone she carried in her pocket and ran her fingers over once in a while. She would never throw the stone away, but neither would it ever preoccupy her the way these disturbing, rough-edged feelings for Nathan did. Falling in love with Rob had been easy, fun; she'd been at an age when everyone was pairing up, and he was handsome, intelligent, made her laugh.

Why did it have to be so difficult this time around?

Patrick was asleep. She gently touched the furrows between his brows. Then, before she moved him, she sneaked a glance at Nathan. As she'd known he would be, he was looking at Patrick, too. Or at her breast. When he lifted his gaze to her face, his mouth had a twist she couldn't interpret, and his eyes smoldered with dangerous emotions.

Just like that a question popped into her mind: what if, back when she'd met Rob, Nathan had been there, too? Which brother would she have fallen in love with?

The answer was one of those rough edges. It came without a trace of doubt, leaving guilt in its wake. Worse yet, what if she'd met Nathan while Rob was still alive? What if the two had reconciled? How would she have reacted to Nathan?

Her hands shook a little as she lifted Patrick to her shoulder and then reached to fasten the flap on her nursing bra. Nathan's eyes, unwavering, held a molten glow; tension came from him in waves. Fumbling, she lowered her shirt and patted her son's back until a small burp rewarded her. With a jerk, Nathan turned his head to stare at the TV. Otherwise, he was so still it was unnatural.

Her legs trembled when she stood. "I'm going to put him to bed and see what Mandy's up to."

He didn't even look at her. "I'll clean the kitchen as soon as the news is over."

She nodded meaninglessly and fled.

Another week passed in much the same way. She needed Nathan, wanted him, didn't know if she could bear to go on this way. She could hardly talk to him anymore. What was he thinking? She couldn't be imagining the way he looked at her! Why didn't he say something? *Do* something?

Like kiss her. They were both single. Unattached. Together they'd created a baby. She knew he loved Mandy, as well as Patrick. So why couldn't they fall into each other's arms, get married and go off into the sunset hand in hand?

There wasn't a reason in the world. Which meant she *was* imagining things. He was here out of a sense of obligation. He wanted to prove he really intended to be a parent to Patrick. Maybe he was fascinated by the sight of his son nursing. Maybe his expression didn't have anything at all to do with her.

As the next week went by and March arrived, her thoughts circled around and around. He wanted her; he wasn't the slightest bit interested. Typical was one afternoon when Beth had just convinced herself of his indifference for the tenth or twelfth time. She went down to the kitchen for a before-dinner glass of juice. Nathan was there chopping green pepper on the cutting board with unnecessary ferocity. He looked up and his eyes pinned her.

She almost took a step back. "I, um, just came down to get something to drink."

"I'll pour it for you." He set down the knife.

"I'm not helpless," she said mildly. "It's nice enough that you're making dinner. Why don't you let me do it tomorrow night?"

His jaw muscles flexed and he picked up the paring knife again. "Fine," he said curtly.

She had to pass him to get to the refrigerator. The

quarters seemed too close, even though the kitchen was a good size. Belatedly Beth wished she had let him pour the juice for her.

As she opened the cupboard and reached for a glass, she momentarily closed her eyes. If he didn't either move out of her house or kiss her in the next hour, she would go crazy. Stark raving mad.

"Excuse me," she murmured on the way back.

He seemed not to hear her, turning suddenly so that his denim-clad shoulder bumped her just as she passed, sloshing the juice. "Damn," he muttered, and grabbed her with his free hand.

A meaningless touch. And he'd been this close to her dozens of times. Hundreds of times. So why did pure longing shoot like a drug through her bloodstream? Why were her knees buckling?

Nathan froze, still gripping her upper arm. His eyes sharpened like a camera lens focusing and zeroed in on her mouth. She stared up at him, mesmerized. His throat vibrated as he growled something, and then his head bent slowly. Her eyelids sank shut, her lips parted and she tilted her head back.

The next thing she knew, he released her so quickly he might as well have shoved her away. When she opened her eyes, she was looking at his back. After a second the chop, chop, chop resumed as he turned the diced green pepper into unusable shreds. Beth fled. Again. Running away was getting to be a habit.

Had Mom and Uncle Nate had a fight or something? They hardly talked at all or looked at each other, except sometimes when he sat staring at Mom like…like he was mad at her. Except that wasn't quite right. Mandy didn't know *what* he was thinking. She only knew that things weren't going the way she wanted them to.

Mandy sat brooding on her bed. Calvin and Polly wrestled around her, tumbling and squeaking when teeth sank in too far. Sometimes she'd reach out and stroke one of them, and they'd pause for a second before springing back into battle.

She'd been so sure Patrick would be fun, even though she should have remembered that little babies weren't. He was kind of cute—well, cuter than he'd been at first, anyway. Not so red. When he grabbed her finger and held it tightly, his own so incredibly tiny but really strong, she felt a surge of sisterly pride. He liked holding on to *her* better than anyone.

She might have enjoyed helping with his baths, except he hated them and screamed and screamed. Inside the bathroom with its tiled walls, his crying hurt Mandy's ears. At first she felt important when she changed his diaper, but when he'd pooped, it was gross. Other times the diaper was so soggy she hated to touch it. And, since Mom was nursing, Mandy couldn't even give Patrick a bottle. Mom said she'd introduce one soon, so other people could take care of him sometimes, but she hadn't yet. So what use was a big sister?

Uncle Nate didn't ignore her just because he had his own kid now, but he wasn't fun like he used to be, either. For one thing, he and Mom were always tired. Patrick slept more during the day than he did at night. And he really could yell. Mandy knew that both Uncle Nate and Mom napped when she was at school, but it didn't seem to help that much. Maybe not enough sleep explained why they were both grumpy. And when Uncle Nate wasn't mopping the kitchen or making dinner, he was in Mom's office working. If she had a question about her homework, he'd answer it, and she helped him with dinner and did more chores than usual, but he never wanted to play games or just tell jokes and be dumb like he did before.

Sometimes she almost wished Patrick had never been born. Except…she had that selfish reason to be glad he had been. And if it hadn't been for him, Uncle Nate wouldn't have been living here at all. Mandy kept wondering if he was going to stay for good, even if he and Mom didn't fall in love and get married like she'd dreamed they would. But she didn't ask; she was afraid she'd remind him that he really ought to go. Because she *liked* having him here. She just wished he'd lighten up.

By the time she heard Patrick awaking from a nap and then her mom's murmurs, the cats had worn themselves out and were curled together sleeping. She bent down and kissed Polly's white tummy and Calvin's creamy yellow one. Then she went into the hall and knocked on Mom's bedroom door.

"Come in," her mother called.

She sat cross-legged in the middle of the bed, Patrick lying on his back in front of her. She was changing his diaper and tickling his toes. When Mandy stopped beside the bed, she saw that his eyes were a little wider and brighter than usual. At least he looked interested, even if he didn't know how to smile yet.

"He's still so little." She dropped to her knees and rested her elbows on the bed so she was eye level with her baby brother.

"He *was* a little premature. He weighed almost two pounds less than you. He's just barely catching up." Mom bent over and blew on his toes. Patrick's eyes got even wider and his arms waved.

"Are you enjoying him?" Mandy asked dubiously.

"Enjoying?" Mom laughed. "Yes. Except at certain interludes in the middle of the night."

"What's to enjoy?"

Mom took the question seriously, tilting her head to one side as she fastened the tapes on the diaper. "When you have your own baby, it's…special. He needs me. That makes me feel all mushy inside. And…oh, it's exciting, the way he changes every day. The first few years are like a race. If I look away for even a minute, I miss some of it."

"I'm changing every day, too," Mandy said, trying to sound gloomy but not sure she meant it. Having her body change so fast sometimes scared her, but sometimes made her feel like she was really grown-up. Just yesterday she'd noticed Colin Hillman staring at her chest. He'd turned bright red when he realized she'd seen him.

"Changing… Oh." Mom smiled. "How's the leg shaving going?"

"It's okay. I don't cut myself very often." Mandy hesitated. "Do you think my breasts will get very big?" It was weird thinking about stuff like that now that there was a good chance she might not die.

Mom buzzed her lips against Patrick's bare tummy. All his limbs waved again, like sea anemones on the bottom of the ocean. "Hard to say," Mom admitted. "Mine aren't especially large. And Grandma wasn't busty. Look at pictures of your other grandmother. I think maybe she was. But since you get genes through your grandfathers, too… Heck, who knows? Will you mind if you do?"

"I'd hate it!" Mandy said vehemently. "Krystal Peters at school already wears a C cup—she *brags* about it—and she bounces up and down every time she moves. You ought to see her in PE. The boys can hardly takes their eyes off her, but even if she likes having big boobs, *I* think they'd be uncomfortable."

Mom made a face. "Maybe a little. Besides, I had a buxom friend in college who swore she'd marry the first guy who looked at her face before her chest."

"And did she?"

"If she didn't change her criteria, it took her a while to find him. She didn't get married until she was thirty."

"Oh." Mandy thought about it. "Is there anything I can *do?* Like exercises, or…or…"

"Sorry." Mom grinned and leaned over to kiss her nose. Patrick gurgled, as if the attention should all be his. "How about keeping your fingers crossed?"

"Yeah, like that's going to help," Mandy grumbled. But she supposed if God let her live but made her have big boobs, she shouldn't complain too much. And she *had* sort of liked it when Colin noticed she was…well, a girl.

Mom just smiled again. "Can you reach that sleeper?"

Patrick was so little Mom didn't put him in real clothes yet. He always wore those knit one-piece pajamas with feet. This one was bright blue and had an elephant embroidered on the front. "Cute," Mandy said, handing it over.

Patrick didn't want to get dressed. He kicked and wriggled and arched his back and even screeched when Mom insisted. "Silly boy," she cooed. "It isn't warm enough to stay naked. Wait'll summer. Then you can sleep in nothing but your diaper. I promise." His face just scrunched up like a troll's. Mom laughed softly.

"When I was a baby, did I look like him?" Mandy hoped not.

Mom finished snapping up the front of the sleeper. "A little. Prettier, though. You seemed to be more cheerful about life."

"You said I was your sunshine." Mom wouldn't forget stuff like that now that she had another baby, would she?

Her mother immediately began caroling, "'You are my sunshine, my only sunshine!'" Mandy joined her for the rest.

When they'd finished and were smiling at each other, Mom added, "Actually I think you looked more like pictures of me when I was a baby, even though you have your dad's coloring. If he'd ever quit frowning, I suspect Patrick looks more like baby pictures of your dad. And your uncle, of course."

From the doorway Uncle Nate said, "Considering he's my son, not Rob's, it's nice of you to tack me on."

Mom's head shot up. "It's Rob's baby pictures I have in an album, not yours."

He stayed in the doorway. "We were together in most of them."

"Probably, but nonetheless they were my husband's. The last time I looked at them, I didn't know you. I didn't think, oh, Nathan's eyes aren't shaped like Mandy's. It was her dad's face I paid attention to."

Feeling anxious, although she wasn't sure why, Mandy tried to distract him. "You looked exactly alike, anyway, didn't you?"

His eyes didn't waver from Mom's. "We may have looked alike. But we weren't alike."

"Mandy." Mom sounded pleasant, as though there wasn't anything wrong. But there was. "Will you take Patrick downstairs? You can put him in the bassinet if you want. Just keep an eye on him. I'd like to talk to your uncle for a minute."

"Okay." Her chest tight, Mandy picked up her brother, carefully supporting his head. Neither adult said a word until she'd left the room and closed the door behind her.

She thought she could hear Mom's voice as she started down the stairs.

A sick feeling in Mandy's stomach told her that, if Mom and Uncle Nate hadn't had a fight yet, they were having one right now.

Chapter Fourteen

The moment the door quietly shut behind her daughter, Beth asked, "Was what I said that offensive?"

"It didn't strike you as a little strange?" Nathan asked, teeth gritted. Maybe he was overreacting by making such an issue of this, but finding out she saw Rob even in Patrick's face had played into all his worst fears. "Comparing our son to your first husband, instead of his father?"

Beth scrambled off the bed to face him. "You were identical twins! All I was doing was comparing Mandy, who looks more like me, with Patrick who I think is going to look like you and Rob. Where's the harm in that?"

"Goddamn it, he's *my* son! Not Rob's!" With shock, Nathan realized he'd shouted.

She planted her hands on her hips and shouted back, "I know he is!"

"Do you?" he asked more quietly.

Beth gasped. From rage, hurt, he didn't know. "You still think I see Rob every time I look at you, don't you?"

He swore. "I don't know."

"I'll take that as a yes."

He slapped a hand down on the crib rail. The whole crib jumped and the mobile hanging above it swung wildly. "Take it any damn way you want!"

She backed up a step and stared at him with huge eyes. In contrast, her tone was almost musing when she said, "The question is, why do you care? What difference does it make to you whether your brother's widow is still pining for him?"

All that rage and anguish bottled inside him broke free and he stalked forward. "You're playing games. You know why."

She could have retreated a few more steps, but didn't. "Do I?"

Throwing his own questions back in his face wasn't calculated to soothe the wild beast she'd unchained. He swore again, took one more stride, snatched her into his arms and captured her mouth with his. He'd quit thinking, was blind with desperate hunger and bone-deep hurt. The kiss wasn't gentle; but, oh God, she was so soft, her taste as potent and smooth as fine scotch, the small sounds she made driving his frenzy.

Even in his mindless state, he slowly noticed that she did no more than stand passive in his embrace. Her lips were parted, her breath came quickly, her eyes had fallen closed, but she wasn't kissing him back. Her arms stayed at her sides.

A groan tore its way from his throat, which felt raw. He pushed her away and backed up until his legs hit the bed, where he stood swaying, rubbing his face with his hand.

"You didn't really answer my question," she said in a voice that would have sounded composed had it not been for a husky note.

He looked up incredulously. "What question?"

"Why do you care how I feel about Rob?" She paused. "Or you?"

Now he knew he was going crazy. Maybe the kiss hadn't happened. He'd imagined it. He shook his head, trying to clear it. "You can't tell?"

"I can tell you want me." For the first time her gaze lowered, her lashes shielding her expression. "Is that all there is to it?"

He muttered a profanity and sank onto the edge of the bed, burying his face in his hands. How had he blown it so badly? He'd wandered into a nightmare. No, he'd created his own nightmare.

The only thing good about it was that he had nothing to lose now.

He looked up again, eyes painfully dry and jaw clenched. "I love you."

Her lashes swept up and, pupils dilated, she stared at him. For a moment he'd have sworn her mouth softened, and emotion deepened the gray of her eyes. An instant later her face twisted and she turned away. She was drawing deep ragged breaths, her head bent, and all he could look at was the slender line of her neck and the heavy weight of pale hair carelessly knotted above it. He wanted to put his lips against that soft skin, nuzzle her curls. He wanted...

His fists knotted and he closed his eyes. Waiting.

He didn't open them until she spoke, voice firm, unrevealing. "You need to move out, Nathan."

He nodded dumbly.

"Of course you can visit Patrick and Mandy."

But not her. She would take care to be elsewhere. He knew it.

"I wish..." Her voice faltered the tiniest bit. "I wish you'd find some way to forgive Rob. Or yourself."

"For what?" He sounded hard. Unforgiving.

"I don't know." Her breath came out in a sigh. "Him for being too much like you. For being jealous of you. Yourself for cutting him off."

"You don't think he deserved it?"

"I don't know," Beth said again, face sorrowful. "What I do know is that he was a good man. Not perfect. But who is? And he loved you."

Intense grief hit Nathan with all the force of the head-on collision that had killed his brother. A part of him looked on in astonishment as a huge sob convulsed his chest. He fought it, throwing back his head and clenching his teeth and thinking about anything—everything—but Rob. His other half.

A gentle hand touched his arm. "Nathan—"

"No," he said harshly. "Leave it."

Beth took her hand back. Her magnificent eyes sparkled with hurt and pride. "That's your philosophy, isn't it?"

"What the hell is that supposed to mean?"

"You've just…shut away whatever it is you feel for Rob. Until you open that door and take a good long look, you aren't going to be ready to love anyone else. Especially not someone he loved. You need to resolve your feelings for him."

He got up and paced away from her, swung back and said bitterly, "You're a psychologist now? You're sure there's some deep meaning to the fact that we competed and ended up hating each other's guts? Life can be that simple, you know."

Her knot of hair slipped when she shook her head. "I don't think so. Not when you were twins. Each half of a single egg."

He uttered an obscenity.

Her eyebrows rose. "Fine," she said tartly. "Go wallow

in hate. But don't do it here. I won't have you glaring at me because you *imagine* I'm being sick enough to pretend my dead husband is alive in your body!"

"I never said—"

"Yes, you did!" Flat-out anger flushed her cheeks and glittered in her eyes. "And you call what you feel for me *love?*" She said it with loathing.

"Yes." He'd make her believe that much. "I love you. Heart and soul." He gave a bitter laugh. "I guess it goes to show that you're right. Even our damned brain cells were identical. Rob and I couldn't help loving the same woman. All I want to know is that I'm not second-best. That he's gone and it's me you see."

"Not second-best? What you mean is, you want to be sure you came out first. Won the blue ribbon. Beat out brother Rob."

She was wrong. He'd never been the one who cared about winning. "Your opinion of me is heartwarming. I don't even know why we're having this discussion." His jaws ground together. "Why didn't you just say you don't love me? Never will?"

Her gaze fell from his. "Because," she said softly, "I do."

He quit breathing.

Her lashes lifted again to reveal eyes as clear as the purest mountain lake and utterly honest. "I haven't been able to figure out why we didn't just fall into each other's arms. Go off into the sunset." She made a small helpless gesture. "Now I know."

Fear clawed at his chest. "I love you."

"Love," she said unhappily, "makes you so terribly vulnerable. It can't work unless you trust each other. Because of Rob, you can't trust me."

He felt as if he'd chosen to climb a mountain unroped,

and now his fingers were slipping from holds on a steep rock face. Hoarsely he said, "I know you'd never betray me!"

"Except in my heart, where you think I'm betraying you every day." She shook her head hard when he took a step toward her. "No. Go back to your condo. Or…or even to Portland. Figure out why you can't believe that I've let Rob go. Figure it out for your own mental health, if nothing else. But, please—" her voice shattered "—go. Today. Now."

He went, blundering from her room to his, throwing his things in his suitcases, forcing them shut. He walked straight out of the house without looking into the living room where he knew Patrick and Mandy were. And he drove away, not knowing whether he'd ever be able to come home again.

The door creaked open. "Mom." Mandy's voice came hesitantly. "Uncle Nate…Uncle Nate *left*. He took all his stuff."

Beth should have been sobbing. Instead, she stood in the exact same spot she'd been when he walked out of the room. Lot's wife, turned to a pillar of salt. Her eyes were gritty and her insides were as arid. She scarcely felt anything. She had to be numb. Surely it would hurt later.

"I know." The words scraped out. "I asked him to go."

Mandy's face crumpled in shock. "You *asked* him?"

Pity was the first emotion to trickle through the crystalline salt that was her heart. "Honey—"

"I liked having him here!" her daughter cried. "He liked me!"

"I know." She should have hugged Mandy, held her, comforted her. Instead, Beth sank onto the edge of the bed and sighed so deeply she felt hollow. She patted the spot beside her. "Come here."

Mandy sniffled. "I left Patrick."

"In the bassinet?"

A nod.

"Then he'll be okay. He can't exactly climb out and toddle off."

"But if he gets unhappy…"

"We'll hear about it."

"Oh. Yeah. I guess so." Still Mandy didn't come. "I need to blow my nose."

"Go get a box of tissues."

Mandy nodded again and went. Beth wondered if she would come back or go hide out, maybe at the willow tree or in the barn. She undoubtedly didn't *want* to be held, not by her mother the betrayer, who had driven away the man who was her father in all but name.

Dear God, did I do the right thing? Beth asked, but got no reply. Maybe all Nathan had needed was time. Reassurance. Hadn't she herself been confused early on? She'd admitted as much. And it wasn't as if she'd ever announced one day, "I'm over Rob. When I'm having erotic dreams, I no longer get confused over which man I'm dreaming about."

But how could Nathan not have known? Her confusion had been shortlived. He *wasn't* at all like Rob, not in any of the ways that counted except being a good parent. He must know that. Did he think that she was an idiot, that she couldn't distinguish between the two of them?

No, her brains had nothing to do with it, she thought unhappily. Nathan was so wrapped up in his own jealousy he'd never see her straight. Or was it guilt that made him unable to believe in her love? Did it matter which it was? She wasn't going to walk into a relationship where the man suspected her of infidelity, even if it was with a ghost.

She'd done the right thing.

Maybe for herself, but not necessarily for Mandy. Never mind little Patrick, who was going to have to do with one even wearier, crankier parent.

Mandy appeared in the bedroom doorway, box of tissues in hand. She stood there uncertainly until Beth patted the bed again.

"I put Patrick's little mirror in with him. He's looking at himself."

"Vain already."

Mandy's glasses rose high on her scrunched-up nose. "How could he be?"

"Give him a month or two. He'll be beautiful." She hesitated. "Mandy—"

At the precise same moment her daughter said, "Mom—"

They both stopped. Beth squeezed Mandy's hand. "You first."

"He did *everything*. I mean, he cooked and washed clothes and drove me and… I can't cook. And I'm always forgetting to take stuff out of the dryer, so it's wrinkled, and—"

"Sweetie." Not quite daring to test their relationship with a hug yet, Beth squeezed Mandy's hand again. "I'm healthy. I can do most everything I used to do. We've managed fine all these years, haven't we?"

"Yeah, but…" Mandy ducked her head.

"But what?"

"It was cool with him here!" she burst out. "More like a real family!"

Knife to the heart. "Yeah, it was, wasn't it?"

"*Why* did you ask him to go? I don't understand."

Only for a second did she consider…well, not lying, but telling less than the truth. She and Mandy had finally learned to be honest with each other. She wasn't going to risk that gain because it was hard talking about her feelings, not to mention adult love and sexual attraction.

"It's complicated."

Mandy waited, that too-old expression on her face.

"He thinks he's in love with me."

Shock replaced the skepticism on the twelve-year-old's thin face. "And you don't love him?"

"I do love him. No—" she held up her hand "—listen. You know he and your dad got angry enough at each other not to speak for fifteen years."

Mandy nodded.

"Well, as far as I can tell, Nathan still resents your dad or feels guilty because they didn't make up or something. Have you noticed how he doesn't talk about your father anymore?"

Her daughter's brow creased as she thought about it. "I guess," she finally said. "I mean, I hadn't noticed, but—"

"It took me a while, too. Anyway..." One more hesitation. This was the hard part. "He's convinced that I still love your dad and that I'm attracted to him because he looks like your dad. He thinks he's a substitute."

Mandy's mouth opened in a circle. "But...but..."

"My reaction exactly. The thing is, I can't convince him. So I told him to resolve his feelings about Rob and in the meantime I didn't want him around the house glaring at me."

"Oh."

"Do you think I was wrong?"

Her daughter gave a small, "I don't know."

She shouldn't have asked. She was the adult. "You'll still be seeing him," Beth said bracingly. "Just because he moved out doesn't mean he won't be here often."

"He didn't even say goodbye!" Mandy flung herself into her mother's arms, sobbing.

If she'd been made of salt, she'd have dissolved like the Wicked Witch of the West, because the next thing Beth knew, she was crying, too. Her grief was almost as terrible as when she'd lost Rob. She'd only loved two men in her life. One was dead and now she'd driven the other away.

Mandy's shoulders quit shaking at last; she rubbed her tear-streaked face on Beth's shirt. Beth gave a choked laugh and wiped her own tears on Mandy's curly hair. But still they held each other.

"Do you think he'll really come back to see me?"

"Yes," Beth said with certainty, "I do. He wouldn't desert you or Patrick."

Under her mother's chin, Mandy nodded. "But what about you? Will he ever see that you love him, not Dad?"

She hadn't thought she could cry another drop, but tears burned again in her eyes. "I haven't a clue." She blinked hard. "I did love your father, you know."

"I know." Mandy, her face blotchy, pulled back to look up at her mother. "But Dad's been gone a long time. I mean, I loved him, but that doesn't mean I can't love Uncle Nate, does it? So why can't you, too?"

Why indeed?

"Kiddo," Beth said on a sigh, "you're smarter than he is."

For the first week, he was angry. She'd sent him away because she *loved* him? Apparently she didn't want honesty from him; if he'd kept his fears to himself, he'd be putting a ring on her finger right now. But no, she wanted him to enter therapy to "resolve" his feelings for his brother so he didn't have to wonder anymore whether Rob's widow might be just a little confused, when she woke up in the middle of the night, about which brother's head rested on the pillow next to hers. Was that so unreasonable?

The next week he was so goddamned depressed he could hardly make himself roll out of bed every morning and stumble to the shower. For the first time since college, he got falling-down drunk one night, but instead of anesthetizing him, the booze made him maudlin. Beth was the love of his life; he'd lost his little boy; Mandy would die and never know that he felt like her father. He even dialed their number with the intention of drunkenly telling them how devoted he was. Thank God he dialed the wrong number and reached some total stranger's answering machine.

The third week he pulled himself together enough to call Mandy and offer to drive her to drama class. She accepted with such pathetic eagerness he hung up feeling like a crud. Big man, sulking for two weeks.

As he'd expected, Beth was nowhere to be seen when he picked up Mandy. His niece did take him into the living room to visit Patrick, who was awake in his bassinet. The dark hair was fluffy now, the cheeks plump and pink, the brown eyes bright and focused. Seeing how much Patrick had changed was like a fist in Nathan's stomach. He was missing his son's life. But obviously Patrick was thriving. He didn't need his father.

Beside him, Mandy bounced. "Tickle his tummy. He really likes that."

"Okay." Hiding his gloom, he forced a grin and trailed his fingers over a stomach almost as round as the cheeks.

Patrick wriggled, his arms and legs waved, and then his mouth opened in a huge toothless smile.

"He's smiling," Nathan said foolishly.

Mandy bounced again. "Isn't it cool? He smiled for the first time a week or so ago. Mom screamed and I came running into her bedroom. Of course he wouldn't do it again, and I didn't believe her, but then in the morning, the second he saw me he smiled. It was, like, the most exciting thing ever!"

He should have been here. He hid his pain and swung Patrick up in his arms, tickling and grinning until he'd earned enough smiles to store away for the lonely evenings at his condo.

At least Patrick's achievement had kept any awkwardness from developing between him and Mandy. They talked like always during the drive each way. It was another evening where he got to watch part of the class, but this time he felt like a fraud among the parents.

He didn't come into the house with Mandy when he took her home, even though she invited him. What would have been the point? All he'd have achieved would be to make Beth uncomfortable—assuming she didn't see him coming and go into hiding first.

Sometime after that night Nathan started having dreams about Beth and the kids that were vivid enough to stay with him when he woke up. At first the dreams were innocuous, just little snippets of him rocking Patrick while Mandy chattered, or of Beth breastfeeding Patrick, or of all of them wading in the stream by the willow tree in some sort of perpetual summer.

But after a few nights the dreams started getting weird. He'd be staring at Patrick feeling hostile because his son looked like Rob, instead of him. Once, Rob was there, and Nathan knew himself to be invisible, watching his brother with his family. The kicker was the night *he* was Rob, feeling smug as all get-out about his beautiful wife and cute kids.

That time, Nathan's eyes shot open and he stared uncomprehendingly into the darkness. He swore and sat up, putting his feet on the floor. What the hell had *that* been all about?

Beth's accusation, he thought grimly, running his hands through his hair. He'd hardly thought about Rob in the past three or four months, and then she'd decided he was obsessed with his brother. Now, courtesy of her, he apparently was.

Yeah, but what did the dream mean? He wanted to *be* Rob? On some level he and Rob were one and the same?

The thought was less than comforting.

Nathan wished he had a really close friend he could talk to. If it'd been summer, he'd have called Matt and suggested they swing their packs onto their backs and head into the Alpine Lakes. On a two- or three-day hiking trip you found yourself talking, maybe with the sun hot on your back while you put one foot in front of the other and felt the peace of the high mountain country, or maybe when you were sprawled on your sleeping bag staring at the fire as it died into coals and left such pure darkness the stars shone brighter than city lights. But it wasn't summer. It was March and raining like a son of a bitch.

Finally, out of desperation, he picked up the phone, anyway. His friend, home in Beaverton, Oregon, sounded glad to hear from him. They talked about work for a minute, then Matt's wife and kids.

Out of the blue Nathan said, "You knew I had a brother."

He could almost see the raised eyebrows. Then, "Yeah. A twin, wasn't he?"

Nathan grunted. "Turns out he's dead. Killed in a car accident three years ago. Left a wife and daughter."

Silence. "You didn't know?"

"I last saw him fifteen years ago. We had a hell of a fight, and…time passed." Even to him, that sounded weak.

"Fifteen *years?*"

"His, uh, widow tracked me down. Their daughter, Mandy, has leukemia. She needs a bone-marrow donor."

"Are you a match?"

"No. That's when I got myself into kind of a mess. The donor registry couldn't find anyone, either, and they were about to give up hope. Other relatives didn't work, and Mandy had no sisters or brothers, which are the best bet. So I, uh, fathered a son. Genetically he could be Rob's."

"And?"

"He matches. Mandy can have the transplant in about five months, when Patrick's old enough."

"But you're not celebrating," his friend said shrewdly.

"About that, I am. It's… Oh, hell. You don't want to hear this." He was suddenly sorry he'd called. What good would it do to dump all this on someone else?

"Yeah, I want to hear it. What are friends for?"

Nathan pictured Matt, relaxed in the leather chair in his home office, size-twelve feet in battered running shoes on his desk, which would be overflowing with undone paperwork, as usual. He might have his glasses on, which vanity made him reluctant to wear in public. Given that it was Sunday, he'd be wearing rumpled khakis and a University of Oregon Ducks sweatshirt over a brawny chest and a waistline that was getting just a little soft.

"I'm in love with Rob's widow," Nathan said baldly.

"Yeah?" Matt's voice sounded genuinely perplexed. "So what's the problem? There isn't any kind of law against marrying her, you know. In fact, it used to be tradition for a man's brother to marry his widow. He was taking care of her."

"The problem isn't one of legalities." Nathan swiveled his chair to gaze, unseeing, at the framed photograph of dead leaves clogging a stream. "It's the fact that Rob and I were identical twins that bothers me. What if it isn't me she wants? What if through me she's recapturing her relationship with Rob?"

A long silence was followed by the rumbling sound that indicated Matt was thinking seriously. "Do you have any reason to think that's what she's doing? What—did she blow it, call you by his name in a moment of passion?"

Which moment of passion? Their one and only?

"I thought she did. She denies it, and… Oh, hell, I'm undoubtedly being paranoid. She probably didn't. She thinks—" he had to force it out "—she thinks I have, quote, unquote, unresolved feelings for Rob. She doesn't want to see me until I do something about them."

"Ah. Is it true?"

He swore. "I don't know."

"You plan to find out?"

"How? Spend ten years in therapy?"

"A few sessions might not hurt."

"You think she's right."

"I think it's a little strange that you've hardly mentioned your twin brother to me in all our years of being friends. That you didn't even know he'd gotten married, had a kid, died. I mean, are you still angry with him, or what?"

Nathan squeezed the bridge of his nose. "No. Not angry. I just… Hell. I don't want to find out I'm not enough on my own." He heard himself with shock.

This time the silence fairly vibrated. "Not enough *what?*" Matt finally asked.

Still stunned, but thinking hard, Nathan said, "As a kid I felt that way. I would have sworn I didn't anymore." He stopped, blank for a moment. "I don't. I'm a successful businessman, I managed to get married and divorced on my own, I have a decent life."

"But now you feel linked to your brother again because this woman loved him and now she loves you, too."

Nathan made a rough sound in his throat. "You're in the wrong business."

"You kidding? Lawyers are glorified therapists."

"Okay. I'm afraid of being lumped with Rob again. 'The twins.'"

"Not the worst thing in the world to have someone who'll go back-to-back with you, knows what you're thinking, always cares."

"And screws your girlfriend because he thinks it's funny she can't tell the difference between you. Or maybe because he doesn't like you having something he doesn't have, too."

"Ah," his friend said again. "Yeah, that's pretty crappy. It'd make me mad. But what was he? Twenty? Twenty-one? A kid. Both of you were. Kids do dumb, unthinking things."

Blind to his surroundings again, Nathan saw the scene when he'd confronted Rob. Saw that face, handsome but still unfinished. No lines carved by experience. A boy's face. They'd done two years at the local community college, so that junior year at the university he and Rob had been away from home for the first time. Nathan's nature was the steadier, more earnest, Rob's the more reckless. He'd partied more than Nathan thought smart, drove faster, dated more women. No, not women. Girls. Rob had mocked him sometimes when he chose the library over a fraternity party. That had irritated him. But, God almighty, why had the one stupid stunt lit such a fuse?

Because he was looking for an excuse to shed his twin brother, find out if he could stand alone?

"Including me, apparently," Nathan said dryly. "Do dumb, unthinking things, that is."

"Yeah, well, think about it now," his friend advised. "Maybe that's all this woman you love is asking."

Nathan hung up in a daze. Maybe Beth was right. Maybe he was overdue coming to terms with everything his anger at Rob had cost him.

Like a brother. Someone who'd always stood back-to-back with him. Family.

Oh, yeah, he'd found out he could be self-sufficient. He'd learned that so well he had damn near forgotten that he'd once feared he alone was incomplete, that without Rob to drive him, to provide the qualities he didn't have, he'd be inadequate. What he'd never noticed, until he'd found Beth and Mandy, was that self-sufficiency was damned lonely.

Would it be so bad to go back to being one-half of the McCabe boys? To guess that, once in a while, Beth saw them in double exposure?

To know that she'd loved Rob, too?

Chapter Fifteen

He hadn't been here in fifteen years, and it was all as familiar as if he drove by it every day. Except that changes kept jumping out at him: the Murrays' house on the corner was gone, replaced by a convenience store. Somebody had added on to the Howards' place—an awkward second story. They should have hired an architect. The streets were still too narrow and lined with parked cars. Bicycles lay in the one-car driveways, which were cracked with age. Basketball hoops hung on the small detached garages. When Nathan was a kid, people stayed their whole lives in this neighborhood. He was willing to bet that now, these were "starter" homes, that families moved when their incomes rose.

He took the last turn, seeing nothing but the house in the middle of the block. A bungalow, still white, with a deep front porch. The boxwood hedge wasn't as neatly trimmed as Dad had insisted on keeping it; shoots straggled out. Paint on the house peeled. Dad would roll over in his grave.

He had died soon after Rob and Nathan had left for college. With a speed that had taken them aback, Mom sold the house they'd grown up in and bought a condo out Wheaton Way that let her walk or take a bus everywhere she wanted to go. It had a spare bedroom; they'd been able to come home for Christmas, but it wasn't really *home*. And then Mom had died, too, quickly and unexpectedly. No longer bound to Rob by anything but blood, Nathan had been able to walk away from his brother without weekly letters or phone calls from Mom keeping him up-to-date, without having to hide his enmity over Christmas holidays.

If Mom had still been alive, he suspected, the quarrel would never have solidified into permanent silence. Chances were, he'd have been there at Rob's wedding, held Mandy when she was tiny, carried one corner of his brother's casket.

Hated Rob anew for having the woman he wanted.

Or maybe he never would have let himself realize that he wanted her. He hoped not.

He stopped the car at the curb right in front of the house and sat there, wondering what in hell he was doing here. How was looking at the house he'd grown up in going to resolve anything? Last night, after talking to Matt, the idea seemed to make sense; if he physically went home, perhaps emotionally he could, too. Tap into something deeper. Pull up memories he'd repressed.

Now he sat here behind the wheel of his car and felt... old. Incredibly remote from the boy who had lived here, mowed that lawn, sheared the hedge once Dad deemed him responsible enough.

At that thought a wry smile twisted his lips. Rob had been really steamed when Dad handed the shears to Nathan one day and said, "You've seen me do it enough times, boy. Go for it."

"What about me?" Rob had asked.

Dad had shaken his head. "No matter how often your mother asks you to use a cutting board in the kitchen, you can't be bothered. You've ruined the Formica. So, first you have to prove you're ready for a job with sharp tools."

Face flushed dark, Rob had stomped off. Of course, later he'd come out to mock Nathan for being stuck with a sweaty tedious chore he'd avoided.

He'd even succeeded in making Nathan feel he'd gotten the short end of the stick. Rob had been good at that.

By the next summer, they'd sheared the hedge together, each starting on one end and meeting in the middle. The first time they'd tried it that way, they'd met to find that Rob's half was cut more ruthlessly. There'd been a three-inch difference. But he'd helped Nathan go back and trim some more, until it came out even. Actually they hadn't made a bad team.

Nathan's fingers tightened on the steering wheel. Good God, he hadn't thought about that in years. Hadn't remembered...

Hell, maybe there was something to this, after all. But what did he do now? Go knock on the door and ask if he could wander through the house? Right.

Still, he did get out of the car and slam the door. Leaning against the fender, he gazed at the house. Behind the dormer window up above had been their bedroom. As teenagers he and Rob might have gotten along better if they hadn't had to share. In college Nathan had had a different roommate. Except for nights spent at friends' houses or in hotels when the football or track team was on the road, it was the first time in his life he hadn't fallen asleep to the sound of his twin's breathing. Somehow his roommate's was different. He'd told himself it was liberating. All the same, he hadn't slept well at first.

"Hey." A kid's voice jarred him out of his memories. "You want something, mister?"

Holding a basketball, a boy, maybe eleven or twelve, stood in the driveway by the end of the hedge, blond hair cut in a bowl shape. He wore jeans and a T-shirt with the logo of a rock band printed on it.

"Not really." Nathan smiled crookedly. "Sorry. I must've looked strange. You live here?"

"Yeah." He sounded pugnacious. "My brother and me. With our mom."

"I grew up here." Nathan nodded toward the house. "I haven't been back in years. I was just…curious."

"Really?" Interest wiped out the edginess. "You mean, when you were a kid you lived here?"

"Yup. My brother and I shared the bedroom upstairs. Dad built in bunkbeds."

"Hey." The boy's eyes widened. "They're still there. My brother and me share 'em."

"How old's he?"

"He's ten. I'm twelve. Next week."

"Rob and I were twins," Nathan offered. "He died a few years ago. Car accident. It's him I was thinking about."

"Oh." The kid dribbled the ball a few times. "Do you miss him?"

For the first time, even to himself, Nathan admitted, "Yeah. Every day."

After a moment of silence, presumably to respect Nathan's grief, the boy asked, "Was it you who built the tree house?"

"In back?" Nathan found himself grinning. "In the big maple? Yeah. Jeez. Is it still there?"

"It was kind of rotting, but when we rented the house,

Mom bought some lumber and nails and stuff and let my brother and me work on it. It's really cool!"

"Do you sleep out there sometimes?"

The boy nodded. "You want to see it?"

"Would your mother mind?"

"She's not home right now." A belated recollection of safety lectures must have struck him, because he added hastily, "The neighbors are home. In case I need something."

Nathan nodded solemnly. "Sure. I'd like to see it."

As they circled the house, the boy asked, "Did you put that big hole in the floor of the tree house? I wondered what it was for."

"The pipe's gone?"

"Like a fireman's pole or something?" Satisfaction flitted across his face. "That's what I figured. My brother thought maybe you had a rope you swung from."

"Nah, we slid down a metal pipe." Looking up at the circle cut in the tree-house floor, he could still feel the texture as his hands slid down the cold pipe, the thud as his feet hit ground, the thrill.

"Must've rusted. Maybe we could get a new one. How'd you get it to stay there?"

At the boy's invitation, Nathan scrambled up into the tree house. His size made it feel cramped, but when he closed his eyes, he was ten again, swelled with pride because he and Rob had built it with hardly any help from Dad. In summer you could be up here without anybody knowing since the broad maple leaves grew so thick. It was quiet and green and secret. They'd hauled their sleeping bags up and stayed out here almost every summer night that year, then the next and the next. They could say anything they wanted, make up gory stories and plan pranks and, later, talk about girls and wet dreams and feeling like shrimps.

He and Rob had talked about things other boys kept to themselves. Sharing something with Rob wasn't really like telling another person; it was more like *thinking* it. In those days they were that inseparable.

Nathan showed the boy how they'd drilled a hole just big enough for the pipe to slip into in the big branch above their heads; it was no more than a scar now. He explained how deep they'd sunk the pipe into the ground, and how they'd tamped around the base until the pole didn't even quiver when they swung onto it.

The boy listened raptly and finally nodded. "Cool! I bet Mom'll let us do that, too."

"Don't take shortcuts. Make sure it's rock solid."

The boy nodded again and walked him back to his car. "I guess you could come in," he said doubtfully, "if you want to see the house and all."

"Thanks." Nathan smiled. "But that's okay. Your mother wouldn't like it, and...I don't need to go inside. I found what I came for."

"What's that?"

"Memories." He opened his car door. "Rob and I as kids."

"I bet you had fun. I wish my brother was my age."

"Sometimes it was great. Sometimes not so great. But having a brother is special."

The boy made a face. "I guess."

"Someday you'll appreciate him."

"Yeah, sure."

Nathan laughed, started the engine and with a wave pulled away from the curb. He took one last look in his rearview mirror.

"'Rock-a-bye baby, in a treetop,'" Beth sang softly, for the fifteenth or twentieth time. Patrick liked to fall asleep to soothing repetition, not a variety show. "'When the wind blows, the cradle will rock.'" A peek showed her that his mouth had gone slack around his thumb, and she didn't finish the lullaby, instead rising to put him in his crib. She tucked the blanket around her infant son, lingered for a moment to watch him sleep, then turned off the lamp and left the bedroom.

He usually napped for a couple of hours in the afternoon. Time for her to do laundry and put in an hour or so preparing the Tillicum Creek tax return. "Oh, joy," she muttered. "Maybe I should take a nap, too."

The idea was seductive, but… No. She was trying to get out of the habit. Patrick was eight weeks old now and sleeping through the night, if you could call midnight until six in the morning a night's sleep. It was now spring. In the next few weeks she would have to be out in the fields weeding and mulching, not snoozing away her afternoons. She'd already arranged for a half-day babysitter, a nice woman in her sixties who watched two grandchildren, too.

The phone rang before Beth had done more than throw the first load in the washer. Her heart stilled when she heard Nathan's voice.

"Beth, I'd like to talk to you." He didn't give the impression of being angry or upset. Nor was his tone demanding. Still…

"All right," she said warily. "Now's okay."

"May I come over?"

She hadn't seen him for a month, except for stolen looks between the curtains. A coward, she'd hidden every time he visited the kids. Dumb, considering they'd have to see each other regularly for the next eighteen years or so. But she hadn't been sure she could bear to exchange a few pleasant words, watch him snuggle Patrick, laugh with Mandy, nod a cool goodbye. Not when she missed him so terribly.

"I...can you tell me what you want to talk about?"

"I'd rather do that in person." He sounded so calm, noncommittal. What if he wanted to see more of Patrick, maybe intended to discuss getting a court order setting out visitation?

She licked dry lips. "All right."

"Mandy's not home?"

"No, she's at school."

"I'll see you in half an hour, then." Click. He was gone.

She had thirty minutes—forever—to wait and wonder. What did he want? It frightened her that he preferred not to say whatever it was in front of Mandy. Unless... She pressed her fingers to her mouth. Oh, God. Was there any chance he'd decided to file for joint custody, take Patrick away from her half the time?

She was shaking. She made it to a kitchen chair before her legs collapsed. Her eyes sought the kitchen clock. Twenty-five more minutes.

What if that was it? He'd loved being with Patrick, and when she'd asked him to leave, he'd probably felt as if she was taking his son away, too. She'd never intended... But how could she go on living with him almost as though they were husband and wife, when all the time he thought she was pretending he was Rob reincarnated?

He'd gone away so angry. She couldn't even kid herself that there was any hope he'd do as she'd asked and deal with his feelings for Rob. Why should he? He thought it was normal still to be painfully jealous of a brother who'd been in his grave for three years. Nathan probably figured *she* was the one with a problem. If he had ever really loved her, she doubted he did anymore. This could end up like the most bitter of divorces, with them fighting over the children.

And they had been so happy. Could be so happy...

"Don't think about it," she said aloud. In these last painful weeks she'd grieved, just as she had for Rob. She'd admitted no hope, didn't dare let herself feel any, because then it would mean starting all over with tear-soaked pillows and sleepless nights. She'd almost gotten numb, except those times when she knew he was coming, or could hear him downstairs, or waited for him to bring Mandy home. And then she felt the slicing agony of having to share a part of her life with the man she loved and couldn't have.

But if he took Patrick from her... Suddenly she leapt to her feet and began to pace. What would she do? Could she afford to fight him in court? Did she have any chance of winning? Did he want Patrick that badly? He claimed to love her—how could he do something like this?

The doorbell chimed and her heart took a sickening jump. He was here.

"Calm. You can be calm." Her fingers writhed together. She took long deep breaths, willed her heartbeat to slow down. And then she went to the door and opened it.

She had a flash of déjà vu: opening the door that first day to find a man on her doorstep who could have been Rob.

And now she saw only Nathan, dark, broad-shouldered, intense.

He shoved his hands in his pockets and nodded. "Beth."

"Hello, Nathan." She hesitated, then stood back. "Come in."

In the hallway his head turned. "Patrick asleep?"

"He naps every afternoon about this time."

"Am I keeping you from *your* nap?"

Oh, how polite they were being! "No," she said, leading the way into the living room. "I've given them up.

I'm working on my taxes and I've arranged for half-day babysitting starting next week. I've got to be outside—we're setting out new strawberries and expanding our raspberry fields, and everything has to be weeded and mulched. Anyway, I figure for part of the day he can be in a playpen in the shade or in the barn with me, but we're going to try having him go to Mrs. Heyer's, two properties down, just for three hours to start with."

"You're giving him bottles now."

"Mandy feeds him once a day. He doesn't mind." Nathan seemed to be waiting for something. She looked around vaguely and realized they were standing in front of the couch. More politeness. "Please, sit down."

He nodded, waiting only until she'd chosen the wing chair facing the couch. He didn't lounge the way he had when he lived here; he sat more like a businessman biding his time.

Civilities were over; they looked at each other.

What he said was unexpected. "I've missed all of you."

Beth focused on her hands, folded on her lap as though she were a little girl at a tea party. "We've missed you, too."

"Patrick seems to be doing fine without me."

She lifted her head in surprise. "The fact that he's healthy doesn't mean—"

"I want to be here with him."

Her heart began to drum. "What do you propose? A separate apartment for you—"

"I want to marry you." His voice lowered a notch, acquired a hint of huskiness. "Live happily ever after."

"Mandy and Patrick will grow up. Leave home."

"Not for them. For us."

Abruptly she was trembling again. She stood, went

behind the chair, gripping the back to hide the tremor in her hands. "I can't," she said desperately.

He rose to his feet, too, although he didn't come toward her. Thank God—she'd have crumpled. As it was, the hunger in his eyes shook her to her core.

"I've been thinking about what you said."

"Nathan—" His name caught in her throat.

"The other day I visited the house where Rob and I grew up. In Bremerton." Mouth wry, he looked away from her toward the fireplace. "A couple of boys live there now. I talked to one of them for a while. He let me go up in the tree house Rob and I built."

"You mentioned the tree house."

"Seeing it brought back the damnedest memories. You know, I don't think we ever went up in it again after we turned…oh, fourteen, fifteen. Partly because we'd physically outgrown it." The wryness became more pronounced. "And partly because we couldn't share it anymore. Good God. I don't know where we went wrong."

She was almost afraid to breathe, but she had to say something. "Hormones?"

"Yeah. Hormones and Mom." He fell silent for a moment. "She loved us so much. She was so proud of us. I think…she was trying to encourage us to develop individual identities. I don't know, maybe she was afraid we'd wear matching business suits when we were forty if she didn't drive some kind of wedge between us. I guess we were pretty close when we were little. Must have scared her. We actually had our own language for a while. Rob ever tell you that?"

Beth shook her head.

If Nathan saw, it was out of his peripheral vision, because he was still looking the length of the room toward the photographs on the mantel. Toward his brother.

"Mom couldn't have afforded a psychologist, so she used a little old-fashioned competition. You notice I don't say 'healthy.'"

Beth wanted to wrap her arms around him, feel his control break. "No," she said. "Not healthy."

"By the time we were in college I hated him. It was like—" his jaw muscles knotted "—he was me. The side of me I didn't like. Dr. Jekyll and Mr. Hyde. I was the classic good kid by then. He was the screwup. Only, I had more stake in his screwups than a brother usually would. He was me. I was him." Nathan laughed humorlessly. "He must have resented the hell out of me. No wonder—" He stopped abruptly.

Her fingers bit into the chair upholstery. "No. There's no excuse for what he did. It wasn't funny, or even just careless and insensitive."

Nathan turned his head and his eyes, dark with emotion, met hers. "Rob was angry. He must have been."

"You know," Beth said quietly, "maybe each of you going your own way was best. When I knew Rob, he was…oh, sometimes a little lazy, sometimes unthinking, but good. Mostly he was funny and sweet. He adored Mandy. If he just hadn't been so sure he was immortal…"

"He was always reckless. That made him a better athlete than I was." Creases between his brows, Nathan was silent for a long time, seemingly thinking. "For years I told myself it was best. We were better apart. But hell, all I was doing was justifying my own rigid unwillingness to forgive." He gave another bark of grim laughter. "Ironic if I was right."

She came to him at last, stopping a few feet away. "Does it matter anymore either way?"

The creases came back. "Matter? You're the one who was saying it did."

"No." She drew a painful breath. "How you remember Rob matters, not whether you were able to forgive him."

Nathan's voice was harsh. "You're saying that what can't be changed should be shrugged off?"

"No. Only that it's done. Over. And you know…" Was she foolish to remind him? But she must. For their sake. "Rob and I had a good marriage. He cherished his daughter. In fact—" one last hesitation "—I suspect he was happier than you've been."

Nathan looked at her, layers of protection suddenly stripped away to reveal heartbreaking vulnerability. "I suspect you're right."

Her heart increased its drumbeat until it filled her ears. "We could change that." Did she sound as odd to him?

"Oh, God, Beth…" His voice broke and he had to clench his teeth. "Can you believe that I love you?"

"If…" She had to stop, press tremulous lips together, try again. "If you can truly believe that I love *you*."

Still several feet separated them.

The love and fear in his eyes nearly undid her. "I've been an idiot."

Oh, damn, she was crying.

One step closed the distance between them. His arms engulfed her with bruising force, as though he was afraid she'd slip away. She leaned her cheek against his chest and wept. Only a few tears, these ones of happiness.

"I can't promise I'll never be a jackass again." He moved his mouth against her hair. "Just…slap me down and forgive me?" When he heard his own choice of words, his muscles went rigid. "God. Who am I to ask anyone for forgiveness when I denied it for so long?"

Beth drew away, meeting his eyes squarely. "Rob didn't look for you, either. Remember that. He talked about you, he missed you, but…I think he was just as afraid as you were of starting the whole vicious cycle over. Maybe, for both of you, self-preservation didn't allow forgiveness."

His mouth twisted. "Now you sound like me. Sugarcoating it."

She'd gained enough confidence to add a hint of tartness to her voice. "Are you going to torture yourself for the rest of your life?"

"Just as long as I don't torture you." If he'd meant the words to sound light, he'd failed; he was raw, stripped bare for her.

No more talk of forgiveness. "I love you," she said shakily.

He snatched her to him again. Under her hands, she felt his heart slamming against the wall of his chest. Her own raced so hard she was dizzy. She expected a kiss of passion, desperation; she got one so achingly tender her knees buckled. Nathan didn't just hold her up, he lifted her into his arms.

She clutched his shoulders.

The light that flared in his eyes warmed any chill left from her lonely nights. "I don't think I can wait any longer," he said roughly. "Do you have any idea how hard it was to turn down the chance you gave me last year to make a baby with you in that bed upstairs?"

"No," she whispered.

"I've been cursing myself ever since." He carried her into the hall. "When I had to produce sperm in that damn clinic…"

"I had to sit in the waiting room imagining you fantasizing about busty love goddesses. I hated them."

He set her down on the stairs, wrapping his hands around her hips. "Do you know who I fantasized about?"

Beth leaned forward and kissed the base of his throat. "Do I want to know?"

"You." His eyes smoldered. "All I could think about was what it would have been like with you."

Her breath came out on a sigh that he drank in with a second kiss, this one urgent and devastatingly sexy. Her lips parted, she tasted his tongue, felt his arousal pressing against her belly. She gasped for breath when he took his mouth from hers only to string kisses down her throat and along her collarbone. Her back arched, her head fell back, and her fingers twined in his hair.

"Nathan."

In response he unbuttoned her flannel shirt, unhooked the catch of her bra, groaned when he cupped her breasts in his hands.

"God, you're beautiful. I loved watching Patrick nurse."

She gave a faint laugh. "You looked like you hated watching. You glowered."

A reluctant grin caught his mouth. Freed from its reserve, his face was wickedly sensual. "Oh, I liked watching. But there's something a little cruel about making a man watch his son suckle on breasts *he's* never touched, don't you think?"

"I seem to remember you touching them."

"Like this?" His thumbs flicked her nipples, traced taunting circles around them.

"No," she whispered, remembering the tug of his mouth. "Not exactly."

His hands gripped her waist and lifted her up a step. He leaned forward and kissed her breast, teased it with his tongue, and then he moved up one step, too. This time he peeled her shirt and bra off altogether and tossed them. One more step up, and his attentions turned to her other breast. They were so sensitive heat coiled between her legs with stunning speed.

By the time Nathan and Beth had reached the top, she'd pulled his shirt over his head and discarded it, too, only a small part of her mind shocked by the sight of her bra dangling from the banister.

He backed her against the wall and kissed her deeply, grinding his hips against hers. A dark flush ran across his cheekbones, and the look in his eyes was molten.

"Am I dreaming?"

"No," she whispered. "If you were, we could use my bed. As it is, I'm afraid a twin bed will have to do."

"Oh, my God. Patrick. I forgot him." The dismay was curiously gratifying. "What if he wakes up?"

"Let's just be very quiet," she suggested. She wanted Nathan *now,* not tonight, not tomorrow when they could be alone together again. Right this second she didn't think she'd ever forgive their son if he kept Nathan from finishing what he'd begun—or had she begun it?—that day last summer under the willow tree.

They made it into the spare bedroom before they shed the rest of their clothes. The twin bed there looked so narrow, so prim, a gurgle of laughter lodged in her throat. The next second Nathan bore her down onto it, and the laughter died in a rush of need so intense she forgot where they were and what had come before. All that existed were his broad shoulders above her, his weight pressing her down, his mouth, damp and hot, moving on her breast.

She wrapped her legs around him, felt the muscles in his back bunch as he began a maddeningly slow thrust.

"If only," he said in a voice barely recognizable, "we'd made Patrick this way."

"Yes." She sucked in breath as he filled her completely. "Oh, yes."

What they did together on that narrow bed was glorious. He plunged and withdrew and she followed him, led him, coaxed him. They kissed and whispered and she looked up at Nathan's face, altered by passion, the angles of cheek and jaw sharper, the shadows more exaggerated. And, oh, the way he looked back at her, with tenderness and desire and love, made her hurt inside even as his every touch, every shift of weight, felt incredible, like nothing she'd ever known.

As he thrust harder, faster, as the rhythm became a frantic dance, the bed squeaked and Beth heard whimpers and words that could only be coming from her. She was pleading and promising and demanding. It was nothing like her—nothing, but wonderful. At the end, he smothered his own ragged bellow and her cries with his mouth. It was a kiss that didn't end even as his muscles went slack, and then he rolled onto his back and pulled her atop him.

At last he cradled her face and lifted it enough for her to see his lopsided smile. He looked...boyish, she realized in astonishment.

"Will you marry me?"

"Sir," she said in mock outrage, "I assumed I'd already been asked."

The smile deepened. "Let's make it official."

He'd slipped out of her. She scrambled away and sat up, clutching a pillow to hide her nakedness. Nathan rolled onto his side and braced his head on his hand. He looked older, apprehensive.

"I didn't think about Rob," she said.

He swore. "Damn it, Beth, I didn't ask!"

"No." She smiled tenderly. "But let me say this, just once. Rob and I had a good marriage. A *nice* marriage. But...I never felt anything like I just did. I love you, completely and utterly. Which is probably redundant, but that's okay." It was harder to smile this time. "Rob is a memory. You're my life."

He wasn't taking it well. His eyes frowned and his voice was taut. "Believe it or not, it never occurred to me that you were thinking about Rob." He muttered another obscenity. "Is this going to hang over us forever?"

"Nope." She grinned, letting him see her joy. "I would love to marry you, father of my son. I just thought that, once, you ought to know you did win the blue ribbon."

The warring emotions on his face would have been comical if they hadn't moved her nearly to tears. "Damn it, woman." He wrapped a hand around the back of her neck and pulled her close for another kiss, as sweet and lasting as a marriage vow.

She came away from it, laughing. "And by the way, father of my son. You're being called."

Nathan went still, listening to the grumble that preceded Patrick's piercing siren wail. Then he cocked an eyebrow at her. "What are you going to be doing while I'm performing diaper duty?"

"Picking up the clothes littering the hall before Mandy gets home."

"Jeez Louise." He erupted from bed. "Get a move on, woman!"

She watched as he yanked on his jeans. "We can work anything out, can't we?"

"Like diaper duty?"

"No, I mean…" She didn't know what she meant, except in an inchoate way.

But he did, because he gave another crooked grin. "Yeah. We can work it out. How can we fail? We're a family. And I never make the same mistake twice."

Family. Treasuring a last hard kiss, Beth collected the pieces of clothing littering the staircase and hall, then slipped into her bedroom past Nathan, who was now changing Patrick's diaper on the bed. He was cooing, and Daddy was cooing back. Unseen, she stood in the bathroom doorway and watched them. Father and son.

Her heart cramped. Oh, yes. They could be happy. They would be.

She could hardly wait until Mandy came home.

Epilogue

Mandy swallowed a sudden surge of nausea and clutched her middle. The sun didn't feel warm, although it was August and Mom wore a sleeveless dress. They all sat out on the front porch steps pretending they were soaking up the sun, pretending they weren't going anywhere important. A baseball cap shaded Patrick's eyes. He bounced on Mom's knee, laughing, his chubby legs kicking. On Mandy's other side, Uncle Nate gently squeezed the back of her neck with his big hand when he saw her double over.

"It'll get better," he said quietly. "Even if you are facing a cruddy few weeks."

She nodded, wordless. The strange thing was, she ought to be dreading those weeks. And she wasn't.

Today was the big day. Mom and Uncle Nate and Patrick—her *family*—were delivering her to the bone-marrow-transplant unit on one of the top floors of the hospital. Because her immune system had already given up, she'd be placed in sterile isolation while she went through a round of chemotherapy and radiation to kill her existing bone marrow. That meant she wouldn't be able to touch anybody for a long time. Mom and Uncle Nate and Patrick would be able to see her, but only through a transparent wall. No hugs or kisses, no hand holding hers. She knew how sick she'd be. She could even die there behind that clear wall. What the doctors would be doing to her could damage her organs, or she could get an infection no matter how careful they were. Or, once Patrick's cells had been introduced into her, they might reject and attack her body. And she'd be alone in a way she'd never been. Always she'd had Mom beside her, holding the basin when she threw up, washing her face afterward, massaging her back, laying a hand over hers. But not this time.

The pain in her stomach eased and she lifted her face, despite her shivers feeling the sun's warmth. For a second she leaned against Uncle Nate, and his arm came around her in silent support. She turned her head and saw that Mom was watching her, this incredible love in her eyes. And even Patrick grinned at her. Mom was right, Mandy thought; he *was* cute. Except when applesauce dribbled back out of his mouth.

What had she been thinking about? she wondered vaguely. Oh, yeah—the fact that she wasn't really scared. And she didn't feel alone. She knew she wouldn't be even if nobody could touch her. Because she had more than Mom now. She had a whole family. Including a brother whose gift of life she absolutely, positively would not waste by dying. Besides, he needed her. Neither Mom nor Uncle Nate knew what life was like for a kid these days. She had to be around to teach Patrick.

And at the end of school last May, when everyone knew she was going to have the bone-marrow transplant this summer, Colin Hillman had come up to her and asked her to go out with him. To be his girlfriend. So *he* would be waiting for her to come back, too.

Nope. She knew she was going to get better, this time once and for all. What she had was faith. Knowing people loved you enough gave that to you.

"Okay," she said. "I'm ready to go."

* * * * *

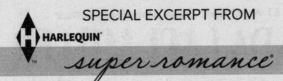
Remembering That Night

By **Stephanie Doyle**...

Liza woke up and waited. Waited to remember her tenth
birthday, or her high school graduation. Nothing.

Still, today was different. Different because she knew her
name even if she didn't exactly remember who she was.

She heard a noise coming from another part of the house and
remembered last night. Greg had stayed with her, distracted
her. They had eaten pizza and talked. Since she didn't have
much to offer, he did most of the talking. First about his family.
Then about his job and the work he did detecting when people
were lying.

By then it was so late he accepted her offer to stay the night.